THE FINAL VICTOR

FATE'S INMATE
BOOK 3

L. BLAISE HUES

Stag
Beetle
Books

To Gwendolyn, Harper, Holden, Hudson, Josef, or whatever your names would have been if things had worked out:
You taught me about the dangerous balance between hope and fear; pain and purpose.

To Adi and Brooke:
Thank you for showing me what I have is beautiful, magical, and so much more than good enough! You are the source of my greatest joys. You fill my heart and soul with endless love.

CONTENTS

THE FINAL VICTOR

1. Sasha Popov — 3
2. The Fall of Zalar — 17
3. New Tattoos — 23
4. Junior Lieutenant Drivick — 33
5. Retribution — 43
6. Trust and Slag — 55
7. Kasia's Squad — 62
8. The Guards at Vazenia — 74
9. Triage — 84
10. Not The Worst Plan — 93
11. Destruction Zone — 100
12. Burning Canvas — 109
13. Commander Alekin — 116
14. The Yellow Doctor — 122
15. The Cuvacs — 133
16. The Neighbor's Warning — 142
17. DavatNoc — 152
18. Bitka — 162
19. Outpost 5D — 171
20. A Deeper Red Than Crimson — 178
21. The Monster — 187
22. Head Warden Molnar — 193
23. Korporal Turuk — 200
24. The Final Victor — 207
25. Mr. Preemptive Officer — 213
26. Explosions Are Loud — 224
27. Black Tears — 232
28. The New Oscar — 240
29. A Single Memory — 247
30. A Bloody Scar — 262
31. A Reasonable Cruster — 274
32. An Unworked Section of the Mine — 281
33. Be Bold — 286
34. No More Pretense — 296

35. Burning and Memories — 305
36. Scars — 316

From the Author — 327
From the Publisher — 333
Also by L. Blaise Hues — 335

THE FINAL VICTOR

I'D ALWAYS BEEN DANGEROUS, BUT
NOW I'D BECOME A THREAT.

CHAPTER 1
SASHA POPOV

THE VEHICLE SLOWED and then stopped. Markos pressed the brake and turned to look at me and Roman.

Outside, the stars and moon reflected on the snow, bringing enough light in through the windows for me to see his expression. Resignation and apprehension crossed his face.

"I was a Test Criminal," Markos confessed, shooting a glance at my wrist before looking back to my face. "I'm… skudge it. I'm Victor-1."

I'd heard many impossible statements over the past several months. Roman had told me I could block pain and heal. Lockbox had told me about a legion of lurpers used as soldiers on The Outskirts. Roman confided to me that he was an unmarked Kilo.

Of all the impossible statements I'd come to believe, this was the most impossible.

Commander Markos was a Test Criminal. He was a Victor just like me.

His daughters, Emberly and Milena, were lurpers just like me.

I should have suspected when Emberly wanted to attack Erik or when she'd heard what I'd whispered to Alex.

But Commander Markos—former head warden of Rhosivi Mine and Prison, chancellor on the Judgement Board—a Test Criminal?

Roman sat staring, slack-jawed.

"I'm glad you're surprised. Didn't skudge that up at least," Markos said. He kept his eyes trained on the dark road in front of us even though the truck was stationary.

We were only a few kilometers outside of the entrance to Khizmit, on our way to The Outskirts.

Had Emberly made it back to her mom and sister? Would she tell her mother the truth about how I'd killed Velky? I worried that even though she'd called me her Victor, maybe having seen me murder would make her second-guess her interest in me.

I was a murderer. But Emberly—she was a Victor and had no idea. Completely unaware that the reason her father wanted her to stay away from lurpers was because she was one. If they tested her blood, it would reveal not only what she was, but what Markos was.

In the best-case scenario, both she and Milena would be sent to Vazenia. In the worst-case scenario...

The acrid taste of bile filled my mouth. Markos had certainly considered that. He'd considered what danger his daughters were in at this moment.

"Emberly..." I trailed off.

"Yes," Markos said. He finally looked at me.

He'd heard my conversation with Velky. *Had he heard my conversation with Emberly?* Did he know that I'd kissed her, long and passionately with my hands tangled in her silky hair? If he did, his expression didn't give it away.

"Commander Markos," Roman said. "All this time—what you've been through—what you've witnessed..."

Markos cleared his throat and looked back out the front window.

"Get Lockbox up here. I don't want him freezing back there and I'm only telling the story once," Markos said.

Roman opened the door and hurried to the bed of the truck. I followed, concerns and curiosity swirling around me like the snowflakes.

Roman grabbed a crowbar and pulled the lid off a crate in the center of the bed. At first glance it held blankets.

"Lockbox," I called. The blankets shifted and Lockbox sat up, his eyes still faintly milky.

"I think I dozed off," he said with a chuckle.

"How are your legs?"

"Not great."

"Commander Markos has…" I trailed off and turned to Roman.

"Commander Markos wants to tell us something," Roman said. "He told us something and he wants to tell you, too."

I reached in and scooped Lockbox into my arms before jumping down from the back of the truck.

Roman tacked the lid to the box back down.

A flash of white fur sent my heart racing, but I turned to see a large white dog with floppy ears at the side of the road. He growled once, a warning, and then as I looked up I realized that some of the white around us wasn't snow, but the backs of sheep. The Cuvac barked once, watching me closely while I helped Lockbox into the back seat of the truck.

"Good boy," Roman said, "or good girl." He pulled the door shut and the dog backed away. Lockbox settled into the bucket seat beside me in the cab of the truck.

"Can I guess?" Lockbox asked as soon as Roman shut the door. Markos started the engine again.

"Guess?" Roman asked.

"I have three theories. Theory one: Commander Markos was a guard at Zalar and witnessed the cruelties against the inmates there which filled him with compassion for the criminals. He survived the breakout and made it his mission to right some of the wrongs done that day."

"No," Markos said.

"Theory two: Your wife was a Test Criminal. You didn't know when you married her and maybe didn't find out until later, but when you realized that made your own children lurpers, you decided to help us."

"No," Markos said.

"Theory three: You—"

"I was a Test Criminal," Markos said.

Lockbox turned to me, his expression full of glee. "I considered that!"

"We can't skudge this whole thing up with the Lurper Legion, so let me fill you all in and then we'll get our stories straight before we arrive."

———

Eighteen-year-old Sasha Popov said in his own words, "I'm not leaving Khizmit to die in a ditch alongside a bunch of skudging strangers." It wouldn't be long before he'd be shipped off to the front lines. He and his friends, Pedrick Markos and Stefan Krajnak, knew the next wave of deaths would lead to another draft of able-bodied boys and men in Khizmit. It was only a matter of time before they'd be forced to join the army and give their sanity and lives for the Khizmit enclave. According to the rumors, Latvani had overtaken their neighboring Enclave, Dovaberg and the Dovas joined the Latvanians in battle, united to overtake Khizmit.

Sasha wanted nothing to do with the war. He, and everyone else, knew the stories of what happened at training. Running, climbing, shooting, crawling beneath barbed wire through mud while keeping your rifle clean. Quite the contrast to the life he'd become accustomed to.

Sasha, Pedrick, and Stefan enjoyed lives of fleeting pleasure, often involving petty theft, harmless flirtations, hookups with beautiful girls, and inordinate amounts of rakia and vyco.

The three orphans had personal reasons for hating the war. Their fathers died in half-frozen ditches a hundred and sixty kilometers south of their wives. Sasha's mother died from a blood clot, and he moved onto the streets a few hours later. He never asked Pedrick or Stefan what happened to their mothers.

Sasha, Pedrick, and Stefan figured they'd only get a few more weekends in town, and with the holidays coming up, they thought they'd have some fun. After a few rounds of hot rakia, much of which they'd spilled down the front of their shirts, their mortality seemed distant. They decided, with minds muddy and ignorance dialed up, that they'd show Khizmit how they felt about getting sent off to war.

They vandalized five block centers before anyone caught them. While the three young men would have stood a chance on a normal night, the excessive drinking left them all slow, physically and mentally. The guards, aided by their palkas, a few years of seniority and experience, arrested them. Sasha, Pedrick, and Stefan spent the night throwing up, nursing headaches from the alcohol and the palkas, and considering what punishment might await them.

Sasha had the distinct impression that he was going to be shipped off to the war right away, after all, they'd made it clear how much they loathed the idea.

However, they didn't get sent to the front lines like they'd feared, which Sasha decided made sense. It wasn't wise to arm three young men who'd just expressed the utmost dissatisfaction with their enclave and its leaders. That could lead to a coup. That idea began as a seed, planted deep in Sasha's mind. A coup, he decided, was the only thing that would change Khizmit for the better.

Sasha, Pedrick, and Stefan were chained, cuffed, and shipped to Zalar Correctional Facility. No trial. There wasn't any time for that. Besides, they'd been caught red-handed. Their peers, had they been polled, would have voted for the worst for them anyway. They'd painted messages about how they hated Khizmit. How they didn't want to live here. How unfair the war was. On top of it all, the language they used was far from polite.

Zalar Correctional Facility was the first facility of its kind. The three men, who'd acted far more like boys, shared a cold cell and huddled together for warmth during the long, long nights. With most of the men on the front lines, only a few guards could be spared for Zalar, which meant the prisoners remained in their cells, only rotating out weekly so they could clean themselves and their cells under the shadow of a muzzle and a hungry trigger-finger.

After only a few weeks, Sasha begged the guards to give them another chance. He said he'd changed his mind and that he'd go to war. Even death would be better than this hell. Stefan didn't bother, knowing it was futile, and Pedrick had become too ill to protest anything anymore. Zalar, while a prison, housed more than a few guards and a thousand prisoners. Men and women in lab coats occupied the well-lit rooms, and their conversations sometimes echoed down the hallways and into the cells.

Word began to creep around Zalar Correctional Facility, carried by the rats—the prisoners. Because they'd learned that's what they were: lab rats for the scientists' whims.

Four months after the trio had been arrested, the prison came to life. The scraping of chains and chairs rang through the hallways. The scientists, who'd worked for months in whispers, began to celebrate and threw off any pretense of secrecy.

One by one the guards pulled the prisoners from their cells and took them to the center of the facility, a giant cafeteria, where the inmates would have taken their meals if they'd been fed regularly and if the prison had had enough guards to keep them under control. Each prisoner was chained to their chair, their cuffs double-checked, and then left.

Sasha, the most mentally clear of the three counted the sections of chairs as the nearly one thousand inmates were dragged, pushed, or herded into the room before being chained down, causing Sasha's heart to pound, blood roaring in his ears.

"Keep this control group clean until we see the effects," a woman in charge said, addressing the guard and pair of scientists in front of Sasha's group.

At the same time, creaky carts laden with needles and vials and all other sorts of disconcerting medical equipment entered the room, accompanied by scientists and doctors dressed in lab coats and expressions of joyful anticipation.

The guards sectioned off a group, called it the Alpha Group, and then the scientists got to work injecting them all with unknown substances. One man protested, threw his arm up and caught a scientist in the jaw. Immediately, and without warning, the guard nearest him smashed him over the head with a palka. The crack was so loud, Sasha, who sat across the room, gritted his teeth and grimaced.

They proceeded to another group, arranging them all and labeling them from A through Z.

But his group, V, was the first group without a team of scientists.

Sasha watched the groups of inmates submit to either getting a shot in the arm from a syringe or a shot from a Lugar in the head.

For two days Sasha sat in the chair, half-starved, desperate for a drink. The stench of excrement and body odor would have been enough to drive anyone to insanity, which is how some would explain the scientists' behaviors. Each group that had been injected with serums had been, in turn, taken to another room. Tested. Prodded. The scientists themselves had gone without food as they frantically worked, recorded information, and made decisions in their sleep-deprived enthusiasm.

Sasha woke up in the chair, dazed and confused as guards worked their way down the rows of inmates to ladle water into their mouths. The metallic, warm water, barely registered as bitter to Sasha. He would have guzzled the whole bucketful if given the chance. He would have dunked his head into the water and swallowed it or drowned himself in it for how happy he was to have it at all.

But that would have taken energy to do, and he didn't have any to spare. It took almost all his strength to register the two carts that scientists wheeled into the room. A lean, gray-haired man picked up the first syringe, labeled V-1, and approached Sasha.

"Please mark down Victor-1," the doctor said to a woman with a clipboard. She scribbled away.

Just then, a few rows away, a man started screaming. Suddenly, a guard raised his rifle and fired once, and with the blast of the gun, the scream died.

Those wearing lab coats barely glanced at the prisoner, because they knew it wouldn't be the last prisoner to die today.

A guard then announced what Sasha deemed to be obvious: "You can either submit or get shot. Those are the only options." The woman working in front of Sasha grinned at his words and then wrote something on a paper.

Sasha's seat up front put him first in line and only vaguely, he realized he was receiving two shots, simultaneously given in each of his shoulders. They blazed like fire, and he cried out as it burned and pinched. Dizzy and surely dying, Sasha screamed. His shoulders felt like they'd swollen up. His muscles spasmed through his body. He didn't scream alone for long. The inmate beside him began to cry out as soon as he received his injections, and then the woman after him joined in, her voice higher, her scream sharper.

Sasha thought he'd screamed himself to death, but when he awoke in a back room, he found he wasn't so lucky.

Water spewed at him with the force of a tidal wave. Two guards outside of the giant cell aimed a wide orange hose toward him and the other inmates from the Victor group. The water woke them all immediately. Some tried to scramble to their feet as the water ripped across their arms and faces, only to have their legs swept from beneath them. Sasha sat up, shielded his face, and tried, mostly in futility, to drink some of the water as it dripped off his arms.

Finally, the guards turned off the water and the room echoed with the splash of inmates lapping it up from the floor and panting as they licked the droplets off their arms and legs. Sasha took a deep breath. His arms no longer ached, he peered at his shoulders, only to find them a bit hard, not swollen like a bruise.

Enough light came from the hallway to illuminate three guards, each with a large sack. They opened the door with a screech from the hinges and threw the bag in. The way small sphere-like objects spilled from the bag told everyone it was food. Unsure if they were potatoes or rolls or onions, Sasha leapt at them and took a bite, surprised to find they were apples. Mushy and bruised and undoubtedly riddled with worms, Sasha snatched an armful and moved to a far corner to eat them.

It had to have been a few hours later when the guards approached the fence.

"We need Victor-1," the guard said.

A flash of white, a lab coat, caught Sasha's attention. He peered closer only to see that it wasn't a guard. It was a scientist. Maybe the woman from before who'd given him one of the shots. His mind was clearing slowly, but not quickly enough to understand.

"Sasha Popov?" the lean man asked, glancing at the paperwork in his hands for the briefest moment.

Sasha didn't move. He didn't respond at first.

The guard rapped his palka against the bars and the

weapon sang out a threat, discernable in any language. The man barked out his name. "Sasha Popov. Identify yourself!"

"Why?" Sasha said, dully.

"Come to the gate. No one else can approach or you'll be shot."

Slipping a bit on the cold, wet cement, Sasha approached the gate. The guard opened it, pulled Sasha out, and locked the door behind him.

They went only to the next room and disoriented as he was, Sasha couldn't tell where they were. Sasha looked around for his friends, but they'd been taken to other sections. He couldn't remember if they'd been put in U or W or moved to M. Sasha looked for Pedrick and tried to remember when he'd last seen him. Pedrick Markos had been, he thought, in the back corner, in an unmarked section. *And Stefan?* The flash of a spinning palka out of the corner of his eye demanded his attention.

The guard didn't hit him.

Sasha tried again to clear his mind. He sat in a metal chair bolted to the floor of a small cell, maybe identical to the one he'd been in, but it was hard to tell without moving around. Two doctors, the same ones who'd injected him, stood in front of him, behind the thick bars discussing him in low voices. Two guards, both with palkas at the ready, stared at him with malice and suspicion; he knew better than to move.

"The Romeos showed signs within hours," the lean scientist muttered. "And the Uniforms reactions have varied."

"When will the Romeo be here?" the woman asked, glancing briefly toward the door.

One of the guards spoke up. "They're on their way."

Sasha decided to stand and test his legs. He felt, somehow, that as he became more alert, he became more aware of his surroundings than he had been before being injected. He had the fleeting impression that if one of the guards opened the door, he could use the slippery floor to his advantage. He could rush the guards, slide across the floor, and knock them both down before climbing on top of them and taking their palkas before—

Sasha shook his head and jerked his head suddenly to the door. The image had been bloody and violent and completely uncharacteristic. Insanity was common among inmates, so he felt that's what had happened to him.

Insanity was infecting him. Emboldening him.

He wouldn't move when the door opened. The situation changed anyway when they brought a livid inmate down the hallway. The man stood as tall as Sasha. They'd obviously picked some of their most imposing guards to escort him down the hallway.

The guards in the cell with Sasha opened the door, directed the large inmate they were calling Romeo in, and then shut it. The large guards stayed, and seven pairs of eyes stared in at Sasha and the Romeo.

"Fight," the scientist said, with the same tone as if he'd just asked them to sit.

Sasha glanced at the inmate with little more than a curious indifference. *Fight?* He thought, and with the word alone, an idea came to him.

He could drop to a knee and grab behind the man's leg before sliding his own weight to the side and tossing the man to the ground with his own momentum. If he could get the man up high enough, he could drop him on his own head which might kill him right away.

Shocked again at the image, Sasha shook his head. He locked eyes with the inmate and felt he could see similar violent images sprouting behind his eyes.

"Dr. Bolest," the woman said to the lean scientist beside her. "How will we get the Victor and Romeo to fight?"

"Respectfully, Dr. Fransson, we'll kill them both if they don't."

A hulking guard stepped from the shadows. The blade at

his waist designated him as a captain. "Fight," he said. "And one of you will live."

"Please mark down Victor-1," Dr. Bolest said to Dr. Fransson. "And Romeo-03."

It was with some confusion that Sasha accepted that on the paperwork, he'd become Victor-1.

The captain outside the cell pulled out his Lugar and clicked the safety off. "You have to the count of three before I shoot you both. Fight, you skudging rats!" he screamed. He emphatically hit the bars with the palka in his other hand.

The ringing sound emanating was like a bell, announcing the beginning of a battle as Romeo-03 raised his fists up near his eyebrows and began to circle Sasha. He threw out a fist, and his arms were longer than Sasha expected. He caught Romeo's punch right in the mouth. His teeth cut his lips. When he smiled, deep red shone from between his teeth.

His face throbbed immediately as he tasted the metallic tang of his own blood from the deep cut on his bottom lip.

Romeo didn't hesitate. He stepped forward, lunging for Sasha's leg, and Sasha instinctively pulled it away just in time to circle to the right, and grab a fistful of Romeo's collar. He yanked Romeo down, catching him off balance, and followed the directions as they entered his mind. He sprawled out, putting his weight on the back of Romeo's neck and upper back. His opponent fell to his knees and Sasha looped his arm around Romeo's neck, making sure his arm slipped tight below his chin. He fell backward. Pulled his arm tight. Wrapped his legs around the Romeo so he couldn't stand. He couldn't fight back.

Romeo threw a few punches wildly into Sasha's ribs as Sasha pulled him tighter, diving the bones of his arm into the blood vessels of the other prisoner's neck.

Romeo kicked once. Then twice. Then he became still.
Wholly still.

Arms shaking, Sasha released Romeo. He stared at the

body on the floor. The words from the observers came to him as if from a fog.

"Victors are proving to be much more dangerous."

"He made quick work of that."

"Imagine those abilities, in a soldier rather than a rat."

Sasha snapped to attention. He rolled the Romeo over and looked at his face.

He'd killed him. Killed a man, and not even an enemy. Guilt swam into his throat, making it feel tight. He'd avoided going to war because he'd found murder to be reprehensible, and now he'd committed it. He'd killed a man from Khizmit.

The room seemed to spin around him, faster and faster, and the floor seemed to rock back and forth. He looked back at the man, his vision swirling, swimming, spinning and then, suddenly, Sasha threw up all over the floor.

The chunks of partially chewed apples and brownish water splashed over the corpse and Sasha turned, sickened at how he continued to defile the man. Pinkish patches of blood speckled the floor with the vomit. The acid from his stomach burned the cut on his lip.

"Victor-1!" a man shouted. Sasha made him repeat it twice more before he looked up. "Victor-1!" Dr. Bolest shouted again.

Sasha wiped his face off and looked up, enraged at what they'd made him do. At what they'd turned him into.

"Your lip is injured," Dr. Fransson said quietly. Calmly. As if she hadn't just witnessed manslaughter. "Heal it. Think about healing it."

"You think telling him to heal it will make him heal it?" Dr. Bolest questioned.

"It worked for the Uniforms."

Sasha knew what they'd done. They'd changed him. They'd given him something, some poison, to turn him into a murder machine. They'd injected him and changed him.

"It's already working," Dr. Bolest said. "All subjects who

didn't receive a variation of the seventh serum have experienced exceptionally high levels of pain."

Sasha assumed his lack of pain was due to adrenaline, but when he considered his lip, he felt a whisper of pain, as if waiting for him to give it permission to scream at him.

Through a hateful gaze, Sasha surveyed the doctors. *He could heal? Just by thinking about it?*

As improbable as it sounded, he'd already seen how the injections had changed him. What was healing compared to changing the way his brain worked and assessed threats? He told himself simply to heal the cut on his lip.

It felt cool for a moment, like an invisible hand was dragging an invisible block of ice across his face, and in that moment, the swelling disappeared. His tongue searched for the cut, only to find smooth skin.

The doctors laughed as they watched him. Thrilled by their creation, they actually laughed and turned to their clipboards to scribble down notes.

Sasha glared at them, glanced at the corpse again, and then swore under his breath, "You won't laugh for long."

CHAPTER 2
THE FALL OF ZALAR

SASHA SAT on the floor of the giant cell surrounded by the other Victors. The guards had come and taken one at a time out of the room, and more often than not, they came back later, with a tremble in their hands, but no visible injuries.

One woman the guards called "Victor-27" returned with wide eyes and three deep scratches across her face.

She slumped to the damp floor beside Sasha, trembling slightly, still trying to catch her breath.

Sasha waited until the guards' footsteps faded to a dull echo around a distant corner before addressing her. Even with the angry red gashes on her face, Sasha had to take a moment to build up his courage to address her, intimidated as he was by her beauty. She had small eyes, wide with worry, and she had her lips pulled tight into a thin line across her face. But he didn't address her because she was beautiful. He mourned with her, guessing at what she'd done in the other room. The same room that Sasha had been to.

"I'm Sasha," he said. She didn't react at all at first. Didn't look his way. Didn't acknowledge him in the slightest. She just stared at the floor near her filthy shoes with glassy eyes.

"It should hurt," she finally murmured. "My face should hurt. I know she raked it with her hand, like a wild animal."

She hesitated and Sasha let her think for a few seconds before continuing. "I saw the blood and for a moment, a quick moment, it did hurt. But then that woman, that doctor, told me I shouldn't be able to feel pain. And now I don't."

The two sat for a moment on the hard floor as whispers of other conversations echoed like a distant wind around the large cell.

"They also told you that you can heal?" Sasha asked.

"Yes," she said, her face still mortified. "But I don't want to. I refused to."

Sasha knew not to ask her if she'd killed someone in the back room. Her hands trembled because of what they'd done to someone. He reached out slowly, sure she saw his movements, and placed his hand on top of her small one.

What could he say? He had no ideas. He held her hand not as a lover, or a gateway to other physical actions of affection, but as an action of comfort. As a way to say, "I'm here. I'm with you. You're not alone."

He hoped she understood and it seemed, by the slightest movement of her mouth, that she did.

When the sirens began to wail, few in the room reacted at first. They'd heard sirens before on the few occasions that an inmate had tried to escape. A flicker of envy coursed through Sasha.

Escape.

Then hope replaced the envy. An idea, as detailed as the instructions on how to fight, entered his mind. A plan of how to escape. Now that he was a changed man, he could feasibly get out. Maybe he could get out while the other breakout occupied many of the guards.

As Sasha stood, he realized he wasn't the only one with the idea. All of them appeared to be plotting paths to the same future.

They rushed to the bars, some stripping off their shirts in the process. By the light of the dim lanterns in the hallway, they swarmed the doors. Some began wrapping their clothes around the thick unyielding bars, twisting and trying to pry them open.

In the distance, gunshots and shouting combined with screams grew from distant and indistinct to a near cacophony as a mob of inmates burst through the door.

At the sight of the Victors struggling with the bars, three of the men and two of the women stopped and, with their bare hands, pulled the doors off the cell. Their strength was inhuman and now all the Victors were free. Sasha pulled his new friend to the side, unnecessarily, as she skirted around the rushing mob. For a brief moment, they shared a smile.

"Good luck," she said, and disappeared into the flowing mass of inmates.

For a second Sasha almost followed the group out to the open world, but then he paused. The pop and crack of guns behind him screamed a warning of his safety, but his friends could still be back there, in a cell, getting altered.

Pedrick had been so sick.

Sasha took a deep breath, and turned back into the building, toward the sounds and the darkness and the flickering light of small fires.

He walked carefully through the hallways, stepping over the bodies of guards and inmates, not looking too closely lest he fuel the fear in his chest. His heartbeat made his hands feel numb. This is what he'd wanted to avoid in war. Death. Loss. Gore. The desperate rattle of men's final breaths.

This was worse for him—this shouldn't have been war. These were all people from Khizmit. Among the dead and dying were women. Women he felt in his gut he should have been protecting. Women who'd been taken and mistreated and manipulated now lay in pools of their own blood on the floor of the prison.

Anger and revulsion swelled inside him in equal measure.

He bent down and took a flashlight and a Lugar from a corpse.

Sasha had to focus, still placing one foot in front of the other as he looked for his friends. The flashlight's beam cast a strong circle of illumination, and a long grey line down the middle where the glass was cracked. The facility seemed, for the most part, to be empty of all living. Scientists lay on the ground, their lab coats sticky with the blood they'd altered. Their lives were taken by the hands they'd made capable.

Sasha stepped gingerly into a room and searched through the rubble of some filing cabinets and scattered paperwork with the broken beam. His friends weren't there. No one was.

He continued on, hoping they'd have escaped. Maybe Stefan had made it out, but Pedrick had seemed too sick. Maybe they'd given him a serum.

Maybe the serum had killed him before the breakout.

Maybe Stefan had found Pedrick and helped him outside.

Sasha gasped as his beam found a tangle of dead women, their hands full of each other's hair, their faces fixed in angry twisted expressions even as they'd each taken bullets to the head.

It was nearly an hour before Sasha found Pedrick.

Pedrick sat in a cell with three other men, all pale and sickly. Sasha wasn't sure if one of them was dead or not.

"Pedrick," he knelt beside his friend who lay curled on his side. Sasha placed an unsteady hand on his shoulder. "Let's go."

The shake of his head, though small, was clear.

"I'll carry you," Sasha said, more determined. He went to set the flashlight on the ground, but Pedrick reached over and grabbed Sasha's wrist. His feeble grip did more to capture Sasha's attention than a vice grip would have.

"They'll track you down. I heard them talking. They always intended to kill us all after the tests. We were only ever to be lab rats."

"What did they give you?"

"Nothing," Pedrick said. "They left us here to die. We were too weak to use a serum. No food. No water. They've left us with nothing."

"But I'm here now. I'll get you out."

"I'm already dead." Pedrick said, his face somber. "I can feel it. Death is patient. It's sitting with us now, waiting for me to reach out and take its hand."

"Take mine instead."

"I would if there was any hope for me. But there isn't."

"There is!" Sasha insisted.

"Listen carefully to me, please. They gave you a serum?"

Sasha nodded.

"They'll find you and they'll kill you for what they've made you into. As long as you stay in Khizmit, they'll know. But if you can find the files and change our information, then you'll be safe."

"What do you mean?"

"Become me," he said, with more foresight than Sasha had expected from him.

"What? Why?" Sasha heard himself asking.

"They'll see from the records that I was never given a serum. If any records make it out of here, they'll know you were given one. That you're one of the inmates."

"I'm not one of them."

Pedrick coughed. "In war, there are only two sides brother. With them or against them. Until you can win the war against them, you better make skudging sure they think you're with them."

Sasha understood what Pedrick meant for him to do. He had to become Pedrick Markos and let Sasha Popov die here in a cell. If Sasha assumed his identity, then when he was found, they'd know he'd been here. That he knew what had happened. And he could claim he'd escaped when everyone else did. He could convince them that seeing it changed him and made him more loyal to Khizmit. He could even, dare he think of it, help track down some of the inmates.

"But Stefan? What about him?" Sasha asked.

"You can't both be me. And he isn't here," Pedrick said. He knew Sasha well enough to know that he understood the need. The dilemma.

"Go make a name for us, Pedrick," Pedrick said, laughing even as his face turned ghostly white.

Sasha knelt and pulled his friend into a tight embrace. "I'll burn them to the ground."

In the midst of the bedlam, Sasha wove his way through rubble to the files. Ignoring any cries for help, delirious with adrenaline as he moved huge pieces of that prison out of his path. He went back to the room with the filing cabinets and dug through the files in a fervor. He took the grainy, black-and-white picture from his file, pried it off with shaky hands, and placed it underneath his friend's name in his file. Pedrick Markos.

He'd been right. They'd labeled him too sick for the study. Too sick for the serum.

If they ever found the files, they'd never recognize Sasha for who he was. Sasha was dead.

The new Pedrick Markos wiped off his hands, grabbed the Lugar and the flashlight, and left the prison a changed man.

But not in the way that Khizmit would ever suspect.

CHAPTER 3
NEW TATTOOS

"As far as anyone is concerned, Sasha Popov died that night. I will never forget him, but it's best if you do," Markos explained.

"You were brave. You've always been brave," Roman said.

"I was young, reckless, and lucky," Markos said sheepishly. More sheepishly than I'd ever seen him before as he nervously scratched the back of his head. *Was it shame? Embarrassment? Or was he feeling a pain that couldn't be numbed?*

By now the sun was rising, illuminating dozens of triangular outlines on the horizon. Markos sped along. He turned the wheel to the right and we passed a few piles of debris and a broken vehicle. He slowed then stopped.

The engine died, leaving us in a temporary silence. This was the beginning of something new. The beginning of the coup. Markos threw the truck into park and sighed.

"Roman will have to process you, Lockbox." Markos offered Lockbox a sympathetic look. "I'm sorry. You're still a lurper here. Roman will change the 17 so you won't be the missing Oscar and we'll do our best to keep your injuries a secret without aggravating them."

"Tie me to a desk," Lockbox suggested. "That way it'll

look like I'm not moving because I'm not allowed to. Just for a few weeks."

"I'll consider it," Markos said. "I'll forge the paperwork stating that your transfer here was approved if anyone asks. You're here as a key strategist."

"Yes, Sir. Whatever you need."

"We can't do this without you," Markos said.

Lockbox laughed sardonically. "I hope to be as helpful and knowledgeable as you imagine I am."

The four of us climbed out of the car and this time Roman assisted Lockbox. With one arm around Lockbox in what, from a distance, was a possible hold common when escorting prisoners, Roman walked toward the tent in front of us. Markos grabbed a few bags off the back of the truck and hoisted them over his shoulders.

Almost as soon as Roman and Lockbox had disappeared behind the loose tent flaps three soldiers hurried over. Two men, a high captain and a captain. One woman, also a captain. I stiffened at the sight of their rank patches.

"Commander Markos, Sir," the male captain said. He had a few blonde curls coming out of the front of his ushanka. "Happy Koliada!"

"Captain Gaborik," Markos said, probably for my benefit more than anything else.

"We weren't expecting you back yet," Captain Gaborik said. He threw a cursory glance my way and then began unloading supplies alongside Markos.

The female captain didn't say anything. She was lithe and nearly as tall as the other captain.

Markos took a few steps away from the truck. "I'd have preferred to stay but I'm not always in charge," he said. If they wondered why he wasn't in uniform, they didn't ask. Was it as odd for them to see him dressed like a normal man as it was for me? I glanced at my clothes. Did Markos find it odd to see me outside of prison clothes?

The wind suddenly gusted around me and slammed the open door of the truck shut with a bang like a gunshot.

Only the woman glanced at me. Following their lead, I walked to the bed of the truck to assist with unloading the supplies.

I lifted one of the wooden crates and trailed Captain Gaborik, Commander Markos, and the other two officers down a worn path on the small hill toward a tan tent.

Markos set the supplies down outside the tent. The high captain followed and then clapped him on the shoulder.

"Happy Koliada, Sir," he said. The high captain had a reddish beard and looked at me with an expression that wasn't altogether unfriendly. "Who's this?"

"This is Luka," Markos said. His gaze briefly flitted down to my hands, which were safely gloved for the time being. "He'll be working with Captain Kral."

"He's back then?" the high captain asked. He was careful with his tone. If he knew the rumors of why Roman had been sent to Predvoi, neither his tone nor expression revealed it.

"Captain Kral fulfilled his assignment at Predvoi honorably. We're lucky to have him back. He'll take back his position as Commander of Third Company." Markos nodded to me, and all the officers stared. "Luka, this is Captain Gaborik, High Captain Toth, and Captain Sakrova."

Captain Sakrova smiled, revealing a missing front tooth. I didn't allow any surprise to enter my expression.

"Take care of the supplies," Markos said. "We'll regroup this afternoon."

High Captain Toth, the bearded officer, began issuing directions to the other two.

I could nearly feel the questions in the air as Markos and I turned to walk away. My questions hung in the air, unspoken. These soldiers weren't like Captain Crease or Lieutenant Ivanov—they respected Markos too much to question him.

Markos stopped at the truck and grabbed a large, brown

duffel bag. I thought, momentarily, that he'd ask me to carry it, but instead, he slung it around his shoulder and kept walking. By the time we reached the entrance of the commander's tent, the officers down the hill had unlocked the door and moved most of the supplies inside.

Roman and Lockbox sat in the center of a tall tent stationed in a semi-permanent military camp. Roman held a needle to Lockbox's wrist, his attention so fixed he didn't look over when Markos and I entered. Occasional gunfire broke the air in the distance, to the south.

"They're training at the range," Markos explained as if reading my mind. He took a seat and gestured for me to sit on a small wooden trunk, not unlike the ones issued to lurpers.

The four of us sat alone in the tent, if it could still be called a tent. I'd always pictured tents to be small, fragile, temporary things, but this made all those assumptions look idiotic. Huge wooden beams supported the thick canvas and had to be dug into the ground very deep to make the structure stand up against what I'd come to learn were occasional but strong bursts of wind down near The Outskirts. Roman finally dropped his hands leaving a few small beads of blood to dry on the inside of Lockbox's left wrist.

It now read O-16. Roman had become his aunt's son. Sasha Popov had become Pedrick Markos. Lockbox had become Oscar-16.

Had I become Luka? It didn't feel as much like me as Victor. I would forever be Victor, no matter how long people called me Luka. I was both.

A gust of wind tugged at the flaps over the windows, but they held. In the distance, the rip of fabric informed us that one of the other tents hadn't.

I couldn't help but notice that Markos had also named my father among his friends that night. I'd kept quiet, knowing better than to interrupt, but now that he was done, I let the question out.

"My father, Stefan Krajnak, did you see him again?" I asked, but Markos shook his head. He bent over some paperwork that he hurriedly scribbled on.

"No," he said. "What do you want me to put as your name?" Markos looked up to Lockbox.

"Can I keep Lockbox?"

Markos hesitated. "Yes."

"Are there risks?"

"We're in too deep. I've spun too many lies. Everything becomes more delicate by the hour. Whether you go by Peter, Lockbox, or Ivan, it won't make a difference at the end of the day. There are other threads that lead to me." Markos sounded worried. It wasn't like him.

It was clear from Lockbox's expression that he had more questions. Questions about Zalar. Questions about being here, or forging paperwork, or if someone could change their identity so quickly, but he didn't voice any of them.

Or maybe, I considered. *Maybe he doesn't have questions. Maybe he has more answers.*

I looked at the needle in Roman's hands and the fresh ink in Lockbox's wrist. The tattoos on Roman's fingers had been the work of his own hands, hands so steady he'd tattooed the numerals on all his knuckles with equal skill and precision.

"It looks good," Markos said, standing. "Because you're the only Oscar here, you'll stay here, in my tent. I can keep an eye on you here. It'll simplify coordination. While it's only a matter of time until the legion learns we have an Oscar, I have no intention of announcing it to anyone outside of my cadre."

"Your cadre?" I asked. "Those officers I met?"

"I'm the commander of the Lurper Legion, but I don't run it alone. I can't. High Captain Toth is my second-in-command. We have three companies, and each company commander is a captain who has a second-in-command who is usually a lieutenant."

"You said Roman is a company commander."

"Captain Gaborik is the commander of First Company. Captain Sakrova is the commander of Second Company. Now that Roman is back he'll resume command of Third Company."

I gaped. "Skudge, you really left your position of company commander to come to Predvoi?"

Roman wiped the blood off Lockbox's wrist. He didn't look at me. "Worth it," he said.

Something Roman had told me back in Khizmit entered my mind. Lowering my voice, I asked, "Then what did you mean when you said people didn't know you and Markos were working together?"

Roman raised his eyebrow at me.

"When you needed a reason to go to his home and you and Emberly...you know...went back together. You said people didn't know you and Markos were working together. But you were a company commander in his Legion. You obviously worked together."

Roman leaned in. "They didn't know we were working together on things regarding a coup. Obviously, we worked together out here. Everyone knew that."

"Then they'd know that you knew who Emberly was."

"Not necessarily, but that is a topic that's been debated. Some people say I was a slaghead for not doing my due diligence and asking more questions about the girl I followed home. Others have claimed that I targeted her specifically thinking it would somehow win me some favors with the commander. Can you just believe me when I say that she and I did the best we could trying to navigate potential gossip? We opted for killing our reputations rather than risk drawing attention to the coup. People would rather assume a scandal than an insurrection."

I nodded. The explanation would have to be enough.

Markos pulled over his brown bag and unclipped the

opening. He dug around for a moment and pulled out a thick black folder.

"If anyone looks closely, this deception will be obvious, but let's not give them a reason to," Markos said, stuffing the paperwork into the folder. "But at least if High Captain Toth wants to look over the paperwork, he'll have something to see regarding Lockbox."

Markos rummaged around his heavy bag and began organizing a few things on the desk.

"They don't know?" I asked. Roman hadn't even known what Markos was.

"No one knows. Just us."

"Are there any other hidden lurpers or Test Criminals among the cadre?"

"No," Markos said. "I don't believe so."

"How did you discover what Roman was?" Lockbox said.

"Observation," Markos replied with a chuckle. "I knew what to look for. I confronted him."

"Respectfully, he scared the slag out of me," Roman said. He moved his gear over to me and with a scrape, dragged his chair beside mine. Was he going to re-ink me too? Was I back to being a Victor? This time a Victor-17? Victor-29?

"Who am I now, Sir?" I asked Markos. I'd play whatever role I needed to. He'd told me at his home that he needed me to be a weapon. He needed me to be dangerous.

"You're always you." He met my gaze. "You wear masks, and you have different sides you show to different people, but whatever name you go by, you're you. Don't lose sight of that."

I nodded.

"You are Luka and I need you to become a member of my cadre."

His words meant the impossible. I stared at Lockbox whose blue eyes were much clearer now. I could tell that he could see me now, at least clearly enough to read surprise on my features.

"First, you have to get rid of that tattoo for once and for all." Markos continued shuffling through papers behind his desk. He set a few pages aside and continued to flip through maps and charts.

"I could burn the rest of the ink out," I suggested. I'd even considered the ghastlier option of cutting out the ink and regrowing the skin. Painless as it would be, the idea left me nauseated.

"No," Markos said.

"The biggest mistake I see Victors make is disrespecting themselves because they can't feel it. Your body is still human, Luka. Respect it. Our ability to heal is a gift and an advantage, but not a show. I'm convinced that even when we heal, our injuries scar us somehow. There's still a cost. Maybe it's mental."

He stopped what he was doing, to drive the warning home. "You still need to be careful with yourself. With your mind."

"Yes, Sir." I looked at my wrist and handed it over to Roman. Clearly, he and Markos had discussed a plan.

"It's faint, but without any other ink around it, it's still legible," Roman said.

"Other ink?"

"We need to put more ink on you to cover this. You don't want a tattoo?"

I felt I'd been inked enough and would have preferred never to have seen a needle again. But that wasn't one of my options. What was the punishment for having another tattoo as a lurper? What was the punishment for giving a lurper ink other than their designation? We were well past that now. Well past worrying what they'd do. We knew. Roman knew what he'd risked coming to Predvoi.

Roman tapped a finger to the V.

"Do you know why they ink your wrist?" Roman asked.

"So they can identify us?"

"I mean why there? Why not across your forehead?"

I'd never considered that as an option. I briefly imagined V-27 across my cheek instead of the scar that had been there for five years. The scar I'd erased at the first opportunity.

"I'm sure one of the reasons is that tattoos are painful, but the real reason is because you see your own wrist all day. They wanted your label where they could see it, sure, but the most important thing to them was to put it somewhere *you* could see it."

The crusters had thought it out. Roman went on: "So, you'll want something on your wrist that's worth seeing all day. Something that represents people or ideas that mean a lot to you."

"Nothing means a lot to me," I said instinctively.

"That's not true," Roman said.

My few friends mattered to me. Emberly mattered. Even the beautiful parts of Khizmit. I summed up what I valued most. "Freedom. But I don't want that word across my wrist."

Roman chuckled. I mulled over a few ideas, but nothing seemed good enough to permanently ink into my skin.

"What do you think?" I asked Lockbox.

Lockbox shifted in his seat and pain flashed through his eyes for a moment. He knew I saw it.

"I'm okay," he said. "There's a lot of beauty in symbolism. A star with eight points represents hope. That lends itself nicely to a V."

A star wasn't the worst thing I could get on my wrist.

"This is a date," Roman said, showing me his index tattoo. "This is my mother's birthday." He gestured to another one. "This is the day I went to live with my aunt."

He pointed to another series of numbers. "This is my father's birthday. And this is the day they executed him."

Roman's hands told a story, not just in the scars along his

fingers, and the dirt beneath his nails, but in the ink he'd deliberately placed there.

I was immediately sobered. Of all the times I'd stared at his hands. I'd never realized they were dates. I'd never bothered to think about it.

"When I look at my hands, I see these dates, and it reminds me of the sacrifices and people who got me where I am today. It motivates me to do what needs to be done. Sometimes that means I pull a trigger when I'd rather not because I'm seeing the big picture."

I nodded, still thinking. What mattered to me was freedom. Not just my own, but Lockbox's, and even a bunch of the other slagheaded lurpers I'd met who I didn't like, but still deserved to have a life outside of the mines. Freedom to run when we wanted to. Freedom to keep what we earned. Freedom to have relationships.

My thoughts went back to Ember. Markos had to know that I'd kissed her, even though he hadn't said anything about it. *What was there to say? Tell me not to do it again?* She was back in Khizmit, and now I had a whole legion of inmates to get to know and help train for a military coup.

"Have you decided what you want?" Roman asked, readying his needle.

"No," I admitted. "But I want something to cover this."

"Do you trust me?" Roman asked, and I met his gaze.

"Yes," I said.

"Then hold out your arm."

CHAPTER 4
JUNIOR LIEUTENANT DRIVICK

PINE TREES. Detailed, shaded pine trees grew along the horizon of my wrist and extended up my forearm. Pine trees like the ones I'd watched and wandered through when I'd slipped outside of Predvoi.

I didn't say anything as I choked on some emotion. The complete lack of pain had made me think the tattoo would be small. Since Roman had tattooed dates on his hand, I figured maybe he'd turn mine into dates, but obviously my body had subconsciously blocked the pain and healed the tattoo even while he did it. The tattoo, though far more extensive than I would have picked, stirred emotion in me.

The trees reminded me of my rebirth. I traversed the woods and came out a new man. Not an inmate. Not a boy. Not a threat.

I was Luka now. Not Victor. A soldier, not a prisoner.

It was all I could do to just nod. *What would I say to Roman? Tell him it touched me that he knew me well enough to pick a tattoo that would be so meaningful for me?* There wasn't a way to put it into words. I had a friend. A brother.

"You like it?" Roman said. I nodded again. "If not, you could always stick your arm back into the fire, burn out the ink, heal up and I'll try again."

Markos didn't look up from his desk. He and Lockbox had been poring over documents, muttering under their breath while Roman had worked away at my arm. I could have listened, and maybe they wouldn't have minded if I did, but most of what they would talk about was most likely too diffi-cult to follow without seeing what they were looking at. Markos had asked about the mountains to the west of Khizmit and Lockbox had recited examples from history when men had tried to cross, only to disappear or lose half the members of their party.

"I like it," I said to Roman. "You do good work," I added, admiring it. Roman no doubt knew he'd done great.

Several thick trunks streaked up my arm with detailed branches. There was absolutely no way to tell that beneath this ink, this forest of pines, a faint V-27 had existed. It was no longer faint; it was gone.

"If you're done, it's time to meet the troops," Commander Markos said, standing. Lockbox sat on a bench with wheels. I wiped the blood and then accidentally healed it before showing it to the two of them. Markos glanced at my wrist and I held it out for him, reminding me of the many times I'd done so for him to read V-27 before shuffling me between rooms. He chuckled, letting a small grin sneak across his face.

"Looks good. Suits you," he commented.

"It's better than a star," Lockbox said.

Markos pulled two brown parcels from his bag. He handed the smaller one to me. On the top, in his scribbled cursive it read, *Happy Koliada, Luka.*

"This one is from Zuzana and I both. But I confess it was mostly her idea."

I took the box into my hands, half-wanting to wait and try to guess the contents, but curiosity forbade me from waiting. The paper crinkled loudly beneath my hands as I pulled away the brown paper, revealing a wooden chess board. As I flipped it around in my hands, I found a drawer and the small metal knob screwed into the end. Small, carved white wooden pieces filled the space and I pulled them out, counting them. Excitedly, I flipped the box around and found a second drawer, full of matching pieces but in black.

A full chess set. I could have cried if I hadn't been in the presence of Markos and Roman. Maybe if I'd been back with Zuzana and Emberly. Instead, I swallowed the lump in my throat and sniffed discreetly.

"Thank you," I said. I almost asked him how he'd known but I didn't need to. Markos had been watching me. He'd known I'd tried to gather all the pieces to a chess set and had finally given up. Besides not having the pieces, I'd never been able to find someone willing to play with me. Not before Lockbox, and not since. Not that there had been time since.

"Rematch?" I asked Lockbox.

"Only when you want a lesson in humility."

I'd never looked forward to getting beat more.

"I was going to give it to you back home," Markos said. "But…you know…plans change."

"Thank you," I said. "Thank you, Sir."

Markos gave half a grin and then shoved the second brown package my way, only giving me a moment to set the chess board on the small table before the mess of brown paper landed on my lap.

This one was soft, not boxed. Something like clothes. I tore into it finding I was right.

It was clothes. Not a striped prison uniform. Not something worn and used that labeled me as less-than-human. This was a promotion to humanity. Gawking, I held it up.

A uniform to match Roman and Commander Markos, except for the ribbons and rank. A brown uniform with long sleeves and brass buttons, the Khizmit Flag already sewn onto the shoulder of the right sleeve.

"Thank you," I said, trying to keep any and all emotion from my voice.

Markos smiled. "Put it on."

I dressed quickly, only fumbling with the shiny buttons for a moment. I'd have thought that donning the uniform of the guards who'd harassed me my whole life would make me angry, but the words from Pedrick Markos, the real Pedrick Markos, came back to my mind.

"Until you can win the war against them, you better make skudging sure they think you're with them."

Markos pulled another uniform out of his bag and passed it to Lockbox. "Happy Koliada, Lockbox," he said.

While my friend dressed himself, I tried not to notice how long it took Lockbox to get the pants on with his injuries.

When I stood, fully dressed in my new uniform, Markos grinned at me before his expression turned serious again. He called me over to the center of the tent to stand beside a Khizmit flag which hung from the top of the tent canvas. Roman moved Lockbox closer. I couldn't believe the four of us, all altered by Khizmit, now wore the uniform.

Markos spoke to me in a low voice, so none of his words could carry outside the tent. "You'll go by your birth name. I take it you'll want to keep Luka?"

I nodded.

"What last name do you want?"

My father's last name was Krajnak. Perhaps it would have been honorable to take his name. Maybe I should have, but I didn't want his name. I didn't know him. He was nothing to me.

"Lockbox," I said, turning to him. "Will you give me a name?"

Lockbox looked more shocked than he had when I'd told him about killing High Warden Velky.

He didn't ask me if I was sure. He didn't even hesitate

more than a moment. He just glanced at Markos, got a ridiculous grin on his face, and said, "Drivick. Luka Drivick."

As he said it, I laughed. I loved it.

"I see what you did there," I said. I looked to Markos to see if he noticed. To see if he cared. "Do you…mind?"

"Mind?" Markos said. "I would be…honored."

He knew what Lockbox had done. Pedrickivick would have been translated to "son of Pedrick." But Drivick was distant enough that no one had to know. No one except for us.

"Attention," Markos said. Though it was only me, Lockbox, and Roman in the room, he'd said it like an announcement. His accent became richer as he spoke in his serious voice. The one I'd heard most often at Rhosivi. Roman snapped to attention and I tried to imitate him.

"I, Commander Pedrick Markos, acting on behalf of the Government of Khizmit, do hereby promote Luka Drivick, who has proven himself to be trustworthy, diligent, sound of mind and body, and who has demonstrated necessary qualities of a leader, to the rank of Junior Lieutenant in the Khizmit National Ground Force. Effective today, the 27th day of the twelfth month in the year 1915."

Markos stepped closer and slapped the patch onto my sleeve with such force that I nearly fell over. Roman grinned and motioned for me to salute Markos. I snapped my hand up, he adjusted the angle of my thumb, and I did it again.

"Congratulations, Junior Lieutenant Luka Drivick. At ease." Markos nodded to me and stepped back so Roman could step forward. I expected him to either clap me so hard on the shoulder that it nearly knocked me over or for him to shake my hand.

He did neither.

Roman stepped toward me, wrapped his arms around me, and said, "Congratulations, JLT."

"I'll take care of the paperwork, Sir," Lockbox said. He got to work at the desk, beaming.

Markos slung an arm over my shoulder. "When you're ready, I'll introduce you to the legion. They're probably not what you're expecting."

What was I expecting? On one hand, I expected rejection and looks of fear and distrust, but these weren't inmates. At least, not in the sense of inmates at Rhosivi or Predvoi. These were soldiers, just as dangerous, if not more, as me.

But they wouldn't know what I was. To them, I was a Junior Lieutenant. A cruster.

Luka Drivick. Junior Lieutenant Luka Drivick. I'd gone from a letter to a whole name, title and all. Roman and Markos stepped back and I took a moment to admire the small gold threads that made up the birch leaf on the patch.

My face grew warm either because this was the furthest south I'd ever been and the uniform was warm, or for a different reason—something to do with feeling emotions that I'd never felt before. Even if the nummers back in Rhosivi and Predvoi had been made to quell these feelings, there'd never been a need. It had to be some swirling combination of delight, disbelief, and surprise.

It was one thing to wear a uniform and feel like a fraud, but it was a completely different thing to wear the rank of a Junior Lieutenant knowing nothing about the Khizmit National Ground Force.

Markos called me over to the desk which was now almost entirely covered in a map. I recognized a few points on it, Rhosivi, Predvoi, and Khizmit. I'd never known the location of Vazenia before now. It sat nearly parallel to Rhosivi, but in a valley between two large mountains, almost equidistant from Predvoi and Rhosivi. Markos gestured for me to take a seat.

"The Penal Legion, more commonly called The Lurper

Legion," Markos began, "isn't exactly a legion. It's a battalion." He tapped his finger on the edge of the table.

"What's the difference?" I asked, refusing to let my ignorance embarrass me.

"There are three soldiers in a team. Three teams in a squad. Three squads in a platoon. Three platoons in a company. Three companies in a battalion."

Lockbox did the math immediately. "Are there really 243 soldiers here in this battalion?"

"No," Markos said, stiffly. "They try to keep it exact, but I keep requesting more soldiers, if only to get you out of the prisons."

"I never thought there'd be so many of us, the lower ones in the alphabet," I said.

"It's hard to get approval for anything other than Victors, Whiskeys, X-rays, and Yankees. We have a few Charlies around to keep order and our newly acquired Oscar." He winked at Lockbox.

"How are there so many? Enough for a battalion?" I asked.

"When they made the Test Criminals, they administered the serums in groups of 40. 40 inmates per group and 7 main serums, three variations of each resulting in 21 groups of 40. Then they got risky and mixed some of their successful serums and gave those solutions to the rest of their test groups. 40 inmates in 26 groups, but all the Zulu's died, resulting in an even 1,000 Test Criminals. Some died. Some were captured." Markos lowered his voice. "But many of us escaped and went on to live normal lives. Especially those of us who got more than one serum because it made us more dangerous. More slippery. There were 160 Victor, Whiskey, X-ray, and Yankee's combined originally. Is it any surprise we have about 230 of their kids in this battalion?"

He explained the math more patiently than Lockbox might have.

"Some doctors have theorized that the Yankee serum increased fertility in the female patients, because of how many Yankee children have been found. Most of them are female too. But, ultimately, none of that matters to us. You need to know enough to be passable as a Junior Lieutenant, second in command to Captain Kral."

I nodded, understanding the structure but none of my responsibilities. *Second in Command?* I didn't know slag from silver out here.

"We're defending this line. Latvani soldiers have sent over a few spies. We have one held hostage. They have a couple of our soldiers too, assuming they didn't kill them on sight. We're waiting to see if they agree to our terms of exchange. We sent a message with an X-ray over three weeks ago and haven't heard back."

"Will you retaliate?" I asked.

Markos pursed his lips. "No. Our job is to hold this line of defense, and we can do that easily. If I cared about winning the war against Latvani, I would have done so as soon as I became battalion commander. I'm interested in taking down Khizmit. That's where my real war is."

Roman leaned back, and his chair creaked loudly. "Yes, but I don't know if we'll send another couple of soldiers over."

"Why's that?" I asked, looking at the map where X's marked the camp of Latvani soldiers not too far from us.

"It's not safe. Or wise."

"You think there's any chance the X-ray deserted?" I asked. I would have run away from Rhosivi if I'd had a chance. Maybe these soldiers saw this as their prison, desperate to get away at the first opportunity.

"No," Markos said. "I think he was captured. I think they're disinterested in getting their soldiers back right away. They know we won't kill them."

"Why won't you—we—kill them?"

Markos stared me down. "For one, they aren't my enemy and for another thing, I want to recruit them. I want them to fight with me. If I treat them well and come to trust them, I can use them. I can't take Khizmit with a single battalion, even with the most gifted soldiers. If we're going to attack in a coup, we need more people with us. More guns. More eyes. More everything. And if all else fails, we can do a prisoner exchange."

I didn't understand completely why Markos needed Latvani's help in a military coup. Khizmit had walls, sure, but there were relatively few guards at the gate and within the city. Once they breached the entrance, they could secure themselves inside and defend it against a much larger force. It didn't seem like getting in would be that difficult, but I knew better than to voice anything like that.

"If you want Latvani to join you, why don't you just ask them? Sign a treaty about this current war and tell them your plan. They want to take over Khizmit. You want to take over Khizmit. Do it together."

Markos shook his head. "War and politics aren't so simple in practice. I wish they were."

I didn't say anything else since I knew it would only make me look stupid.

"The leader of the unit across The Outskirts is Commander Alekin. He's arrogant, outspoken, spiritual, vulgar, demanding, and unyielding. He takes what he can get where he can get it and he's a skudging good leader for it all."

I considered those traits. The legacy he was leaving for himself in Latvani and Khizmit alike. Demanding. Unyielding. *Spiritual and vulgar? Was that possible?*

Looking at my hands and the ink on my wrist I wondered how I'd be described twenty years from now.

Dangerous. That one was unavoidable, but could I pick some for them to add. What did I want? How did I want the soldiers here to describe me?

Unyielding, sure. But more than that I wanted them to know I was motivated by more than anger, rage, revenge, or desperation.

I was motivated by hope. Hope that I could be better. That the world could be better. Hope that these lurpers could be more than fodder in a war.

CHAPTER 5
RETRIBUTION

"Come on," Roman said, getting to his feet. "It's time to meet the company. They're bound to be anxious to get to know the new Junior Lieutenant."

"Who was your second-in-command before?" I asked.

"The X-ray who went missing."

"Who was the company commander in your absence?"

"The company commander for First Company stepped in. Pulled double duty."

My heart beat harder, and I hoped Roman couldn't tell that I was nervous. I'd faced Bolest, Velky, Dulka, and a Judgement Board who had given the vote for my death. I could face my fellow lurpers...But they expected me to be a leader, and I found that I expected them to be my friends.

"Luka," Markos said, and I could tell by the way he addressed me that it wasn't as a commander to a lieutenant, but something else. Something that I finally identified as the way that I thought my father would speak to me. "Sorry to reiterate the obvious, but you can't use your other abilities around them. Be compliant. Don't block pain. Don't heal. Don't fight. Most of these soldiers aren't out to get you, but some hate Khizmit, and since you're an officer representing that army, some will hate you."

The news painfully struck me. By coming here as a cruster instead of a lurper, I wasn't one of them. I was an *other*. An officer. An enforcer of Khizmit rules and regulations.

In time they'd see me for what I was, but that time wasn't yet. For now, they had to hate me.

"Captain Kral," Markos said.

Roman finished putting his supplies away and turned to Markos.

"We'll be back in a few minutes," he said.

As soon as Markos and Roman exited the tent, I hurried over to Lockbox.

Lockbox sat with the biggest grin.

"You're entirely too happy for someone with broken legs," I stated.

"You had my back." Lockbox reached an arm around me. "You went looking for my mother, thinking it was a clue."

"I'm not an Oscar, clearly," I said. "Have you filled in the rest? What happened after you left?"

"Most, but not all."

I hurriedly told him everything he'd missed, including, to my own surprise, my kiss with Emberly.

"Is this what you want? To be here, working again. I'd hate to think that I freed you from one prison to bring you to another one."

Was he less of an information slave here than he had been back at the palace or Predvoi?

"I want to live up to my potential. I'm good with information and strategy. To ignore that, to avoid using those abilities, would make me less of myself. It would be like asking you not to fight, not to be strong. The difference as I see it is, imagine you were taken as a slave by Latvani and thrown into a pit to fight another Victor to the death, the way they made Markos fight the Romeo back at Zalar. That's not who you want to be. Not how you want to use your talents. Here on the frontlines, you can become a weapon for good. Fight how you want, when you want, because you believe in a better future."

"People will think you're a slave here."

"I've never cared what people think. That's a very Victor-ish trait."

I chuckled.

"This is where we're supposed to be, Junior Lieutenant Drivick." He said it with a knowing smile.

I chuckled. "You'd be better at impersonating an officer."

"First of all, Luka, you're not impersonating one. You are one. Markos just made you a legitimate JLT. And second, you're easily passable as an adult. I don't look a day past fifteen, and I'm self-aware enough to admit it."

"Fine," I consented. "Do you…do you have anything to share with me?"

Lockbox glanced at the door. "I have a theory regarding one of the threads Markos mentioned that lead to him."

"And?"

"Do you remember how Bolest had been examining your blood and said it had changed?"

I nodded.

"But you told me you never gave blood at Rhosivi."

The wind ruffled the flaps of the tent.

"Someone else was giving blood to Doctor Bolest in your stead. Another Victor."

The wind howled again and Roman and Commander Markos stepped back inside. They'd changed into their uniforms, and both were now armed.

Lockbox had said enough for me to understand now. Commander Markos had been sending his blood to Doctor Bolest to study while I'd been incarcerated at Rhosivi. But once Bolest had gotten ahold of my blood, he'd noted the difference. He knew my blood was altered by the Victor and X-ray serums.

He knew that the blood he'd studied for a decade belonged to a different Victor.

I understood completely the worry on Lockbox's face. If he'd figured it out, it was only a matter of time before Doctor Bolest did too.

———

Roman and I exited Commander Markos's tent and headed down a slope where we overlooked the semi-permanent military base campsite.

"Our camp has been affectionately called 'Camp Chaos' because, as you might imagine, things can become a little bit unruly here," Roman said. "To the north is Camp Wolf, where the Wolf Legion is situated. To the south is Camp Bear, where, as you can guess—"

"The Bear Legion is situated."

"Yep." Roman gestured to both sides. "It's safe to assume that they try to gather intel on us, but it's a bit harder for them to infiltrate us than it is for us to infiltrate them."

"But wait, if they're from Khizmit, don't all three legions or battalions or whatever they are just share intel openly?"

"Luka, what did I warn you about back at Predvoi? Khizmit is not the utopia you dreamed it would be. You're a lurper. They're never going to trust lurpers. Even if the Lurper Legion somehow defeated the Latvani Forces, permanently secured our borders, and ended this skudging war, Khizmit would never accept you."

"But you're—"

"A lurper, too?" Roman whispered and flashed me a grin. "I know it. But Khizmit doesn't. Khizmit Ground Forces don't trust this legion, which is why they've stuck us between the two other legions. If they weren't so busy fighting Latvani troops, I think they'd come try to wipe out this whole legion if only so they could sleep soundly at night. No, we have a few spies planted in Bear and Wolf ranks, the same way we have some back in Khizmit. The Delta we've got set up in Wolf ranks can run faster than most of the Echoes we've got now, and he can get back here, share intel for Markos, and return to finish his shower before anyone takes note of his absence."

"I'd expect most of the spies would be Juliets or Kilos so they can listen in."

"We send out teams when we can, where Markos can sneak them in. Obviously with the tattoos, it can be complicated, but you're not the first one who's got a fancy new sleeve." Roman chuckled.

I asked, "Do you worry that some of them here might listen in to our conversations?"

"We don't have many of them here. And the Juliets, Kilos, and Lima's we have in the battalion are either more dominantly good with sight, like me, or they've been reassigned, like you guessed, as spies."

I still had the impression I should watch what I say to some extent, but it highlighted something I hadn't realized I hoped for. Even among other lurpers, I was special. I caught myself grinning as I looked down at Camp Chaos. Roman pointed out the main features.

At the center of the circle were large white tents, comprising the medical station, mess hall, armory, chapel, and communications center. The six companies comprising The Penal Battalion circled the white tents, in clusters of green canvas. To the far north, up the slope, was Commander Markos's tent. To the far south was a range, with eight lanes. In the distance, I could still hear the drumming of rifles without enhancing my hearing. The wind blew up the scent of gunpowder and campfire smoke.

"I'll call the company to attention to introduce you. The platoon leaders will direct their squad leaders to take the soldiers back to training so the five of us can chat and catch you up to speed. I recommend you keep your mouth shut so they don't know what you don't know. Keep your scrappy hands to yourself because I promise you, they'll bait you."

Fifteen minutes later, the Third Company stood at attention in a small field beside a cluster of green tents, much smaller and less stable than Commander Markos's. Though they'd set the tents up beside a clump of shrubs and small trees, it didn't seem to be as effective at blocking the wind as they'd hoped. From where I stood, I could see a few large tears in the tents, especially along the doors and in the corners where small holes had turned into large holes which had been evidently, haphazardly patched up.

I kept my face stoic as I'd seen officers and guards do my whole life while I looked at the company. Though I knew there would be some women in the group, I didn't really know what to expect. They stood along the ranks, mixed in, as if there was nothing at all odd about them being there—I knew there shouldn't have been, but I'd never seen it. Girls stood beside boys, and the boys didn't even glance in their direction.

I turned to Roman as the platoon leaders took accountability.

"I wanted to ask; do you give them nummers?"

"Some of them," Roman said, shrugging. "But we don't give them to most of the soldiers in our company. Markos wants to wean them off so they can learn to control their urges themselves."

"But what about the fact that girls are here?" I almost felt myself blushing at the stupidity of my comment.

"What about them?"

"I mean…I was on the nummers until I left Predvoi and it was, well, quite an adjustment for me to be around girls."

"The girls have their own tents separate from the boys."

"But they're just tents. They aren't cells."

Roman leaned over, obviously understanding my confusion and concern. "Markos isn't about to drug his whole battalion just to keep his troops from sneaking into each other's tents in the middle of the night. If the soldiers are consenting adults, he doesn't care what they do."

A lieutenant approached us and saluted. He had wild eyebrows pulled low over his eyes as he surveyed me. He stood nearly as tall as I did, with wide, muscular arms. The complete lack of scars on his face and hands left me wondering if I was looking at a Sierra, Tango, or Uniform. Everyone had scars. Even I'd left some even if just to remind myself that, despite my abilities, I was still human. I saluted the soldier back, alongside Roman. "Captain Kral, Sir, all are present and accounted for in first platoon."

"Thank you, Eleman."

The soldier nodded and stepped back toward his platoon. Under his breath, Roman whispered, "He's an X-ray. You'll like him."

A second soldier stepped forward: a woman with dark hair and a tight-lipped expression—I caught myself looking twice each time I saw a female in uniform. She made it look great, better than the female captain I'd seen wearing it. I glanced up at the company to give myself a moment away from her gaze, then back to the girl who had inky black hair pulled in a ponytail so tight I wasn't sure she could have changed her facial expression even if she'd wanted to.

"Captain Kral, Sir," she saluted him quickly. "Junior Lieutenant," she nodded to me. I might have accidentally smiled at her. "All soldiers in second platoon are present and accounted for."

"Thank you, Lynx," Roman said quickly. To me, he whispered what her tattoo would have told me. "She's a Yankee."

Lynx stepped back in front of the second platoon and another girl stepped forward.

She was decidedly feminine somehow, despite her short blonde hair. I think it was her petite features. She had the smallest face of anyone I'd ever seen since my young child-hood. Small eyes, small nose, small lips, and small arms. But the curves of her body announced her as a woman. I snapped my attention back to the lieutenant as she spoke. Her voice wasn't as small as her stature.

She saluted Roman and then me. "All members of third platoon are present and accounted for."

"Thank you, Kasia." Then to me, "her tattoo is mysteriously faint, and she won't tell anyone how, but if you look closely enough, you'll see it puts her as a Whiskey."

I gawked after her. She was Lockbox and Ice together. My heart continued to pound as she locked eyes with me and grinned. I looked back at her. *Why was my heart racing as if I'd just finished eight kilometers on the mills at Predvoi?* Kasia was nearly as dangerous as I was, and no one looked at her with fear. Just respect, and maybe, if I read the expression on a few of the soldier's faces, longing.

Once she stood back into formation alongside her platoon, Roman shouted out. "At ease!"

The fifty or so soldiers moved as one, with more precision than I'd seen among the guards at Rhosivi and Predvoi. I began to speculate why some men had been sent to guard a prison instead of the border. The group of soldiers contained children and adults, men and women, but in the few minutes that I'd watched them, I understood why Khizmit had let us live and fight for them. Together we formed a machine. A deadly force. Precise. Determined. Nearly invincible.

"Third Company, this is Junior Lieutenant Luka Drivick. He's spent time at Rhosivi and Predvoi, as well as serving a brief tour in Khizmit before having the opportunity to come here." Roman would have kept going with an introduction if he hadn't been interrupted.

"Is he a lurper?" someone shouted from the third row of the third platoon. The voice struck me as familiar. Familiar enough that my heart almost seemed to seize up.

"Junior Lieutenant Drivick has a nice face, doesn't he?" Roman called out.

"Yes, Sir," the soldiers answered in unison.

"Don't fall for it. Drivick here was handpicked by Commander Markos. He will put you in line if you feel the inclination to toe it."

"But is he a lurper?" the soldier asked again.

Roman stepped to the side to look at the soldier. "Come forward."

The soldier stepped around the people beside him and scooted around to the front of the line where he stood beside his platoon leader, Kasia. He dwarfed her. It appeared that he could have tipped her over with minimal effort.

But it wasn't his height that made me catch my breath.

It was his eyes. His voice. The way he stood.

I knew him.

Romeo-22 from Rhosivi stood within four meters of me for the first time since having jumped me back when I was twelve.

"What's your name?" Roman asked.

"Most people call me Flak, Sir. A Romeo. Romeo-22, Sir."

"And do you have a question, Flak? Something worth interrupting me to ask?"

"Yes Sir, I'd like to know if Junior Lieutenant here is a lurper like us."

"Why do you ask?"

"Because I think I saw him. I think I know *Drivick* here." He drew my name out. The way he'd used to call me 27. It threw me back to when I was 12. The memory cut into my mind's eye with the same slick sharpness as the shiv that had sliced into my face all those years ago.

"Skudge off!" Flak said. "When I'm done, you can see if there's any left for you."

"That's not how it works, and you know it." I smiled as if that

would change his mind. He didn't even look at my face. "A quarter kilo man. C'mon."

"Get lost, 27."

"Don't call me that." I clenched my jaw. "My name is Victor."

"You don't have a name. None of us do. What, you think you're special?"

My heart pounded down into my hands, and I clenched them into fists.

"You don't have a name because you don't matter."

A moment later he lunged and shoved me down to the rough ground and two of his friends rushed over to his side. For a moment, the sun glared into my eyes and I couldn't see the attackers. Flak's voice reached me. "Stay down, or I'll break your hands. We'll see how many bags you fill with mangled fingers."

Flak grabbed a bent piece of metal that protruded off the side of the cart holding the remaining rocks. He stepped closer, gripping the shiv with a look of glee, and spoke to the captain.

"Sir, we have rules in this prison. Prison rules." I could nearly taste the blood even from the memory of his last words to me before gashing open my cheek. *"The rules demand retribution."*

"Drivick," Roman said, a tone of entertainment in his voice.

I turned to him, shaking off the memory. "Yes, Sir?"

"Do you recognize this lurper? Have you ever seen him before?"

I stared at Flak, as if examining for any trace of him in my memory. As if his voice didn't elicit trauma. I wanted to reach up and check my cheek to make sure the wound hadn't reopened after all this time. I still tasted blood. It had been five years, but in that time neither of us could have changed beyond recognition. Sure, I wore a uniform now, but so did he. Yes, I'd healed my face, my hair was longer, but he knew me. Even though my voice was deeper and my arms were bigger than his now, I knew he recognized me, and no matter what I said, it wouldn't change that.

"A face like his would be hard to forget," I said, through gritted teeth. The desire to fight him now nearly sent me hurtling in his direction. *The rules demand retribution,* I thought bitterly. I could show him retribution in a thousand different ways.

The edges of my vision flashed crimson. Soon my hands would be.

His face would be.

I could—

Roman placed his hand on my shoulder and my attention lurched away from Flak. Roman gripped my shoulder tighter and gave me a small nod. His eyes darted briefly to the Lugar at his waist and then he pulled his arm back.

Roman spoke loudly enough for the entire company to hear. "Flak, how many times have you been concussed?"

Flak struggled to look away from me to direct his words to Roman. "What, Sir?"

"Slag, did it affect your hearing too, Private? I said, how many times have you been concussed? How many concussions have you received while stationed here?"

"At least seven, Sir."

"And would you say your memory is crystal clear?"

"No, Sir."

"Can you describe the situation surrounding your latest concussion?"

Flak finally looked at Roman to answer. "No, Sir."

"Are lurpers allowed to be promoted as officers?"

"No, Sir."

"And yet, you're asking me if Junior Lieutenant Drivick is one," Roman scoffed. "Are lurpers allowed to have tattoos other than their designation?"

"No, Sir."

Roman inclined his head and I pulled up the sleeve of my uniform far enough to show the trees.

Roman's voice had a hint of amusement now. "I suggest,

Flak, that since your mind and memory are not reliable, you shut the skudge up rather than humiliate yourself by publicly highlighting your mental impairments."

Snippets of laughter began to roll out of the company of soldiers, which emboldened a few more to laugh openly. I kept my face a stone.

Flak looked at me, then back to Roman.

"Yes, Sir."

"Take your place back in formation, lurper!"

While Roman introduced me to the company and gave orders for where the platoons would be training today, I made every effort not to look back toward Flak.

CHAPTER 6
TRUST AND SLAG

FLAK'S FACE seemed to be branded in my mind, addling me while Roman gave me a tutorial on how to handle a firearm. I wasn't sure if thinking about Flak and reliving the moment he'd shoved a shiv through my face would motivate or distract me while I learned to handle a pistol.

Roman and I would have the range to ourselves for half an hour while the company cleaned up the campsite. There would be enough rumors about me sweeping through the ranks without the need to add my complete inexperience with a firearm to the fire.

I'd only ever held a firearm with the intention of tossing it out of reach. Back at Predvoi when I'd disarmed some guards, I'd briefly held their pistols in my hands, but never planned to use their weapons. Never with the intention of learning how they worked.

This gun was mine. Assigned to me by its serial number. The metal wasn't cold in my hand, because Roman had been holding it. For how small it was, it felt heavy.

"Close your left eye and focus on the target with your right," Roman directed.

With my right arm straight out and the tip of my right index finger on the trigger, I took a deep breath. My left index finger overlapped my right to steady my aim. Why did such a little weapon require both hands to hold?

"The kickback is minimal," Roman said. "Breathe slowly. Pull the trigger so slowly that it's a surprise to you when it goes off."

I breathed slowly as Roman continued to coach me. Far down the range lay the target. Red in the center, blue around that, and then concentric lines going outwards like ripples from the bullets Roman had planted so perfectly in the center during his demonstration.

"Line up the dots. Get the one at the end right in the middle."

I squeezed, held my breath, and the gun exploded.

Although Roman was right about the recoil, I still found myself keeping an almost too firm of a grip on the gun. Vanity coaxed me into trying to fire it with one hand, but the gun jerked to the left just before the bullet left the chamber and didn't hit the target at all. Roman chuckled and I laughed with him, still trying to shake the uncomfortable feeling of coming face-to-face with Flak.

I would have talked with Roman, but the ear protection would have necessitated that I yell, and my history with Flak at Rhosivi was hardly something I wanted to broadcast. I said nothing, just fired fifty rounds, getting faster at reloading the magazine each time.

It didn't take a lot of practice to get near the center of the target every time. It was, as a matter of fact, in my blood. I was born to kill and fight, and my abilities made wielding a gun easy. *How strange,* I mused, *that with the simple pull of a finger, I could take a life.* And I'd thought it was easy to kill someone before that.

"How do you know him?" Roman asked as we walked from the range to the small distribution center for a sleeping bag and other supplies for me. I knew he was talking about Flak. Maybe I'd pictured his face in the center of the target with such accuracy that Roman had seen it briefly flash across the red circle.

I told Roman what had happened to my cheek, probably with enough detail that he could tell how it still haunted me.

"Markos pulled him off you?" Roman verified.

"Yes," I said. "Which begs the question as to why he let this happen. Why did he let Flak stay here after he'd decided to bring me here? He puts everything at risk!"

"I have to believe that Markos has a plan. He's no Oscar, but he's got enough experience with strategy to not be blind-sided by this."

"I don't want him here," I muttered.

"I could arrange for a training accident," Roman offered, and I honestly wasn't sure if he was joking or not. I'd seen him pop a bullet into Smoke's head as casually as if he'd been cutting his fingernails.

"No," I said, decidedly. "But after I get my equipment set up in the tent, I'm going to speak to Markos. He could have warned me at the very least!"

———

As soon as I entered Commander Markos's tent I hissed, "You didn't tell me Flak was here."

Lockbox dropped the papers that had been in his hand to the desk. Markos was standing behind him. He straightened.

Lockbox flashed me a take-a-breath sort of look, so I did.

"I mean, Commander Markos, Sir, you knew, didn't you? I'm sorry for barging in here, but Flak—how could that have slipped past you?"

"It didn't slip past me," Markos said. "Of course I knew. I recognized Romeo-22's name as soon as I took command, but my options were limited, Luka. What did you want me to do, get him killed so you wouldn't have to face him?"

"Roman offered." My tone was dry.

Markos tilted his head slightly as if he were about to scold me. "Flak's an adult who didn't qualify to become a vaznov. Rather than hand him to the firing squad they sent him here for training and more work as a lab rat to see what Romeo's could handle since they don't heal like you can."

Markos had called him Flak. It wasn't hard to see why Markos sympathized with him. They were both used as lab rats.

But this was Flak. This was different. "He's going to blow my cover. What are we supposed to do about that?" This time I looked at Lockbox. He was the key strategist. Granted, this might not be as important as figuring out how to get a battalion into Khizmit, but it mattered to me.

"Can we send him somewhere? Maybe reassign him?"

Markos clicked a pen. "Flak's almost 20 years old now. He can't go back to Khizmit. I can't fake paperwork making him a vazzie. They see him only as a bullet block for the soldiers in Wolf or Bear Unit. The same way they see all the lurpers here."

I threw my hands up. "Well, couldn't you have put him in a different company at least?"

"Even if he'd been in Fourth or Fifth Company, he'd have seen you eventually, and this way you were able to confront him immediately without giving him a chance to spread ideas or rumors around the camp."

"Oh, I'm sure he'll be spreading the story far and wide!" My heart raced in my rage. For a moment a voice in my head told me to throw a few punches Markos's way so I forcibly relaxed my hands.

"And what will he say, Luka? That you're the Victor he knew at Rhosivi?" Markos said, and I couldn't tell if he was irritated with me or frustrated at the situation in general. "That he slashed your face when you were twelve? His story won't convince anyone of anything other than that his brains have been shaken inside his cranium too many times."

"But unlike the inmates at Rhosivi and Predvoi, these lurpers know that Victors can heal. Not only will they know about my past, but they'll know I'm a Victor or a Sierra or—"

"You're focused on the wrong things." Markos's voice lost any hint of patience. "That was then and there. This is here and now. Flak paid for that crime and a thousand others he didn't commit during his eighteen years at Rhosivi! I'd have expected a little more compassion from you. You've been in those rat holes. You've dug through those rocks and been shot at by guards. You've been hated and judged and isolated."

Compassion. I balked. "Compassion for the kid who'd slashed my face open when I was 12?" But then I heard myself. *The kid.* He'd been a kid. Still, I'd been a younger kid.

Markos dropped into the chair beside his cot and exhaled. I hadn't asked what he'd done today. If he'd heard from his family. I worried that if I did ask him then he might think I only wondered about Emberly for selfish reasons. *Did I?*

"Any word on Velky's death?" I asked.

"Nothing yet. I'm sure they've found the body. Probably beginning an investigation."

"They'll bring in the Oscars at the palace," Lockbox said.

"Will they figure out it was me?"

"Depends on if you left any blood at the scene," Markos said.

I didn't think I had. I'd healed quickly and I'd buried the blade that had borne my blood into Velky, tainting the two of us.

A horrible idea emerged.

"Sir, is there any chance that putting a small portion of my blood would..." I stopped. It was insane, wasn't it?

"What?" Markos asked.

Lockbox understood. I could tell by the look in his clear blue eyes. "Your blood isn't a serum. There's no way you could share your healing abilities with someone by giving a small amount of your blood to them."

"What if I gave a large amount of blood to them?" I considered the bag of blood Velky and Bolest had taken. *What if they'd put it in someone else? What if they hadn't given it back to me?*

"Not probable. If you gave your bone marrow to someone, it's possible they'd begin to make more of your blood than their own, and would share some of your abilities, but that's not really what we're talking about, is it?" he replied.

I glanced at Lockbox's legs.

"I don't need your blood, Luka," Lockbox said. "I'll heal up. It'll just take a little while. I'm not in a rush anyway."

I was in a rush. If we'd gotten him out sooner, he'd be able to walk. I wasn't convinced he'd ever be the same again.

"I'll let you know when I hear anything about High Warden Velky," Markos said. "In the meantime, you'll have to take the situation with Flak one day at a time. He's sustained enough brain damage that he might second-guess himself."

Brain damage?

"What are you working on?" I asked it quickly to fight back any concern that had entered my mind at Markos's words.

Markos nodded to Lockbox, giving him permission to share information with me.

"We're trying to coordinate a coup with a commander of enemy forces who has no intention of conversing with us. We also need to find a way to mobilize the lurpers at Rhosivi, Vazenia, and Predvoi and have them join our ranks before breaching Khizmit."

The way I imagined that working out was nasty at best. *Literally all of them? Every single one?* "How would we keep them from completely revolting? From killing innocent people?"

Markos raised an eyebrow at that.

"I'm not suggesting all of us are unhinged, but we're

dangerous," I said. "I don't understand how you keep any of these soldiers from shooting up the whole battalion."

He wants to arm people like Ice?

He'd armed Romeo-22. My jaw was clenched so tightly it began to hurt.

Markos answered. "A lot of it comes down to respect. Out here I can do that more than I could at Rhosivi. Here I can show my soldiers respect, and most of them give it back to me. A little respect and trust can go a long way with anybody, but especially with people who have never been given any."

Suddenly I felt bad for interrupting. If they could deal with trying to get the Latvani commander to open communication, and coordinate getting lurpers out of all three prisons, I could deal with Flak. With a slow exhale, I took a few steps toward the door. I wanted to ask Markos if he knew I'd kissed Emberly. If he had any idea what I felt for her, how I worried about her, and that I'd do almost anything to see her again. If he got a letter or message from his family, would he tell me?

I kicked the toe of my boot into the dirt and then started for the door.

Lockbox shifted behind me. "Sir, you might want to tell him…"

I stopped and looked at Markos.

He scowled before sighing. "Give me some time to think about what we should do about Flak. It's a little bit…complicated."

I waited but neither of them elaborated. "What?"

Lockbox answered this time. "Flak won't be the only familiar face you see here."

CHAPTER 7
KASIA'S SQUAD

Roman and I had finished dinner and were heading back to our tent when the group of soldiers sauntered out from the shadows. Their eyes practically glowed with malintent. The sun was setting on my right, casting enough of a glare that I had to focus to see very well.

It was exactly who I'd worried it would be.

Flak spoke, his low voice reminiscent of the grinding of wheels on the mine carts back in Rhosivi Mine. "I've been hit in the head and blown a few hundred meters at a time, so I don't remember everything… But I remember *you*."

Another voice, just as familiar, reached me before I could see his face. "Victor-27. I figured they'd killed you years ago."

The young man stepped closer, and we locked eyes. The top half of his face was obscured in the shadows cast by the sweaty clumps of hair that hung low, near his eyebrows. He was bigger than he'd been back then. Taller. Thicker neck. A single black earring glinted from one of his ears.

"Raph?" I said, a single word that could be taken for a full confession.

"Skudge yeah!" Raph said, coming closer.

I lifted my hands to fight only to realize that he wasn't throwing hands at me. The one who'd helped Flak attack me in the yard back at Rhosivi was throwing his arm around me. He clapped me on the back, and I stiffened.

"He remembers me!" Raph shouted to Flak and the other two silhouettes in the night.

As the other two people advanced, Raph turned to Roman.

"This guy knocked me down cold when he was just twelve! Gave me this!" He slicked back the hair over his forehead, but I couldn't see much in the dwindling light. "What are you, Mr. Invincible?" Raph asked, clapping me on the back again.

My body was as stiff and cold as the loaded pistol at my hip.

"Junior Lieutenant Invincible," the next boy announced himself.

It took me a moment to identify him. His hair was much longer than it had been at Rhosivi, pulled into a small bun at the top of his head. The bottom half had been buzzed close to the skin.

"He busted three of my ribs with a halfhearted kick!" His hand immediately went to his side, and I worried that he'd pull out a knife, though he clearly hadn't been issued one as a private.

India-07 from Rhosivi Prison hooted. "Could have kicked my soul right out of my body if he'd tried!" He extended his hand to Roman, who I knew was willing and able to shoot any one of these guys if it became necessary. "Name's Clink. I'm in second platoon."

Roman eyed the India, now called Clink, making no move to extend his hand from where it was occupied on his waist, just shy of his sidearm.

Clink, Raph, and Flak had me on three sides just as the fourth person stepped forward. His face, sullen and reserved, was unfamiliar to me.

"Seems you're a legend, Drivick." His voice was almost melodic, the way he dragged out his vowels.

I wanted to ask who he was, but the urgent problem regarded my safety instead of his identity. *They wouldn't be dumb enough to jump two officers, would they?* While I didn't see any palkas on their hips and they'd had to return their firearms to the armory, I didn't doubt they had something hidden.

Flak had used a piece of metal to hurt me. Scar me. In more ways than one. My mind took quick stock of the dangerous weapons within the vicinity. Rope—could hang me, tie me, choke me, bind my feet, trip me, etc. A tent stake—easily driven through my temple, jugular, hands, jammed between my ribs.

At that moment I knew their plan. They'd mentioned the injuries I'd given them. They held their grudges against me closer than Roman held his pistol. Clink would break my ribs, they'd tie or stake me down, then Flak would re-create the scar on my face, maybe finishing up what he'd started all those years ago. Then Raph would knock me out. Or perhaps Raph would knock me out first so that I wouldn't be able to heal.

Would I? Sometimes I healed unconsciously. Would that keep me safe if they somehow disarmed Roman? My gaze flicked back to Roman. He'd be their first target.

"Did you know?" Raph asked Roman in a raspy whisper. "He's a Victor."

"He's not a Victor," Roman replied, and if he was scared or shaken in the slightest, it didn't show.

"Like skudge he isn't," Clink piped in, stepping closer.

The impending fight played out in my head. Flak posed the biggest threat to me, but he stood the furthest away. I'd have to take down Raph first, assuming Roman would disable Flak the moment he moved.

My hands twitched, anxious for it to begin so I'd know

which threat to address first. On defense, I had an advantage —one I wasn't willing to forfeit.

"I'm Spikes," the fourth one volunteered.

My mental focus wandered for a moment. *Spikes? As in, Lockbox's roommate before me?*

"From Predvoi?" I said, my shoulders loosening. I'd been so sure they'd executed him.

Spikes held his hands up dramatically. "The same! Commander Markos brought me in."

Of course he had. He'd wanted me and Lockbox to work together as roommates and the best way to ensure that was to get Spikes assigned here.

The combination of tension and joviality left me confused. I needed the fight to start while I had adrenaline rushing through me. Raph stood with his arm still on my back and I braced myself for a takedown.

But it didn't come.

"Junior Lieutenant Drivick is not a Victor," Roman announced. "He's a lurper all right, but not like you."

"Like Spikes said, he's a skudging legend! We already knew he's not like us."

Flak flexed his fist. "I always assumed it was the Victorness in you, but I've met other Victors since, and they've got nothing on you."

"Then what's he on?" Raph asked Roman, then gave my shoulder a squeeze. "What serum have you got running in your blood?"

A quick glance to Roman gave me the approval I needed.

"My mother was a Victor. Which as you know, is—"

"A Romeo and Uniform," Flak said. "I didn't know then. Didn't know until recently; you know how it is at Rhosivi. But I should have known you were my brother." Flak stepped up and slapped me on the shoulder, but I grabbed his wrist, ready to break his arm when my brain processed the last word.

Brother.

Brother?

My brother.

I dropped his wrist.

The adrenaline drained out of my muscles with such speed I nearly fell over.

They weren't here to kill me.

They were here to welcome me.

———

"I'm a mutt of a lurper," I explained once we all stuffed ourselves into the tent I shared with Roman. The two-person tent bulged at the sides as the six of us crammed in, but being so close made it easier for us to whisper and still hear each other. Spikes, Raph, Flak, and Clink sat enraptured at my history, my parentage, and my travels around Khizmit. I explained my trip back here as if it was Roman who'd convinced Commander Markos to take me in. Roman jumped on that story right away.

"I got to pick my second-in-command, and when I ran into Luka in Khizmit…Well, I knew what he was because of how I'd seen him move—I knew I needed him out here. Once I stabbed him, we arranged to meet up in Khizmit. I may have swapped some paperwork to get him approved, but Commander Markos wouldn't care if we have another lurper here."

"You lied to the commander?" Clink asked.

"Not exactly. Don't get hung up on the details."

If any one of them had been in the Oscar category, they'd have unraveled the poorly spun tale, but they didn't seem to care about how I got here as much as they wanted to know about the prisons. My escape from Predvoi. We told them as much as we could while they bombarded me with questions.

"How was Predvoi?"

"What did you do at Predvoi?"

"Why did they transfer you?"

"What happened to your tattoo?"

Flak, Clink, and Raph had a hundred questions for me, and I answered all the ones I could that didn't have any connection to Markos.

Spikes had only one question for me. "Did Lockbox get out?"

I nodded.

"Where is he?"

"He's here," I said. "Up with Commander Markos."

Spikes shrugged, "There are worse crusters to be an info slave to."

"You broke him out of prison?" Flak asked.

"Actually, he was in the Grand Palace," I said. I'd reiterated the need for secrecy so many times I wanted to punch myself in the throat. Markos had left me few options with these guys. Lying wasn't one of them.

"You got him out of the Grand Palace?" Spikes guffawed.

"If anyone could do it, it would be this lurper!" Flak said, shoving me sideways playfully. I bumped shoulders with Raph who steadied me.

He steadied me.

I'd chosen to trust them with the truth but the hair on the back of my neck still stood up, warning me about being too close to these lurpers.

"Those Latvanians won't know what hit them next battle," Raph commented. "Drivick here will crush them. We'll end the war."

"And what, go home? What home?" I asked.

Flak shrugged, "What's so bad about staying here? Just send Wolf and Bear Legions back to Khizmit and we'll live in The Outskirts."

"We'll die here," Clink said casually as if telling us what

time of day it was. "But we'll all die someday anyway. Khizmit won't thank us for our service."

Khizmit might. The thought hit me like a punch. *The people might.* Once we took over the Grand Palace and placed Markos in charge, then we'd own Khizmit. It should have been our birthright.

After only an hour of chatting with these soldiers, the warning sirens in my head became completely silent. I ached to tell them the whole plan, somehow believing that they were, in fact, my brothers, just as much as Lockbox was. But I didn't tell them about the coup.

I didn't get close to Markos's secret even as we laughed together while the air grew colder, the wind intensified, and the dark of night crowded around us.

"Captain Kral," Flak said, turning to Roman. "Seems like a good time to rearrange the squads, don't you think?"

————

Sometime the next day Roman passed the message to Markos that all was well regarding my previous acquaintances, and that they wouldn't make a scene of me being there. Despite our histories together, I trusted them not to tell as much as I trusted them not to stab me in the back. Not that I'd give them a blade and free access, but my gut relaxed.

I'd have gone to his tent myself, if for no other reason than to check on Lockbox and see if he thought I was a fool for my new friendships, but as a Junior Lieutenant, I wasn't exactly supposed to be seen with Markos one-on-one very often.

The next morning at formation, I stood a little more relaxed at Roman's side. After only a day, the salutes came more naturally to me.

Roman's voice carried far as he announced, "While we wait for more soldiers to join our company, I've decided to rearrange a few squads. First Platoon, Fourth Squad will merge with Second Squad. Second Platoon, Fifth Squad will send two soldiers to Third Squad, and the rest will join First Platoon, First Squad. Third Company, Third Platoon will merge with Second Platoon, and Junior Lieutenant Drivick will be joining you."

Though I'd been looking between Flak and Clink as he made the announcement, my gaze caught a reaction on the platoon leader's face. Kasia. Her features, though small, revealed…something. *Excitement? Concern?*

As we broke into squads, I think I understood why. Our squad consisted of me, Kasia, Spikes, Raph, Flak, and another girl. We were assigned to work together, just like they'd requested.

"I'm Tally," the last girl said, holding out her hand to shake mine. I found myself more interested in catching sight of the mark on her wrist than shaking her hand. For a moment I prepared myself to lean in and kiss the air beside her cheeks, as they greeted one another in Khizmit, but as I moved forward incrementally, she stayed still. I probably looked unsteady on my feet as I rocked back.

"If you want to know what I am, just ask," she said, sounding annoyed. She yanked up the sleeve of her uniform and showed me the letters. "X-ray-12," she read it aloud. "Tally because I keep track of all the Latvanian soldiers I've flattened."

"Flattened?"

"Sure. Flattened. Crushed. Stomped. Thrown. Dismembered. Do you want me to be more direct?" Her voice was more monotone than any other girl I'd met, at least until she started listing verbs.

"I get it," I said.

"Killed."

"Right, I get it—"

"Slaughtered. Maimed. Disfigured."

"Okay Thesaurus, I get it."

She narrowed her eyes, and I figured her arm was flexing beneath her uniform as I saw the fabric bend and rustle. "What did you call me?"

I grinned and found myself looking over to Flak. Though he was smiling, he didn't seem to have a clue what I was talking about.

Raph tried to back me up. "He called you a dinosaur!"

"No! Slag, you guys really should have read some books!" I shook my head.

Slag, I wish Lockbox was here too.

I decided to placate Tally. "I didn't call you a dinosaur. A thesaurus is like a dictionary, but it has synonyms. Words that—"

"I know what a synonym is, slaghead!"

Kasia stepped in. "Tally, you will not speak to Junior Lieutenant Drivick in that tone, or you will be subject to disciplinary action."

"Yes, Ma'am," Tally said, tossing her long brown ponytail over her shoulder. "Junior Lieutenant Drivick, Sir, contrary to what you might have learned in your education, I grew up in a cell."

Her voice was crisp, her words sharp as the dagger on my hip. "Unlike you, I didn't have access to *thesauruses*. I didn't have access to clean water or a warm bed, not that you'd know slag about that. Maybe where you're from the girls are dumb, walking artwork for men, but you'll find that the female soldiers here don't give a *skudge* about what you learned in your books. And, given the opportunity, any one of us could absolutely wreck you."

Kasia's voice rose. "Tally!"

I stared at Tally, processing what she'd assumed. What she'd accused. The disjointed way she'd gone about trying to make a point. I didn't think I could find a physically attractive girl so unattractive as I did her. Ever since I'd left Predvoi, I'd worried that all girls would make me weak in the knees and send my heart racing.

I realized at that moment that I'd worried the girls here might distract me from Emberly. Might make me forget how much I liked her. Ember was, after all, the first girl I'd met. But now, looking at Tally, I realized I was decidedly wrong. Girls like Tally made me that much more appreciative of Emberly.

Tally had all the makings of beauty, but the venom, the venom in her words and face and intentions made me want to fight her. Fight a girl. Throw her down. Not bloody her up, but forcibly put her in her place. That's how I deal with dangerous things. When they bare their teeth or fangs, I show them that I'm deadlier. As dangerous as they think they are, I'm the bigger threat.

I could have, to use her verbiage, flattened Tally, despite her strength and confidence, because I was an X-ray like her, but I was also a Victor. I was willing to bet that beneath that uniform she had quite the physique. Not that I'd have wanted to know or see. She'd be a fun sparring partner if I could have trusted her enough to risk such a thing.

Flak should have kept his mouth shut, but he didn't. He knew exactly what he was doing when he said, "Tally, are you snorting dust? Drivick here could chew you up and spit you out without breaking a sweat."

Tally didn't have a short fuse. She had no fuse at all. No warning. No build-up. She was an absolute powder keg waiting for the slightest spark to set her off.

She lunged at Flak and caught him around the throat in a choke. Flak fell forward on top of her to ease the pressure on his neck and then scrambled to the side of her only to find that she'd thrown her legs up, trapping his arm. He threw his knee up, barely brushing against her face as he tried to get his arm free.

"Enough!" Kasia shouted and once again I was impressed

at the volume that she could yell. She looked at me, exasper-ated. "Are you going to separate them, Sir?"

"I'll get Flak," I said. "You get Tally."

She nodded and within three seconds we had our squad mates separated and subdued. Flak, to his credit, didn't fight me in the process.

"You keep talking slag, Flak, and next time I'll snap your arm clean off," Tally spat.

This time I should have kept my mouth shut. "He's not talking slag. I *could* wreck you. But we're a squad, aren't we? Brothers and sisters in arms. We aren't each other's enemies."

"My brothers are lurpers," Tally spat. "Not Khizmit meat sacks like you!" She glanced at my wrist as if to make sure a designation tattoo hadn't magically appeared there while she'd been shouting.

I looked down at my wrist, the trees there, the intricate work at Roman's hands, and for a single flicker of a moment, I missed the V-27. Even though it had been inaccurate, and I'd fought it for my whole life, I was a Victor. I was a lurper.

This tattoo was a mask, but maybe an essential one. At least for now. I shifted my attention back to Tally, who was breathing heavily, her shoulder bobbing up and down slightly.

"So, what about Flak here? You just attacked him," I said, gesturing to Flak who was unphased by the attack on his airpipe.

"I went easy on him," she grinned, and I thought I saw some blood between her teeth. "If the opportunity arises, I won't be so gentle with you."

"Enough!" Kasia shouted, directly in Tally's face. A few droplets of spittle flew out and landed on Tally's cheeks, but Tally only smiled and raised her hand to salute Kasia.

"Apologies, Ma'am. It won't happen again."

Despite the promise, Tally looked at me with an expres-sion that absolutely promised it would. That maybe soon she'd jump me, expecting me to submit. Expecting to flatten me or whatever other word entered her brain at that moment.

She'd try to pin me down, lock my shoulder, and choke me out, and—honestly—I looked forward to showing her just how impossible that was.

When it came time for our squad to use the range, I didn't humiliate myself. *Thank you, Roman,* I thought as I sent all sixteen rounds through the center of the target. Granted, it was only twenty meters. Thinking back on the shot Roman had made at Predvoi directly into Smoke's skull, made me shudder. Roman was good. Too good. I'd been impressed at the time but now his precision floored me. I should have known he wasn't, as Tally had put it: a meat-sack from Khizmit.

As expected, I required minimal training, earning me nick-names like Legend, Eagle, Bone Crusher, and Prodigy. Kasia eyed me with suspicion and made me second guess doing my best in the field training, but she never asked me anything directly. A few times I caught her looking at my wrist, and once I was sure I saw her looking elsewhere before I turned around.

"You're a nice shot, Drivick," she said, and it was clear she wanted to see how I reacted when she dropped my rank from conversation.

I hesitated before correcting her. I had to be a cruster. That didn't mean I had to be a slagsack about it. If she called me Luka, then I'd draw a line. Then I'd enforce a boundary.

Instead of telling her to call me "Sir," an idea that made me physically nauseated, I smiled. "Thanks."

CHAPTER 8
THE GUARDS AT VAZENIA

With how routine the next few days were, sometimes I found myself forgetting that we were all prisoners here. The lack of bars and chains certainly aided that. That didn't mean that everything was peaceful though; fights like I'd seen in Predvoi or Rhosivi would break out sporadically. Usually among soldiers who hadn't spent time in either prison and had, in my opinion, a complete lack of gratitude for how good we had it here. Latvani hadn't attacked once, excluding a few rockets launched too far east to cause any problems for us.

In the evenings, Kasia and Tally returned to their side of the camp. I spent evenings sharing jokes with Clink, Raph, Flak, and Spikes. Khizmit didn't ship any vyco to the Penal Legion, the same way they refused to send an actual medic to our legion, as if there was any clearer way to say, "*Skudge the lurpers, even those fighting for our Enclave.*" But some of the soldiers snuck into the neighboring legions and took their supplies, distributing their spoils evenly.

Flak, Raph, and I were washing up before dinner when I saw a spurt of red flash across my vision over by the tents for Second Company. I sprinted over to find a soldier leaning over, his hand over his midsection as blood squirted out. Every time his heart pumped, the blood flew, splashing the ground as it went. I reached over to put pressure on it before catching his expression. He laughed as he saw my concern, and when I looked back down, the injury was completely healed. Blood stained his hands and dripped from his fingertips, but the wound—the gaping, grizzly wound—was gone.

"I'm a Tango, meat-sack. Does that mean anything to you?" he asked.

He'd healed it. *But what had caused it?* I wished I hadn't wondered because at that moment the soldier took the bloody knife and stabbed it through his hand again, gasping as the small bones in his hand crunched. He gasped, in temporary agony before he numbed the pain.

My stomach spun. He pulled the blade out and watched, almost transfixed as his blood poured out again from his hand.

"Heal it," I said, my voice more demanding than I meant it to be.

"Sir, yes, Sir," he sang sarcastically and saluted me with his bloodied hand as he healed the skin. Watching it done by someone else was as surreal as when I'd healed myself. The bones crackled as they snapped back in place.

"What are you doing?" I asked. "Don't do that. Your hand…" I trailed off.

The soldier smirked. "I know it's hard for your brain to understand, but I can heal. I don't feel pain." He slashed the blade up suddenly; I nearly didn't catch its movement. I saw, in horror, as two of his fingers dropped to the ground with a muted *plunk!* into the dark puddle he'd created from his first injury.

He raised his hand in front of my face, and I found myself staring at the bright white bone briefly visible before it was flooded by his blood.

Slowly, casually, he bent over, picked up one of his fingers, and held it back against the stump. Three seconds later, he wiggled it and reached for the other one.

"Don't do that," I demanded.

"Is that a direct, order, Sir?" he sang, as he attached the other finger and then wiped the blood off on a rag. "I'm not hurting anyone."

"You're hurting yourself." My stomach twisted at the flippancy. I glanced again at the wet ground before meeting his narrowed gaze.

He cleared his throat and spat into his own blood. "The thing is, *cruster*, it doesn't hurt. Nothing I do to myself hurts. I can't feel any of it, so no, Sir, I'm not hurting anyone."

A question snuck out before I could stop it. "What if you hadn't been able to reattach your fingers?"

"Oh, I can do that. I can reattach and heal my eye. After fingers, legs are easy. Would you like to see?"

I reached for the knife and had it in my hand before he could move.

"You're about as much fun as Kasia is. That is to say: you're no fun at all," he said.

The call came for dinner and the soldier stood up, approaching the spigot to wash off his bloody hands.

"That's Axe," Flak whispered. "One of the few lurpers here that actually scares me."

I clapped Flak on the shoulder as if to say that I had his back, that I'd keep him safe, and I almost couldn't believe it.

Flak. I'd keep *him* safe. Laughing uneasily, in part from the insanity I'd just witnessed and the shock of what I was thinking, we walked back toward the mess hall. I threw the knife into my tent as we walked past it, and then I washed my hands again with the small pebble of soap resting beside the faucet in the ground.

I kept Axe in my sight the whole time, just in case he had other ideas with that knife of his.

————

I couldn't sleep that night. Roman had gone up to the commander's tent for a cadre meeting that I'd been too curious to avoid listening in on. Neither Markos nor Roman had asked me not to, so I figured maybe they expected it.

I wandered up the hill and took a seat on a flat rock in the bare earth beside the locked supply tent. A lieutenant stood guard outside Commander Markos's tent. I faced down the hill, where I had a view of the dancing lanterns and could hear the laughter and conversations of soldiers carried my way on the wind. From my position, I was easily able to eavesdrop while the cadre discussed plans and, to my discomfort, me.

"He's young for a junior lieutenant," Captain Gaborik remarked. "How's he been with the troops?"

"That's one of his biggest strengths," Roman replied. "He keeps them in line. He's found a good balance between keeping things friendly without compromising his reputation as an officer."

Captain Sakrova commented next. "I heard he's a good shot, but nothing like you."

Roman laughed.

"You're really comfortable keeping the Oscar in here while we plan?" High Captain Toth asked.

"If he's going to help us win this war, and I believe he is, he needs to be privy to as much information as we can afford to give him. I don't see him as a risk. Do you?" Markos asked.

"Not him directly, but he could pass information to someone. Buy his freedom," High Captain Toth said.

"He seems content," Markos said, engaging in one of the habits from Rhosivi and Predvoi that enraged me most. They discussed Lockbox as if he wasn't there. "He won't go back to Khizmit; that's where they broke his legs. He wouldn't fare better with Latvani. I've let him see the reports of what they've done to some of our soldiers before dumping their bodies."

Lockbox swallowed so loudly I heard it.

"Not sure he'd fare well among the troops either," Captain Sakrova said.

"I heard about the incident today," Markos said. "She's still receiving medical treatment. She might pull through."

"What happened?" Roman asked. "Was it the Quebec in your company again?"

"Yes," Captain Sakrova. "He attacked one of our soldiers. Lima-07."

"He's in confinement?" High Captain Toth asked.

"Yes, Sir," Captain Sakrova said. "Every time we let him back out, something like this happens. We can't keep letting this happen."

"He's nineteen?" Markos asked.

"Yes, Sir."

Markos sighed heavily. "Since this was his third offense, we have no choice."

"Yes, Sir. Understood." Captain Sakrova said.

I knew what had to happen, but I prayed Roman would be the one to pull the trigger this time.

They'd begun talking about strategy, referencing a map that I assumed was on the desk, when the crunch of boots on the dry ground demanded my attention.

Kasia climbed the hill toward me. She waved as I looked over, and I raised my hand in response.

"Were you looking for some solitude?" she asked. "'Cause I can go…"

"No, it's fine. You're welcome to stay."

She took a seat beside me, and we both looked out over the tents.

"I take it you were listening in." She jerked her head back toward the commander's tent.

"That would be ambitious," I said.

"Not for someone like you." She got a knowing look in her eyes. "I went to Captain Kral your first day here, just to see if he was tracking."

"Tracking?"

"Tracking that you weren't a cruster. I assume you know he's a lurper too by now."

I said nothing. Confirmed nothing.

"Here's what I have figured out: Markos knows Captain Kral's secret, as well as yours. Markos wanted you here for some reason and sent Captain Kral to get you from either Rhosivi or Predvoi, fix up your wrist, and promote you to an officer."

She stared at me. I stared out at the tents.

"Are you going to deny it?"

"Deny it?" I sounded stupid. "I'm not saying anything. I'm just looking at the stars and the sky and the people out there.

"You're Victor-27."

That got my attention. I turned and looked into her eyes. She had something of a twinkle in them as she smiled back at me.

"You Oscars," I mused. "Is there anything you don't know?"

"Always. Plenty," Kasia said. "I take it the Oscar in the commander's servitude is a friend of yours?"

"I wouldn't call it servitude."

"Markos is a good leader. I'm sure he's fair."

I had to assume she didn't know about Markos.

"I'm not going to tell anyone, just so you know." She flashed me another smile, this time showing some of her teeth. "But I wanted you to know that I know. Just in case you wanted someone to talk to about…anything."

My first instinct was that she wanted intel. But as I stared at her I caught the emotion in her face. Loneliness.

She was incredibly lonely.

"Was it so obvious?" I asked.

"No. I like to flatter myself, saying that I'm clever or something. I can't exactly claim it as a talent, since it's instinctive."

"Sometimes I swear you Oscars can read minds."

"Not quite," she said. She placed her hand in the dirt near mine. An invitation. I looked back out to the tents, glistening with frost in the moonlight.

"We didn't have names in Rhosivi or Predvoi," I commented. "Some of the soldiers here have names and some of them don't. Why is that?"

Kasia scratched in the dirt with the tips of her fingers. "We all had a last name at least, since the Task Force had to have identified at least one of our parents when they tatted us. When Markos took command, he set up a team to find the last names of all the soldiers and inform them what he knew about their parentage. I saw it as an initiative to help humanize the inmates. He cares about us, doesn't he?"

I shrugged. He identified with us, but it was the last thing I could tell her. She caught on to the fact that I had nothing to say and kept talking.

"Some took their last names and began using them. A few have even placed their names on their uniforms, I'm sure you've noticed. You can get one sewn on if you want. A few of the girls from Vazenia are willing to sew, but most of them will stab you with the needle before consenting to stitch another patch. I'll do it if you want though. It wouldn't take long."

Her offer was generous, to say the least, not because of the act itself, but what it represented. It would be like if I'd offered to go into a mine for her and bring back a bit of coal. She was willing to travel back, mentally, to her time at Vazenia, to sew me a patch.

"Thank you, but no. If I decide I want one, I'll figure it out." I offered her a grin and looked quickly away again.

"Luka," Kasia whispered. "There is one thing I can't figure out."

"Yeah?"

"You seem somewhat interested in me. Sometimes you give me a look like you think I'm pretty or clever. You did a moment ago when I called you Victor-27."

I had?

"But you fight it. You fight it as effectively as if you were fighting an Alpha or a Delta."

She'd caught on to that too. Oscars really were the most terrifying of us all.

"Is there someone else?" Her breath smelled sweet as she asked me the question. I imagined it would taste the same. Fruit and flowers and vanilla. I looked away from her mouth to her small hand, resting centimeters from me. Her fingers would have been so fragile in mine. I could have scooped her up and kissed her mouth for as long as I wanted to. But I didn't want to.

"Yes. I suppose you could say that I kind of have a girlfriend."

Markos would have preferred if I gave in to the temptation to kiss Kasia. He'd asked me to stay away from his daughter. He trusted me. Commander Markos, who had saved my life, repeatedly asked one thing of me and I hadn't done it. I couldn't do it.

Markos would have been happy if I brought Kasia back to my tent to discuss the universe and keep me warm.

"When did you even meet a girl?" Kasia asked.

"What do you mean?"

"You and Markos know one another. At first, I thought you knew him from Khizmit, but then I figured out you had some abilities. You must have been at Rhosivi while he was head warden there. But I know you've been to Predvoi because you know Captain Kral better than anyone else, which is how I figured out who you are. I won't pretend to know a lot about how Rhosivi and Predvoi are managed, only what I was able to piece together listening to guards at Vazenia who'd come and go between the prisons."

I'd never realized they had male guards at Vazenia.

"Were all the guards male?" I asked.

"Yes." Then Kasia threw a smile at me. "You understand now, don't you?"

And I did. How she knew, I wasn't sure, but I suddenly understood Tally. She'd been imprisoned in Vazenia. Drugged like me, chained like me, cast out like me, ostracized like me, and all these were done to her by guards. By soldiers. By men. The only men she'd ever met had shouted at her, beat her, imprisoned her, and told her how worthless she was.

And I was a man. By default, I was culpable in her suffering, especially since she didn't know I was a lurper. Being a man alone would have given her reason to fear me, but being a meat-sack, as she'd so kindly called me, made me worse.

I was immediately grateful I hadn't taken the opportunity to throw her down and show her that I was stronger. That I was smarter. That I was dangerous.

Because Tally needed me to be kind and gentle. To let *her* be strong and dangerous so she could feel safe.

Safe.

She needed to kill and protect herself because she believed no one else would do it. She believed I was like the guards at Vazenia who'd hurt her.

"Tally," I whispered and Kasia nodded. It seemed, for a moment, that she had tears in her eyes. "But you're part Oscar, so logically you could sort the good men from the bad men. Logically, you reasoned that not all men were bad. That not all men were out to hurt you."

She nodded, smiling, showing straight white teeth.

"I'm sorry," I said, and I meant it. "You are amazing. Strong. Vivacious, brilliant, and...tempting." I should have picked a better word. "But when I was in Khizmit, I met a girl."

I could have told Kasia about Ember's gold earrings and her laughter like the bells decorating the squares for Koliada. I could have told her about her kiss. Warm, reassuring, all pleasure that electrified me. She'd kissed me and sent me out of this world, away from all the pain I'd felt. Away from all the doubt. All the fear.

She, of all people, had made me feel safe.

Safe in the way that we all deserved to be. She'd kissed me and ignited hope that as a slave for Khizmit, I was living far beneath my potential.

The way that all of us deserved to feel. I placed my hand on top of Kasia's.

"I don't deserve her and if she was smarter, maybe she'd be with someone else. She cared for me when no one else did. She trusted me when she had no reason to."

I would have gone on, but Kasia flipped our hands over and gave mine a little squeeze.

"I understand," she said gently. "I don't want to be a… temptation. Just…an option." She giggled. And for a moment, I could see her like the girls I'd seen giggling in the parade in Khizmit, instead of a soldier in a uniform with a firearm slung over her shoulder.

"Thank you," I said. "I—"

A siren began to wail, nearly shattering the night sky and dropping all the stars upon us. When I looked up, I found that it wasn't stars dropping from the sky. The fiery trails were artillery.

CHAPTER 9
TRIAGE

I was on my feet, staring at the trails of fire in awe. Before I could blink, Roman was dragging me down the hillside until I snapped back to attention and kept pace on my own.

He shouted directions to Kasia, who in turn shouted them to her troops. In a flurry of adrenaline, I was handing weapons over to Flak, Spikes, and Raph—and in the next moment, Roman ordered our squad to the forefront.

I followed Kasia, who understood the instructions more clearly than I did. The overlapping crack of the constant gunfire that surrounded us made it hard to hear; I found myself dampening my hearing just to think more clearly. As we moved through the camp, I took a glance around to ensure that everyone in our squad was accounted for.

Kasia led us around the tents, beyond the range. The wind blew dirt into my eyes I had to try and blink out, hurrying after Kasia. Bursts from rifles ripped through the air. Grenades exploded as they fell from the sky. Dust and debris flew into the air. My hands were sweaty as I gripped the handle of my rifle.

Kasia pointed to a long row of sandbags piled only a couple of meters high in front of us. She gestured to them, Flak nodded, and then she and Tally ran forward. The rest of us trailed behind as the sky continued to flash with red and white.

Tally and Kasia huddled behind a pile of sandbags. Spikes, Raph, Flak, and Clink held their rifles at the ready. Flak's eyes were muted, not unlike Lockbox's had been when we found him. His fingers twitched as he loaded his rifle.

Raph's face became a stone. He popped up, fired off a couple of rounds, and ducked back down, mechanically, mercilessly.

Ignorantly I thought I'd know what to do here—that my instincts to fight would translate to the battlefield—but all the sounds surrounding us created chaos that left me feeling frantic and confused.

In prison, I was used to one enemy at a time. A group of them at best, but I could always see them. I only had to fear their hands, their fists.

There were hundreds of enemies now, all armed with guns and grenades.

Kasia scooted her way over to me, dragging her knees across the ground for part of it to stay low.

"Take a breath, Luka," she said with compassion. "Our job is to hold position and provide cover while the Tangos go in." She pointed out a few silhouettes of soldiers slipping through the shadows toward the battle zone.

I could heal too. I should be with them.

Kasia must have read my thoughts. "We need you here," she said.

Raph continued to pop his head up, pull the trigger, and reload.

It was as if my gut knew something was about to happen because I was staring right at the back of Raph's head when the bullet tore through it, leaving the ground to catch him as his body collapsed.

Flak screamed so loudly I heard it over the blasts of both the grenades and Clink's rifle. Tally shrieked, angry and pained at the sight of Raph, motionless, bleeding out into the dirt.

"Get up," Kasia said as Flak dropped to the ground beside Raph. "Get back up!"

Flak didn't cry. Didn't bend over. Didn't reach out to touch Raph. He sat with his legs folded beneath him, quiet, calm, still. He just stared at Raph's open eyes.

"Raph," Flak whispered. His face was so pale it nearly glowed in the waning moonlight.

Bam! Bam! Clink's shots kept coming. Raph was dead. Flak incapacitated. This was my squad, and I was failing them.

Tally launched herself over the sandbags and began sprinting through the dark toward the enemy.

Kasia called her back, but Tally didn't stop. Spikes wiped at the dirt which had turned wet on his sweaty face before looking through his scope again.

I could be a machine. A tool. A weapon. I looked back at Raph, the red on his forehead, and let the crimson tint take over.

I leapt over the sandbags after Tally, sprinting with my rifle in hand. I focused my hearing on the enemy, picking up the shifts in the dirt as they repositioned to aim.

I pulled the trigger first—then again and again.

Tally tore a few soldiers from their foxholes and tossed them like they were nothing more than a pile of clothes. We both noticed the enemy didn't wear the Latvani uniform. They were soldiers from Khizmit. Grown men, wearing the same uniforms and patches we did.

It made me angrier. I emptied my magazine, paying no mind to the bullets that scraped against my legs and arms.

Tally was ahead, her back to a group of three soldiers. My magazine was empty, and my hands were—for the moment— too injured to reload.

"Tally," I said, rushing toward her.

"Don't touch me!" Tally roared. She reached back with her right arm and swatted at me, tripping over a body.

The barrage of bullets flying toward us left me with no choice.

I leapt, tackling her to the ground.

She stared at me, horror and rage as palpable as her sweaty arms beneath mine. She fought me, twisting her hips and bucking like her life depended on it.

But her life depended on me staying exactly where I was.

"I'll kill you!" she screamed. "I'll skudging kill you!"

"Okay," I said quietly. I didn't feel her skull crash into mine. I didn't feel her fingernails dig into my wrists as she fought me.

I was numb and the stream of bullets biting into my back felt like little more than heavy rain. I took the Lugar off my hip and aimed. It took four shots, and then the artillery died down. The air became still.

I waited another moment, listening for enemies, and heard only Tally's racing heart and ragged breaths. The moment I got off her, Tally reached back, and I ducked out of the way of her fist.

"How dare you?" she screamed. She came after me with all the rage I'd expected. She came at me fueled by the pain of her time at Vazenia, letting her hatred for the guards there drive her as she tried to close the distance between us.

I skirted around her, too tired to explain myself. She darted at me again, and I danced between her blows. When I spun to get out of her reach again, she froze, dropping her hands to her side.

"Turn around," she said, her voice suddenly chilled.

I sighed and slowly turned. She gasped. I turned back to see the rage melt out of her eyes.

I knew what she saw. My entire back was riddled with holes and soaked in blood. I'd healed as fast as I could, but I had to push the bullets out before sealing up my wounds, which I knew had left my entire back a wet, bloody mess.

"You—" She took a few steps toward me. "I—"

I didn't want her to thank me or apologize for having been so angry.

"I'm sorry I scared you. I didn't want you to get killed—"

"Shut the skudge up!" she said. "You're a...what are you?"

"I'm...a lurper."

She almost grinned.

"You saved me. I wouldn't have tried to save you."

"Then it's a good thing I didn't need you to."

Tally had several deep gashes on her legs which adrenaline had numbed for her, but now that she and I walked back to the rest of our camp, she began to grimace. I didn't say anything when I stepped closer, but she understood the offer and stiffly looped her arm around my shoulders to offset some of the pressure on her legs.

I'd have carried her if her pride would have allowed it.

I understood why it didn't.

On our way back into camp we passed where Raph had died, but his body wasn't there anymore. I walked alongside Tally until we got close to the crowds. Picking up on the sound of labored gasps even at this distance, I was able to figure out where the medical tent was. I pointed it out to Tally who gave me an incredulous look—of course, she already knew where to go.

I, on the other hand, couldn't accompany her there. The bloody back of my uniform would divulge my secret to everyone if I didn't get into a new one, and Tally seemed to understand. She shoved my hand off her shoulders and hobbled in the direction of the medical tent while I slipped back to mine.

With the chaos of the aftermath of the attack, no one

seemed interested in me. Groups of soldiers moved injured or dead lurpers across the field.

The tang of blood was potent in the air even as I ducked into my tent.

As soon as I had a partially clean uniform top on, I rushed over to the medical tent.

Kasia hurried out, assessing injuries in the line, only sparing a glance for me.

"What are you doing?" I asked.

"Triage."

"Which means?"

"Deciding who needs help first. Who can wait."

"Can I help?" I felt like asking was already an inconvenience.

"Go in there. The surgeon could use a hand."

The surgeon sat beneath a bright bulb holding sharp metal tools in his small hands. I didn't dare utter his name, lest he slip while pulling a bullet from the shoulder of the inmate on the table.

Lockbox's hands were quick. The bullet made a *plink!* as it hit the bottom of the metal pan and Lockbox reached over for a bottle of clear liquid that he dabbed onto a piece of gauze. The kid at the table groaned and bit into the cloth harder as Lockbox cleaned the wound. I stared as he stitched up the hole, cut the string, and motioned for the next patient.

"Luka," Lockbox said, some hint of relief in his voice. "Get me over there!" He pointed to a girl who was lying face down on a cot.

I lifted the whole chair and brought him over to her.

"When did you become a surgeon?" I asked.

"Today," he muttered. I tried not to look closely at what he was doing. "I heard there was an opening. Figured I'd make myself helpful."

Doctor Bolest had been the last doctor here, and since he'd

been away, I'd assumed Khizmit had sent another one. I'd assumed wrong.

"I read what I could. Shared the rest of the material with the other Oscars here." Lockbox motioned to the roll of gauze. "Hand that to me, would ya?"

I did.

"I can't promise to fix everything, but I can do a lot better than Doctor Bolest did," Lockbox said.

Kasia hurried in and said something to Lockbox about hemorrhaging and a tourniquet.

"Luka," Lockbox said. "We need Commander Alekin to help."

The commander of the Latvani Ground Forces wasn't going to join our coup easily. "I know," I muttered. I passed the antiseptic over to Lockbox. "How?"

"Someone has to go tell him the truth. Someone must get through to him."

"Markos has sent people."

Lockbox stitched up another deep cut and pointed to the next patient. I carried him over. Spikes had his hand wrapped in a bloody cloth. When he removed it, most of his middle finger was crushed.

"We have to remove it," Lockbox said. "It won't heal."

Spikes just nodded. Lockbox pointed to a syringe in a medical kit and a vial of vyco.

He carefully measured a dose and injected it at the base of Spike's fingers.

"You're going to cut it off?" I asked. I choked at the idea.

"I'm going to save his hand," Lockbox said. "Sometimes you have to sacrifice something, to save something else."

"Be direct."

"Someone needs to speak to Commander Alekin. That someone needs to be you."

"Why?" I asked. Spikes continued to sputter in pain as a Charlie tied him down.

"It's to keep you from moving while I do the procedure. Okay?" Lockbox explained to Spikes. Spikes nodded.

"I've run the data. I've gone through the intel we have. There isn't enough time to wait for Alekin to come to his senses. We have to take calculated risks."

"And that risk is that I go see Commander Alekin?"

"You risk death. You risk success," Lockbox said. He pointed to a metal device with sharp blades on the edges. "I need that."

"Luka!" Roman called from across the tent.

"I can help here. Captain Kral needs you," Kasia said, hurrying over.

I didn't look over to Lockbox or back at Spikes. I tried not to listen to the sound of the tool as it snapped the bone away at the joint. I heard it anyway.

The sounds of the clinic faded as Roman led me up the hill to Commander Markos's tent.

"What are we doing?"

"Meeting while we can. In the aftermath of the attack, it won't be suspicious for us to meet. Markos needs to talk to us."

"Does he know?" I asked.

"What?"

"Does Markos know that I kissed Ember?"

Roman furrowed his brow looking like he might laugh or yell at me. "You're worried about that? We've got death all around us and you're worried about a kiss?"

It was strange for me to worry about that right now. Maybe it was my mind's way of distracting myself from what Lockbox was doing to Spike's hand down in the tent.

"You did say you thought he'd kill you for something."

"What?" I asked.

"That night, when you were with Emberly, you said, 'He'll kill me for that.'"

I didn't take another step. "You heard that? What else did you hear?"

Roman smiled faintly. "We didn't hear much. We heard her say you were her Victor. We heard you say that he'd kill you for something."

I swallowed hard.

"And?"

"He wasn't as mad as you might have thought. I think he suspected it. Hell, he sort of set it up. He said you were her bodyguard. He gave you permission to hold her hand. Besides, Emberly's not the sort of girl who's going to wait for permission to do something. Markos knows that."

"That's not what this is about?"

"Come on," Roman said, giving me a shove.

We continued our climb up the small hill toward Markos's tent.

"Have some spatial awareness! No, that's not what this is. Markos was in touch with the other commanders," Roman said through gritted teeth. "Markos demanded answers, and they're calling what just happened a *training exercise.*"

"I imagine they lost quite a bit more than we did."

"We? Why aren't we all included in that? It shouldn't be us versus them. We are all from Khizmit. We wear the same uniform."

"But we don't bleed the same blood," I said.

"If Latvani was smart, they'd just wait us out. They'd wait for us to kill one another off before invading again."

Khizmit forces were going to kill us off before we could unite with Latvani. Before Commander Alekin could hear Markos's plan. We had to do something. We had to take calculated risks. Someone had to do something.

Lockbox believed that someone was me.

CHAPTER 10
NOT THE WORST PLAN

"Do we have a plan yet?" I asked. "For getting Commander Alekin to listen?"

"No," Roman said. He stopped a short distance from Commander Markos's tent, and we looked back down over the camp, trails of smoke still hanging in the sky overhead.

I noticed a member of the cadre, Captain Gaborik, patrolling outside Markos's tent.

"What's he doing?"

"The commander of the Lurper Legion always has a personal guard to discourage assassination."

I felt my heart start to race. "Why do they think someone would try to assassinate Markos?"

Roman answered directly. "Because that's what happened to every other commander of the Lurper Legion. Some lasted a few days. Some lasted a few months. It's the fate of the commander of the volatile and gifted."

The volatile and gifted. Axe's face flashed through my mind when he'd cut off his own fingers only to reattach them with that sickening grin. "Does he have bodyguards?"

"He trusts a few to take shifts outside his tent at night. He doesn't want to make a big show of a bodyguard because it demonstrates distrust. He's worked with lurpers like us his whole life, but it isn't his Achilles heel if you know what I mean. He's got a soft spot, but he won't expose it. Besides, he's got something the other commanders didn't."

Markos was a Victor. Markos would heal from an assassination attempt. He would dodge the bullet, and if he caught it with anything other than his head or heart, he'd heal.

As we approached Captain Gaborik, I saluted, and he saluted back. We didn't speak, but the unspoken tragedy of the night's losses was unmistakable as we passed him and entered the tent.

Markos spent his days planning, what I had to assume was a way to get Alekin's attention long enough to convey his plans. His plans for betraying Khizmit. His plans for taking over the Grand Palace and freeing all the lurpers in the Enclave.

When we entered his tent and I saw him for the first time in a few days, the bags under his eyes and the dangerous edge to his voice sent torrents of anxiety through me.

"Thirty-two deaths so far," Markos said. "Thirty-two skudging dead and for what? For them to call it a training exercise." He ran a hand across his unshaven face. Time was ticking.

Did Khizmit suspect him?

"Have a seat, Luka."

I dropped into the chair that I'd occupied when Roman had tattooed my arm. Markos sat on his trunk and pulled out some papers.

"Lockbox suggested that we use horses to go over the mountains and enter Rhosivi from the west."

He unfurled a map and traced his finger along the route. "There are no guards on that side of the prison, and if we could get word out, lurpers could congregate during their shifts in the mine."

"Do you have horses, Sir?" I hadn't seen any.

"No, but Latvani does."

Latvani. We relied too heavily on them.

"If Alekin joined you, and gave you horses, would they survive in the mountains? Would the inmates from Rhosivi survive long enough to get to Khizmit?"

"Most of them," Markos said. "Alternatively, we could attack Rhosivi from the west, hoping that the lurpers would see our forces as allies and overthrow the guards and command there. Then we could all walk and take any vehicles on the road down to Predvoi to do the same."

"What's wrong with that plan?" I could tell by the way he'd said it that he didn't like it.

"If we cause a prison riot, word will get to Khizmit. Bear Legion and Wolf Legion will come to defend the Enclave and our chances for success diminish significantly."

Roman poured a cup of what smelled like sveetin into a mug and handed it over to Markos.

"I favor Lockbox's initial plan," Roman said, dropping into a chair beside me.

"Which is?"

"Ideally, Latvani forces will occupy the Wolf and Bear Legions down here in The Outskirts while we send three small forces up to the three prisons. Plan a simultaneous riot on all three. Get all three groups of lurpers to converge at the north of Khizmit while the Lurper Legion comes up from the south."

I tried to imagine it. Tried to picture all the lurpers working together under Markos. His risk of being assassinated would increase tenfold if he freed inmates. I wanted inmates to be free. I knew how much I wanted to be free, but not everyone could be trusted with freedom. The reality was that many of them were dangerous.

"What happens when some of them turn on us?" I phrased the eventuality as gently as I could.

"Some will have to go back to prison, but it will be for crimes they commit instead of proclivities they possess."

The tent flaps rustled, and High Captain Toth poked his head in. "Sir, we have more casualties."

"How many?"

"Seven more, Sir."

Markos's expression dropped.

"When can we act?" I asked as soon as Toth ducked back out of sight. "Will you tell your cadre?"

"I will tell them when the time is right. We can't act until we have Alekin."

"What will it take to get him on our side?"

"An ambassador. A successful ambassador." He'd sent ambassadors to speak to Commander Alekin with the Latvani troops beyond the destruction zone, and none had come back.

Something inside my head stupidly demanded that I go myself. That I speak to him myself. Some dumb part of my brain was convinced that if I went to him and told him about my time in Rhosivi, Predvoi, and Khizmit, and asked for his help, he'd grant it. Lockbox had said so. Lockbox knew a lot of things.

Something idiotic inside me was convinced that he'd make peace after decades of war all because of me.

Markos and Roman continued to discuss some details but I couldn't focus. Not now that I had the idea in my head, nudging me.

I had to go.

I had to ask Commander Alekin to open communication with Markos and assist in a military coup to take over Khizmit.

"Sir," I said, interrupting Markos as he'd been speaking to Roman. "I'm going to be your ambassador. I'm going to see Alekin."

"No," Markos said. "I haven't heard back from anyone else I've sent. I'm not willing to risk you."

"It's not your choice." I shocked even myself with how forcibly I said it. "It's my choice. I'm willing to go."

"What's your plan, Luka? Walk over there and ask politely? Fight your way through their ranks until you find yourself face-to-face with Alekin?"

"No. I'm going to ask Lockbox."

Markos sighed and took a long drink from his sveetin. His eyes were shut when he said, "I told him not to ask you to go."

"I will do it. I will go and I will meet with him."

"You're going to leave your brothers and walk away, right into the hands of the enemy?"

"We can't do this without Alekin, and nothing else has worked."

"What makes you think they won't blow your brains all over the field as soon as they see you? What makes you think they'll hesitate before they flay you?" Markos set his empty mug down and leaned forward to stare at me.

"I don't know." The words sounded weak, and I quickly tried to accompany them with some degree of confidence. "If we don't succeed in the coup, we're all dead anyway. All the lurpers. You. They're killing us for training exercises. Eventually, Khizmit will find out about you." With that last comment, I was afraid I'd shown my hand. Markos had risked his reputation and identity time and time again for me. To keep me safe. To save me from a firing squad.

I worried about Roman and Lockbox, and I even found that I worried about Clink, and Flak, as insane as that was. But the idea of Markos getting hanged outside the city center in Khizmit made my intestines knot up so tight I almost felt the need to heal some fatal internal injury that hadn't been inflicted yet.

I think it was because Markos guessed at my true motivation that he shot down the idea entirely.

"Absolutely not," Markos said, dismissing me with a wave of his hand. "Return to your tent and await orders."

"Markos—"

"Do you see any other junior lieutenants saunter their way over here for unscheduled conversations?" His voice rose to a roar. "As a matter of fact, do you see any lieutenants approach me even when I'm doing inspections around the camp?"

I didn't say anything. Then, "No, Sir." He raised his eyebrows as though to challenge my answer. "But I'm not—"

"Junior Lieutenant, don't think for a moment that you're calling *any* shots here." Markos rose to his feet and began to shout. "Your chain of command goes through Captain Kral."

Suddenly I was Victor-27 again, looking for a cot to sit on or climb beneath.

"I will not discuss it with you again." He dismissed me and I walked away, biting back the words, "Yes, *Mr. Chief Preemptive Officer.*"

This place was a prison, wasn't it? This Legion was a prison and he, as the commander, was still the warden. But I was no longer an inmate. My wrist didn't say V-27. It had trees. And it was about time I saw some again.

"You're not a skudging prisoner, Luka. This isn't Rhosivi. Leave whenever you want." He turned his back to me.

I stood up and straightened my uniform. It wasn't the worst plan. "Sir, tomorrow morning I'm going to go south, through the zones. I'm not deserting. I'm not abandoning the unit. We need Latvani's support, and we can't keep waiting."

Markos turned back around and stared at me for a long moment before meeting Roman's gaze. Neither he nor Markos spoke a word. I didn't speak again.

Markos finally said, "I won't be able to help you. I won't know if you're dead. I won't know if you're alive. I want you here."

"I'm going tomorrow. Lockbox can give me directions. I'll leave at dawn."

Markos wasn't mad. He was disappointed. He'd be more disappointed if our coup failed because we didn't have enough soldiers.

Markos finally shook his head and scoffed, "It'll be a skudging waste if you die."

CHAPTER 11
DESTRUCTION ZONE

"I respect your autonomy."

"I trust your judgment."

"I support your decision."

Any one of those sentences would have been welcome when I'd announced to Commander Markos that I was going to Latvani.

Roman and I later discussed Markos's reaction and decided it was permission enough. I packed up a bag, brought only a pistol as a weapon, and followed the directions through the battle zone, weaving over trenches and debris from past battles.

I'd asked Markos if I could bring the Latvani prisoner back as a show of my good intentions, but he said it was too risky.

With some strange combination of courage, determination, and fear, I walked away from camp, setting my back to the Penal Legion, knowing that they weren't going to follow me into enemy territory. Latvani and Khizmit had been at war for decades and here I went thinking that a single conversation was going to make any difference at all.

But I had to try. We didn't have time to wait and to send letters back and forth. We didn't have time for Commander

Alekin to agree to a meeting with Commander Markos. They'd been trying. I could go in though. Even if they shot me, chances were, I could heal and still say what I needed to say. My specific abilities made me the perfect candidate and I believed that eventually, Markos would come to see that. I wasn't disobeying his orders or defying him. I was being proactive. I was doing this for him. For us. For Victors and all other inmates.

For the good of Khizmit as Khizmit should be.

I knew there was a slim chance for my success. I walked on toward Latvani despite the fear and the uncertainty because I had something. Something Lockbox had reminded me time and time again was a tool and a gift. Something I'd fought for and resented for years.

Hope.

Hope that things can get better in Khizmit. Hope that I'd see my friends again. Hope that Commander Alekin would be a reasonable man and that he'd give me a chance to speak to him. Hope that Latvani and Markos and his legion could unite and lead an assault against Khizmit. Hope that I'd see Emberly again. That I'd get to hold her close to my chest and smell her hair as it tickled my face.

I walked all day, mindful of the body's tendency to eventually walk in a circle, and checked Roman's compass often. Roman believed in me, at least enough not to stop me. At least enough to get out of my way.

Lockbox said I risked death, but also success. He didn't give me percentages. He said he didn't have enough information to.

After crossing through the destruction zone, I came to clear land, though evidence suggested troops had stayed here not long before. It looked like this was where most of the forces who'd attacked us had set up their base.

I stepped around large boulders, followed narrow paths carved by the small deer that populated the area, and rested only long enough to swallow a small amount of water every few kilometers.

My thoughts threatened to stop me as I walked toward the unknown.

But it wasn't truly unknown. We knew that Latvani soldiers hid ahead. We knew they had an X-ray as a prisoner. We knew they hadn't sent back a message.

What would they say? What would they do?

The only reason Commander Markos had let me go was because I'd practically begged him to let me. I had to help.

My whole life I'd been reminded, emphatically and often violently, that what I did had to contribute. I'd believed it. Not for the good of Khizmit as Khizmit was, but for what Khizmit could become.

The Latvani Legion had set up camp on the opposite side of a river, knowing the difficulty anyone would have in approaching them without putting themselves at risk. I wasn't trying to be discreet. I walked alongside the river in plain sight of anyone who might be watching me from the trees. The thin layer of black mud beneath my boots squeaked and squelched as I walked. Each little suction, from each time I pulled one foot from the mud to put in front of the other, announced to the enemy that I approached. Though the plan required that I not be stealthy, the voice in my head that told me how to fight also demanded that I walk more quietly. That I keep to the shadows. That I approach with caution.

Any semblance of secrecy or stealth could result in a speedy death. A slow death may not result in death at all, given my abilities. If Latvani soldiers had any idea what I was, though, they'd kill me quickly rather than risk me healing and killing them.

As soldiers out here in a war with the Penal Legion, Markos had warned me they'd met soldiers like me who could heal from injuries. They'd met soldiers like me who could fight and maim and kill with minimal effort. Their fear of our unnatural abilities made them kill first and never question if it was the right move.

Markos had believed that Commander Alekin was putting together a list, a key, linking the tattoos on soldier's wrists to their abilities. But my wrist was concealed. They'd met Charlies and Victors, but they'd never met me. I prayed that could be to my advantage.

The trees thinned here and, rather than tall, strong trunks that supported heavy branches, only pathetic shrubs and stooped trees grew. The gusts of wind that flew down from the distant mountains attempted to bend me over too, but I stood straighter because of them. I walked proudly, fighting the wind while keeping my pace.

For several moments the wind howled so loudly I doubted I'd hear anything over it, and when I crossed the open space to the new tree line, I heard a distinct click.

"My name is Junior Lieutenant Luka Drivick. I'm here as a representative of the Khizmit Penal Battalion under the command of Pedrick Markos. I carry this pistol, clearly visible at my waist, and bring no weapons other than myself. I have a message for your commander, Alekin." I sent my words boldly into the trees, even while adjusting my hearing to the quieter hum within the woods.

There were at least four soldiers around me. With my eyes, I tracked the trees they hid behind. I glimpsed what might have been a black boot disappearing into a pile of orange needles.

"I will comply with any bodily inspections or safety measures you want to employ to ensure the safety of your camp."

The soldier stepped out from the tree, his rifle trained on me as he took deliberate steps toward me. I raised my arms higher, then stilled any movement.

His uniform wasn't entirely different from my own, but a darker grey, with intentional blotches of brown and green which made him camouflage much better with the surroundings. Rather than the Khizmit flag on his shoulder, he wore what had to be the Latvani flag, in deep blue with yellow stars around a black ship or a rounded blade, I wasn't sure which.

With movements that were obviously meant to be fast, but came predictably slowly, all the soldiers stepped out from the trees. The soldier on my far right manifested the most fear as his hands trembled. I stood completely still as the soldiers approached.

In a language that sounded almost like a shorter, slang version of mine, the soldier in charge, a captain by the looks of it, gave orders to the two soldiers nearest me. In synchronized movements, they both handed their rifles back to a soldier behind them and then approached us. It wouldn't have been much more difficult to take the rifles, but it made them feel better keeping them out of my reach.

The captain gave another order and the soldier nearest me pulled out a green bag, apparently made from a parachute, and pulled it over my head before binding my hands together.

Still, it would have made for a fun challenge to disarm the group, despite their efforts to contain me. I wondered briefly if there was a way Commander Markos could make a training exercise like this.

The bag on my head smelled strongly of sweat, and my breath made it uncomfortably warm. They began pulling and pushing me toward their camp and I followed, compliant, non-threatening.

We walked for about twenty minutes, occasionally making loops around the trees, which mostly succeeded in confusing me, but I still believed I could find my way back to Markos if need be.

When we arrived, they walked us past large groups of

soldiers who murmured, sometimes in a language I understood, and sometimes in their coded speech.

I was pushed to the ground where I sat for another ten minutes until I heard a group of approaching footsteps.

At the command of a new voice, someone grabbed my wrists and slid the rope to the side to check my wrist for a lurper's tattoo.

The bag made it difficult to see anything, but I could have sworn the silhouette of a soldier behind me lifted the butt of his rifle and although I knew what was coming, I decided not to dodge it.

If they saw me as a threat, they'd never trust me and they'd try to kill me. They wouldn't have to be too creative to be successful at that.

The butt of the gun smacked into my head sending momentary waves of pain throughout my whole body. I dulled the pain instinctively, even through the daze the impact had caused. Through the haze of the dizzying ringing in my head, I felt them bind my wrists and drag me across the hard, dry ground.

I woke up right after a soldier threw sludgy water on my face, maybe as much from the stench as from the shock.

"What are you?" a captain demanded in a deep, coarse voice.

I hadn't expected it though I should have. They knew we had abilities. Maybe they even knew what it would mean if I told them I was a Victor.

They didn't ask *who*. Or what I wanted. Just what I was.

"I'm an emissary from The Penal Battalion," I said.

"But *what* are you?"

"I am a soldier. A boy. I was a prisoner for most of my life. Khizmit kept me in Rhosivi Prison, where I mined coal. Then I spent time at Predvoi before coming here."

"What do the trees on your wrist mean?"

"They don't mean anything. They mean freedom to me.

Freedom from the prison." Speaking with the bag over my head made it more difficult to breathe. While oxygen could get in through the fabric, it became stuffy and uncomfortable. "Can I speak to you face to face? I'll answer your questions."

Their response came as a sharp, deep pain slashed across my arm, near my bicep. I felt my blood pouring out over my arm.

I bit back cursing and took a moment to tell my brain not to heal it. This was a test to see if I could heal. To see what I could do. I held back the impulse to mend the injury and instead bit back tears.

They watched long enough to determine that I wasn't a threat to them without the ability to heal and someone removed my boots and socks.

Rough hands grabbed at my uniform, tearing it from my body. With the use of their knives, they stripped me naked in less than a minute, leaving multiple cuts across my body from their reckless hands.

Someone put a rope around my hands and then lifted me so brutally that for a moment I was suspended by my wrists. They lowered me slowly until my feet barely reached the floor before removing the bag from my head.

Four soldiers stood in the room around me. My uniform lay in tatters on the floor near the walls of the thick canvas. Looking up I saw the rope holding me looped around a beam in the ceiling.

I could have pulled myself up, climbed the rope to the rafters, dropped down to the other side, and then used the rope to strangle the men who'd done this to me, but instead, I stood there as goosebumps prickled up all over my skin from the gusts of wind that burst through the large holes in the sides of the tent.

The cut on my arm wasn't bleeding much anymore, maybe because it was elevated far above my heart. The other few cuts drew red stripes down my body.

I could kill them all, I reassured myself. But what would it accomplish? It wouldn't win the war. It wouldn't help the coup.

The captain had a looming forehead, and if the name *Gorog* hadn't been stitched into the front pocket of his uniform, I'd have called him something after his forehead. If he'd turned to the side, I think it would have jutted out on his profile. He didn't turn. He didn't look away from me. I wasn't sure he even blinked, but the effort it took not to follow my instincts to heal, fight, or be free was greater than I expected.

Unfamiliar with the rank of the Latvani army, I didn't know what the other soldiers in the room were, but they all had lines and dots on their uniforms beside their names.

"What are you?" Captain Gorog asked me. He'd been the one to ask me before.

"I'm an emissary. I'm a friend."

Something sliced across my back. One of the other soldiers had whipped me.

Angry as the red line bloomed across my back, I bit my tongue.

"I'm a soldier from Khizmit. I was a prisoner—"

"You *are* a prisoner." Gorog cut in. "And you will tell us how to get past the defenses of your army and into Khizmit."

"I'll let you into Khizmit. I'll lead you there. That's why —" another lashing across my back cut off the rest of my words.

"What are you? If you were a prisoner, then you're one of them. What does your wrist say beneath all the ink?"

I took a deep breath, certain my response would merit another lashing. "Beneath all the ink is skin. Beneath the ink I'm a boy, trying to become a man in a world that didn't want me here at all."

Gorog surprised me by holding up a hand to stop the soldier with the whip. The whip was made of leather and metal. Maybe metal with more give than barbed wire but not much different in other ways. I was sure if he whipped it against the side of the tent it would have ripped it wide open.

Suddenly the huge openings in the walls made sense.

He had.

Someone had.

"Did you desert?" Gorog asked.

"No, I did not. I am here as a messenger to speak to Commander Alekin."

"You will never get near him. You will die here, *Khis*, only after you have betrayed everyone you think you're loyal to now."

Khis, I was sure, had been said with all the hatred of a slur, but as it was just another combination of sounds to me, it didn't have the desired effect on my emotional state.

I can leave anytime, I reminded myself. *I can get out whenever I need to.*

Unless they kill me.

CHAPTER 12
BURNING CANVAS

IF I SLEPT, it was a half-sleep, half-torture state of chill, pain, and apprehension. I woke up many times with my arms and shoulders numb, not to mention the other parts of me that had nearly frozen off during the night. The hardest part was right before dawn when cold dew began to settle all over my skin.

Give it a few more days, I told myself, only to shorten my timeline a few hours later in the night. *If today goes poorly, escape tomorrow night.*

The temptation to escape now rather than later dangled in front of me, baiting me. But I wouldn't take the bait. I hadn't accomplished anything. Not daring to heal anything or block pain because of how it would show my abilities, I took a deep breath and attempted to see in the dark. I listened for distance and caught parts of jokes and bits of conversation in what I assumed was Latvani language. It was similar enough that I understood most of what they said, but it sounded like one of my roommates who'd had most of his teeth knocked out and had a swollen tongue for a week.

Sometime later, I drifted off again.

Someone was whispering. I cracked my eyes open. The whisper came again, and I knew it came from a child. A girl.

It was a distinct sound so surprising that it jolted me wide awake—as alert as I could have been, having been deprived of food and water.

Another child whispered and I turned to look through the largest of the holes in the tent where two small faces poked in staring at me. One boy and one girl. They could have been twins or maybe the girl was older. They shared the same dark hair and eyebrows. Both had long eyelashes and wide, curious brown eyes. The boy had a dimple in his chin and even though the feature seemed like it would have made him look older, it didn't.

The boy whispered to the girl again, and I listened closer this time.

"He's a spy."

"But why's he's naked?" The girl remarked.

"Because they had to make sure he didn't have any weapons."

"And he's bleeding."

The boy didn't say anything. He stared right at me, seeing that I was awake, and jumped back. Based on the sound, he'd fallen over. The girl caught my gaze and held it.

"Are you a spy?" she whispered, the tremble in her voice making it nearly impossible to understand the question.

"No," I whispered back. "I'm a boy."

"I can see you're a boy," she said, no longer whispering.

The boy tugged at her arm, speaking quietly in the not-quite-same-language—again, I could understand the general meaning of what he said, but I couldn't have spoken it back.

He was afraid of me. He'd called me a spy.

A spy. Of course they assumed that. *Why would they believe I was anything else?*

I waited all morning for someone to come and check on me. Though I didn't have any expectations, I did wonder if I'd get water or food of any sort. I watched the legs and boots of soldiers march past all morning, allowing me to occasionally listen in to conversations about the war. By listening to distant conversations, I became somewhat familiar with a few of the temporary structures around me. If all else was quiet, I could hear people talking at a normal level almost five kilometers away, but if I was listening to such a distant conversation and then some other, closer sound blared in my ears, it usually resulted in a ringing in my ears for a few minutes.

Based on a conversation between two nurses, I knew the medical tent was behind me, to the southwest, at least two kilometers. The commander's tent, if I was right in what I'd overheard, lay almost three kilometers to the south. There were a few women around the semi-permanent military base. Some worked as nurses and some worked as soldiers, but their barracks were much farther away from me. However, it sounded like some tents housed entire families. Once or twice, I thought I heard a child's voice, but they were harder for me to hear from a distance, especially with all the other sounds: artillery in the distance at what must have been the range, the scrape of shovels, the spray of water.

Water. I almost escaped just to get a sip of water. I entertained the idea of leaving and getting something to drink and returning, but the risk was too high.

Occasionally while eavesdropping, I heard conversations that pertained to me.

"He's not healing, and he doesn't seem too strong or smart. The best we can tell, he's not a lurper. He's an officer and hasn't shown any inhuman abilities—" But shouting on the other side of my tent forced me to draw back.

By midday, there was no part of me that didn't ache, and I nearly gave in to the temptation to deal with some of the tearing that had surely happened in my shoulders.

I half-stood, half-hung there by my arms all day. The cuts the soldiers had inflicted the night before itched, asking to be healed.

Not yet. Not yet. But soon, I said to myself.

At lunchtime, I risked calling out to see if anyone would speak with me.

"My name is Luka Drivick. I have a message for Commander Alekin from Commander Markos. Please, someone come listen to me. I have a message for your commander."

Gorog came in with his soldiers and narrowed his already small eyes at me.

"Luka Drivick. You were close with Commander Markos. Our intel indicates that you stayed with him in his home over the holidays. That you, as a junior lieutenant, have been privy to many conversations with him. It's unfortunate."

I didn't wait long to talk, despite the dryness of my mouth and throat.

"What's unfortunate?"

"All of it." Gorog's voice didn't convince me. It had something of a playfulness to it. "It's unfortunate that you trusted the man who sent you here and that you'll share all his classified intel before you die."

"What is it you want to know?"

"The truth," Gorog said. "Why did he really send you here?"

"The truth," I tried to readjust my arms, but it was futile. My brain told me six ways I could have killed Gorog. "The truth is that Commander Markos didn't send me. I came here on my own. I came because the previous messengers didn't come back and I need to speak to Commander Alekin. Commander Markos didn't want me to die."

"Then you'll continue to be a disappointment to him," Gorog said.

His soldiers left more gashes across my back before they left.

"What do you want to know?" I shouted after them. I began to think they didn't want to know anything. They just wanted to kill me.

A thought, dangerous and merciless, came into my mind as I waited for the sun to set. I was meant to be a prisoner. Born a prisoner, it was only right that I'd die a prisoner. I preferred prisons with a cellmate, a prison that required manual labor to hanging my arms in a tent alone. I preferred skinning rabbits to this. Was that all I was good for? Being a prisoner? The trees on my wrist mocked me. I'd left them. I'd come here on my own.

I'd drifted off, tired from my hunger, when the screams woke me. At first, I thought it was a windstorm but realized from the dancing light that it wasn't the wind that caused people to shout and scurry outside the tent.

A fire roared outside, growling as it consumed tent after tent, the wind picking it up and carrying it across the sky.

I stared, contemplating when to escape as the fire drew nearer. Then a cold blast of wind brought a burning piece of canvas right to the side of my tent and then heat slammed into me as the tent ignited. In the blink of an eye, two sides of the tent around me were ashes and the wind took the fire and carried it to the next tent while the rest of mine only slowly burned.

Had it burned the rope or the wooden poles of the tent, I'd have had a reason to escape, but it had already moved on, and the wind blew it out on my tent. I now had a full view of the chaos outside as tents blazed and soldiers ran around with buckets and hoses. The dance of flames entranced me for a few moments as the growl of the fire and the hiss of the wind sang a song of demolition.

Then someone screamed. Wood splintered. The frame of the tent beside me collapsed, dropping burning canvas right on top of the two children. I turned my head back and forth to see who would come to their rescue.

The girl's scream was high-pitched and desperate. The boy grunted as he tried to move the flaming log off them. For a moment I couldn't see them, but the canvas burned through and once again their heads became visible.

"Help!" the boy screamed. The two of them worked together but screamed again every time they placed their hands on the log to push it off their legs. The boy was stuck deeper, and, from my angle, I only saw one of his arms reach out and try to move the blazing log away.

I saw the scene unfold the same way I'd seen countless scenes unfold before. Instructions as clear as those that had helped me disarm guards at Predvoi guided my actions and I pulled myself up by my wrists, took the rope in my hands, and shimmied up to the top of my beam. I untied the knot and stood, running along the top of the next beam before leaping off toward the children. I hit the ground hard, knowing at that moment that the adrenaline rushing through me had healed all my injuries. I became like fire myself. I reached into the flames, feeling the rush of the heat in the back of my mind as I lifted the whole log up before tossing it to the side. I didn't even see their faces. With a child in each arm, I sprinted away from the flames toward where I'd heard a female's voice discussing medical procedures. I didn't see a soul until I arrived at the front of the tall white tent.

A woman in a folded hat stared at us in horror.

"Do you have a cot or a bed I can put them on? They probably have broken legs."

Then I heard the gunshot.

I never felt it, but I watched as my arm gave out, and there was nothing I could do to stop the boy from falling onto his face.

Almost as suddenly as the first bullet hit my arm, another

tore into my stomach. I dropped to my knees, trying to set the girl down carefully.

"Stop!" Someone bellowed and the gunfire ceased. "You've killed him."

I gasped in a breath and looked down to see the bullet fall out of my gut before the skin healed itself back together.

A man, wider than Commander Markos but solidly built, walked over. He stared down at me impassively. In the dark, I couldn't read his name patch, but the authority he held himself with alone led me to believe that I'd found Commander Alekin.

"He isn't what we expected."

"He's a Whiskey?" the man who'd shot me approached, his gun still at the ready.

"At least that."

The man who'd shot me told me to come with him, and I did, while more soldiers in the distance got the fire under control. This man, a lieutenant, guided me to what appeared to be an empty barracks tent based on the sheer number of sleeping pads inside. He threw a uniform at me and told me to dress. I did.

He directed me to wash my face using a bucket of water outside of the tent. I did.

"Are you going to kill me?" he asked, and I assumed that he understood how little his gun would help him if I had other plans for his future or lack thereof.

I walked in the direction he led me. "Are *you* going to kill *me*?"

He didn't answer.

CHAPTER 13
COMMANDER ALEKIN

WE WALKED up a small hill to a tent that, other than location, was identical to the rest of the tents in the small valley below. A huge Latvanian flag hung from the front, lit by a spotlight staked into the ground.

"Was it an electrical fire?" I asked. The soldier ignored me. "Is that symbol a ship or—"

The man stopped and jerked his thumb toward the entrance.

"Commander Alekin would like to speak with you."

I wanted to ask if that was who I'd met earlier, but knew it was something I'd discover shortly.

"It is my understanding that a single bullet in your head will kill you."

I nodded. "Yeah, that's my general understanding too."

"But I'd rather not do it."

"Then we're on the same page." I'd have tried to smile at the man, but apprehension kept my face tight.

I'd have to walk in first, and this soldier would follow, his gun pointed at my head. I took a breath and parted the entrance of the tent.

A few blankets spread across the side made for a bed, and three trunks, not that different from mine at Rhosivi and

Predvoi, sat along the sides of the tent where the thick canvas was staked down. There were no visible papers or maps.

"Luka Drivick," the man in front of me said. The dim light inside his tent was sufficient to tell that the man I'd seen before was, in fact, Commander Alekin. The commander was at least as tall as Commander Markos, but not as broad in the shoulders. He was clean-shaven with short, well-kept black hair beneath his cap. The gaze he fixed me with reminded me of Warden Velky's—suspicious, wary, and reserved. It might have intimidated someone less experienced than me.

His uniform matched those of the soldiers who'd brought us here, only his had many ribbons along the front in yellows, reds, purples, and burgundies. Along his right front pocket, I read his name. "Alekin" in wide gold letters.

"Commander Alekin," I said, saluting him briefly out of respect.

He didn't hesitate to respond. "What are you doing here?"

"As I've told your soldiers, I'm here to discuss a proposition. Commander Markos didn't send me, because he feared for my safety, but I am loyal to him and the cause we have is important enough to me to take the risk."

Alekin stared at me. He didn't scratch at his face or play with the handle of any weapons. It appeared at first glance that the only firearm in the room was the one currently pointed at my head.

I paused, not because of his expression or the sudden change in my status as a prisoner, but out of shock.

I didn't immediately have thoughts of ways I could kill him.

Wait.

Well, now I did, but I hadn't before. My immediate reaction to standing in front of the commander hadn't been full of ways I could have disarmed the man behind me and used the weapon against the commander.

"You're not here to kill me," Alekin stated.

"No, Sir," I said hurriedly, pushing away the image of silently choking him unconscious from behind. I stayed silent. Waiting for an invitation.

Alekin pursed his lips slightly as he looked from me to a paper in his lap.

"Why are you here? I assume you want to negotiate peace."

"I'm not here to negotiate peace." I didn't want to leave the sentence there, lest it sound like a threat. "We have shared interests, and you may find what I have to say difficult to believe. What I propose is dangerous, but not especially to you."

"I'm curious," Alekin said. "But I have no reason to trust you."

"That's true," I said, adjusting my position on the floor. "But I promise I will answer anything you ask me truthfully. I came here with answers. I don't know what you already know, and you can cross-examine what we say with what you know about our battalion and Khizmit's history."

Alekin nodded as if deciding how to phrase what he'd say next. "I heard the kids screaming. I saw their tent collapse and then I watched you escape from your bonds as if it was nothing. I had you in my scope, but the timing of your escape made me curious enough to wait and I watched as you healed yourself only to go to the aid of the children of the men who'd harmed you. You came face to face with the most vulnerable members of our ranks and you threw the burning beam away from them as if it was weightless. Why?"

His question could have referred to any part of my actions, so I set out to answer all of them.

"I didn't escape before because I wanted to speak to you. I didn't heal because I didn't want to put myself at risk of death if it appeared you couldn't hurt me any other way. I escaped when I saw the children in danger because I've seen enough kids hurting, bleeding, and dying in Rhosivi and

Predvoi who I couldn't help. Now I'm in a position to help and I intend to help as many as I can."

"Even Latvanian children?"

"All children. Any children."

Alekin let a brief smile cross his face. "Do you know why Latvani and Khizmit are at war?"

"Not exactly, Sir, no." I waited for him to tell me. He didn't.

"You say you're here to ask me something on behalf of Commander Markos."

"Yes, Sir."

"How do I know that you aren't baiting us for a trap? We've been at war with the Lurper Legion of the Khizmit ground forces for years. In a standstill. How do I know this isn't an attempt to change the tide of war?"

I adjusted my position on the floor. "Our intel suggests that you and Commander Markos have the same goals. As I've already said, I'll answer any questions honestly."

Alekin didn't conceal his suspicions.

"Then tell me what you are." Alekin narrowed his eyes at me and leaned forward. "I was under the impression Khizmit didn't allow their lurpers to hold the rank of an officer."

"No, Sir, they do not typically."

"The abilities you demonstrated could put you as a Victor, or an X-ray, or maybe a Whiskey. What are you?"

Our gazes were locked for a moment, maybe longer before I decided to be as transparent with him as possible.

"You've never met someone like me." I said it calmly, not as a threat. I repeated what I'd said time and time again. "I'm a boy. I'm a prisoner. I'm a victim of TPI. I'm a soldier and a miner and a fighter. But that's not what you want to know." I took a deep breath.

"I should begin at the beginning. At Zalar Correctional Facility." I told him about the serums, intended to make super soldiers. The breakout and success. The hunt for those soldiers and the subsequent incarceration and labeling of their children.

Alekin's expression didn't change as I spoke, making it impossible for me to know what he already knew or suspected. Nothing seemed to shock him.

I paused as my mouth had become dry. Alekin motioned for his soldiers to bring water and they handed the bottle to me. I swallowed it slowly and thanked him. Then I picked up by telling him what Lockbox had told me about the serums, their variations, and what the different labels meant.

"I can write it down for you if you'd like." I offered.

Alekin gave an order to a soldier behind him who grabbed some paper and a pen. "He'll write it down."

He wrote down the various abilities: Compliance, Speed, Strength, Enhanced Senses-slash-Premonition, Memory-slash-Intelligence, Reflexes-slash-Violence, and Healing.

"And what about V-Y?" Alekin questioned. Undoubtedly, he'd seen most of those, since that was what made up the majority of the ranks in the Penal Legion.

"Victors," I said, disassociating myself from the title, "Have Reflexes/Violence and Healing. Whiskeys have Intelligence/Memory and Enhanced Senses/Premonition, X-rays have Strength and Enhanced Senses/Premonition, and Yankees have Compliance and Reflexes/Violence."

Alekin glanced at the paper as the soldier finished filling out his chart. He nodded. The three soldiers behind him spoke in code, but I took it to mean that it all corresponded with what they already knew and had discovered.

"What are you hoping to get in exchange for this information?"

"Your trust," I said.

Alekin didn't laugh. He blinked. He stared. He took a deep breath. "That's a high price."

"It's not all we want." I continued.

"Not all?"

"We want something else." I rephrased it. "We need something else."

Alekin stared. Waiting.

It all came down to this. The future of Khizmit. My future. I tried not to overthink it, so I spoke clearly and matter-of-factly. "We need your help overthrowing Khizmit. Commander Markos wants to incite a military coup."

After the initial shock passed over Alekin, he called in the rest of his command team, as well as dinner. He talked to them in coded speech while a woman served us bowls of creamy bean soup. It had a smoky taste and I'd almost eaten my whole portion before she came back with a piece of crusty bread for me to dip in the remnants.

"Khizmit and Latvani didn't always have a contentious relationship. At one point we traded furs and linen for coal. But when Ilya Dulka took over, all trade ceased, and we didn't know why. When word reached us of human rights violations, we dedicated resources to learning more about the situation and the government. But then Dovaberg invaded. We had to dedicate our resources to that war. We needed the coal desperately then and sent a few small-scale invasions into Khizmit to get some."

"What happened to Dovaberg?" I asked.

"They built ships and left. By then they'd developed iron hulls that were able to break through the ice in the Lednoy Sea. We haven't heard from them in years."

Alekin's willingness to confide in me gave me optimism that he was going to help us.

"Wait a minute, human rights violations? You invaded later because of human rights violations?"

"We heard they were testing serums on their own people."

"You invaded…to help?"

Alekin sounded exasperated. "We've *always* been interested in helping."

CHAPTER 14
THE YELLOW DOCTOR

GETTING BACK to Commander Markos was not simply a matter of retracing my steps because of the way Khizmit defended the open border between the Hebulka Mountains and the Lednoy Sea. Three main Legions defended The Outskirts, and the Penal Legion was the least trusted of the three. For that reason, Khizmit placed it between the other two units. On the east camped The Wolf Legion, and on the west, The Bear Legion. Sandwiched between was the Penal Legion, more dangerous than Bears or Wolves.

For all I knew both those legions had set mines throughout the Destruction Zone, even possibly up into the Battle Zone, even though no current battle waged. There could be spies from either the Wolf or Bear Legion, and if one of them spotted me it wouldn't matter if I was Latvanian or Khizmit-born, as a lurper, or a child of the TPI, they'd kill me for fun anyway.

Alekin shared a map with me that led through the trenches most of the way through both the Battle Zone and the Disruption Zone. In a pack on my back, I carried a cipher with instructions for Markos to locate a radio signal that he and Alekin could use for communication.

I traveled quickly, anxious to get back to my friends. How was Flak faring after Raph's death? How was Spikes managing without his finger?

As I skirted my way around mounds of earth and rusty, half-buried lengths of barbed wire, my thoughts went to Emberly. Lockbox would have known she was a Victor. She'd heard me whisper. She'd wanted to fight Erik. At the time it didn't seem unusual to me. I wanted to fight Erik too. Anyone with half a conscience would have wanted to serve him some humility.

I traveled all night, my path lit by the sliver of moon left. By the time I got back to the southern end of camp, I stopped walking with care. I could hear the camp in the distance waking up, the low hum of voices on the horizon, the crash of pots, the occasional smack of a hammer on a tent spike.

When I heard the bullet whizzing through the air, it was too late to do anything. It caught me in the shoulder. I fell onto my back, screaming before I numbed the pain and pushed the bullet out.

Skudge! I was wearing the uniform Alekin had given me. I looked like I was from Latvani. I shouted to the empty field, "I'm a lurper!"

No reply except for another bullet sent my way.

I hoped whoever was pulling the trigger could see that I'd healed. That should give them undeniable evidence of my abilities.

Whether they noticed or not, they kept shooting. Shoot first, think later. Anger was a tool I could use. I steeled myself and then jumped out of the foxhole, sprinting, weaving my way toward the trigger finger. I maneuvered around the few bushes, using them to my advantage. I counted the shots, knowing when I'd have a longer window to run while they reloaded.

I was nearly there when their last shot caught my knee.

The bone shattered and my vision flashed crimson. With my good leg, I leapt over the sandbags and tackled the shooter.

It was a boy, younger than me, with sweat trailing down his face. I held him down, noting the tremble in his arms.

"You skudging shot my kneecap, you slag head!" I cursed. I steadied myself and focused on healing my leg. It took more concentration than the shoulder had. As I finished, a headache began to grow in the back of my head. Once healed I looked down and found the kid's face full of terror.

"You're a good shot," I said, climbing off. "But you didn't need to do that. I'm a lurper."

He didn't get up when I climbed off. I reached a hand out to help him up, but he didn't take it.

"Listen you're not a slag head. I just—you shot my knee, okay? Obviously, since I healed it, I'm one of you." He blinked at me, fear and defeat in his eyes. "Forget it. Get back on patrol," I said before turning my back to him.

As I walked to Commander Markos's tent, I sighed. Everything I ever wore ended up covered in blood.

I'll stop at my tent, I decided.

I heard the voices of the platoon leaders from Second and Fourth Companies shouting at their soldiers.

I began to strip down as I walked, knowing I'd get less attention for that than walking around in a Latvani uniform. By the time I got to my tent, I'd passed a few groups of soldiers who'd looked at me and then saluted, apparently recognizing me. I saluted back, as awkward as it felt in the wrong uniform. The lack of attention made me uneasy. I tuned in to listen to some of the voices of the platoon leaders, catching a few words in the jumble: "rapid tests" and "doctor." When I stepped out, hurriedly fastening the buttons across my chest, I heard a call.

"Luka!" Roman shouted, running down the hill toward me. His Lugar bounced on his hip, but it wasn't in his hand. If there was a threat, it couldn't have been too serious. "You made it back." He took only a quick moment to look me over before clapping me on the back. "I saw you," he explained.

"What is it?" I asked as a few soldiers came over beside us. Flak and Clink came over and welcomed me back briefly. Clink slapped himself in the face to wake up.

"Want me to help?" Flak said in jest to him.

"What is it?" I asked, pushing Flak out of my way. "What's happening?"

"Blood Analysis. Chancellor Eldrat wanted the Lurper Legion to use the Rapid Tests."

I sucked in a breath. I could hide. Surely, they didn't intend to use their precious rapid tests on each one of us.

"We have to assemble our company for randomized testing," Roman said. "They'll check the results against their tattoos. As cadre, our responsibility is to ensure our soldiers comply with orders, and that they do not approach the scientific team with any weapons. Commander Markos has ordered us to put down any threats against those administering the tests."

Flak scoffed. "Send Axe in. He'll happily donate a limb and try to grow it back before he bleeds out."

"It's randomized," Roman said, looking sideways at me. I could have kicked myself for not realizing sooner. If they tested either of us, we'd be dead. Lurpers couldn't be officers. Lurpers couldn't have tattoos other than their designation tattoos. Lurpers had to be registered. The multitude of ways we threatened them would leave either of us in mortal danger.

Roman and I exchanged a look. They had no reason to waste a test on us. They'd assume we were loyal to Khizmit. That we'd been assigned here to harass and haze lurpers. While I didn't know what sort of plans Markos had been working on in his tent, this was certainly not the time for me to show any sympathy for my friends. For my brothers.

"They can't know," I said, needless as it was.

"I'll comply," Spikes said. "I've got nothing to hide."

"Hell, I'll volunteer," Flak said.

But what if they did test me? What if they tested Roman?

"Third Company!" Roman called the company together and asked the platoon leaders to take attendance.

We marched in formation over to the field, where First and Second Company had already assembled.

If they'd been inclined and united, they could have easily slaughtered our whole cadre. At least, those of us who weren't secretly lurpers too.

Axe alone could have done a lot of damage, but the lurpers complied. I could only assume they took orders because the alternative was actual chaos. Khizmit wouldn't send food rations. They'd have complete anarchy among themselves and inadequate forces to take over Khizmit.

All the lurpers stood at ease as Commander Markos walked down the hill alongside ten soldiers and a single doctor. Doctor Bolest's yellowed lab coat stood out like a spot of piss on fresh snow.

The sight of him made me want to hurl. Memories of him made my arms tense.

"I am sure you know what I'm here to do by now," Bolest announced. "We have developed tests that tell us what mutation you have in your blood. You may wonder why we do this since you have already been marked on your left wrist, but as you might not know, there are some mistakes. People make mistakes." His gaze flashed over to Commander Markos. "I'll have a few words with your commander, and then we will begin the randomized testing." Bolest coughed after the effort of projecting his voice for all to hear.

In a fluid motion, all the soldiers in Bolest's armed escort pointed their rifles directly toward Markos. A few gasps of surprise rose from the ranks.

My ears calibrated to listen to Bolest's conversation, which I never would have been able to understand otherwise.

"I wondered, while doing the blood work on Victor-27 how it could have changed so drastically. I'd been studying his blood for nearly a decade, which you and few others knew. As soon as I looked at it the first time at Predvoi, I had my suspicions, but not of you."

"Doctor Bolest—"

"I know what you did. I know what you are." Bolest cleared his throat and shouted to the battalion again. "Before our randomized testing, we will take a sample of your good commander's blood." Bolest directed his announcement to the cadre. "So far, these tests have shown 100% accuracy at detecting a skrag and 90% accuracy in identifying one of their monstrous offspring.

"Will you be so kind as to show these lurpers how it's done? Will you lead by example?" Bolest faced Markos.

Markos extended his hand for the finger-prick. Bolest pulled out a razor blade instead of a needle. He thought he was fast, but both Markos and I saw his plan long before he did it. Bolest sliced the blade dragging a deep, bloody canyon through the meat of Markos's hand.

Markos's eyes instantly became watery. He must not have numbed the pain. If the test didn't work, he didn't want to show what he could do.

"Why are you doing this?" Markos asked.

Bolest's voice was low and vicious. "I like to watch Victors bleed. I like to watch Victors' eyes when they're in pain. I think it's fun to see how much a Victor can take…"

Markos drew back his hand. Gritted his teeth. Blood trailed down his fingers as he moved his arms back to his side while Bolest shook up the vial.

"Positive," Bolest shouted. He held up the vial as if we could read the small markings on the test strip. "Positive for Victor."

The troops stirred. Most of the whispers expressed disbelief and confusion. Others, awe.

"You skrag!" Roman shouted at my side. He marched out of position toward Commander Markos and Bolest. "You skudging skrag!" Roman pulled out his Lugar and pointed it at Commander Markos with such convincing rage it nearly worried me.

"Captain," Bolest said as Roman approached. "I hadn't realized you were back here!"

"I hadn't realized lurpers had snuck into positions of power in our ranks!" Roman spat, getting closer still to Markos.

Markos's gaze flitted from me to the rest of the battalion, to Bolest, and back to the officers who all had their guns trained on him.

"He tricked me! He lied to me!" Roman screamed.

Bolest gestured to the officers in his escort not to take their rifles off Markos even as Roman approached.

"I'll kill him!" Roman screamed. "Let me kill him!"

Bolest's mouth broke into a grin. "So much time around Victors…are you sure you haven't caught some of their bloodlust?"

"I didn't catch bloodlust from them. Just *for* them."

"I heard what you did with Victor-27," Bolest said.

My chest was taut as he spoke.

"I know how to dispose of them. Let me take the shot," Roman pleaded. "After a betrayal like this, I—I want to be the one to pull the trigger."

Bolest slowly began to nod.

"Yes," he agreed. "I'd want it to hurt, but with Victors like him, there's no point. Make it stick."

Whispers began to roll through the formation more loudly, confusing my hearing so I couldn't listen to Bolest as he ordered the officers with him to aim at us, the soldiers, while Roman directed Markos to back up, away from anyone else. Bolest alone approached Markos.

He must have demanded that the officers restore silence because they began to shout at us.

"Shut up!"

"Don't move a centimeter or you'll be shot."

We quieted.

Bolest's voice came across the field. "Pedrick Markos, who apparently isn't this man, is dead. And this man, who I believe is named Sasha Popov, has committed crimes against Khizmit. If he were a true officer, he would require a trial, but as a skrag, and as the test shows, a Victor, I need no cause to kill him."

Bolest stood close enough to Markos that I wondered briefly if Markos would leap out and tackle him.

Blood continued to drip from Markos's fingers. I struggled to stay where I was; if Bolest noticed me, I'd be next, and Markos wouldn't have wanted that.

"When you're ready, Captain."

"I'm ready," Roman said. He lifted his Lugar, took a deep breath, and squeezed the trigger.

The pop echoed.

Doctor Bolest dropped to the ground. He howled in pain.

"Drop your weapons or I'll kill him!" Roman yelled.

Some of the officers, mostly junior lieutenants and lieutenants by the look of it, dropped their rifles to the ground and raised their hands. A captain turned his rifle on Roman, who shot him in the leg. At that, three more of the officers dropped their guns.

A high captain turned his rifle to Markos and fired four shots directly at him.

The fourth shot, as it turned out, was Roman. The high captain's silver pinecone patch swam in red.

Three circles of blood bloomed across Markos's body. A chunk of his neck had been blown out. We stared in shocked silence for only a second, watching as Markos healed the wounds and marched toward us.

"Battalion," he called. "I am Commander Markos. I am Sasha Popov. I am Victor-1." The bullets had torn holes in his uniform and his blood darkened the cloth near the wounds. The bleeding stopped.

He stood over Bolest, who whimpered on the floor. "We have suffered too long at the hands of our enemies. We have slaved and died for Khizmit, with no rights and no rewards. I volunteered to lead you, not with the intention of freeing Khizmit from Latvani, but freeing us lurpers and skrags from Khizmit."

Markos's cadre was slack-jawed.

"I invite and implore you all to join me in creating a truly free Khizmit. If you choose not to join me, I ask that you turn in your rifle. We will keep you in the main tent under supervision until the coup is over, at which time you will be released unharmed if you have not tried to sabotage us. We want everyone in Khizmit to be free, Test Criminals and lurpers alike. If you do not share this vision, you still deserve freedom, unless you fight against us."

Markos walked toward the group of soldiers Bolest had brought. "Will you join us?" The first of them shook his head and walked away from his rifle which was already on the ground.

"Captain Kral, please escort them to the main tent. Assign guard duty from your company."

"Yes, Sir," Roman said.

As he went to guide the soldiers to the tent, one of them turned back.

"I...I will join you," she stammered. She fidgeted with the front of her uniform and then looked up to Markos in what clearly took a lot of bravery. "I do not agree with TPI. I never have."

Markos, in a move that surprised her and the rest of us, hurried over and embraced her. "Thank you," he whispered.

He picked up a rifle and handed it to her in what I thought to be a rash gesture of trust.

I looked back to Bolest as he stirred. I stepped out of formation, getting closer to him. I wanted him to know I was still alive. That he'd been wrong.

As Markos talked with a confused High Captain Toth, I walked closer to Bolest.

"Doctor," I said.

He looked up at me, his pain temporarily buried in his rage. "No," he gasped. "Not you."

"Markos did cover for me. He did protect me. Because I was a child. Meanwhile, you ran tests on me. Can't you see who the monster is?"

"They'll find my notes. They'll come for his family now. I will get to his daughters," Bolest swore. "His daughters are Victors. I will run tests on them for the fun of it. They don't know what they can do. I *like* to watch Victors bleed. I like to see how much they can take before they either—"

Pop!

I lowered my Lugar.

Bolest lay on the ground by my feet, a trickle of blood running from his head, his eyes wide and yellow.

"What the skudge just happened?" Markos bellowed, stomping over to me.

"Bloodlust," I said, and it wasn't completely a lie.

Markos revealed very little in his expression as he looked from Bolest's body up to my face.

My jaw was pulled tight. My eyes were narrow. The edges of my vision tinged with crimson, and I trembled inside, in my core, knowing what danger Emberly and Milena were in.

Markos looked at me like I was dangerous but not with fear. With respect. With delight.

"I'm going to Khizmit," I said. "If they knew about you…"

Markos nodded, concern showing in his eyes for a moment.

"Get them safe. Bring them here."

"Yes, Sir," I said.

"And Luka," he added. "If necessary, make the skudging crusters pay."

I was dangerous just like everyone had always told me. But even *they'd* underestimated what I could do.

What I *would* do if anything happened to the Markos girls.

CHAPTER 15
THE CUVACS

The truck screeched to a jolting halt at the base of the hill.

"Slag," I cursed as the motor died.

The quick tutorial Roman had given me for driving the hunk of metal had been thorough, but shifting and pushing the clutch at the right time didn't come naturally to me. I turned the key again, released the clutch less-than-smoothly, and started back on the road.

Roman wanted to come with me back to Khizmit, but Markos needed him to stay and help him talk to the cadre. By the looks High Captain Toth, Captain Sakrova, and Captain Gaborik had about them when I left, they were more upset by the deception than learning that their brave commander had once been a prisoner by the name of Sasha.

I would have liked to have Lockbox for company, but he was still less mobile than he'd have liked, and the mark on his wrist would have revealed him immediately as an Oscar to the soldiers on guard patrol.

It wasn't safe for him to be in Khizmit, even if we found a way to sneak him in.

Because of the wrist tattoos, I couldn't bring Flak, or Clink either, and as strange as it was, I'd sort of liked the idea of having one of them watch my six.

Markos gave me three options. I could take a Charlie who was registered and make him my comrade. I could take someone like Axe who had successfully cut out his tattoo completely before re-healing his arm, or I could go alone.

I presented him with a fourth option.

"Are you sure you don't want me to drive?" Kasia asked as the car stalled again.

"I—slagging piece of metal," I dropped my hands from the steering wheel and reached for the door. "Go ahead."

I walked around the car while she climbed across the center console into the driver's seat.

Though Markos had found it ill-advised, Kasia was someone I knew, someone I trusted, and her tattoo was faint.

Roman had turned the tattoo into a small book and scattered pages from the book up her arm clear to her elbow. Despite the rush we were in, Kasia asked for a small flower for the back of her right hand, near the base of her thumb with a stalk that extended down to her wrist. Roman made quick work of it and didn't ask her any questions.

Maybe she wanted to see something else when she looked down. Maybe she thought it made her look more like a cruster than a lurper. The mere presence of it meant she wasn't a lurper.

By the time we'd packed a few supplies and loaded them into the truck, my heart was racing.

Bolest had been thrown onto the pyre with the lurpers killed in the training exercise since the ground was too frozen to dig graves. Markos had secured anyone disinterested in the coup into the main tent and was discussing details with Lockbox and his cadre in his tent. I'd have eavesdropped if I wasn't so worried about Emberly and Milena.

Bolest had threatened them. He was dead, but was his research? Had he coordinated the release of information in the event of his death? Or had he been so bold, so sure of his guards, that he'd kept it to himself? I hoped that he'd wanted to enjoy the glorious moment of revealing what Markos was to Chancellor Dulka himself upon his return.

He'd wanted evidence, right? He'd wanted to prove it before acting. Without proof, he'd have no reason to give Ember or Milena a rapid test.

Kasia drove much more successfully than I had. Although she drove as fast as the truck would safely carry us over the dry ground, the road was long.

We were convincing as officers in our uniforms with fresh junior lieutenant rank patches.

"I suppose I have to thank you for the promotion," Kasia said, breaking the silence.

"If you weren't a lurper, you'd have been one by now. Can I ask you something?"

"You can ask whatever you want. It doesn't mean I'll answer."

"How'd you fade your tattoo, anyway?"

Kasia cocked her head to the side as if deliberating over telling me. "Magnifying glass and the sun."

I grimaced. "You burned it out?"

"Little by little. Day by day. One of the girls at Vazenia had broken her glasses and I snagged the lens. Used it as a magnifying glass primarily and secondarily to burn the ink. It's not advisable, obviously."

Compared to shoving my hand into a furnace her approach was smart. Cleaner. Significantly saner.

"Another question: what flower did you get?"

"Lily of the Valley." She paused then gave me more explanation. "It symbolizes hope and happiness. It can survive a harsh winter. It has healing qualities and, if left unchecked, it can become quite invasive."

Invasive. Like us. Like the lurpers would become.

I looked out into the vast emptiness, remembering Bolest's face and his threats. I should feel bad for what I'd done. He was already disabled from Roman's shot. Maybe Markos could have gotten more information from Bolest, but if Markos was upset with me, he'd concealed it well.

"I don't feel bad for shooting him," I said.

"Okay," Kasia replied.

"I should feel bad because I shot him, point blank in the head."

Kasia kept her eyes on the road.

"It wasn't as though it happened by accident. I pulled the trigger. Nothing forced me to."

I waited for Kasia to say something.

"I'm glad I did it. I know how that sounds, and maybe it makes me a monster in my own right, but I'm glad I killed him."

Kasia glanced at me.

"Bolest is responsible for the deaths of dozens of kids. He's the man who started all this. He was there when they injected Markos at Zalar. He's the one who developed the tests."

"What do you want me to say?" she asked.

"I don't know! Tell me I'm a monster for killing him and feeling like I've done the world a service."

"Maybe I should thank you."

I gritted my teeth. "That's not what I'm looking for," I muttered.

She drove on, in silence.

"He would have hurt Emberly and Milena. I know it! If he'd come back here somehow, or sent a message back somehow, and they got hurt, I'd feel the weight of guilt. If I had let him live, any blood on his hands would be on mine."

"I'm not going to tell you you're wrong. I'm not going to call you a monster. You know what you are."

"And what am I? Dangerous?" I shouted.

"The world needs dangerous people, Luka. There's no moral virtue in saying, 'I am weak and fragile, so I am harmless.' That comes from being able to say, 'I am dangerous, but I am not a threat to you.'"

"You're saying I'm morally virtuous?"

"You can't be brave if you're not afraid. You can't protect if you aren't dangerous. In my opinion, you're a little too hung up on being dangerous. It's a privilege to be what we are. To do what we can do."

The engine whined as we crested a hill, and far in the distance, I caught sight of the huge wall surrounding Khizmit. Out here in the field, there were a few flocks of sheep and shacks housing shepherds, some of whom were bundled in wolf coats the way I had been briefly.

The Cuvacs were out too, barking as they herded the sheep off the road ahead of us. I raised a hand to the shepherd nearest us and he waved back as his giant white dog bounded across the road behind us.

"A privilege?" I asked.

"Yes. Not to be treated how we have been, caged and turned into cautionary tales for our peers in Khizmit, but it's a privilege to be powerful. To be dangerous. We must be so we can fight for the good of Khizmit. For the innocent, the meek, and the weak.

"I think we're the Cuvacs—the sheepdogs. Without us, there will still be wolves, but there will be no sheep."

Her point was clear, and it did have a way of making me feel better. She reminded me of Lockbox in that way. There was a correlation between retention and wisdom.

I decided to tell her that I was also an X-ray. If we understood each other's abilities, we'd work better as a team.

"Four serums. Color me impressed," she said. There was a hint of flirtation in her voice that I chose to ignore.

I chuckled. "Thank you for coming with me. For helping me with this."

"As I said, it's a privilege."

"Even though we're going to help Emberly. The girl that I..."

Kasia full-on smiled as she shifted gears. We cruised down a short hill.

"I'm not the jealous type," she said. "I like Commander Markos. I have since the day he showed up and took over." She shifted again, smoothly, seamlessly. "How long did you know he was a Victor?"

"Not long. Did you know? You knew *I* was."

"I suspected something, but not that. He has been uncharacteristically compassionate to the troops. When we had to execute a soldier, he seemed resigned to it. I thought maybe he'd just come to humanize us after working with lurpers his whole life."

I didn't have to mourn Doctor Bolest. Killing him hadn't taken a bite out of me. I'd killed a wolf before he could hurt anyone else.

I hoped.

Though talking with Kasia had put me more at ease, as the silhouettes of the guards at the gate came into view, my palms grew sweaty.

Markos said they might not even ask for paperwork. I hoped that was the case since my sweaty fingers would smudge the ink in their current state.

"Commence operation 'Cuvacs in Wolves' Clothing,'" I whispered as we approached the gate and Kasia slowed the vehicle. It got a grin out of her, hopefully putting us both at ease.

We rolled to a stop and the captain on duty asked us to step out of the vehicle. Both of us left the doors open behind us as we climbed out. I rolled up my left sleeve, hoping the motion looked mechanical.

A lieutenant walked over, and I saluted him.

"Where are you coming from?"

"Lurper Legion, Sir."

"Got any lurpers concealed within your vehicle?" he asked.

"No, Sir."

A captain and a korporal searched the truck while the lieutenant looked over my wrist.

"That's some great ink," he commented.

"Thank you, Sir."

"Think you could refer me to the artist?"

I considered dropping Captain Kral's name. "Sorry, I was slagged as skudge on rakia at the time. I don't remember who did it."

The lieutenant and captain laughed at that. They checked Kasia's wrist and told us we could get back into the truck.

"You new?" the captain asked Kasia.

"Yes, Sir." Her voice was bold.

"Have we met?" he asked.

"No, Sir," she said, and her voice became flirtatious. "I wouldn't forget if we had."

He smiled at that and leaned in the window.

"Trust me," she said, and I think she threw him a wink. "You'd remember, too."

The captain licked his bottom lip and stood up.

"I'm Captain Zakharov, but once you're out of uniform you'll be free to call me 'Zak.'"

"Oh, really?" Her voice was coy.

"Will you be in town for a few days?" he asked.

"Just a couple."

"You ever frequent DavatNoc?"

"I'm familiar with it. Haven't been. That's not to say that I won't go if I have a reason to." Her voice was almost unfamiliar with how sweet she made it. How slippery she sounded.

"I'll be there tonight around nine."

"Interesting." She simpered.

"Will you?"

"Maybe I will, maybe I won't."

She started up the engine.

The lieutenant backed away and hurried to open the gate with the korporal. Kasia raised one hand as we drove through.

I'd heard of DavatNoc from guards. It was something between a brothel and a bar. A place for drinks—like rakia, borovicka, slivovica, brandy—and promiscuity. I assumed Kasia had heard of it too, but her response didn't sound as disgusted as she should at the invitation. I wasn't going to mention how strange I'd found it for her to suddenly be so interested in that man. That cruster.

Then the truth of the situation hit me like a palka to the back of the head.

"Holy slag," I said. "You *did* know him, didn't you?"

Kasia's jaw was clenched tight. Her knuckles were turning white from how tightly she gripped the wheel.

"He was a guard at Vazenia."

"Yes," she whispered.

"And you flirted with him to throw him off? To disassociate you now from you then."

"I helped him to see someone else. Focus on something else." She sighed.

"I'm sorry that you had to do that. That you had to act… like that…like you were…" I stumbled over my words so clumsily.

"You don't have to apologize for them or feel pity for me. I don't want your pity."

"I don't pity you." She stopped the car and looked at me to see if I was lying. "I respect you."

"I appreciate that," she said, and her grip relaxed. "Now I have a question for you."

"About my tattoo?"

"No."

Kasia turned to face me, her shoulders drawn back. "Where is Commander Markos's house?"

CHAPTER 16

THE NEIGHBOR'S WARNING

We walked quickly through the streets of Khizmit, and I took more than one wrong turn. Kasia didn't tease me, but she seemed to have a familiarity with the city that confused me.

"Have you been here before?" I asked her when she told me to go right when I wanted to go straight.

"I've seen maps."

"And you memorized them?"

"Naturally," she replied.

The streets looked different now that most of the decorations for Koliada had been taken down. There were still candles in windows, not lit since it was so bright outside, and some garlands strung between the narrower alleyways.

"Do you know his address? I can find it if you tell me what block it is."

I stopped walking outside of a small embroidery shop that displayed shirts in the clean window. Emberly had told Erik she and I were from the same block when I first arrived in Khizmit.

"Block..." I hadn't been listening to her very closely; having her near me had been distracting, to say the least. It was the first time I'd seen her face, and smelled her hair in the breeze. She'd pressed her leg to mine.

"Sector Four?"

"I can work with that," Kasia said, and turned around to walk back down the street we'd just come up.

A few patrons of an outdoor café looked up at us as we passed, either because of our uniforms or because we'd wandered past them moments earlier.

"Do you know what DavatNoc is?" I asked as Kasia rounded a corner, taking us past a stone fountain. It was familiar. Maybe.

"A bar of sorts."

"Of sorts?"

"A bar where lonely men and women go to become less lonely."

"I suppose that's most bars, right?" I said, my face warming.

"In a way, yes." Kasia took a sharp right, and I stepped over a pile of broken bottles.

Something glinted in the light in the middle of the path, something not glass. I bent, picking up the small piece of gold with my fingertips.

"What's that?" Kasia asked.

"An earring."

It reminded me so much of Emberly's. She liked small gold earrings. I decided to give it to Emberly as a gift. Maybe it would be a token to show her that, despite my showing up here with a girl—a decidedly beautiful girl—I was loyal to her.

Kasia didn't ask me why I stuck it into my pocket. She didn't ask a lot of questions. Either she knew why, being part Oscar, or she knew enough to mind her own business.

Two more turns and I found myself looking at the street the Markos family lived on. One of the neighbors was outside smoking a pipe. He stared at us, unashamed as we approached. I waved and he stared back. Maybe he didn't recognize me as the boy who'd stayed with the Markos family a few weeks prior.

I stood in front of the door, heart hammering at the prospect of seeing Emberly again. As I reached to knock, my gaze fell upon the frame.

It was splintered.

Small pieces of the wooden frame were scattered in the dirty, slushy snow at the base of the door.

My heart began racing.

I placed my open palm on the door and gave it a gentle push. It opened, creaking on its slightly crooked hinges.

"Forced entry," Kasia said, noticing what I had.

I didn't look back at the neighbor as we entered the Markos's home.

"Hello?" I called. I shut the door behind me, but it didn't click into place. The knob was broken, the latch bolt was bent. "Zuzanna?"

I removed my boots and dropped them into the basket beside a single pair of worn, sheepskin boots that I hadn't seen either Milena or Emberly wear. Kasia, following my lead, dropped her boots into the basket as well before we climbed the stairs and entered the living room.

"Ember?" I called. Her name grated against my throat. "Emberly?"

The house was empty. My ears told me that. I calibrated my hearing to listen for anything, a scuffling of feet, heavy breathing, a cry; all that could be heard were conversations in the neighbor's home.

"They aren't here," Kasia said.

I hurried down the hallway, throwing open the bedroom doors. Zuzanna, Milena, and Emberly were gone.

The optimistic part of me hoped Emberly and Zuzanna were at work and Milena was at school. After all, it was the middle of the day.

But Milena's school bag sat in her room at the edge of her bed.

"Emberly works at City Hall," I said, meeting Kasia in the kitchen. "We'll go there next. Can you find your way there from here?"

"Luka," Kasia said, and the sympathy in her voice made me tense. "The food is spoiled. They haven't been here in at least a week."

A week.

A week wasn't that long. A week was something I could work with.

I had to work with.

Maybe they'd made a run for it. I hurried back to Emberly's room and opened her dresser.

I wasn't intimately familiar with her clothes, but there didn't seem to be many things missing. If she'd packed a bag, she'd packed light.

"Skudge," I muttered. I pulled the small gold earring from my pocket and placed it on the dresser. "We can still go to City Hall. They might know what happened."

Kasia reached out as if to touch my arm, to comfort me, but dropped her hand. "We have to ask carefully. If Doctor Bolest left information about Markos being a Test Criminal, his family might already have been arrested."

"But where would they hold them?"

Kasia shook her head. "The maps I've seen didn't tell me that. There are lots of places to keep people in Khizmit. Lots of holding cells in places like the Grand Palace, or the basement of City Hall. There are cells in the barracks and in random buildings throughout Khizmit."

"If they've been arrested, we'll break them out. I got Lockbox from the Grand Palace."

"We can't rescue people if we don't know where they are."

My voice lowered in an effort to conceal my fear. "We'll find them."

I turned out of Emberly's room and hurried down to the entryway where I pulled my boots back on. I pulled the laces too tight and steadied my breathing.

"The neighbors might know something," I said, memories of delivering treats fresh in my mind. "They know me."

"If you say so, Lieutenant." Kasia said it not as a mockery, but as a sign that she was taking this seriously.

I pulled the door shut, noting how it didn't click into place, and marched over to the neighbor with the pipe.

"Hello," I said.

He nodded, breathing through his nose as he sucked on the pipe.

"We're looking for the Markos family." I felt stupid saying that since he'd just seen us enter and exit their house.

"You're late," he said. "They haven't been home in a while."

"Where are they?" I asked.

"Dunno," he replied.

"When did you last see them?"

He took a long breath through his nose, considering my question. "I'm not sure."

I wondered if he was hung over, or if he was completely too high to understand me.

"Have you seen anyone else over at their house?"

"A few soldiers came by asking after them, just like you two. Maybe you'll have better luck."

We weren't the only soldiers looking for them.

"How long ago did other soldiers ask after them?"

"What day is it?" the man asked, narrowing his eyes into the distance.

Kasia told him and he pulled his eyebrows closer together.

"A few days ago, I think."

I wanted to grab him by the collar and hoist him up, demanding that he tell me something with certainty.

"What is it you want them for, anyway?" he asked.

"Can't say," Kasia said, and turned to the side.

I moved closer to her.

"He's no help at all," I groaned.

"He doesn't know anything."

"He's too high to be of any help!"

"So, let's move on."

I scowled at the man and walked across the street to the neighbors who seemed to know the most when we'd visited.

Brita Yatsenko seemed to know everything that happened on this street and even though I'd killed her nephew Goyle—Dimitar—I had to speak to her.

I knocked three times, harder than necessary.

The door opened a few centimeters.

"Yes," Brita said, her voice wary.

"Brita," I said warmly. "How are you?"

She opened the door a little wider and looked me over.

"Do I know you?"

I was about to answer when she opened the door completely.

"I do know you. You were with the Markos family. A friend of Pedrick or a friend of Emberly's. Both?"

"A family friend," I said. "Do you know where they are?"

Brita looked up the street, then down the other way, leaning her head out of the doorway to get a better look. "Come in," she whispered. "Come in quickly."

I was reminded of Lockbox's mom and how she'd brought me inside before calling for soldiers to arrest me. Going into her house had resulted in imprisonment at the hands of Captain Crease.

Risky as it was, I needed answers. Perhaps getting arrested would land me in a cell beside Emberly anyway. Kasia was right; we couldn't rescue someone we couldn't find.

I stepped over the threshold into Brita's house, Kasia right behind me.

Brita's house looked nearly identical to when I'd last been here except her husband was gone, and with just the three of us, it felt smaller and colder. I tediously unlaced my boots and climbed the stairs into her living room.

"Where are they? Have you seen Emberly?"

Kasia gave me a look that clearly told me to slow down. I had to see this as a conversation, not an interrogation.

"Lovely home," Kasia said. "Thank you for inviting us inside."

"Take a seat," Brita said, pointing to the couch.

It was torture hearing Kasia introduce herself, and hearing Brita tell three short stories only somewhat related to the one Kasia had made up about how she'd joined the Khizmit Ground Forces. Brita threw a tray of buns in the oven and served them to us as she asked Kasia about her previous assignments and her childhood and how it was becoming a female officer.

Kasia was the most natural liar I'd ever met. Her story was convincing, with just the right number of details to make it seem like memories.

I was on the verge of insanity when Brita finally got to talking about Emberly.

"There have been strange things happening here since Koliada," Brita said, surreptitiously. "High Warden Velky was murdered!"

I held my breath. The crunch of Velky's sternum beneath my hand came back to me as the logs in her fireplace settled.

"And that's not all! The chancellor supreme resigned her position as high warden of Predvoi Prison after what happened in Vazenia."

"What happened in Vazenia?" Kasia asked. She leaned forward, eyes wide.

"We don't know! No one has any idea what's happening, but the soldiers who were supposed to come home for

Koliada never did. I've talked with the ladies in town, and they haven't heard from their sons in weeks!"

"None of the guards from Vazenia were in town for Koliada?" Kasia asked.

"Not one that I know of."

"But the Markos family—"

"First there were the rumors about Emberly Markos and a captain." Brita looked at me as if checking for an indication of jealousy. "Some indiscretion, not that I blame her. I bedded a few good-looking soldiers in my day." Brita winked at me then. It made my stomach churn. "But the whispers about her changed. Some suggested she'd been involved in helping an Oscar escape from the Grand Palace. They never found him, by the way, not that I know of."

I grew impatient with every word she spoke. "My own nephew was killed, you know. The lurpers have been getting more out of hand. I can only imagine what's happening at Vazenia. You two don't happen to have any additional information about it, do you?"

I turned to Kasia. Her voice was stoic. "Not me, ma'am. You know they don't let female soldiers work as guards up there."

"Of course not." She shook her head, disappointment in her gaze. "How about you? You were at Rhosivi though, right?"

"I'm afraid I don't know much about Vazenia at all."

"But you have friends there, don't you?"

"A few, yes."

"Have you heard anything from them?" she leaned in.

"No, actually, now that you mention it, I haven't heard anything from them."

"It's all very odd. Somehow, I get the feeling the Markos family is more involved than they let on. I don't mean to incriminate you in this, Luka. I mean it more as a warning. Look at all the evidence. It can't be a coincidence that

Emberly Markos became intimate with more of the officers and then High Warden Velky ends up dead in the streets. Commander Markos disappears before Koliada. No one has heard from or seen any guards from Vazenia in over a month. An Oscar escapes from the Grand Palace. The Chancellor Supreme gives up her position at Predvoi. And then, the Markos family goes missing!"

"What does it have to do with the Markos family?" Kasia asked.

"I've heard whispers, you know how I do, about Emberly starting a group that sympathized with lurpers. If it's true, and it seemed to be true, then where did she learn that? I hate to say it, but it does make one question Pedrick's loyalty. Where would she get such a fool-brained notion?"

Brita extended the plate of baked buns to me. I took one, knowing that refusing food was the fastest way to offend someone.

"Thank you," I muttered, biting into the warm dough.

"You know how dangerous those lurpers are," Brita commented. "You've seen them. Probably put a couple down, haven't you?"

"Yes, ma'am," I said. "Do you know where Emberly, Milena, and Zuzanna are? I want to ask them a few questions myself."

"I'm sure you do!" Brita said, growing indignant. "But I don't know where they are. They went missing a few days after Koliada. I have it on good authority that Emberly wasn't at work, and Milena never returned to school."

"Were they arrested?"

"I don't believe so," Brita said, grinning. "Because a few days later a whole squad of soldiers came down the street and broke into their house. They came down the street asking if we'd seen them and even checked my back rooms to make sure I wasn't hiding them. I'd take in Zuzanna, but between you two and me, I'd worry about associating with Emberly."

I chewed the bun more aggressively than necessary.

"You're a good boy, a handsome boy. She's a flighty thing, beautiful but dangerous," Brita gestured to Kasia. "You two would make a cute couple. He's a striking boy, isn't he?" She nudged Kasia playfully. "Are you two a couple?"

"We aren't," Kasia said.

Brita chuckled. "I heard the regret in that. Didn't you? Get someone loyal to Khizmit. Stay clear of the Markos family. They're deep in this somehow." Brita sighed. She finally relaxed into her seat.

"Thank you," Kasia said. She moved to stand.

"If you find out what happened to them, would you come back and tell me? It keeps me up at night, worrying, wondering."

"You've been wonderful to us," Kasai said. "If we learn anything, about any of it, we'll let you know." She placed a reassuring hand on her shoulder.

Brita gave me two more of the stuffed buns for the road and waved goodbye as we walked down the street, away from the Markos's home. We walked until we were completely out of sight of the street and found an empty bench at the end of an alleyway. The corners of the alley were full of garbage, wrinkled papers, broken ornaments, and several partially crushed cans.

"Someone must know where they are. *Someone* knows something," I said, anger in my voice.

"Maybe the higher-ranking officers in town have information. They have soldiers who questioned the neighbors."

"True," I said. "But how would we get them to talk to us?"

Kasia leaned her head into her hands and shut her eyes tightly. "We will go to DavatNoc tonight." She sat up, opened her clear blue eyes, and stared at me resolutely. "I'll get High Captain Zakharov to tell me what he knows."

CHAPTER 17
DAVATNOC

It was the middle of the day, but Kasia and I slept. I took the couch in the front room and Kasia went into Milena's room and locked the door. I expected to toss and turn on the couch, stirred by the memory of killing Velky, the pop of the gun when I'd lodged a bullet in Bolest's skull, the callous look on Brita's face when she told me about Emberly, but I was too tired. There was nothing helpful I could do until we knew where Emberly, Milena, and Zuzanna were.

I slept for hours, undisturbed until a gust of wind threw open the door. As it crashed into the wall, I leapt to my feet, finding my dagger in my sweaty hand as I stared at the empty doorway and a darkening sky.

My heart was racing as I walked down the steps and shut the front door again, this time lodging it shut with the basket for boots.

Kasia poked her head out from around the corner.

"We should get ready," she said.

———

Kasia looked positively stunning in her dress. It wasn't her dress, not really. It was Emberly's. Maybe that's why I didn't feel as bad staring at it, gawking slightly when she'd stepped out of Emberly's room with it on. It was dark blue with sheer long sleeves, slightly lower cut in the front than anything I'd ever seen Emberly wear, and came down to her knees.

There were turquoise and golden birds with long golden tails as large as my hand sewn into the bodice and along the base. She spun, genuinely giddy, and the dress flew up, giving me a clear view of most of her thighs until she realized and stopped immediately.

"Sorry," she said, patting the dress down again.

"You're beautiful." I tried to say it as a statement rather than a compliment.

"I didn't mean to...you know...show my legs like that..." She blushed.

I hadn't minded, but maybe I should have looked away. Even if it had been Emberly, I probably would have looked away.

"Are you sure about this?" I asked. "Showing up at a bar, wearing that, Zakharov is going to have...thoughts."

"I need to distract him from our goal. This will work, won't it?"

"He'll be distracted," I said, finding myself looking at the bodice of the dress again. Her body. The way the dress hugged her waist.

Kasia had also found Emberly's makeup and now wore black eyeliner and blush. "We need information. It's a matter of life or death, isn't it?" She was scared but I wouldn't tell her I could tell. I knew fear though. I'd worn it like a second skin for almost eighteen years.

"We have to find Zuzanna, Emberly, and Milena," I said. "I just don't like the idea of using you as..."

"Bait," she stated. "I'm the bait. But I agreed to this." She squared her shoulders. "You can't decide what you think, can you?"

"Huh?" I asked.

"You flicker from looking absolutely mortified at the sight of me to looking like you're about to come over here and… and kiss me or something."

I laughed. *What else could I do?* "I'm worried. You are… breathtaking, Kasia. He wanted you when you were in your uniform but in this you look…"

"What?"

The words that came to mind were inappropriate for a number of reasons. "You look good. Striking."

"Well, as long as he's within striking distance, that shouldn't be a problem."

I'd come to see her as an Oscar without considering her abilities as a Whiskey, as a Juliet. She could be a weapon, and even I'd forgotten that looking at her. Zakharov didn't really pose a threat to her, especially because he'd underestimate her.

"Is there any chance he'll recognize you?" I asked.

"He knew and harassed a Whiskey in Vazenia. A girl with a feral look in her eyes, blood under her fingernails with tangled hair who only spoke in vulgarities." The image she described didn't match her at all. "I don't even recognize myself. He doesn't stand a chance," she said, stepping into the blue heels she'd pulled out of Zuzanna's closet.

"He doesn't stand a chance," I echoed.

"You don't look half-bad yourself, Luka," Kasia said, securing a short blade to her inner thigh. I looked away.

Markos's clothes fit me pretty well since my time in Rhosivi left my arms nearly as big as his. It appeared that he'd brought most of his clothes with him to The Outskirts, but I'd found an oversized white shirt with gold embroidery to wear beneath a red and gold kaftan. It came a little past my wrists and midway down my thighs with nearly as many buttons as the uniform top had. I wondered briefly if this expensive textile with all the embroidery had been made in Vazenia at the hands of lurpers like Kasia.

"This feels very formal for a bar," I said.

"From what I understand, there will be a wide range of outfits there, but no uniforms."

"Where did you get your information?"

"Guards at Vazenia."

I'd heard guards talk about the women they'd met at DavatNoc, and the drinks they'd had, nights they only partially remembered, but nothing about the attire.

We'd have to come back to the Markos's home for our uniforms, and I prayed the next time I came here it would be with Emberly's hand safely in mine. I would have been lost without Kasia there with me. When I'd asked Commander Markos to let her come with me, I hadn't known she had a map of Khizmit stored in her photographic memory.

She led me through the dark streets of Khizmit, and occasionally I saw buildings I recognized. We walked past Pekaren, the bakery where Ember had bought me vyco upon my arrival. We passed the square where I'd joined Ember in the parade, throwing her ex-boyfriend to the icy ground with a laugh.

We didn't pass the place Emberly and I had kissed, or the place where I'd dropped Velky's bloody corpse.

A small group of guards openly gawked at Kasia when we walked past their patrol. She didn't seem to notice—not enough to say anything about it.

When she stopped outside of a plain brick building with steps that went down, instead of up, she descended the first few and then turned back to face me.

It seemed a sin to bring someone like her to a den like this as bait just so I could find Emberly, her mother, and sister. But Kasia wasn't helpless, and she didn't need my protection, though she had it all the same. I'd kill again before I let that captain or anyone else lay a hand on her.

There were two large men standing guard outside the doors to DavatNoc, dressed in all black, meant to look imposing. They bore similarities to Hotels, but I doubted a graduated lurper would be given this job. What did I know about Khizmit though? Not enough.

The man on the right hooted at Kasia as she approached the wooden doors and leaned forward to pull the handle for her.

"If you don't find what you're looking for in there, maybe you can check back outside?" he asked. She kept her face forward, giving no indication that she'd heard him. I passed between the two makeshift guards, glancing up at the yellow letters spelling out the name DavatNoc.

As soon as we stepped into the bar, the smells of alcohol, leather, and something like wood stain spun through the air with the music that came from the far corner of the stage to my right.

Two guitarists stood on the far side of the stage, their music emanating from the shadows as if produced by a mystical force rather than fingers and string. If there were other musicians alongside or behind them, they were too well concealed in the dark for me to recognize.

Kasia had been right about the attire. There were dresses in every color, mostly dark shades, some more revealing than others. The men wore kaftans and cloaks, but there wasn't a single uniform in sight.

It was a jarring sight, almost like I'd been transported to another planet, and I had to catch myself before I gazed too long. My life had been uniforms and prison stripes, followed by more uniforms. Here it wasn't like looking at a room of lurpers or soldiers.

They were just people.

Then we saw him: the captain with the short beard who'd invited Kasia here. Zakharov.

"There he is," Kasia muttered, making sure I was close. "Here goes nothing."

"Zak," Kasia said, striding across the smooth wooden floor to the man in the blue kaftan.

"Skudge," Zakharov wiped some excess rakia off his chin where it had dribbled into his beard. "You came!" He stood up, bumping into the table in his haste.

"Don't sound so surprised or I'll think you didn't really want me here." Kasia flipped her hair.

"Oh, I want you. I want you here." Zak leaned in and kissed both her cheeks. The muscles in her back and shoulders visibly tensed. The situation already made me sick. This ruse was absolutely slaggy.

"Come over, sit with me here." Zak sidled into a booth and practically set her on top of his lap. She gracefully slipped to the side, a demure smile on her face as she put some distance between them.

"I'm Kasia," she said. "But maybe you aren't interested in my name."

"I'm interested in your name. And this dress, skudge, you make it look good." He ran a hand across one of the birds above her hip.

I made room for myself on the bench across from Zak where two other men sat. They clearly didn't want me there from the way they resisted scooting down.

"You brought your friend?" Zak asked, glancing at me briefly.

"Brought? I wouldn't say that. He has a thing where he doesn't like to let me out of his sight."

"That's a bit overprotective for a comrade, don't you think?" Zak asked me. He waved to a woman serving drinks and she began wigging her way through the patrons toward us.

"What do you want?"

"To drink or tonight?" Kasia said.

Zak's mouth twisted up into a grin again.

She was good. If I'd stumbled in here and looked at her, heard her speak to him, I'd think she wanted to be with him.

"Another round, please," Zak said to the server. She made a quick note on a piece of paper in her hand and made her way back to the bar.

"What brings you to Khizmit?" Kasia asked. "You assigned here currently?"

"Yes, thank skudge! You heard what's going on in Vazenia, haven't you?"

"No communication?"

"I think it's a prison riot. There'd been whispers of one happening when I was there, but it never turned into anything we couldn't control."

"You were at Vazenia?" Kasia said, and I heard her voice catch.

"Three years. Surprised?"

"How was it?"

The woman set five drinks at the table. Everyone at the table, Kasia included, reached out and took a glass. She sipped, eyes fixed on Zak as she lowered the glass. The last drink sat on the thin metal tray, beads of rakia spilling over the edge, waiting for me.

"It's a slaghole full of lurpers."

"Well, we all know *that*, Zak," one of his friends said, guzzling half his glass at once. "You didn't hate your time there. You said some of the lurpers were—"

Zak kicked his friend underneath the table.

"My time there was good for promotion. Got me where I am today so I can't complain." Zak reached out and tucked a loose strand of hair behind Kasia's ear.

"The only other way to advance around here is locked up!" Zak's friend said, earning him another swift kick from beneath the table.

"What does that mean?" Kasia asked.

"Don't worry about him. He's already drunk."

I leaned into the friend. "What did you mean?"

"You'd think skudging the commander's daughter would land you in slag so deep you'd never walk again, but I swear to Veles I know a guy who did and got promoted!"

He had to be talking about Roman and Emberly.

"And you said she's locked up?" I asked.

"What's it matter to you?" Zak asked.

I shrugged, trying not to be too intense or insistent. "I'm not posted at Vazenia, and don't want to be anytime soon by the sound of it, so maybe I'm just looking for options for promotion. Why do you care?"

Zak leaned closer to Kasia, evidently sold on my comment. "So, you two aren't together, I take it?"

Kasia shook her head. "We aren't—"

"We sort of are," I interjected. "We could be. We might be." I sounded pathetic and Zak chuckled at me before reaching over and putting his hand around Kasia's shoulders.

"You aren't if she says you aren't."

I didn't know what to say. The music in the corner grew louder, now definitely accompanied by some percussion.

"Don't worry, Junior Lieutenant. I'm sure if you request Vazenia they'll send you there. Assuming anyone survives."

"Survives?"

"Okay, I said it might be a riot, but I know it is. It's been overrun by the lurpers. The Chancellor Supreme said they'll starve them out. They can't get past the electrified fences, so they'll kill each other off in there, and run out of food in a few weeks."

Kasia's face visibly darkened, a haunted expression passing over her eyes like a thundercloud.

"I'd never criticize her approach, but it sure as skudge makes me happy I'm not there now." Zak was oblivious to Kasia's pain.

He was oblivious to everything except her beauty.

The Chancellor Supreme, Dulka, knew no love, no mercy,

no pity, and no loyalty. She'd let the female inmates slaughter the guards at Vazenia, and each other, by the sound of it. As far as she was concerned, the threat to Khizmit was contained, her own people be damned.

But then, they were all her people. All citizens of Khizmit. Most of them were children, whether she wanted to see them that way or not.

It was no wonder darkness gathered in Kasia's face. I wondered if she, like me, saw crimson when her desire to fight was strong.

Maybe it was bloodlust after all.

"Kasia," I said, trying to keep her grounded the way Roman had helped me.

"Vazenia is far away. You don't need to worry about them." I hoped she understood my true meaning which was *"We're too far away to help them right now. You don't need to worry about your friends. They'll take care of each other."*

I'd get this intel to Markos when we brought his family back. Maybe he could tell us how to disable the electric fences and get the inmates out to join our coup. He could send a few squads up, maybe all of Third Company, to deliver food and help the lurpers there.

"What were you saying about the commander's daughter?" I said, bringing the topic back to the reason we were here. "Which commander?"

"It's classified," Zak said, glaring at me.

"Oh, come on, I don't think we should start this relationship off with secrets, do you?" Kasia asked.

Zak licked his teeth. He looked feral. "What if we play a game of it?"

"A game?" I asked. Every time I spoke and drew attention to myself, I felt Zakharov put his defenses back up.

"A game between me and Kasia," he said.

I leaned back in the booth, trying to blend into the shadows like Zakharov's friends had.

"I like games," Kasia said.

Zak laughed. "Here's the game: I ask a question and you must answer honestly. Then you can ask me one and I'll answer honestly."

"Okay," Kasia said, trying to sound enthused.

"No lies. No deception. No holding back."

"Fair."

"And nothing is off limits," Zak added.

"Fine." Kasia tried to relax in the seat, but her shoulders still looked tense. She only glanced at me briefly before looking back to Zak, a fake smile on her face.

Zak shifted in his seat, trying to get a better look at Kasia in the unsteady lights of the room. "First question: Have we met before?"

CHAPTER 18
BITKA

My heart raced. *Would she lie?* Kasia certainly couldn't tell Captain Zakharov the truth, but his question meant he suspected her.

Kasia didn't hesitate. She sighed, as if conceding. "Yes, we've met."

"When and where?" Zak asked.

"One question. One answer," she said. "Let me ask a question on behalf of my comrade here with the hope that if his curiosity is satiated, I can pursue more interesting topics: What did your friend mean when he said the only other way to advance around here is locked up?"

"Of all the things you could ask, and you pick that?" Zak asked, incredulous. "I'll answer a bit more thoroughly than you did, and maybe you can remember that when I ask my next question."

Kasia shrugged playfully. "I might."

"Commander Markos's family was arrested. He's under official investigation, but I don't know what for. The comment was with regards to his daughter, but I don't know her name or which one, but I think he has two and the older one has something of a reputation with soldiers."

Kasia pretended to be impatient with me when she asked, "Good enough?"

"Thank you," I said.

The server wandered over with a small plate of cheeses and roasted sausage. Three dollops of sauce, horseradish, mustard, and one that smelled like pickles, sat in the center of the plate.

"Get that, would you?" Zak asked his friend. His friend scowled but dug into his pocket, and pulled out a few koruna that he handed to the server before she walked away.

"My turn," Zak said, grabbing a small piece of cheese and twisting it between his fingers. "What were the circumstances surrounding our first meeting?" Zak asked Kasia. His friend nearest me gestured to the untouched drink in the middle of the table.

"Are you going to have that?" he asked.

"No," I said. He reached for it with greedy fingers.

Almost as greedy as the ones playing with the hair at the base of Kasia's neck.

Kasia reached for a piece of sausage and casually stuck it in her mouth. Her nonchalance impressed me. "The first time I saw you, you were in uniform. You were a second lieu-tenant, and you had your Lugar drawn. I was in line for lunch. The first time you saw me and spoke to me, I was outside, shivering. You asked if I was cold, and I said that I was." She took another drink, surprisingly unaffected by the alcohol.

"Was this at a training? Were we in the field?" Zak asked.

"I gave you your answer," Kasia teased.

"Do you have any other information about the arrests? About the Markos family?" I asked.

"You're not part of the game," Zak said. His friend reached for two pieces of white cheese at once. Kasia took another piece of meat off the table and cocked her head at me.

"If I ask your questions, will you finally give me a turn?" Kasia said, feigning irritation.

I sighed. "Yes, but don't pretend that you're not fascinated. Commander Markos under investigation? That's big news." I followed her lead and took a piece of cheese. Refusing to drink was one thing, but refusing to eat made me look suspicious.

"There are more interesting things we could talk about," Kasia said. "But fine. Zak, please tell me any more information you have regarding the Markos family so I can get to some more entertaining topics."

Zak sighed. "I know they arrested one daughter first and had difficulty finding his wife and other daughter. They found them a few days later and arrested the woman who'd been harboring them."

"Why'd they arrest her?" Kasia asked.

Zak shrugged, as if lives weren't on the line. "She knew they were under investigation from the chancellors. She tried to fight off the guards who'd come to arrest her."

My heart raced at the image of a woman standing over a threshold, trying to keep soldiers from entering while Zuzanna and Milena snuck out the back.

"Where are they being held?" I asked.

"I don't know!" Zak said impatiently. "In a small holding cell that won't draw a lot of attention. Chancellor Dulka doesn't want people to know that Markos is being investigated and so she's arranged for his family to be kept somewhere discreet rather than a bigger holding cell."

It was probably all he knew. As much as he wanted to anger me, he wanted Kasia's attention back on him.

"Where did we meet? What did I say to you?" I could smell the horseradish on his breath from here.

"We met briefly at Vazenia," Kasia said.

She was telling the truth there. Why was she taking the risk? I realized how warm I felt at that moment.

Kasia had admitted to being at Vazenia. But there were no female guards there.

It suddenly felt like the piece of cheese I'd eaten was fighting with my stomach.

Zak looked as alarmed as I felt. "Vazenia?" he repeated.

Kasia's expression was playful. "Since you're sharing secrets, I can share one too." She leaned closer to him and lowered her voice. "Chancellor Dulka had heard rumors of the lurpers in Vazenia planning a riot. As a result, she recruited a few female officers to go undercover and try to gain information."

"Are you slagging me?" Zak asked.

"You volunteered for that?" the slightly less inebriated of his friends asked.

Kasia turned to face Zak. "When you met me, you thought I was one of them. My assignment demanded secrecy above all else."

"I can't have been kind to you," he said.

"You thought I was a skudging lurper! Of course you were unkind! But when you harassed me, it helped me to build rapport among the inmates. It encouraged some of them to open up to me. Really, I should thank you," Kasia said.

"Thank me?" Zak asked. "Didn't I hurt you?"

"That's another question and it's not your turn," Kasia's voice had a slight bite to it.

"I didn't know there were officers among the lurpers."

"Only Dulka and High Warden Rolfe knew. It was too risky to confide in anyone else. I spent four months undercover and then they pulled me out. Reassigned me to the Lurper Legion."

Zak looked half-impressed and half-mortified. "I knew I'd seen you there. I could have sworn I'd seen you behind bars, wearing those stripes."

"Don't remind me," Kasia said. Her hand clenched into a

fist and then, slowly, she released it. "It's my turn for a question."

"Ask anything," Zak said. It was clear he wanted her to ask something inappropriate.

Kasia leaned in close to his ear and whispered. I tuned in, which made the music and nearby whispers too loud in my head.

"Can you help me lose this slaghead comrade so we can have some fun?"

Me? What was she planning?

Zak laughed. "What did you have in mind?" he spoke loud enough for everyone at our table to hear.

Kasia whispered again. "Challenge him to a *bitka*. Loser walks."

A bitka.

That was a game—a joke. It was a term I hadn't heard since brawling as a 6-year-old. In the prison, we used the term for children's fights. It was clear from Zak's trepidation that the word meant something else here.

Kasia leaned in close again, her lips brushing his beard. "Please, Zak. I have so much more to ask you. It would take all night."

"Last question, and then I will," Zak said. He leaned in close to her ear. "I remember one threat I made to you in that prison. Maybe I made a few, thinking you were just a lurper."

"You made a few, but I think I remember the one you're talking about." She visibly struggled to smile. I could almost feel her pain as she glanced toward me before taking a shallow breath. "We were alone in the yard, except for my cellmate, Victor-13. The moon was full. It was spring and I had stitches in my arm."

"You remember it well," Zak said. "As well as I do. That's the strongest memory I have of you. Granted, you looked nothing like you do here. I should have known you weren't slag on the bottom of my boot. Maybe I could tell you were different from the lurpers. Maybe that's why I gave you special attention."

Kasia finished her drink and used the action of putting it back on the table as an excuse to scoot incrementally away from him. "I like to think that was why. Like you could tell by my eyes that I didn't belong there. Didn't stop you from swinging the palka though."

It seemed from the look on her face that the last sentence had slipped out accidentally.

As if to recover from the mistake, she smiled, giving the twisted impression that she hadn't minded.

That the memory wasn't telling her twenty different ways to murder him.

My mind told me plenty of things I could do in the next five seconds that would leave him without a pulse. My personal favorite involved Kasia breaking the glass on the edge of the table and using the sharp edges to spear Zak's throat. She should gouge his eyes out for looking at her the way he did. She should cut off his fingers for the way they clawed at the buttons on the back of her dress.

Zak's lips brushed against her temple. "My question is, if I win the *bitka*, will you let me make good on that threat I made back then?"

Kasia's throat bobbed as she swallowed. A few droplets of sweat beaded along the neckline of her dress, all the way down to the swell of her breasts, slightly visible.

"Why else do you think I showed up tonight?" she asked and stroked his arm. I don't know how she did it without reaching across to kill him. I saw in her face that she wanted to, and I knew she could. She could grab him by the face and snap his neck without breaking a sweat.

Zak licked his teeth and snickered. "Skudge," he murmured. He whipped his attention to me.

"What?" I asked.

Zakharov stood on his bench and clapped his hands together before he shouted, *"Bitka! Bitka! Bitka!"*

The side conversations dropped to a low rumble. The musicians stopped playing. Zakharov spoke again. "I hereby challenge you," he threw his finger toward me dramatically, "to a *bitka.*"

"*Bitka, bitka, bitka,*" the crowd began to buzz.

The server hurried to the doors and brought in the two large guards they'd posted outside. One locked the door while the other walked up to the stage.

"Do you accept?" Zakharov asked.

I was supposed to know the rules of a *bitka.* Asking would make me look like an idiot or make them suspect I wasn't truly an officer, familiar with the rules of the duel.

"Luka," Kasia whispered. "It's a wrestling match. You just have to pin him on his back for five seconds or get him to tap from a submission." Her words were barely audible beneath the echoing chant of *"bitka, bitka, bitka."*

I did my best to look slightly nervous. I swallowed hard and obviously.

"I accept the challenge," I said. The audience cheered and Zak's friend pushed me to my feet.

"Approach the stage!" The muscled man at the stage shouted.

"Send this boy out on his ass," Zak's friend yelled.

Zak and I walked around the tables and patrons of Davat-Noc. Many of them stared at the two of us. Some were lip-locked, and others were half-asleep from their drinks. I'd never had such an audience for a fight before.

The guard centered us on the hard stage. Zak was going to be sore if he got up at all after this.

Zak rushed me, and I let him grab my right leg and lift it off the ground. He tried to push me forward, but I hopped my free leg between his feet, grabbed a fistful of his shirt with my right hand, and sat down. The motion threw him onto his back, and I rolled on top, one of his arms pinned beneath my shin.

He tried to escape by flipping to his side. As much as I'd have loved toying with him, the more skills I displayed, the more at risk I was of being discovered. I had to end this quickly.

I grabbed his arm and rotated myself around his body before dropping to my back on the hard, wooden stage. I had my left foot placed in between his shoulder blades, keeping him from rolling back towards me, and my other leg draped across his face. His left arm was stuck between my legs, held straight out. I applied pressure to his elbow, threatening to bend it the opposite way.

He yelped.

The crowd was silent. Maybe I had worked too quickly. Maybe it didn't matter.

"Where are they holding the Markos family?" I asked quietly.

He didn't say anything, so I applied more pressure to his arm. He yelped again before answering. "I don't know for sure."

"Guess," I demanded.

"Probably Block 22, Building 4G, or Outpost 5D." He sounded like he was about to cry. "Why do you care?"

"I don't," I said. "I just wanted to see how easily you'll share confidential information. You're the one who arrested them, aren't you?"

He was gasping for air, still struggling to escape from my hold. While I threatened to break his arm with my upper body, my leg threatened to choke him, or as Lockbox had often corrected me, strangle him.

Zak answered. "I helped arrest the older girl. I wasn't there when they found Markos's wife and other daughter."

Emberly. *He'd* arrested her. I pulled down on his wrist, making him gasp.

"You can't keep a secret for slag, can you?" I said.

"Tap!" Zak's friend shouted. "Tap already!"

But Zak didn't tap, and I wasn't ready for him to.

"You lost," I said.

"Let me have her," Zak pled his voice muffled as I stacked my leg over his face.

He still thought I was fighting him for Kasia. As if she was a prize. An item to be won. Much as it pained me, I had to let him think that was my motivation. I whispered a vague, lewd comment about her to him, one that I regretted having thought of so easily.

He tried to spit on me, but I drove my knee into the side of his face harder, forcing his teeth to grind together.

"I'll get a turn with her," he said through his tightly gritted teeth.

I believed him.

And then I snapped his arm.

CHAPTER 19

OUTPOST 5D

"I'M sure he'll find some vyco," I said to the few people who expressed concern as I walked away from Zak. He was curled on the stage howling in pain.

"What the hell?" someone said to me.

"He didn't tap," I said calmly and approached Kasia.

She didn't hide her relief.

"Let's go," I said. She looped her arm into mine and we hurried to the door of DavatNoc. The large guard opened the door for us, giving me a nod of approval as we left Zak wailing on the stage.

We decided it would be better to go straight to the addresses Zak had given us even though I'd have preferred to be in my uniform instead of these clothes. I was willing to bet Kasia felt the same way, and not just because it would be awkward to rescue the Markos family wearing their clothes.

"Sorry you didn't get to be the one to break his arm," I said as we hurried through the streets.

"He has another one," she said.

"Are we going to Block 22, Building 4G, or Outpost 5D? Should we split up?"

"While splitting up would help us find them sooner, it

decreases our chances of success. Too risky. We should stay together."

I was still following her as she sprinted down the street. "Where are we going?"

"We're closer to Outpost 5D."

She wheeled around the edge of a building as if she'd roamed these streets every day of her life.

Fortunately, most of the people outside at this time were lost in their drinks or someone else's arms so they didn't give us much attention as we dashed through the blocks across Khizmit.

Kasia stopped suddenly beside a tall brick wall.

"It's ahead. But there are probably guards outside it."

"We can fight them."

"Sure. But we should get closer for some more intel before we move. If they're being held there, we can't risk them getting hurt."

"Or you getting hurt," I added.

She grinned and I was happy there were enough small lights overhead that I could see her expression clearly.

"How do we get closer without being suspicious?"

"We aren't suspicious. We're just two kids out late, having a good time. There are no laws against laughter."

"But to be soldiers, we have to be adults. If we're adults we're supposed to have identification, but it's back at the house."

Kasia quirked her mouth. "You didn't bring your identification?"

"I left it with my uniform."

"Then I guess you better not do anything suspicious while we get closer."

I imagined that her plan would involve holding my hand, flirting with me as we walked closer to the outpost. We could pretend to be lost in each other's attention as we drew nearer to the door. Maybe she'd back up to a wall and I could lean in—

Traitor, I told myself. *You unfaithful piece of slag.*

I was here to save Ember. Not to find a way to justify sharing affection with Kasia. I hated myself for the moment and turned away from Kasia, afraid that somehow with her incredible intelligence, she'd know what I'd imagined.

Maybe I didn't even deserve Emberly. With my eyes closed tight, I leaned against the building. It was cold.

"I'll get close and then come back and see what I can find. I have my identification," Kasia said. "Stay here. I'll be right back."

She stepped out into the corridor between the two buildings, heels clicking confidently as she walked toward the outpost.

"Hi," Kasia said. "I'm wondering if you can help me."

"What are you looking for?" a man asked.

"DavatNoc," she said. "I think I'm a little turned around."

The guard gave her instructions and then asked, "How late will you be there tonight?"

"Don't know yet," Kasia replied. Her voice was innocent as if she didn't understand what he really wanted to know. "Thanks for the directions."

She would have walked back and I would have done what she'd told me to and stayed there, but then someone asked her, "Can I see some identification before you go?"

That someone was Erik.

I stepped out from behind the wall. Hearing him should have made me more determined not to come out of the shadows. Hearing him should have reminded me to be careful who recognized me. His voice triggered a fight-or-flight response, and I only knew how to do one thing.

It made my hands clench into fists and my pulse rise. I would not cower away from him.

"Kasia?" I said, hurrying over.

"Luka!" Kasia said, sounding surprised, though I had little doubt she was confused why I'd stepped out before we could regroup.

"Erik," I said, stopping where I stood to look him over.

"What are you doing here?" he asked.

"It's sort of a long story, but I bet you'd like to hear it." I was trying to sound compliant, but my voice still revealed some anger. I tried to give a better reply with a more relaxed tone. "I'm glad I ran into you, actually. I wanted to talk to you." I lowered my voice. "About Commander Markos."

Erik's eyes were narrow. His whole body tensed for a fight with me.

"Isn't that Commander Markos's kaftan?" he asked.

I looked down and chuckled. "It sure is. Or it was, anyway."

"He gave it to you?"

I knew Erik had information about the Markos family. He was there, which made me even more sure that I'd find the Markos family inside. But if he had any idea where my loyalties were, the plan was dead.

I felt I had no choice but to betray Markos.

"I wouldn't say that. Not sure I'd accept a gift from him at this point anyway. Would you?" I asked. I kept my words quiet, as if worried the other guards would hear.

"What do you mean?" Erik asked. His hand remained on his dagger. No wonder, considering what I'd done with it last time.

"Didn't you hear?" I whispered. "He's under official investigation."

"So, you what, robbed his closet?"

"Why not? His family isn't there and I doubt they're coming back."

"Luka," Kasia said, tugging at my arm. Skudge, she was strong. I couldn't help but look over and grin at her. "Aren't you going to take me to DavatNoc?"

"Of course. This will only take a minute," I said gently before redirecting my attention to Erik and the blade in his hand. I wanted to punch it through his sternum.

I wanted to toy with him, to write my name across his face with the tip.

What was wrong with me? Erik was a piece of slag, loyal only to Khizmit, but he was still a person. A voice, a warning, sounded in my head as I looked at him though. As if my mutation knew something about him that I didn't.

"You mean to tell me," Erik said. "That you don't side with Commander Markos."

"I side with Khizmit. It doesn't sound like Markos does anymore."

"Is that why you're with her? I thought you and Emberly—"

"Please," I said. "I was on assignment. I was following orders. Once I heard the accusations against Pedrick, I had no interest in being affiliated with him or following any directions from him." I lowered my voice even more and scooted closer to Erik to the point that I could see each individual thread on his ushanka. "I heard he sympathizes with lurpers."

"But didn't you know?" Erik asked. "That night we were looking for the Oscar, I swear he was the boy with Emberly."

"You think…" I paused as if replaying the scene. *Had I been near Lockbox?* Markos had just asked Roman to verify that his wrist was clean—not me. I acted like the realization had just dawned on me. "You're right," I said, clapping Erik on the shoulder. "It must have been. You were so sure, and Markos kept insisting that the kid was a private, not a lurper."

"It had to have been the Oscar," Erik growled. "I knew it was, but they just kept denying it. I should have reported him then!"

"No one will blame you," I said. "You and I are loyal. We

wanted to follow orders and he's a commander. What option did we have?"

"Not a lot," Erik said, his gaze wandering back to Kasia. "You moved up."

"Be careful," I warned. "I like her."

Kasia blushed. I wasn't sure someone could fake or force a blush.

Erik turned back to me.

"I thought you were thick with their family."

"I wanted to promote by any means necessary."

"So you really don't care about them?"

"Why would I?" I basically spat the question. "I want to watch them suffer for what they've done. Releasing an Oscar? Markos is someone we trusted."

"But what about his family? You want to watch them suffer too?"

"Of course," I said, and the night felt like it was growing heavier.

"You want to…make them suffer?" Erik asked.

"I'd wager a whole krown that you'd be surprised what I'd do if I found them."

Erik winked a dark eye at me.

"Can your girlfriend wait a minute? I have something I want to show you."

"Wait here," I said immediately to Kasia. "Or go without me."

I glanced at her face. Questions. Plans. I don't know what she was thinking.

Erik turned back to the outpost, which was remarkably similar to the one I'd been kept in briefly under Garlic Man's care after Lockbox's mom called the soldiers on me. Erik put a key into the lock and undid the door.

"Are you telling me they're here?" I asked, letting excitement into my voice again.

"Not Emberly."

"Where's she?"

"They were going to take her to Vazenia," Erik said. The bottom of the door scraped against the floor violently.

I immediately calibrated my hearing and picked up three people moving beyond the second door.

Erik pushed the heavy outer door shut and bolted it in three different places.

"But Vazenia is overrun," I said. "So, what…" I had to make sure I was calm. That I seemed happy to have her punished. I almost decided to duck my head, call Emberly a dumb slag sack, and ask Erik where they'd sent her to rot.

But the idea sent my heart racing.

I barely blinked and the next thing I saw was my hand around Erik's neck. Veins popped out around his forehead and along his throat where my fingers gripped and pinned him to the back of the door.

He couldn't speak, but he tried, and it came out as squeaks.

My voice, on the other hand, sounded inhuman. "Where's Emberly? I'll relax my hold, and you'll tell me."

"What the hell are you thinking?" Erik screamed as I slightly released my hold on his throat. With my other hand, I grabbed his wrist, locking it downward, holding it so a single additional centimeter would snap it.

"Where is she?" I demanded.

"Rhosivi," he coughed. "They sent her to Rhosivi."

CHAPTER 20
A DEEPER RED THAN CRIMSON

MEMORIES OF COAL DUST, clanging, bitter cold, lashes with the palka, and night after brutal night, laying there awake, stomach begging for something to eat, left me shaking.

Emberly was at Rhosivi.

They'd sent her to hell.

Mechanically I tightened my hold on Erik's throat, blocking the blood from his brain until he collapsed, temporarily asleep.

I wanted to hold him longer. Wait until he kicked and flailed and died.

But I was not a monster. I couldn't let myself become what they'd feared.

Using his own belt, I bound his arms behind his back, and as he regained consciousness over the next few seconds, I dragged him to the far corner.

He gasped, confused for a few seconds.

"What do you think you'll accomplish by this?" His voice was raspy. "There are several guards outside. Some of them are in the room. Some are in the streets. Some are hidden. If you take a single step outside this room without me, they'll shoot you. If your friend or whatever she is, is still around, they'll kill her too."

"The only person here in danger of dying is you," I said, my voice cruel. The people on the other side of the second door had become still as they listened.

"Luka?" Milena's voice was distinct.

"I'm here," I replied, jamming the key into the hole. "It's me."

I turned the key and wrenched the door open so fast Milena nearly fell into my arms. She wrapped her arms around my neck, immediately bursting into tears. Her hair was disheveled, the left side of it tangled into what resembled a rat's nest. Her beige dress was dirty and seemed inadequate for how cold it must have been here at night.

"Are you under arrest too?" Milena asked, her voice pitching.

"No, and neither are you. I'm getting you out of here."

Zuzanna stepped out from the darkness limping slightly. Cold air poured from the open door as if the cell had doubled as a freezer.

"Luka," she said, relief flashing in her features. "Did Pedrick send you?"

"Yes," I said, wrapping her with my free arm. Her eyes shone with bravery, but there was an overall exhaustion to her demeanor.

"This is Alba," Zuzanna said. A woman with long, dark curls stepped out from the shadows. She had bruising along her face and a cut, which still oozed some blood, on her right eyebrow.

"You're Luka?" the woman with the cut eyebrow asked. Her voice held a combination of fear and anger.

"Yes." I looked back at her. I'd never seen her before. Of that, I was certain.

The name gave me pause and I looked the woman over again. I'd hoped to meet the love of Roman's life, but I'd planned to do it under slightly different circumstances.

Milena continued to cry, her voice getting louder with

every word. "They took Emberly. They took her to Rhosivi. They wouldn't even tell us why!" Sobs began to burst out of her. It echoed around the small, empty room.

I placed my hand on her back.

"We have to get you out of here," I said. "You were right to hide. It's not safe here."

I turned back to Erik who was flopping in the corner, trying to get his hands free from his belt. He'd have to break both of his thumbs to get free, something I doubted he even realized.

With little effort, I picked up Erik and half-carried half-dragged him into the furthest back corner of the cell.

"Have mercy, Luka," Erik said, his eyes full of fear. "Don't kill me."

"I'm not a monster," I said.

Mercy. I could afford a little mercy. I pulled the door shut, mostly to block out our conversation while we decided on a plan.

I figured if I took long enough in here, the guards would become suspicious, and Kasia would have enough time to locate and disable any guards positioned to take a shot at us.

Zuzanna's voice was too quiet for Erik to hear. "Pedrick is ready to start his coup, isn't he?"

I wasn't sure how she knew, but I wasn't about to lie to her.

"Yes."

"Then I have to do my part of it."

"You're part of it?" I asked. I had some difficulty picturing her with a weapon in her hands.

"You think I'm involved in politics for the fun of it?"

I didn't want to question her, but I'd been given an assignment. "But you're in danger if you stay here."

"I'm not a lurper. I'm not a Test Criminal. I've done nothing wrong."

I cleared my throat. "You didn't turn in your husband."

"I didn't know," she said, but it was clear that she had known. She lifted her chin defiantly. "But she is in danger." Zuzanna motioned to Milena.

"What didn't you know?" Milena asked.

Zuzanna took Milena's face in her hands and leaned in close. "Your father is a good man. A great man. One of the few rare men who history will either slaughter or revere."

"What do you mean?"

"I—It's not the right time to tell you. I can't—" Zuzanna had kept the secret locked away deep. Too deep to uncover right now.

It wasn't my story to tell, but there wasn't time to wait. "Your father was a Test Criminal," I said.

Milena's tears began anew. This time they came silently. "I don't understand."

Something slammed into the door and Milena shrieked and jumped. Alba whipped her head toward the door.

Kasia was on the move.

"Take Milena to Pedrick. Do not come looking for me," Zuzanna demanded.

I listened for the guards outside. Another thud followed by a choked cry from atop the roof was all I heard.

With Milena behind me, I pulled the door open and peeked my head out.

"All clear?" I asked, quickly.

"For now," came Kasia's reply. She was on the roof above me. I'd expected to see the guards scattered across the ground but there were no guards in sight at all.

Where had she put them?

Zuzanna caught me in a quick embrace. "Thank you, Luka." She said, holding me close.

"Zuzanna," I said, whispering into her ear. "I'm a Victor and an X-ray."

I turned to see her eyes widen.

"I know Pedrick didn't want to tell my secret, but I

thought you should know. I wanted you to know before you, well—"

She hugged me tightly again.

"Mom, what did you mean about Papa?" Milena reached for her mom, but Zuzanna caught her hands and took a step backward.

"He'll explain everything when you get to him." Her voice was hurried. "Luka can explain things too."

"Mom, stop!" Milena begged. "Don't leave me. What is a Test Criminal?"

A single tear slid down Zuzanna's cheek.

"We don't have a lot of time," Kasia said. "Three minutes, at most."

"I'm sorry my darling. Listen to Luka. Do as he says, and you'll be safe." She dropped Milena's hands and bolted off into the darkness.

I watched her go, surprise and concern in her every step. I was supposed to bring her back with me.

Alba stepped forward, steadying Milena who reached for her mother.

"I told your father I would take you to him. We have a car. Alba can come with us." I said quickly. "We have to move, though."

I stepped outside first, checking for any movement in the streets. I glanced up, looking for Kasia's outline.

"We have to move!" she said, and I saw her only once she'd leapt from the roof. It almost looked like she could fly, the way her dress billowed around her.

"Come on," I called, and Alba stepped outside, her hand wrapped tightly around Milena's.

Milena hesitated at the threshold.

Alba glared at me and pulled on Milena's hand.

"We have to move, now!" Kasia said.

I heard two pops, soft crunches, nearly too quiet for even my ears to pick up.

"Skudge," I whispered. I sprinted back toward the outpost door which Milena had left open. Milena and Alba turned as I ran toward them as fast as I could.

I heard the blade leave the sheath and the grunt Erik uttered as he threw it.

I was slow. Too slow. The blade flew through the air, and I knew its intended target.

No! I thought, launching myself toward her.

Too late. Milena drew in a wet gasp as the blade drove into her stomach. Another short gasp and she dropped to her knees.

Alba began to scream. Milena's eyes were down, looking at the blood seeping from the blade in her gut.

My vision was deeper than crimson.

In the next second, I held Erik's head between my hands. *Crack!*

I dropped his corpse to the floor without a second thought. His silhouette looked otherworldly from the way his head bent at an impossible angle.

Dead. *He* was dead.

Milena could not be.

She *must* not be. I picked her up like she was made of porcelain.

I blinked. Milena was in my arms, gasping. Suffering.

Alba spared a glance at Erik. "You snapped his neck." Her voice was full of terror as she looked at me and then at my hands. With a shake of her head, she reached for the dagger in Milena, her fingers shaking. "You are a monster. And you'll be the death of all of them," Alba said softly.

"Leave it for now," I said, taking a few steps away from the outpost.

Away from Erik's body. Away from the sticky pool of Milena's blood on the dark earth.

I could scarcely hear the steps of the incoming guards between the rush of blood surging in my ears and the ragged, desperate gasps coming from Milena's little white lips.

"I'll hold them off," Kasia said. "Get her out of here!"

I ran. She was light in my arms.

"Block the pain," I said, remembering the sting so vividly my own stomach hurt. "You're a lurper. That means you have special abilities. One of them is to block pain."

"No," she gasped. "I hate lurpers."

"I'm a lurper. You don't hate me." I hated myself, though. All my abilities and I'd been too slow.

Her face was so white she looked like a ghost. A little ghost in a pretty red dress that had been beige a moment before.

I sprinted, trying not to jostle her as I scooted around buildings, taking routes that were dark and abandoned. Without Kasia to guide me, I was lost.

As I ran, I tried to explain, but my head was too full, and my words didn't make sense to her. "Your father was named Sasha. He was in Zalar, and they gave him a serum that changed him. Changed his DNA. Because of that, you're a lurper."

She shook her head. I stopped beneath a small streetlight that cast a halo above Milena's head. Gently, carefully, I set her on the bench.

"I'm going to pull the blade out and then you need to heal the wound. When I take it out, you'll bleed too much. You have to stop it."

"I can't," she gasped. Her face was so wet, so white, so scared.

"You can heal!" I said, my voice aching. "You're a Victor. You're a lurper!" I grabbed her arm.

"I don't want to be a lurper," she said, her voice breaking at every word.

"You can do this. Your father wants to see you. Your sister wants to see you."

Milena didn't move, but her eyes darted around.

"Where's my mom?" she asked, sounding like a much younger girl than she was. She bit her bottom lip and glanced back down at the dagger in her stomach. "Take that out," she said.

"I will, and then you will heal yourself. Do you understand?"

I knew she didn't. Some lurpers learned about their abilities in the moment. She could do this.

She *had* to do this!

I pulled the blade out, dropped it to the ground, and placed my hands over the wound. She screamed so loudly I was sure it would draw attention from someone. I imagined someone would open a window above us and look down to see my red, red hands pressed against her.

"Heal yourself, Milena. Please!" I continued to put pressure on her hip but every time I pushed she gasped in pain. "You can block pain, and you can heal from this."

She shook her head, tears streaming down the sides of her face toward her ears.

"No, I can't!"

"Please," I begged softly. "Please heal."

"You said you were at Rhosivi," she whispered, shutting her eyes. "I thought you were a soldier."

"I am now. Please, Milena. Please heal yourself. We can talk once you've healed."

"My father was a criminal? He was at Zalar…" She took two quick breaths, her body shaking with every word.

"Think about the skin closing up," I begged. "Tell yourself to numb the pain."

Milena's lips were completely white now. "My dad is not a criminal. My dad would have told me!" She ground her teeth and sobbed. As she shook, her pain became more intense.

My hands were warm, and her body was getting colder by the second.

"Milena, he will explain when we get to him. Heal yourself so you can see him again. You can ask him yourself."

Her voice was a cracked whisper. "I don't believe he's a Victor."

I pushed on the wound again and she gasped in pain.

"You have to believe!" I said, trying to sound fierce instead of horrified. Instead of small and scared and worthless. "You have to believe it for it to work!"

"My dad—" she gasped. "My dad is a hero."

"He is!"

"He is not—" she sobbed. "I'm not a—"

She was fading. Her head bobbed down then up.

"You're going to die if you don't heal!" I said, my voice catching again.

Milena turned her gaze to me and pushed my hand away from her wound.

"My dad—is—a—good—"

Her arms dropped to the ground and her entire body went limp.

"Milena!" I screamed. I pushed at the wound again to plug it. She didn't wince. Didn't move.

Didn't breathe.

I sat up and stared at her as my vision became blurry and everything around us faded into irrelevance.

Milena Markos was dead, and her blood was all over my hands.

CHAPTER 21
THE MONSTER

ALBA WAS silent beside me as I pressed my hands into the wound, trying to project my healing abilities onto Milena.

Trying and failing.

Failing and falling. I felt like I was spinning, spiraling into some dark abyss.

I failed.

I'd been sent to save Markos's daughters, and not only had I failed to save them, Milena was dead.

I sat there, arms extended, until the blood on my fingers froze.

"She's gone," Alba said, scooting away from me.

Defeated, I dropped my hands and reached forward to scoop Milena's body into my arms. I cradled her against my chest and sobbed.

That's how Kasia found us. *Had it been a few minutes? A few hours?*

She had very little blood on her dress. I didn't look at her eyes. I couldn't face her. I stared only into Milena's eyes, lifeless, still, empty.

Kasia dropped to her knees beside us in the alleyway, placing her hand on Milena's head.

I might've sat there until I became as frozen as the tears on my chin and as still as the child in my arms if Alba hadn't prompted me to get up.

"We should take her body to Pedrick," she said.

"Luka," she said, and I only realized then that her hand had been on my shoulder the whole time. "You did all you could."

But had I? If I'd killed Erik sooner, Milena would be holding Alba's hand, riding toward The Outskirts asking a hundred questions.

I'd spared him.

My desire not to be a monster had made me something much worse.

Complicit.

Complicit in the murder of Milena Markos.

I felt a shift in my soul the same way you feel an earthquake or an explosion in the mines.

Kasia must have sensed it too, somehow.

"Luka," she said.

I didn't turn my face up, but I looked at her, my eyes narrowed.

"This isn't your fault," Kasia insisted.

"They told me I was dangerous, and I didn't believe them." My voice was lower than usual. "They told me I was a weapon and I tried to show them I wasn't. I tried to show humanity to those who imprisoned me. To show them I could be tame. Controlled. Compliant. I'd showed them mercy."

"Mercy?" Alba asked. "You're a lurper."

My voice grew louder, and I found that I didn't care if anyone heard me. "Doctor Bolest was right. I was weak. But I am not weak anymore."

"Mercy is not weakness," Kasia said.

"She's dead because I was too weak!" I threw my hand toward Milena. "She's dead because I was afraid to become what they feared. I was afraid." I dropped my voice to a growl. "But I am not afraid of anything anymore."

Kasia stood and took a step toward me. "You aren't what they feared. You aren't too dangerous—"

"No," I said. "You can't be too cruel, too cold, too calculating in this world. You can't be too dangerous, too strong, too callous, too brutal. They've set the standard. They've done this— not me."

"Luka, you aren't some demon!"

"Oh, no," I laughed, a low wicked sound. "I'm much worse."

Milena's eyes were unseeing. I would become as unfeeling as she now was.

"I will bring horror they never imagined," I growled. "I will incite a fear so powerful, so palpable, they will throw themselves on the ground when they see me. They will beg for mercy and I—I will laugh in their faces as they realize that I don't know that word anymore."

"Luka," Kasia said.

Alba's face was fixed in horror as she pressed herself flat against the wall.

They said I was dangerous before, but now I'd become a threat.

"They barely know *half* of what I can do. What I *will* do. The streets of Khizmit will be slick with blood before I'm done."

"Snap out of it!" Kasia said, reaching forward to slap or hit me.

I caught her hand and gripped it tightly, considering all the ways I could flip her onto her back or crack her bones. She didn't fight back. She made no move to defend herself.

"If you hurt me, you will not forgive yourself. You will cross a line that you can't come back from."

I looked at her. Really looked at her. Her eyes brimmed with sympathy. Pain seeped from her nearly as visibly as the tears that streaked down her face.

"Am I scaring you?" I asked.

"Yes," she whispered. "You are not yourself right now."

Alba was trembling from terror and malice. She'd be the first of many.

"Maybe I'm more myself than I've ever been." I still held Kasia's arm in my grip. The possible ways to take her down flashed through my head so fast it should have made me dizzy.

"Can I hold you?" she asked suddenly.

I blinked, sure I'd misheard her. "Can you what?"

"Can I hold you?" Her voice was quieter this time. Gentler. As if she was asking for a favor for herself.

"I'm not a child. Didn't you just hear me? I'm—"

"Luka," Kasia's voice was a beautiful balance between stern and sympathetic. "Let go of my arm and come here."

As if I'd been bewitched, I obeyed. I dropped her arm and took two small steps toward her.

I collapsed, ready to hit the ground when she caught me and held me with more strength than I'd suspected, even with her genetic makeup.

"Romulus told me about you," Alba said, her voice a shaky whisper. I had my face buried in Kasia's shoulder as I asked, "What did he say? That I'm efficient at dispatching rabbits?"

"No," Alba said. "He didn't mention that. He said you're...smart. Strong. Sensible. Determined. But one thing that sets you apart from the other lurpers is—"

"I'm a Victor and an X-ray," I stated, standing back up. "A remarkable combination of Test Criminal chaos."

"No. It's your compassion. Most of the boys from Predvoi and Rhosivi became cold and sharp like the winter. But not you. He told me you didn't want to hurt a rabbit. You protected your friend in the prison. You had compassion for an inmate you barely knew, who had never shown you kindness. He told me," she paused. "He told me what you had to do to escape and how that action haunted you. You had compassion for the guards who'd beat you."

"Compassion isn't going to win a war," I stated.

"Maybe not," Kasia said. "But it will win friends. And you need friends to win a war. As your friend, I want you to at least wait a day or two before reigning terror upon the citizens of Khizmit."

I nodded. There was something to her embrace that calmed my heart. My vision was getting less bloody.

A question popped out.

"Is bloodlust real?" I asked.

"Yes."

My heart sank.

"But I don't believe you're any more prone to it than I am. Or than Roman or Markos are."

I waited for Kasia or Alba to speak and say it was time for us to leave. That we had to get out of here soon. They didn't rush me.

They didn't need to.

I took a breath and stilled myself.

"You need to go," I said.

"You don't tell me what to do," Alba said. "You're not in charge of yourself and you're certainly not in charge of me."

She wasn't wrong. She could see the darkness in me. The darkness that I'd tried to keep at bay.

"Both of you need to go," I said. "Take her body and get to The Outskirts."

Alba nodded, the tension in her neck obvious from where I stood.

"What about you?" Kasia asked.

"I'm going to get Emberly," I said, the crimson in my vision finally clearing. I backed away from her and took another look at her face, her dress, her torn knuckles. "I'm going to Rhosivi."

Kasia told me to take the car. She felt confident that with Alba's help, she could get another one and leave Khizmit.

I gave Kasia one final hug, trying not to notice how much I enjoyed being close to her. Perhaps I just loved non-aggressive physical touch.

"Take care of yourself," I said.

Kasia grinned with her mouth, but her eyes remained pained.

"Tell Markos that I'm sorry."

"Sorry won't be enough," Alba said.

"I know."

He'd never forgive me. I'd never forgive myself. I was supposed to be stronger, faster, smarter than any cruster. Erik had willingly broken his own thumbs to get to Milena. I had to be willing to make those sorts of sacrifices and worse if I was going to win.

And I *was* going to win. I wouldn't tell Kasia and Alba the truth, but I would become a terrible monster.

"Tell him that I'll be back with Emberly, or I won't be back at all."

"Luka—"

"I'll be back with Emberly," I said.

If I failed again, I'd let the bloodlust carry me all the way to The Chancellor Supreme.

I had a plan of what to do with her and it involved an axe, some chain, a tree, and the wolves.

If I failed again, I'd become the dealer of death. The minister of madness. I'd fight until it killed me because I realized that as much as I loved Kasia—and I did love her in a way—losing Emberly would absolutely kill me.

CHAPTER 22
HEAD WARDEN MOLNAR

Though it was early evening, I kept the headlights on, making myself, my truck, easily visible from a distance.

My heart drummed in my chest, warnings beating throughout my limbs with every pulse.

Danger. Warning. Cold. Dark. Danger. I gripped the wheel so tightly that my fingers were nearly numb. *Palkas. Crusters. Wardens.*

I had to slow the vehicle more than once to practice breathing normally.

But it was much harder than knocking on Leticia Varga's door or going into Brita's house again, as traumatic as it had been to hear about her nephew.

I changed the tune my heart sang. *Ember. Danger for Ember. Go help Ember.*

When I approached the gate, thick with boards, c-wire, and spikes pointed inward to the prison, I confess I faltered briefly.

If you die here, I reasoned. *It will be nothing less than you always expected.*

There was no way to steel myself. I parked the vehicle a captain gestured for the two lieutenants beside him to approach me. Rifles in hand, they trudged across the hard snow. I opened my door for them.

"Good evening," I said, saluting.

"Identification, soldier," the guard said.

I pulled out my paperwork and handed it over gruffly to conceal any shakiness my fingers might have betrayed.

"My name is Junior Lieutenant Luka Drivick. I am here on assignment." As I said it, I heard a slight accent enter my speech. It wasn't as if one of these guards would recognize my voice. I didn't change it much, just enough that it didn't quite sound right to me. It was different enough without being too difficult to maintain. However, I accepted the very real probability that some of the same guards here would have been the ones who terrorized me. Maybe disguising my voice would make it more difficult for them to recognize me.

But that wasn't the real reason why I did it. I was getting into character.

I was pretending, to myself, to be Roman. He'd come to Predvoi as a lurper in disguise. He'd gotten out and he'd helped me.

It was time for me to do the same for Emberly.

"We weren't expecting anyone," the soldier said.

"I have news for High Warden Molnar." I'd learned his name from Kasia before leaving her. She got it from one of the soldiers she'd disarmed outside the holding cell. "As you know, Commander Markos used to be the high warden here. He's sent me with a message."

The guards stepped away from the vehicle and a gust of wind screamed in through the open door. The wind wasn't as cold as it had been in my memory.

I pulled my ushanka lower on my head. *Oh yes*, I remembered. This was a far cry from the linen cap the inmates wore.

"Do we let him in?" the younger guard asked.

The captain shrugged. "His paperwork is signed by Commander Markos. We let him in."

They waved me in and directed me to a parking spot, and the huge gate screamed as it shut.

Trapped. I'm trapped. I—

I was here for Emberly. I took another breath and parked the car. I climbed out of the car and passed the keys over to the captain. He had brown hair that extended past his shoulders and an accent I couldn't place, as if he wasn't from Khizmit at all.

"What are these for?" he asked.

"Don't you lock them up so the inmates can't get them?"

"Yes, but how did you know?"

"Commander Markos sent me. He didn't send me ignorant of the rules here." I scoffed. "I've been around lurpers before, Sir." I said "Sir" with such disgust I almost expected a palka to swing my way. The lieutenant merely looked startled, and his younger comrade stifled a laugh.

"Come with me," the captain said, walking me through the front door.

I'd spent a decade at this prison, but this part was as unfamiliar to me as Latvani had been.

A few turns and one miserable flight of stairs later led me to the heavy wooden door of the head warden's office where another two guards stood. The air was stale and hummed with distant mining equipment, the screech of mine cartwheels, and the clang of sledgehammers. I recalibrated my hearing to focus just on this room. Just on the head warden.

Step one was to get permission to be here. Real permission to be here. At any cost.

The lieutenant went in first and told the head warden I was there. Head Warden Molnar's voice was croaky and, to my surprise, somewhat quiet.

"He can come in," Molnar said.

The office was much the way I'd remembered it when Head Warden Markos occupied it. Molnar had decorated it differently, which is to say, not at all. There were no books in sight, no pictures or drawings, no visible notes from his wife, if he had one.

"Good evening, Sir." I saluted and waited in the doorway.

The captain escorting me carried my paperwork over to Molnar's desk while I waited for an invitation to enter.

Head Warden Molnar filled out his uniform in all the wrong places. The sleeves were baggy while the buttons around his middle seemed strained as they held the cloth together. He had only a few ribbons on his chest and his ushanka was so high up on his head that his wrinkled forehead was almost entirely visible.

"You say you have a message from Commander Markos?" Molnar asked, taking a few steps toward me.

"Yes, Sir," I said. "Can I take a seat?"

He took the papers from me and nodded. I dropped into the chair as he perused them.

"It says you were approved for emergency leave in Khizmit. It says nothing about being assigned to Rhosivi. I haven't heard anything about it. Commander Markos didn't sign off on it."

"Can I tell you the truth, Head Warden?" I asked.

"I would expect nothing less." I could smell his breath from here. It had the scent of meat. Old meat.

I lowered my voice if only to make my next words more interesting to him.

I had to get Ember under my protection. *At any cost.*

"Commander Markos is a fraud," I said. "He was an original Test Criminal. Doctor Bolest proved it."

Molnar stared and finally blinked. "You're skudging with me." The man drew back in his chair. The soldiers in the corner shifted at the announcement.

"You'll hear the whispers," I said. "You'll know there's a lot of suspicion regarding what he's actually doing there with the lurpers."

"That's a very serious accusation Drivick." Molnar paused

as if allowing me to rescind my allegation. "Commander Markos used to be the Head Warden here. As his successor, you must know I hold him in high regard."

"So did I," I growled. "Until I found out that he's worse than a lurper. I hope you'll excuse my language, but Commander Markos is a skrag, Sir."

Molnar adjusted his position in his seat, which appeared to be too small for him.

"Give us a few minutes to verify some of these claims."

Molnar sent the captain with long, brown hair away. They had some radio communication with Predvoi and maybe all the way to Khizmit, but I wasn't sure how reliable that was. We didn't speak while we waited.

If they couldn't prove what I'd said, maybe they would lock me up. I could deal with that. I could find Emberly anyway. I could navigate nearly every and any corner of this prison mine in my sleep.

Ten minutes passed. High Warden Molnar got up and asked the two guards at the door to watch me.

Another ten minutes passed.

They wouldn't kill me. They'd hold me somewhere until they could figure out what to do with me.

Unless they figured out what I was.

The scuffling of feet on the floor had me turning around in my seat as a young inmate walked past the open door. I rose to my feet and walked over to the guards at the door.

"Is he from the Children's Detention Center?" I asked.

"Yes. That's who we thought you were with when you came."

"Where are they taking him?" I asked it as if I didn't know. As if I didn't remember my first day here nearly ten years prior.

"First stop, the clinic. Doctor Traft will give him a rapid test and then mark him accordingly. We've got his records, but you can never be too careful. Wouldn't want to throw an Oscar in with a Papa, would we?" The guard chuckled.

"Certainly not," I said, hearing that hint of unfamiliarity in my voice.

The eight-year-old hurried along, his eyes full of fear.

"What is he?" I asked.

"What is he again?" the lieutenant asked his comrade.

"I think they said we were getting a Golf."

I nodded.

Sensing their discomfort, I walked back to my seat to wait for High Warden Molnar.

It was another ten minutes at least before High Warden Molnar bumbled into the room and took his seat across from me.

"Well," I said, "Were you able to verify anything I said?"

Molnar was out of breath. "Doctor Bolest is missing. He took a group of officers to the Penal Legion and hasn't been seen since."

"I know," I said. "I was there when Bolest showed up. He told everyone what he'd learned about Pedrick Markos, who admitted it. Markos now has all the officers who wouldn't join him held as prisoners."

"And Doctor Bolest?"

"Doctor Bolest is dead," I said. "He was shot in the head." *By me*, I thought.

Molnar leaned back. His chair creaked in warning of breaking. "Say you're right. Let's just say, the gods forbid, that you're right and somehow Commander Markos was a Test Criminal. What is he?"

"He's a Victor," I said.

It was too much for Molnar. He shook his head immediately, his ushanka almost falling off at the motion.

"He would have killed by now. He would have been taken over by bloodlust by now. Victors don't just rise to positions of power."

"I swear on the mines that he is."

Molnar was running out of patience with me.

"Sir, his daughter Emberly Markos, she's here, isn't she?"

Molnar hesitated and then nodded.

"Didn't they tell you that Markos was a Victor when they brought her?"

Molnar shook his head. "No."

I couldn't let his response evoke a reaction in me. *He didn't know what she was? What the skudge had I done?*

"Then, Sir," I had temporarily dropped my hint of an accent. I picked it back up. "If Emberly Markos isn't in Rhosivi because of her father, why is she here?"

Molnar looked at me like I was something of a slaghead for asking. "She is here for murdering my late friend, Head Warden Andrei Velky."

CHAPTER 23
KORPORAL TURUK

Ember was here for murdering Velky. My mouth tasted bitter and dry.

She was here because of something I'd done. I refused to let my face reveal my horror and regret.

But I was already too far. *Skudge!* I needed Lockbox. I really did have slag for brains.

"You believe she did it?" I asked.

High Captain Molnar adjusted his ushanka, though it did nothing to make it fit better. "It doesn't matter what I believe. She admitted to it. She was found near the body."

"Can I ask, what the nature of his injuries was?"

"He was stabbed through the chest." Molnar seemed pained at the idea.

I could still hear the break of his bones beneath my hands. "And you think she's strong enough to do that?"

"With a sharp instrument, not a lot of force is necessary."

"Where did she get the weapon?"

Molnar looked at me like I was an idiot. "From Velky."

"You think she could easily overpower him?"

Molnar cleared his throat. "We don't know the circumstances, but we do know that he was found dead near her and she admitted to it."

I let my thoughts come out as words. "And you believe that was cause enough to send her here, to Rhosivi? That was reason enough to turn a girl into an inmate, held alongside male lurpers? That can't add up to you. You're too smart of a man to believe that was the only reason."

Molnar bristled. "You want me to believe that you were a soldier under Markos, working in the Penal Legion. That you were there when Bolest arrived and proved that Markos was a Test Criminal—a Victor, a skudging *Victor* of all things. Then you escaped from The Outskirts under the guise of emergency leave—which I see was granted to you—and you came here with the sole purpose of telling me about Markos's true identity."

I thumbed the handle of the knife at my waist. With the adrenaline at my fingertips, I could dispose of everyone in this room. I could dispose of half the prison, at *least*. I could unlock the inmates, cause a riot like the one in Vazenia, and I could find Ember.

I would be able to get her out, at least.

But at what cost? How much blood did I really want on my hands?

"That's not my sole purpose, Sir."

"What do you want Drivick?"

"Since you're a man who values the truth, I'll give it to you." I offered my most twisted grin. "I served under Commander Markos. I obeyed the orders that skrag gave me! I saluted him!" I let all the hatred I could muster enter my voice. "I found out what he was, and I left! When I was in Khizmit, I rejoiced to hear that his daughter had been caught and brought here. And I got an…idea."

"An idea?"

"It would bring me great happiness if you would assign her as my ward," I said. "I would like to…keep an eye on her."

Molnar grinned wickedly. "You're a vengeful one, aren't you?"

"Not always," I said. "But when it comes to skrags and lurpers..." I shrugged, not sure what else I could say. I did want to keep an eye on Emberly. I wanted to keep her close. Hold her close. Protect her at all costs.

"Why should I give you the position you demand?" Molnar asked, leaning forward in his chair.

"I told you what Markos was, didn't I?" I didn't know if that plan would work. "I do not demand it, Sir. I humbly request the opportunity for some...retribution."

"Retribution. That makes more sense." Molnar said, easing back into his chair. "Markos slighted you, did he? Passed you over for promotion perhaps? And now you're making up a story to try and skudge up his career?"

I rose to my feet, desperation getting the better of me.

"It is far more than that, High Warden Molnar. Markos is an imposter. A traitor! He's made a fool of me and a fool of you."

I hadn't expected Molnar to be capable of the roar that came from him next.

"You're on thin ice, Junior Lieutenant! You go too far!"

I sat down. *Be compliant. Be compelling.*

"Sir," I said, my voice low again. "I understand why you don't believe me. My claims are improbable. Bring Emberly Markos in and administer a rapid test." They had one. They'd just used one on the eight-year-old from Children's Detention Center. "If it comes back positive, you'll know that I'm telling the truth."

Molnar remained on his feet, his chest and stomach heaving with his labored breathing. "If it comes back and shows that she is a Victor, you can have the retribution you wanted. I'll make her your private ward and give you permission to exact any disciplinary measures you see fit! Hell, I'll promote you to lieutenant." He glowered, an evil glint entering his eyes. "But if the test comes back negative, you will not be court-martialed. You will not be allowed to leave. You will be imprisoned immediately, here, with an actual Victor."

His threat, intended to scare me, filled me with curiosity. I couldn't stop myself from asking, "You have a Victor here already?"

"We do. Victor-27." Molnar said my name, my old name, as if it were a threat.

I was too stunned to speak. Too confused to ask why he thought he still had me as an inmate when it had been almost eight months since I'd been sent to Predvoi.

"I agree to your terms, Sir." My mouth was dry.

Molnar turned to the captain in the corner. "Captain Razin, go get Emberly Markos. We'll meet you in the medical center." My heart began beating rapidly.

Molnar turned back to me, his tone becoming vigorous. "It seems either way, you'll get to meet a *real* Victor today."

His words were lost to my thoughts. *Emberly. You'll see Ember.*

A horrible awareness cut through my excitement: She was about to learn the truth about her father in the worst possible way, and it was entirely my fault.

I prayed she wouldn't reveal that she recognized me.

I prayed she would forgive me.

Molnar stepped out of the room, Captain Razin at his side. I listened in as they walked away, ignorant of my identity. Ignorant to the point that they'd used my own name as a weapon against me. I would have laughed if I didn't worry so much about Ember. What she'd say. What she'd feel when I told her about her father.

Captain Razin's strange accent left his words clipped. "Sir, we don't have Victor-27 anymore. When Pedrick Markos was made a commander of the Lurper Legion, his final act was transferring Victor-27 to Predvoi."

"I know!" Molnar hissed. "But Drivick doesn't need to know that!"

"What if the test is negative? Will you really throw him in a cell with a lurper?"

"I will!" Molnar said, his voice growing fainter as he walked farther, and farther away. "If I have to go to Predvoi myself and bring back Victor-27 myself, I will!"

The two guards in the room with me shifted uncomfortably in the silence.

The korporal that had a younger face, and eyelashes so light they nearly disappeared, cleared his throat.

"Is what you're saying true?" he asked.

"Yes," I said. "I wish it weren't, but it is."

That's all he said.

"What's your name, Korporal?" I asked.

"Korporal Turuk."

The lieutenant was clearly uncomfortable with Turuk's friendliness towards me.

"Korporal Turuk, I watched Doctor Bolest die at the hands of a Victor. He was shot through the head, and the one who pulled the trigger looked like he wanted to laugh. Like he was relieved. Like he'd do it again, and again, and again, as if he lived in a world where the word remorse didn't exist at all."

Turuk swallowed hard.

"I understand your suspicion of me, Lieutenant," I said. "You're smart to be guarded. To be cautious. We live in a world of liars and impostors. But you'll see that I'm not lying. Not about this."

I waited until I couldn't sit still any longer.

"They'll be in the medical clinic, right?" I asked, getting to my feet.

"I assume so," Turuk said.

"We should be there," I said, sure to say "we" instead of just "I." Then I gave them a reason to be there, besides satiating my need to see Ember. To know she was really here and really okay. "We need to be there to protect Molnar when the Victor figures out we know what she is." My fake accent grated at my throat. It had to be why my voice was dry.

That and the bitter taste of betrayal.

"She's probably played innocent up until now. Guilty of the crime of killing Velky, but secretly relieved you hadn't tested her. I've seen Victors in action in the Lurper Legion and once her secret is out, Molnar will need more than Captain Razin to protect him. To subdue her."

I'd tried not to make it sound like an order.

Turuk seemed nearly ready to come with me, but the lieutenant hesitated.

They weren't moving. They weren't going to the door. I was intimately familiar with the route between the High Warden's office and the medical center, but I wasn't supposed to know the way. The last option I had was to insult their pride.

"Are you afraid?" I asked. Neither of them replied. "You should be. You should be afraid of Victors. They're every bit as bloodthirsty as Bolest said."

"I'm not afraid of a girl," the lieutenant said.

"I am," Turuk said. "Even before you said she was a Victor, I was afraid of her. She has a look about her, in her eyes, a boldness that even the palka couldn't subdue."

The palka. My vision was immediately red.

"Did you use the palka on her?" I asked, my accent suddenly as harsh as Markos's.

"No, Razin did. She didn't scream. Didn't claim innocence. Didn't ask him to stop."

Razin was dead. *He would be dead.*

I would kill him a thousand times over.

"How many times?" I asked, my balled-up hands getting sweaty.

"Ten," Turuk said. "She didn't retaliate. If she was a Victor, she would have killed him, don't you think?"

Ten times. I'd break ten of Razin's bones.

I had to loosen my jaw to answer. "I think only the test can tell us that."

"You seem anxious, Drivick," the lieutenant said.

I walked over to them.

"Did you serve under High Warden Markos and High Warden Velky?" I asked, nearly nose-to-nose with the lieutenant.

"Yes."

"You've already lost one High Warden to her, Sir. I don't think you should stand idly by while the life of another one is in danger."

I reached for the door handle and the lieutenant's hand went to his belt.

"Molnar doesn't want you to leave this room," he said.

I replied quickly, with the blunt force of a hammer. "Molnar doesn't want to die and when that test comes back positive, he'll be glad I came. If I'm wrong and he ends up throwing me in with your inmate, Victor-27, I'm sure you'll be allowed to watch as he dismembers me or whatever it is Victors do to their cellmates."

Turuk shifted and then addressed the lieutenant. "Sir, I think we should go. Just in case."

The lieutenant heaved an aggravated sigh.

"Fine," he said. "But I'll lead the way."

He strode out of the door, and I followed him, my ears listening in the distance for the first sounds from Ember. A single word. A single sigh.

As long as she didn't scream or cry, I could do this. I could help her. I could maintain my disguise and get her out.

If she cried, well, I'd have to resort to the bloodlust plan and hope she was a quick learner.

CHAPTER 24
THE FINAL VICTOR

A CALM FOCUS came over me, just as it always did when my vision was tinged red. Step by step we made our way to the clinic. I heard Captain Razin and High Warden Molnar. The third voice had to be Doctor Traft.

"I already told you," Emberly said, her voice was shriller than usual. I recognized the fear in it, but it was nearly swallowed in her defiance. "I killed High Warden Velky because he was a creep. He handed me his knife and challenged me to do something about him and I used it. But that doesn't make me a lurper, and I'm sure as skudge not some Victor!"

We burst into the room.

Memories smashed into me. Memories of pain. Being denied vyco. Stitches in my face. I looked at the room. I had to be present.

Grey floor. Grey walls. Two lightbulbs. Four chairs, each one bolted down. One stack of wooden bins in the corner. A wall displaying medical equipment that doubled as interrogation tools.

At least, they could double as interrogation tools.

Doctor Traft took up my vision. His white hair had a curl to the ends. He wore glasses, round glasses, in thin metal frames. His coat had brown stains along the base.

I locked eyes with him. His oval face gave the general impression of someone sad, deeply sad, and too far lost in that sorrow to ever try and come back. His frown stayed fixed in place as he said, "I recommended a rapid test when she arrived."

Molnar turned to me. I only glanced at him briefly before sidestepping Captain Razin to get a full view of Ember.

She was shackled to the chair in the same manner I'd been restrained when Bolest had drawn my blood. Her hair had been cut to her shoulders and her hands were black with coal. She had smudges across her cheeks and forehead. Her feet were bare, and I remembered how cold the floor was. How cold she must be. Her eyes, her beautiful eyes were ringed in red. All her earrings were gone, and she wore the striped prison clothes of my childhood.

Her lips parted upon seeing me and I worried she'd say something, but she suddenly snapped her mouth shut.

Molnar censured the lieutenant and Korporal Turuk for bringing me, but I heard none of it while I stared into Ember's eyes.

It was my fear for her safety that kept me from exploding in rage.

I had to keep her safe. I'd failed Milena. I'd be more careful with Ember. More controlled. More deliberate.

"Junior Lieutenant," Molnar said, addressing me for the third time. "We are about to administer the rapid test."

"You'll want me here when you see the results," I said, turning away from Emberly. I couldn't afford to give her a gentle smile or soften my gaze. I couldn't afford to skudge this up.

Doctor Traft drew her blood. She didn't fight.

"The rapid test won't show you anything!" Ember said.

"Actually," I said, wheeling back to face her. "It will." If she was surprised to hear me speaking with a slight accent, she didn't show it.

She froze. *How did I tell her? How could I?*

Doctor Traft put her blood in the vial and shook it.

I spoke, hoping no one would stop me. "Doctor Bolest used the blood from various Victors to determine the mutation in their blood and finalize the rapid tests. In his studies, he found a trail that led him to your father, Pedrick Markos."

"What do you mean?" Her voice was wary.

"Did you ever suspect that your father was sympathetic to lurpers?" I wanted to show her that there had been signs. That her father was still the man she always knew him to be. "Is that why you wanted to start some covert organization defending them? I heard you helped protect an Oscar."

"Is that true?" Molnar asked both me and her.

She didn't answer. She struggled to remove her gaze from me.

"I'm here because I know the truth about your father. Did you know?" I asked, knowing that she didn't. "Did you know that you're a Victor?"

I almost choked on the word.

Her mouth dropped open.

"I don't—"

"I'll be damned," Doctor Traft whispered. He took a few steps away from Emberly and stared at the vial, comparing it to the color chart signifying the mutations. It matched the Victor line perfectly.

"It's positive. She's a Victor," Traft said.

Molnar erupted with questions. Captain Razin moved Molnar farther away from Emberly. I couldn't take my eyes off her.

In the moment of chaos and confusion, I took a single risk and whispered the words, "Trust me."

She'd heard my threat to her ex-boyfriend in the madness of the parade. She could hear me. A small bit of the terror left her eyes and defiance entered again.

But her change in expression didn't go unnoticed.

Captain Razin looked from her back to me and then to her again. "Do you know him?" he asked her.

"Maybe," she said, as if she wasn't sure.

Captain Razin raised his palka.

I spoke. "Just tell them, *Victor*, that you've seen me before. There's no sense in lying to them."

Ember looked at me, her eyes watery. Her lips narrowed in determination and confusion. Her quick expression asked me a dozen questions: *Why are you here? How am I a Victor? Is my family safe? What do you want me to say? Why are you talking like that?*

"I've seen him," she said, her tone defiant. "But I don't remember where or why. You all look the same in your uniforms, it's hard to keep track."

Razin stepped forward. "You lying—"

"Tell them that you've seen me at your house," I said, sounding angry and impatient as I placed myself between him and Emberly. I tried to make it seem like I wasn't protecting her but that I was oblivious to Razin's intentions. "With your father. You saw me most recently at Koliada."

"Yes," she said. "That's right. You work with my father."

"I worked with him. I worked for him!" I screamed, lacing my words with pain. "Until I found out what he was! What you are!" There were tears at the edge of my eyes as I leaned in close to her, close enough to smell her and I prayed she could guess why I was hurting, why I wanted to cry. "Your father was a Test Criminal." I'd wanted to deliver the news to her myself. I'd imagined telling her in secret, in confidence, but I'd ruined that. "He was a Victor, and that makes you a Victor."

Molnar held the results up again, looking at them in the dim light. "This makes her the last living Victor in Khizmit!" he declared.

"What about Victor-27?" I asked.

"I lied about having him here. Victor-27 was sent to

Predvoi and was later stabbed by the captain who'd been assigned to keep an eye on him."

"So, don't get any ideas," Molnar said to Emberly.

"Since Victor-27 is dead, then she is the final victor," Traft said.

They wanted her to feel alone. They believed she was alone. But she was not the final Victor, and neither was I.

"You were right," Molnar said again as he looked back at the results, still stuck on that fact.

"Sir," I said. "The retribution."

Molnar nodded. "Yes, of course." He cleared his throat. "I officially assign you the duty of monitoring the Victor. If she becomes too much of a threat, it will be your responsibility to put her down. I give you all rights and authority to any disciplinary measures you see fit. She will require constant supervision."

"Yes, Sir," I said, making my voice sound excited and wicked. "I'm counting on it."

Molnar handed the vial back to Doctor Traft. "I'd request permission to send her to the Penal Legion, but given the circumstances, our options are to kill her outright, or wait out Markos's little rebellion. See if we can weaponize her. Better that we keep her as leverage in case Markos does come here…" Molnar trailed off. "You'll need a comrade. I'll assign someone—"

"Korporal Turuk," I said. "I'd like to request Korporal Turuk if that's okay with you, and him."

Turuk raised his blond eyebrows, looking as taken aback as Molnar. Turuk was impressionable. Turuk could be ordered around. I couldn't risk getting Razin as a comrade, or a guard who stood a chance of recognizing me after prolonged time together.

"You can have Turuk," Molnar said with a wave of his hand. Turuk straightened and smiled at me.

I turned my attention to Emberly.

I placed a hand on her shoulder, keeping my touch gentle. It was too gentle. The ruse was too fresh. I had to be mean, or at least, sound mean. I had to resist the urge to scoop her into my arms and hold her, kiss her, tell her everything and how much I'd missed her.

I had to be intimidating. She'd understand.

"Don't worry," I said, and though my voice was sarcastic I thought she could tell by my unblinking eye contact that my words were sincere. "I'll take good care of you."

CHAPTER 25
MR. PREEMPTIVE OFFICER

MOLNAR ASKED me to return with him to his office while Doctor Traft marked her left wrist with a V. They didn't know what number to add, and I sure as slag wasn't about to tell them she was Victor-01. The less ink in her, the better.

Molnar was much more at ease in his office and finally breathing more normally. He and I were alone since I'd proven myself to be trustworthy.

Just one year previous I never would have imagined I'd be alone in this office with the head warden. I never would have imagined this office would be occupied by someone other than Markos and Velky.

Molnar's chair creaked beneath his bulky frame. "It will take me some time to digest this information. I'll report everything back to Riah Dulka tonight. Last I'd heard Pedrick Markos's family was being held. They'll want to send the younger Victor up here."

The younger Victor was Milena. The ghost in a red dress.

I wanted to throw up as the image entered my mind again. I found myself wiping my sweaty palms on my pants, again, and again, and again.

Molnar was oblivious to it.

"With everything going on with Commander Markos, it

may take some time to get the paperwork in order and until then, I won't get enough pay to distribute any to you."

I wiped my hands more, rubbing harder.

"Drivick?" he said my name and I stopped moving my hands. "Are you all right?"

"Yes, Sir," I said.

"Do you still want to do this? Obviously, it's a lot of responsibility and I don't have your file to know what your history as an officer looks like, but based on what you've shown me, you're up for it."

"Oh, I want it more than anything." I folded my hands together to stop myself.

"Retribution?" Molnar asked, a grin playing at the edges of his mouth. He wanted me to be twisted. "As I said, I can't pay you. Not for a while at least."

It pained me to say the next words, but I said them convincingly, I was sure of that. "Watching her suffer, making *her* pay, would be more than enough for me."

Molnar smiled in approval.

"I know you've served in the Lurper Legion, but let's quickly go over the Penal Code for Khizmit Guards before I promote you, as promised. There are, of course, some exceptions working with a Victor, but we'll get to that. I'll do your orientation myself so we can expedite your getting to work. I think we'll all feel much safer with her under constant supervision."

"Lieutenant Drivick, Sir," Korporal Turuk said, saluting me enthusiastically as I left Molnar's office. "I just want to say that I'm honored that you selected me to be your comrade. I hope I don't let you down, Sir."

I barely glanced at him as I walked back to the clinic.

"The Victor will be in the clinic, correct?" I asked as Turuk hurried alongside me, his palka swinging wildly. "Scoot your holster a little to the side so it doesn't swing so much," I said, pointing to his hip.

"Yes, Sir." Turuk adjusted it as we walked along the hallway. "She'll be there. They're waiting for us to escort her to her cell."

"Does she have a cellmate?"

"No, Sir."

"Good," I replied.

I threw the door open assertively when I entered, half-expecting to see Emberly with tears on her face.

Instead, she wore an expression of anger and defiance.

On her wrist, in thick black ink, was a single fat V accompanied by a few drops of dark blood.

Captain Razin stepped forward and handed me a small key ring. "When you're ready, you two will take her to Cell 42 in Block G."

"Tu—" I stopped myself. Molnar had just repeated the rules to me, his meat-scented breath wafting over with each punctuated word. No use of names within the prison. No giving the lurpers anything they might use against us. I straightened. "We'll get her there."

I was forbidden from telling the Victor what the designations meant or expressing any sympathy for her, or from calling her by her name. But because she was my ward, I could decide what her daily tasks included, as long as I didn't arm her.

We wouldn't need much time. I planned to send Turuk on a short trip and then I'd take Emberly with me, out of Rhosivi.

"Victor," I said to Emberly, my tone even like Roman's. "We will unshackle you. You will follow him to your new cell. I will be behind you every step of the way." I hoped she found the last line to be reassuring.

I unshackled her and we got into the formation I'd

explained. In heavy, nearly synchronized steps, the three of us marched away from the clinic, where the air became more stale and the hint of mold in the air brought back memories of scrubbing floors, walls, and guards' boots.

"Can you hear me?" her voice came to me like a gentle whisper.

"Yes," I said, whispering back.

Turuk gave no indication that he could hear us. He wasn't a lurper. He wouldn't be able to.

Emberly tripped. Turuk whipped around to see her get back to her feet.

"Sorry," she muttered, and began walking again.

"Luka...I..."

We passed another cell block.

"To state the obvious, I'm here to get you out."

"I know," she said.

"But you shouldn't be here!" her whisper was frantic. "If they find out what you are—"

"We'll be gone by then. I'll have you free by then."

Her bare feet splashed through water that had pooled at the corner as we took a small flight of stairs down deeper into the cells that were more like caves.

I'd been here once, when I was housed with a November. I'd been thirteen.

"Are you cold?" I asked. It was so stupid to ask.

"Obviously," she whispered back. "But don't do anything dumb to help me. Don't get caught."

Her reminder shouldn't have been necessary, but I had half a mind to give her my boots, my gloves, my ushanka with its new patch from Molnar's office.

"Ember...about your dad," I began.

"I'm not mad if that's what you're thinking. I'm not altogether surprised. I'm...confused. I'm just so confused why he didn't tell me or show me or explain—" Turuk pulled out his baton and knocked it against the bars of some of the cells as we passed. The echoing rattle made it harder to hear her.

She whispered again, louder. "Milena won't take the news well. She thinks lurpers are evil. She thinks…I don't know what learning what she is will do to her."

My mouth wouldn't open. I had to tell her. It was my duty to tell her, but how? When? Was sooner better?

I couldn't let some other guard tell her that her sister was dead. If news of her death got to Molnar, and he was the one to tell her, I didn't think she'd forgive me.

"Emberly, about Milena," I whispered, just as Turuk smashed his palka across another set of bars. The cells were empty, as all the lurpers were mining.

"Luka," Ember said. "I'm glad you're here. Don't be afraid to…you know…sell your status."

I hoped she didn't think I'd hit her with a palka. If she believed I'd do that, even as a ruse, she didn't know me at all.

"I may speak unkindly," I said.

"I can heal…" she whispered. "You told me Victors can heal."

"Don't—" I said it too loudly. Turuk turned around.

"Sir?"

"I was telling her, 'Don't.'" I said as the three of us stopped. The ceiling was low, I nearly had to hunch over to keep from dragging my ushanka along the wet, sloped walls. "She was reaching back."

"We're nearly there," Turuk said.

Emberly and I didn't risk whispering anymore. The walls were too good at projecting sounds and the reality was that both of us were in terrible danger.

Turuk stopped in front of her cell—the smallest one here with a threadbare mattress over a rusted frame.

"This is your home now," Turuk said.

With surprisingly steady hands, I unlocked the door and Emberly walked in, shooting me a scowl for good measure.

"Does she have a trunk?" I asked.

"Yes,"

"Go get it." My voice was demanding but kind. "I want to get more acquainted with our Victor here."

Turuk hesitated.

"Don't worry, comrade. She's contained and I'm armed." I tapped the hilt of the dagger at my waist. "I'm faster than you might think."

"Yes, Sir," he said.

"Victor," I shouted. Emberly turned to me from her pathetic bed. "Is your trunk locked?"

"No."

"No, Mr. Preemptive Officer!" I corrected. The angry, accented voice that came out of my mouth hardly seemed to belong to me.

"Sorry, Mr. Preemptive Officer." Her voice was something between defiant and meek. I couldn't quite place it. "No, the trunk is not locked, Sir."

I turned my back to Ember and directed Turuk to bring only the supplies from her trunk and we'd store them in the trunk here. "She hasn't been here long enough to make bringing the whole trunk here worth the effort."

Turuk saluted and walked away, apparently familiar with where he'd been. I watched him go, listening as the footsteps grew more and more distant.

I rushed to Emberly's cell and unlocked the door. It screamed as it opened, but there was no one around besides us to hear it.

"Ember," I said, not afraid to let my real voice reveal pain.

At the use of her name, she turned to me. I rushed toward her, and she reached out, catching me around the neck. I cradled her, brushing the hair away from her face. My lips found hers, and the taste of coal mingled with hope.

I wrapped my arms around her and let her bury her face in the crook of my neck.

"I'm so sorry," I whispered into her hair. It didn't smell of cinnamon, but I imagined it still did. That it smelled like anything other than the slippery mold that grew on the cell floors here. "It was my fault. I killed Velky—"

"It doesn't matter," she said between tasting my lips.

I moved back. *Would she want to kiss me if she knew what I knew?* "I told them you're a Victor. I thought they already knew. I thought that's why you were here."

"You told them?" She backed up.

"It earned their trust." I glanced into her eyes in the dim light from the lantern on the floor. "I never meant to betray yours."

A moment passed. A second. It felt longer. "I don't care that they know." She moved back to me, and I held her tightly. Closer, closer, I wanted to be closer. "Seems unfair that they would know before I did. Why didn't my dad tell me?"

"I don't know." I pulled her tighter. "But you can block pain and you can heal. Don't tell them you know. They'll keep pushing your limits and if they know—"

"I know," she said. "Luka, I blocked the pain when the captain hit me. I didn't feel a thing, I swear. And I've been healing anything internal, just keeping a few bruises for show." She must have seen the pain in my face. "I swear. I look bad, I know it, but..."

"I love you," I said quickly. "I love you Emberly Markos and I swear on the graves of my parents and on the mine that I'll get you out of here."

"You...you love me?"

"I love you. More than life. More than freedom."

She kissed me again, whispering between my lips. "That better be true since you just gave that up. You risked it all by being here. You should leave while you can."

"Don't say that!" I snapped. "I'm not going anywhere. I won't leave you alone. I'm your bodyguard, remember?" I grinned at her, and relief spread through me when she grinned back. "I will protect you."

"Luka when they find out what you are, who you are, and they will find out, they will kill both of us."

"They won't find out and I won't leave you."

"Why would you risk that?" she asked.

"If these are my last days as a living man, I want to spend them with you."

My mouth found hers again. "I love you too, Victor-27," she muttered against my mouth. "Luka. My Victor."

I lost myself in her kiss. I tangled my fingers into her hair like I had on Koliada, imagining we were back in Khizmit, snow falling around us instead of pieces of dirt and dust.

I was so lost between her tongue and teeth I didn't hear the boots hit the floor until it was nearly too late. No time to reach for my knife. No time to pretend that I hadn't been touching her, holding her, tasting her breath.

I had only one choice.

Korporal Turuk had already turned the corner, putting us in his view. Knowing that he could see us, I pinned Ember's hands to the cold wall of the cell above her head and kissed her again, this time running my tongue across her teeth.

"Sorry," I whispered. And drew my face away.

"Drivick?" Korporal Turuk asked. "What...what are you doing?"

"What does it look like?" I turned and grinned at him, keeping Emberly pinned to the wall. She tugged at her arms, and I held them tighter. With his eyes glued to me, I leaned in to kiss Emberly again and, as if on cue, she resisted.

"Stop!" she said.

With my free hand, I grabbed her chin to hold her face still and kissed her mouth roughly. She kept her lips hard, and her mouth shut. I pulled back again. I hated to kiss her like that. It shouldn't even have been called a kiss.

I resumed my accented voice. "If you give me lip again,

I'll give you lip again. Am I clear?" I hated how my voice sounded. Hateful. Demanding. I dropped her arms and stepped back, forcing myself to laugh as I met Turuk's gaze.

He was in utter shock.

Emberly spat on the ground and wiped furiously at her lips. I stepped away from Ember and pulled out my dagger.

"You may be a Victor, but that doesn't give you any power here. I'm in charge. Don't think otherwise!"

"You really kissed the lurper?" Turuk was incredulous.

I hoped I hadn't given him any ideas. I'd have to kill him if he touched her.

"What?" I asked. "She's still a girl, isn't she?"

"You get that close, and a Victor could kill you. You're lucky." Turuk paused before muttering, "Makes me think she must have liked it."

"Shut the skudge up!" Emberly shouted, her voice echoing.

I hurried over, wagging the dagger in her direction. "You bite your tongue, Victor. Or I'll bite it for you."

Emberly shrank back into the corner. Her body language showed fear, but her eyes issued a challenge. After saying the warning, I wondered if she'd spit back another insult, forcing me to make good on the threat.

She didn't.

With my back to Turuk, I softened my expression. "Forgive me," I whispered, maybe even too quietly for her to hear.

"I'm sorry, Chief Preemptive Officer," Emberly said, and though her tone was submissive, there was understanding in it. Gratitude in it for what I'd done. She stood slowly.

With Turuk beside me, I couldn't help. I couldn't touch her. I couldn't cradle her frozen fingers in mine and blow warm air onto them or let her dig her hands under my uniform top to warm her fingers on my skin. I could only look at her.

Turuk deposited her few items into her trunk and

marched out of the room. I backed out slowly, my heart breaking with each step I took away from Ember.

"I'm okay," Ember whispered.

"Did she say something?" Turuk asked.

"Probably talking to herself," I said. I jammed the key into the hole and bolted the door shut. It kept her in. It kept other inmates and crusters out.

I realized then that I didn't know how many guards held a key to her cell.

I rushed back to her door and gripped the bars dramatically. I wanted Turuk to think I was delivering another threat. Some menacing promise.

"If anyone comes into your cell that isn't me, kill them," I hissed. "Your head will tell you how. You'll have flashes of how to fight. If anyone approaches you besides me, follow the directions your mind gives you."

"Yes, Sir," Emberly replied, her voice sounding more afraid than I'd ever wanted to hear it.

"And don't forget it!" I shouted, walking back to join Turuk.

He and I left the stale air behind us as we turned the corner, enjoying the silence for a few minutes before Turuk stopped and leaned into the wall, breathing heavily.

"What's wrong?" I asked.

"All of this..." he heaved. "The Victor. I told you I was scared of her before I knew what she was. Is that, excuse me Sir, but is that why you asked me to do it? Something about making me face my fears?"

I'd forgotten he'd admitted that to me in Molnar's office.

"It's good to face your fears, soldier, but that's not why I requested you."

"Why did you then?"

"Because I can tell a trustworthy soldier when I see one. I can tell if someone will have my back or not. You will."

We began walking again, en route to our own barracks

where I'd spend the night beneath heavy blankets all while Emberly shivered in a cell.

"Sir," Turuk said. "You went into her cell without a comrade. You aren't supposed to—"

"I know," I said. "But if you'd heard her, you'd have understood. I know I'm not supposed to, but I wanted to send a few messages to her. First of all, I needed her to know that I wasn't afraid of her. By entering and making myself dominant, I sent that message in an unforgettable way. But I took it to the next level by getting up close and personal with her."

"That's one way of putting it."

"I like to follow rules, Turuk. I respect them, but I believe there are exceptions. There needs to be. I'd appreciate it if you don't tell Molnar, or anyone, about any of that."

I imagined how it would sound. *"I turned my back for five minutes and Drivick was in her cell, so tangled in her lips you'd think he was going to drown."*

"Sir, I have your back. I can make room for exceptions."

"Thank you, soldier." I'd wanted to use his name, but while in prison, the rules said I couldn't.

"She didn't fight you much though. Not like she fought Razin when he used his palka."

My whole body tensed. The sooner I could dispose of Razin, the better.

I said the only thing I could think of saying. "It seems her spirit is already breaking, then."

CHAPTER 26
EXPLOSIONS ARE LOUD

No one expected me to watch the Victor while she was in her cell, but it was my responsibility to oversee the delivery of her meals. As one of the higher-ranking guards in the prison, I immediately found that I drew attention. Perhaps I should have told Warden Molnar to keep me as a junior lieutenant.

He might not have listened.

Turuk and I walked back to our room in the guard's quarters, where I found a packaged sandwich waiting for me. Turuk and I entered quietly since there were four other guards in the room, all of whom were asleep.

The idea of leaving Emberly in the cell alone, all night, made me physically ill. I tossed and turned for the first few hours of the night, and then sat up, deciding her escape couldn't wait.

I moved out from beneath the heavy furs of my cot and pulled on my boots, lacing them with ease since my fingers were warm. All night my Lugar had sat beneath my pillow and now I pulled it out, did a quick inspection, and holstered it at my hip. My uniform top hung on the wall beside the bed on hook 14. My items belonged in bin 14.

There was some solace in knowing that even the guards

occasionally went by a number. I was buttoning the top three buttons when someone called me in a whisper.

"Oi," he said. I looked over to the bottom bunk in the corner and met the eyes of a guard with notably bushy eyebrows.

My stomach flipped.

Captain Caterpillar was staring at me.

"You're Drivick?" he asked.

"Yes, Sir," I said, assuming the slight accent I'd used here.

"Molnar told me what you said about Commander Markos. Is it true then? He's a skrag?"

I nodded and turned away, grabbing my ushanka off the shelf.

"Where are you going?"

"I need to get some air," I said.

"I'll come," he said. "You need a comrade."

He had questions. I looked for my preferred comrade. Turuk was asleep in his bed atop mine, snoring softly.

Caterpillar was already dressing.

"That's fine," I said. What other option was there?

There was a risk, a high risk, of a guard like Caterpillar recognizing me. Flak had, despite the change in my attire.

There was less of a risk of inmates recognizing me because they'd take one look at my silver birch leaf rank patch, or the Lugar at my hip, and drop their gazes.

I'd dropped my gaze with Caterpillar before. I wouldn't this time.

Without a plan, I exited the room and took a few steps down the hallway to wait for Caterpillar.

He emerged a moment after me, his boots making soft thuds on the stone floor as he approached. I whipped around and extended my hand to the captain as he finished pulling his own ushanka over his ears.

"What's your name, comrade?" I asked, keeping my voice quiet and accented.

"Captain Oravec," he said. "Peter Oravec."

I shook his hand roughly and then turned.

"You have questions about Markos, I take it," I said.

"Of course."

"I was assigned to the Lurper Legion, and Bolest showed up, announcing that Markos was, in fact, some other man. I wouldn't have believed it except I saw him do what only a lurper or skrag could do."

"What did he do?"

I halted and turned, looking at Captain Caterpillar Oravec's face in the dim light of the few sconces mounted on the wall ahead.

"What do you know about Victors, Sir?" I asked.

"They fight as well as they breathe. I've heard some can block pain or heal, but I never saw it."

"You've worked here a long time then? You must have seen Victor-27 at least once." I had to address the situation right away. Tempt fate into giving me away. Better he recognized me sooner rather than later.

"I worked alongside Markos for seven years, and I never saw him do anything that would make me question his loyalty."

"Did you ever see Victor-27 heal?" I asked, turning my face to him. I had a short beard, no scarf, and enough nerve to stare right into his face.

"He never learned how. That's why the captain in Predvoi was able to kill him. I could have killed him too, if I'd been given the authority or order."

I didn't scoff. He could have.

"Oravec, I watched Markos heal his own hand. I watched him close an injury with a mere thought."

"Are you sure?" The shadow of his bushy eyebrows danced across his forehead as he spoke.

"As I breathe, Markos is a traitor. He is planning a coup."

"Where are we going?" Oravec asked.

"You worked with Markos, so you know about his daughter. I will show you the Victor."

"Can she heal?"

I laughed lightly. "Can she? Undoubtedly, she could, if she knew. But she doesn't know. And we sure as slag won't tell her!" We passed the sconces and turned down the narrow hallway, shutting and locking the grate to the guards' quarters behind us.

"We aren't going to harass her tonight. But I want to check on her, and maybe when you see the fire of defiance in her eyes, you'll be able to tell she's not a mere girl. Maybe you'll see some similarity to Victor-27."

Perhaps I walked to Emberly's cell with too much confidence and too easily for someone who'd just arrived at Rhosivi. If Oravec suspected me of anything, it didn't show. He'd stared me in the eyes and not even a flicker of recognition crossed his face.

In the distance, a few conversations between inmates stopped as we approached. Some feigned sleep, and some stared at us. I glanced through the bars and realized I was looking for familiar faces. Not to say hello, but so I'd know what cells to avoid, when to turn my head the other way while walking down this hallway.

I didn't have a plan, but I knew I had to see Emberly. I couldn't sleep while she was back here in the darkness, all alone.

When we reached the end of the hallway, our footsteps and the steady drip of water from the ceiling to the floor were the only sounds.

Emberly must have heard us coming. When we approached her cell, she was sitting on her cot, staring at us with a blank expression.

"Victor," Oravec said. "Hands up, I'm coming in." Oravec then horrified me by grabbing a key from his belt, sticking it into the hole, and unlocking the door.

How many cells used the same key? Was it the same lock for each cell block? In theory, how many guards held a key to Ember's cell?

I entered right behind.

"Did you know your father is a traitor?" Oravec said.

"Maybe you're the traitor," Emberly said, her voice clear. Had she slept at all?

"Do not disrespect me, lurper!" Oravec said, pulling out his palka. He didn't move to strike her. I didn't move to stop him.

"What are you doing here?" she asked, her gaze flitting toward me before setting back on the palka in Oravec's hand.

"Show me your wrist."

Ember flipped her hand over and showed him. It was easy to see the dark V, even with so little light.

"Is it true?" Oravec asked. "Your wrist has a V, so I assume they tested your blood. Are you sure it doesn't come from your mother?"

"My mother is a counselor in the Parliament House. They were among the first to do rapid tests."

Oravec worked his jaw and twisted his boot into the ground. The small motion sent his silhouette dancing on the inner wall.

"What do you want?" Ember asked again. "You worked here with my dad, didn't you? You don't want to believe that he's a Victor, because then you'd have to think of him as the enemy, but you respected him."

"Shut it, lurper," Oravec said.

"I am a Victor, and my dad is a Victor, and he was the whole time you took his orders and followed his directives. My father is one of the best leaders in Khizmit, which is why they made him a high warden and then a commander!" she shouted, beginning to rouse many of the inmates in the surrounding cells. "Being a Victor doesn't make him the enemy. It doesn't undo all the things you admire about him. He's a Victor *and* he's a good man."

Oravec raised his palka and I found myself between it and Ember at the same time.

"Sir," I said, my tone playful.

"Step aside, soldier," he said through gritted teeth.

"A word first, Sir," I said. "Then you can come back if you want to."

Emberly was breathing heavily; her eyes were frantic as she looked at me.

Oravec spat at her feet and followed me out of the cell. He shut it, locked it, and walked down the hallway with me.

"What the skudge—"

"Sir," I said patiently. "The more often a Victor is hurt, the more likely you are to trigger their defense mechanisms. What I'm saying is that if you beat her, it could awaken her abilities to fight, to block pain or heal. We don't want her to know what she can do. We must do everything we can to keep her ignorant of her potential. If she knew she could heal, she'd risk injury to us, or kill us to escape."

Oravec twisted the palka in his hands. "We must use fear as our primary weapon against her."

"Yes, Sir. That's what Bolest's report suggested."

"You've seen the report?"

"No Sir, but I was assigned alongside Captain Kral while working with the Lurper Legion. He's the one—"

"I know who he is," Oravec said, jealously. "I wouldn't be surprised if he was a high captain by next month, the rate he's going."

"So, we agree, fear is the best tactic?" I verified.

"Yes," Oravec said. "I've seen enough tonight. You coming back to bed?"

"Not yet," I said. "I think I'll keep her awake a few more hours before she has to work."

"Smart," he said. "If you're up for it. You know you have to keep up with her all day tomorrow?"

"Don't worry about me, comrade." I clapped him on the shoulder. "I'll be back soon. I won't open the cell."

Oravec rubbed his hand across the back of his hairy neck. "I never took Markos as a traitor," he said quietly. "I didn't want it to be true. What will become of Khizmit when our best leaders turn out to be skrags?"

I answered honestly. "I don't know."

Oravec walked away, disappointment in his every step.

I was on my way back to Emberly's cell when a small voice from a cell on my right stopped me cold.

The voice was soft but distinct.

"Victor," it called.

I rushed toward the cell, horrified that someone might hear. Someone knew me. Even in this darkness, in my uniform, without the scar—someone knew me.

"Who are you?" I asked, pressing close to the door. A small boy stepped from the corner into the light that came in through the slits in the bars.

"Victor," the boy whispered, his eyes widening. He pulled off his cap, as if in a gesture of reverence, and held it over his heart. "You...graduated? Are you a vaznov?" He asked it so innocently. "Your face. How did you...the scar that was on your face. It's gone!"

"Shh," I hushed him. His cellmate was sleeping, as were the boys in the nearest cells. Oravec was, blessedly, far enough away now that I could only faintly hear his footsteps when I focused.

The boy still had his pants cuffed, but I could see from his shirt that he'd filled out since I'd last seen him.

"Mike," I whispered, having forgotten the number associated with his tag. There was no reason to pretend I wasn't myself. He knew me. "Did you keep my secret? About when I helped you find coal?"

He nodded enthusiastically.

"Then you can keep another?"

He nodded again, a bit less excitedly as a look of concern crossed his face.

"I'm…pretending to be someone else here. I'm a real lieutenant, but I'm here, not as a guard. For other reasons."

His expression lifted. His smile was so big his teeth caught the light from the wall sconce.

"You're going to get us out." He stated it like it was a fact.

Coal is black.

Pickaxes are sharp.

Explosions are loud.

Victor-27 came back to set the lurpers in Rhosivi free.

"Yes," I heard myself say. "I'm going to get you out. But you have to play along. You have to pretend you don't know me. That you hate me. That you fear me."

His smile remained on his face as he nodded again. "I somehow always knew you'd come back."

"I'm here now," I said, glancing over to Emberly. I'd get her to safety, but I had more to do here than that.

I had to get these lurpers free. They'd help us overthrow Khizmit, but even more importantly, they deserved freedom.

Freedom wasn't going to find them. Freedom isn't assertive or aggressive. Freedom doesn't come for you the way fear does.

Freedom must be fought for.

Good thing that I'm so skudging good at fighting.

CHAPTER 27
BLACK TEARS

I NEEDED LOCKBOX. Congratulations to me for being some lurper-hybrid who could throw hands better than any one of the inmates in this godforsaken prison, but I'd need more than that to get Ember and the rest of the lurpers out of this hole. What I needed was a plan, and Lockbox would have been the ideal guy for the job.

I sighed. I wasn't the only one who needed him. Markos needed him more.

Lockbox was good—very good—but he wasn't the only Oscar. I didn't want to interact with too many lurpers here, since I wasn't sure if I'd see someone else who recognized me. With Turuk always keeping a close eye on me, I couldn't exactly go around looking through paperwork for an Oscar without a good reason.

What was a good reason?

I laid awake in my bed for hours after talking to Mike, shifting back and forth, too warm beneath the blanket, too stifled by my concerns to get comfortable.

I needed to find a way to get lots of lurpers out of the prison, and I believed an Oscar would know just how to do it.

If Oravec hadn't intercepted me, I'd have broken Emberly

out. I'd have left Mike and the others behind under Warden Molnar's care.

Care. What a stupid way to put it.

I cared and it was possible that I was the only one who could help them.

But how was I going to get hundreds of inmates out of Rhosivi? A full-on prison riot wasn't going to work. It didn't seem to be working for Vazenia.

I tried to think like an Oscar. The biggest threats to my plan were someone blowing my cover, or someone hurting Emberly, necessitating that I blow my own cover.

Who was most likely to hurt her? I'd stopped Oravec. I didn't think he'd go back to her cell, key or not, to harass her.

Razin had already hurt her. My plan with Razin was to lure him into the mine and disarm him near a Romeo, assuming the Romeo would end Razin for me.

It was risky, but I could play it off like an accident. I didn't have to be the one to dispatch Razin—I could feed him to the wolves.

The image reminded me of Dulka. Of my Victor predecessor at Predvoi. I'd get Razin to come with me, I'd hear his cries for help, but I'd come too late.

Problem solved.

That problem anyway.

The idea of finding Razin all bloodied up brought another problem to mind.

Milena was dead and I had to tell Emberly.

Beneath the furs and blankets of my bed, I dug my hand into the pocket of my pants to find the small pieces of metal I'd placed reverently in my pocket back in Khizmit. I fingered them, thinking they'd give me peace or a plan.

They did neither.

I'd give them to Emberly tomorrow. As much as the news would gut her, I had no right to keep the information from her.

Tomorrow, I'd find an Oscar and ask for his help. I'd tell Emberly what happened to Milena, and I'd set up the circumstances for Razin to have a fatal accident.

Tomorrow, I thought, *is going to be a busy day.*

Emberly was outside, sorting coal and stuffing it into rough 30-kilo bags. The sun was warm, and I hoped it would help her warm up from the frigid night in the mine.

I stood at a distance, Turuk at my side, watching her weigh and reweigh the bags. Watching alone made me want to burn this whole place to oblivion. I was tense as I watched the girl I loved slave away sorting coal for Khizmit.

"Are you okay?" Turuk asked, leaning in so no one, not even the other guards standing nearby could hear.

"I'm fine," I growled.

"You didn't sleep last night."

"I couldn't."

"If you need to—"

"I'm fine, Turuk," I snapped.

He nodded slowly and then I finally looked at him, tearing my gaze from Emberly to do so.

"Drivick, Sir," Turuk said. "I know you're mad. You were betrayed, but you can't let it eat you up like this. I support you in getting retribution, but don't let it ruin you, okay? You're a good man. I can tell that much."

I looked back to Ember.

"If it's going to destroy you, just kill her and get it over with. Move on, eh?" Turuk said.

I snapped my attention to him. I didn't blink. "I don't want to kill her. And make it known that I will mutilate anyone who touches her with a palka or a fist or otherwise. She is my responsibility. My prisoner. My Victor. Is that clear?" My voice wasn't my own. It was savage.

"Yes, Sir," Turuk said. "Sorry, Sir." Turuk shrunk back, and I nearly felt sorry for having scolded him.

But then I looked back to Ember. I felt sorry for *her*, not for the armed crusters who kept her here.

All day I watched her work, all day I barked orders at her, and all day Turuk eyed me with concern.

Once I thought I saw Foxtrot-12, my final cellmate here, and turned the other way.

At noon I decided Emberly had to have a drink, so I announced that she'd earned some water. I had to hold myself back from assisting her in any way I could. I wanted to hand her the bottle, tell her to sit down in the shade, and offer her one of the sandwiches a korporal had brought by for all the officers to have for lunch.

Turuk followed me as I walked closer to Emberly. She was sitting on the ground, her back to a large steel pole that supported the small canopy that provided shade to the offi-cers. I pulled out my palka since it would give me an excuse to get close to her.

She wiped her hand across her face, the small droplets of water making the coal dust smudge in a thick black line.

I had to dig deep to find something to say. All the things that came to mind were questions like "How are you?" and "Do you need something to eat?" or "I hate to see you here." What I finally came up with was, "So, Victors get thirsty, too? Just like everyone else."

I stopped directly in front of her. With the tip of my palka I lifted her chin straight into the air so she would look at me. Keeping a menacing expression, I squatted, so my face would be near hers.

"I hate to see you like this. I don't know how long I can keep this up."

"You have to keep it up," she whispered. "Or we both die."

"Ember, I have to tell you something. It's a bad time. There are people around."

"There will always be people around," she said. "There is no privacy for prisoners."

"It's about Milena," I said, and my voice caught briefly as I said her name. I'd slipped back into my normal voice.

Ember's eyes told me she suspected the worst right away.

"I'm so sorry," I said, my heart breaking all over again. Feeling Turuk's gaze on me, I hardened my expression.

"Sir," Turuk said, taking a few steps closer to us.

"You crusters are all the same," Emberly spat at me. I didn't move. Her voice was barely a whisper. "Luka, I swear to the Gods, you're going to get us killed."

What did she want me to do? In that instant, she was on her feet lunging for the palka. I moved it out of her reach and used my free hand to grab the front of her striped clothes. The metal pole made a hollow ping as the back of her head hit it.

I pinned her there.

"Don't," I growled to her. Turuk had raised his palka, and though it trembled in his hands, he'd been ready to come to my aid.

I gave him a quick nod, letting him know I had it under control and strapped my palka back into my holster. With one hand pinning her in place, I dug the other into my pocket and grabbed the little pieces of metal I'd saved for her.

"You should be careful, little girl," I snarled, grabbing her wrists.

"I'm sorry, Sir," she said loud enough for the surrounding inmates and guards to hear.

"Open your hand and look when you're ready," I whispered tucking the earrings between her fingers into her right fist. "Get back to work," I said loudly. And I pushed her to the ground.

I turned my back to her, heart-breaking in a way that I didn't think I'd ever heal from.

I walked away.

She was right. I risked her life by being kind. I risked being replaced by someone who would be worse than I was.

She needed me to be good at my job. And my job was to keep her in line.

Turuk didn't say a word as he resumed his spot beside me in the shade of the small metal canopy. The mood had been somewhat neutral but now that I'd had my altercation with Emberly, the inmates seemed on edge. The guards fingered their palkas. The two inmates on my right worked faster and their small side conversation about who had vyco capsules stored in the toe of their boots ended abruptly.

"Where is Razin?" I asked Turuk.

"Not sure. Why?"

"Haven't seen him around," I said.

"Do you want me to go ask about him?" I turned to face Turuk. There was something about his face that gave him a look of innocence and sincerity. His white eyelashes were short. His skin was so pale I thought he might burn up at first exposure to sunlight.

"How old are you, Turuk? How long have you been working here?"

"I've been here almost a year, Sir. I'm 22 years old. How about you, Sir?"

"Old enough. Young enough." I said, looking away from him. "Did you know Commander Markos?"

"I met him a few times, yes. I worked under Warden Velky most of the time."

"Something is off here. I get the sense something strange is going on." I said it to give him a reason to get Razin. Maybe then, when things went badly for the crusters, they'd think I'd predicted rather than orchestrated it. "I want to ask Razin a few things."

Turuk nodded enthusiastically. "I'll ask around for him, Sir." He didn't ask if I needed anyone with me while I watched Emberly. There were three other guards at the other end of the tables; whether they'd help me was up for debate, but I didn't need it.

I knew the moment Emberly had reached into her pockets and looked at the small fox earrings that had belonged to Milena because of the soft sob that broke out of her chest.

Maybe I should have waited.

The guards across from me pulled out their palkas.

Emberly dropped to her knees and buried her face in her coal-coated hands to sob. Her cries drew the attention of everyone in the vicinity.

As she was my ward, I approached.

"What is it?" I asked gruffly. "I'm sorry," I whispered.

"Don't touch me!" Emberly screamed, and I couldn't be sure if it was an act or if the guttural demand came from her broken heart. "Leave me alone!"

I stepped away as one of the guards, a sergeant, stepped forward.

"Leave her alone," I said casually. "She'll just be out here later if she wants to waste her time like that."

"Is she hurt?" he asked. *Was his tone strictly curiosity or was that a hint of compassion?*

I shouted just as loudly as Emberly had. "She's a Victor. It doesn't matter, does it? Get back to work, all of you!"

The inmates and the guards all seemed to take their tasks a bit more seriously.

Twenty minutes later, Emberly stood up.

Her tears had left tracks down her filthy face. She wiped it with her linen shirt and began working again.

Between the *thunks* of the coal hitting the table and the shift of the burlap bags, I heard her ask, "How?"

In a low whisper, I began to tell her. With every new bit of information, she took a moment to wipe the fresh tears that streamed down her face.

An hour later, after I'd watched Emberly go through

several more bags of coal, I'd told her everything. I was no ventriloquist, but I'd done my best to keep my lips from moving much as I'd whispered about Kasia and Erik.

Turuk had just taken his place back at my side when Emberly's soft whisper cut through the sounds again.

"Thank you, Luka, for bringing these to me."

For a moment our gaze met, and I bowed my head to her, ever so slightly.

Turuk gave her a long look and then cleared his throat. It was no wonder. She had coal smeared across her arms and face, painted from her tears as if they had been inky rather than clear. Even her red lips had streaks of black across them. Still, somehow, a look of defiance and strength looked back at me from her eyes.

"Sir?" Turuk asked.

"What?"

"I just—" Turuk looked incredulous as he searched for the words. "I just didn't know a Victor could cry."

CHAPTER 28
THE NEW OSCAR

Turuk and I returned Ember to her cell early. I said it was because she'd been emotional and unpredictable. I just thought she needed some time alone. When we left, maybe she'd hold the gold foxes in her hand, remembering how they'd hung from Milena's ears back when she'd been playing the spoons through dinner.

"I found Razin," Turuk said as we turned the corner, leaving Emberly's cell block behind us. "He's interrogating the new Oscar."

A new Oscar. I pictured a small eight-year-old boy, fresh from the Children's Detention Center. Not sure how much help he would be to me, but an Oscar was brilliant. I wouldn't underestimate his mind's abilities.

Besides, I pitied anyone being interrogated at the hands of Captain Razin.

"Where?"

"Medical clinic. Why?"

"I just don't think he should have all the fun," I said.

"Do you want to eat first?"

I smiled, "Food can wait. This can't! You go ahead. The Victor is in her cell for the night. Your time is your own until morning."

With the dismissal, I ran ahead of him, skirting to avoid a few inmates in manacles who were being led down the hallway in the opposite direction.

I threw open the door to the medical clinic, expecting to find Doctor Traft sitting there, his sad, oval face unchanged at my sudden entry.

My jaw could have hit the floor.

Sitting in the chair, cheeks redder than ever, sat Lockbox.

Lockbox looked at me, released an exasperated sigh, and said, "Oh, great, now you're interrogating me in shifts. Looks like your replacement is here, Captain." He sounded impossibly disrespectful for the situation.

"What the skudge is he doing here?" I asked.

Lockbox, here in Rhosivi. Here with Captain Razin.

"Do you know him?" Razin asked.

"No," I said, sparing him only a glance. "I heard you had an Oscar back here. I thought it was from the CDC. Not an older one. Where did he come from?"

What story had Lockbox told? What clever tale had he invented to make his being here make any sense at all?

"It doesn't matter who asks me," Lockbox said, "it won't make my memory come back."

Memory loss. That was his play? Of all the brilliant plans he could have contrived, and he was going with memory loss? I fought a grin. You can't mess up a story if there's no story to tell.

"How would an Oscar get memory loss?" Razin asked me, sounding sincere in his question.

"Maybe he overloaded it?" I asked. "I heard that's what Dulka was trying to do at Predvoi. Maybe this one has a smaller capacity than others and he got burned out."

"Is that possible?" Razin asked.

I shrugged. "Can I question him?" I asked.

"Go ahead."

I stepped back into the clinic and stared at Lockbox. He

was smiling, ear to ear, as if he didn't have a care in the world. As if the bruises I saw blooming on his face were hickies from lovers.

"Who are you?" I asked.

"I don't know."

"Where are you?"

"Well, the sign out front said Rhosivi, so I'm going to go with that."

"The mouth on this one," I said to Razin, who stood by the door.

"Do you know who I am?"

"You look like a guard, a soldier. I'll guess, based on your fancy hat and the way you walked in here like you owned the place, that you're someone important?"

How far was he willing to take his memory loss charade?

"You don't know who you are?"

"No,"

"Listen up, slagsack. I'm an officer. When you answer my questions, you need to say 'Sir.'"

"Why?" Lockbox lifted his chin defiantly. "Do you know who I am?"

"I know you're an Oscar." I gestured to his wrist.

"And what the hell is that supposed to mean?"

"You tell me. Tell me what you know. What do you think about all this?" I couldn't risk ruining his cover story, so I had to know what it was.

Lockbox sighed, oh so impatiently.

"You guys, the ones in fancy hats with leaves and slag and whatever, you're in charge here. The guys like me with ink on the wrist are prisoners. This is a prison and mine. Maybe a social experiment. Maybe I'm a dangerous dude. You seem to think so, based on these!" he held up his shackles. "I woke up getting dragged through the snow and they dropped me here. Your hospitality is seriously lacking, for the record."

"Hospitality?" I echoed. He was bold to take things so far.

"You're an inmate. A lurper. I'm a lieutenant. You do what I tell you when I tell you. You work for me now."

"Sir, yes sir!" he said mockingly.

I threw a warning look his way. Razin was going to beat him if he didn't dial down.

"Why?" Lockbox asked. "Why does it say O-16? Why are you calling me an Oscar? How many Oscars are there? How long will I be here? What do I have to do to go home?"

"This is your home," I replied. "I'm not in the business of answering questions. You'll have to rely on the kindness of fellow lurpers to tell you the rest."

Razin nodded in approval of my answer.

I stepped away from Lockbox, back to Razin.

"In Predvoi Bolest was doing research on placing an Oscar with a Victor," I said. "Captain Kral told me about the studies. To honor Bolest's memory, it is my belief that we continue his work on bloodlust and Oscars."

Razin bristled. "You want this Oscar to room with the Victor?"

"I do," I said. "I'm going to take him back to Cell 42, Block G, and introduce the Victor to her new cellmate."

"We don't have any record of an Oscar-16 here. Or anywhere. Ever."

They'd either never found the original Oscar-16, he or she had died in Zalar, or they'd never had kids. And yet, here we had Lockbox with his new tattoo.

"I'm taking him. No use interrogating someone with no memory. If it returns, you'll be the first to know. I prefer research. I'm happy to leave all interrogation procedures in your capable hands."

Razin shook his head. "You need permission from Molnar to take the Oscar."

I removed all playfulness from my voice. "High Warden Molnar told me I could have anything I needed. Anything I wanted. And I want this lurper with brain rot put in the cell with our Victor."

"I think I know that word. Victor," Lockbox said from around the corner.

I hurried over to Lockbox. "You know what a Victor is?"

He fidgeted with his hands, the way he'd done when trying to remember something. "No, but I think I like it. I feel positively about that word, Victor."

I laughed. Razin uncuffed Lockbox's ankles.

"You really must have brain rot, lurper, if you think a Victor is a *good* thing."

Razin pulled his palka as Lockbox stood. I motioned for the door and Lockbox took a few steps forward. He moved slowly, stiffly. Had he walked here? Impossible.

It was obvious that he was tired. When had he last eaten?

"Come on, you dumb little lurper. You're mine now," I said, giving him a little push. I'd get him food as soon as I could.

Lockbox walked slowly down the hallway, his shadow flitting in front of him and then behind him as we passed a few of the low lights in the walls.

"I'm so happy to see you," I said as soon as Lockbox and I had a moment alone in the hallways.

"Why?" he asked, one eyebrow quirked.

"I missed you! How did you get here? Why'd you come here?"

Lockbox halted.

He shot me a glare, the shadows making his face angry and dark. "Don't play like that with me. I might not know who I am, but I know a fraud when I see one."

"Excuse me?" I whispered.

"You think you're gonna play nice with me now, and I'll start to trust you. The captain back there is supposed to be the bad guy. The villain. You're supposed to be my friend, earn my trust, all that slag. Right? Well, that won't work on me."

His face shone with immovable defiance. He played the part perfectly.

"Lockbox," I said. He must have known something I didn't. He didn't think it was safe here yet. I kept up the ruse. "You think you're so smart, don't you? Well, one of your first lessons here will be humility."

I gave him a little push and walked faster. The sooner we got some privacy, the sooner he could tell me what he was doing here. I wouldn't take him to his cell. Too many ears.

I'd take him somewhere actually private. Quiet.

I took a turn through Block E and then pulled Lockbox through an outer door. The air was mercilessly cold.

Lockbox wasn't dressed for this. We'd have to be fast. At the base of the guard towers sat a small wooden shack with just enough room for two people. Only three of the towers were currently occupied since the inmates were locked up for the night.

I threw the door open on the tower nearest us and Lockbox hurried in, shivering.

There was a ladder in the middle to climb up to the open platform, but the trap door was shut, sealing out the snow and wind. Still, it wasn't much warmer here than it was outside, and the thin wooden walls gave little protection.

A narrow shelf held a discarded fur coat and a broken palka. I threw the fur coat over to Lockbox as he shut the door.

"Here," I said.

"Interrogating me in the cold w—won't change anything. You crusters all have slag for brains!"

"Lockbox," I said, placing my hands on his shoulders. "It's just us here."

"What does that mean? That I should be scared you're gonna lock me in here tonight? Not quite the warm welcome—"

"It means you can drop the charade." I reached out to hug

him and he scoffed before hitting me with his cuffed wrists. "What the hell, man?"

"Don't touch me," he said, genuine fear in his narrowed eyes.

"Where are your glasses?" I asked. "Can you see me?"

"I can see enough."

"Lockbox, cut the slag. What the skudge is going on?"

"What do you want from me? If I say, 'Yes Sir, you're so skudging smart, Sir!' can I go inside? You said there was a cell, and a bed, however slaggy, sounds pretty great right now."

A wave of nausea overtook me, churning my gut. I placed my hand on the wall to keep myself upright.

"You mean," I asked slowly, "that you're not faking it?"

"Oh, I'm faking compliance, and submission if that's what you mean."

"Lockbox, come on!" I said. "No one's around."

"Listen up, Mister Captain, Lieutenant, whatever you are. I don't know you and I don't know Lockbox. Can we just get the skudge out of here so I can get some rest?"

"You don't know who I am?" I asked, my voice as normal as I could possibly make it.

"I know who you are," he said confidently. "You're a skudging dense cruster."

"No, I'm...I'm your friend..." I said. It wasn't smart for me to tell him. I couldn't trust him like this.

Lockbox reached out and looked at my wrist. His fingers were icy on my skin. He looked up at my hat. "You want to take advantage of my memory loss, but there's one thing I know to be certain. You and I were never friends."

CHAPTER 29
A SINGLE MEMORY

Lockbox walked beside me, glowering, questioning my motives. It was fine saying things like, "You'll learn humility here," or calling him a dumb lurper with brain rot when it was part of a ruse. But this was no ruse.

Lockbox really had lost his memory.

How? When? Was it permanent? I'd have asked Lockbox if he had any idea, but he didn't trust me.

What course of action would I take from here? Gain his trust as a lieutenant? Doing that put me at risk. By telling him he and I were friends, I'd already put myself and my whole plan to get us out of here at risk.

He'd become friends with Emberly, and then either his memory would return, or he'd come to trust me through her.

Should Emberly and I keep our relationship a secret from him until he sees me as a friend again? Would he feel betrayed if she wasn't honest with him?

If I took him aside and told him everything from our time together at Predvoi and on The Outskirts, would it help him remember? Or would confessing everything to him just put everyone here at risk?

"There are lots of other Oscars," I said, keeping my slight

accent, but making my tone friendlier. Not too friendly. Not too cruel. "Lockbox is what you'll go by."

"Do you usually name your pets?" he asked.

"Listen, Lockbox," I said, lowering my voice and turning to face him. I didn't want to seem menacing, but I was. I towered over him. I was armed with a palka and a Lugar. My arms were twice the size of his and he could probably tell, from every movement, that I knew how to fight. I knew how to hurt people.

"What?" he asked, impatiently.

"I'm not asking you to trust me. Or believe what I tell you, but I must warn you to be a little more compliant with the other guards. If you publicly disrespect me, I'll have to discipline you."

"Justify yourself however helps you sleep at night," he said.

"Like that! You can't speak like that to the guards here."

"I'm not afraid of you," he said.

"Yes, you are," I said.

He took one faltering step backward. If I didn't scare him, someone else would. "You—Oscars—you protect yourselves by knowing things. By having information people want. You recruit protection by maintaining leverage. But you lost your memory. You lost that advantage. And you must be terrified. You are vulnerable now, more vulnerable than you've ever been. You don't know your name, why you're here, what you're doing. You're lost in your own head! You're terrified."

Lockbox stared at me and blinked his eyes a few times.

"Besides that, your vision is slag. You can't even see!"

"What gave it away?" he asked.

"I know things," I said, echoing one of his lines from Predvoi. "I know a lot of things about a lot of things."

He blinked.

"Just, be careful." I turned him back down the hallway.

"Come on. Bed's this way." He glanced toward me, eyes clearly unfocused, and began walking again.

"What's your angle?" he asked a few moments later. "What do you want?"

I hesitated. "You're smart. I think after some observation, provided we can get you some glasses, you'll figure it out for yourself."

A few more steps took me to the door of Emberly's cell.

Emberly was asleep when I approached her cell door. Usually, she was sitting up, roused by footsteps of approaching guards, but my guess is that she'd cried long and hard even after I'd shut her in.

I had a few misgivings about placing Lockbox in with Emberly now that he didn't have his memories of her helping him back in Khizmit, but he wasn't a mean kid. He was good. Pure. Smart. Losing his memories wouldn't alter his personality, right?

I unlocked the door and pulled Lockbox in beside me. Emberly's eyelids fluttered open. As she caught sight of Lockbox, she sat up.

"What—"

"This is your new cellmate, Victor. He is an Oscar with complete memory loss."

Emberly's gaze went from me to Lockbox.

"Really?" she whispered to him.

"Really," he said, warily.

"His name is Lockbox," I said, unsure what the consequences would be if she revealed she knew it already. "Keep to your sides of the cell. I'll be back in the morning."

I removed all the cuffs on Lockbox and backed out of the cell.

He watched me as closely as he could.

I hurried away, turned the corner, and then stopped. I calibrated my hearing, listening for their conversation.

"Do I know you?" Lockbox asked. He must have dropped into his bed based on the creak of the metal.

"Do you?" Ember asked.

"I'm not in the mood for this."

"The mood for what?"

"Games. Are you really even an inmate? A Victor? Or are you a mole, planted here under the guise of being a Victor to gain my trust."

"Why would being a Victor gain your trust?"

"I told them I had a positive emotional connection to that title. I don't trust that lieutenant."

Me. He didn't trust me.

"I'm not trying to play games with you, Lockbox."

"Then just be straight with me—who are you?"

"My name is Emberly Markos. I was recently identified as a Victor. I grew up in Khizmit, but my father was, apparently, a Test Criminal. He's a commander."

"Markos," Lockbox echoed. "That name feels familiar."

"We've met," Emberly said. "In Khizmit. You were once kept as an Informational Slave in the Grand Palace. You escaped and I helped you. But the name feels familiar because you know my father, Pedrick Markos."

"Pedrick Markos," Lockbox said. "Maybe."

"Does that guard who dropped me here know that you and I have met?"

Emberly didn't reply right away. "I don't know what that guard wants me to tell you and what he wants me to keep secret."

"Why do you give a slag what he wants?"

"Because he holds my life in his hands." Her voice was sincere with just enough fear that I caught it. "Head Warden Molnar gave him express authority to kill me on a whim."

I couldn't see Lockbox's face, but I'd seen him thinking enough to easily picture his lips pursing.

"I'll see what I remember in the morning."

I waited another five minutes listening to some inmates in the distance mutter, cough, and curse in their sleep before I wandered back toward the clinic.

———

Traft gave me five different pairs of glasses. Turuk carried them, and I carried two lanterns from the supply cabinet as we hurried down the hallway to the cells. Morning light struggled to enter the prison, only succeeding in bringing a few fragile beams in through some high windows that had been cut for ventilation. They were covered in ice and snow, but the light came through. Light is persistent. We'd need the lanterns when we got to the mine. Thin glass and wire made it lightweight, and it could have been broken and turned into half a dozen shanks for inmates to swap, but Lockbox and Emberly weren't normal inmates. As long as Turuk didn't object, I'd give the smaller one to Emberly before sending her into the mouth of the mine.

Lockbox and Emberly had clearly been discussing something important when Turuk and I arrived, but they'd cut their conversation short before I'd gotten in range. The other sounds of the morning disturbed the air.

"Morning, lurpers," I said, thinking that a friendly tone paired with an insult made for an appropriate balance. "I brought you a gift," I said, meeting Lockbox's gaze.

At my command, Turuk extended one of the pairs of glasses through the slim bars.

Confused, Lockbox took them and tried them on, blinking a few times.

"Second pair," Turuk said, putting a pair with thick black frames into the cell.

Lockbox swapped pair one with pair two.

"Which of the two is better?" I asked.

He tapped the frames of the second pair.

Turuk and Lockbox passed all five pairs back and forth until Lockbox had tried them each on.

"Which one is best?" I asked.

"The third pair," he replied.

I nodded and Turuk passed that pair of glasses back into the cell.

"And the second?" I motioned to the pair with thick black frames.

"Those are good too."

"Keep both. That way you have a backup."

"Why?" Lockbox said, taking the pair from Turuk.

"If we wanted our inmates to be blind, we'd blind you. You're more helpful when you can see."

"Why are you talking like that?" he asked, adjusting his glasses and giving me a long, hard look.

"Like what?" I said, making my 'w' sound like a 'v'.

"You didn't sound like that last night."

"I don't think you have the most reliable memory," I jibed. "Let's go. Boots on."

With some difficulty, I directed Emberly and Lockbox through the prison and out into the frigid morning air and sunshine with a toneless voice. I pretended not to know or care that Emberly's teeth chattered as we hurried toward the black mouth of the mine. Just like I pretended that I forgot my breakfast.

"Slag," I said, stopping suddenly in the prison yard. Most of the inmates were still waking up or making their way to grab breakfast.

"What is it, Sir?" Turuk asked.

"In my haste to get these lurpers working, I neglected to grab breakfast."

"For yourself, or for them?" he asked. Perhaps he was on to my plan.

"Both, but I'm not worried about them. Lurpers can work

without food for a good long while before it becomes a problem."

Lockbox started, "What the—"

"Shut up!" I said, cutting Lockbox short before he could say something unforgivable. "You'll speak when addressed. Victor, review the prison rules with him."

"Now, Mr. Chief Preemptive Officer?" she asked, arms trembling even as the sun shone off her light skin.

"Yes, lurper. Now!"

I took a step toward her, attempting to look intimidating as I shielded her from the brunt of the wind as she began:

"In order to qualify for graduation, prisoners must adhere to the following rules: One: Prisoners must maintain silence after lights out. Two: Prisoners must keep their cells clean, beds made, and personal items secured within their trunks."

Turuk's breath was visible as he exhaled, glancing between the prisoners, and then back to me.

"Would you like me to go grab breakfast for you?" he asked quietly.

"Unless you want to stay with them while I run back?" I asked. With a glance at the top of the guard towers, I added, "You won't be alone."

Turuk shook his head. "No Sir, I'll get it for you."

"Thank you," I said, turning back as Lockbox began speaking.

His eyebrows were pulled together tight in concentration as he recited a rule. "Prisoners who fraternize with guards, wardens, or other staff members will be subject to severe disciplinary action." He looked my way. *Was his memory coming back?*

"Let's get to the mine." I gave Emberly a nudge and we hurried toward the mine. "Turuk will be back soon, and for all I know, other guards will bring more lurpers down here."

Emberly and Lockbox hurried, stumbling over some of the large chunks of ice in the path.

Heat seemed to come from the mouth of the mine, as I remembered, and Emberly scurried through, beneath the large beams, past the empty mine cart.

"What do you want?" Lockbox demanded.

"A lot of things," I said, dropping my accent. "I want your memory to come back, first of all. I want to know why you're here. I want to know where Pedrick Markos is."

"You want to make out with her," Lockbox said, gesturing to Emberly.

I fell silent. Emberly froze.

"Excuse me?" I asked.

"You told me to observe. Now you're upset that I did?"

I scoffed.

"Inexplicably, she wants to make out with you too."

At this, I laughed, and my voice carried through the mine.

"Oh," Lockbox said. "Again. You have...I...Well, this is awkward. Should I see myself out?" He gestured back toward the mine entrance.

Emberly hurried toward me, and without taking my eyes off Lockbox, I set the two lanterns down on the ground and wrapped my arms around her. "Don't speak a word of this to Turuk," I said to Lockbox.

Lockbox raised his eyebrows as if daring me to tell him what to do, but it was good enough for me.

I kissed Emberly's cold mouth, planted kisses across her cold eyelids, and then rested my lips on the center of her forehead. "I'm so sorry about Milena," I whispered.

"Lu—"

I silenced her with a kiss. "Not that," I whispered into her mouth. "He doesn't believe we're friends."

Emberly dropped her head to my shoulder, giving me a clear view of Lockbox and the mine entrance beyond.

"Well, what do your observations tell you?"

"Plenty."

"Lockbox, give me more than that." I grabbed Emberly's hand, warming her fingers.

"All I see is fraternization to the fullest extent."

"Lockbox," Emberly pled. "Please. Try to remember!"

Lockbox's hands went to fists. "You don't think I *want* to know who I am? Who you are? Who this slaghead is? You think I haven't tried?"

I reached out, wanting to console him.

"Don't you dare touch me again! I'll tell everyone what she is to you. What she means to you. Don't you dare touch me!"

"Again? Lockbox, what do you think I am?"

Lockbox's voice had a snarl to it, something I'd never heard from him before. "You asked me to find a memory of you and I searched all night until I found you. I'm in a prison yard and you approach. You wrap your arm around my neck and pull until the lights go out. You asked me to find a memory and I have one. It's of you strangling me."

"Lockbox—"

"And you know what? I think it's real." He turned to Emberly. "I think he really did strangle me."

"That's not how—"

"I'm sure you have your reasons." Gone was the look of an innocent boy, replaced by the vengeful glare of an enemy. "I don't give a slag about what they are. What they *were*. I'll make a deal with you though. I'll help you find a way out of this prison if you stop acting like we're supposed to be buddies—*best friends*. You needed an Oscar to help you. I'll help you. But that won't make me your friend."

"Lockbox, we *are* friends."

"You are and will always be, my enemy. I don't trust you. I don't like you and I'm warning you, if you try to get close to me, I'll make sure you regret it."

I wished he'd hit me instead. Wish he'd shoved the mine cart over on top of me.

"Deal," I said. "Your job is to find a way out of this prison, not just for you and Emberly, but for as many lurpers as we can."

"Fine," he said. "But don't tell me why. I don't want to get involved with whatever this is." He gestured vaguely to me and Emberly.

"Fine," I said. "I'll set you both to work on a pump. I'll tell you to keep it going to supply air to the tunnel but in fact, it's an unworked section of the mine. You only have to pump when Turuk and I come to check. Otherwise, spend your time figuring out how—"

"Do you always use so much redundancy when you talk?" Lockbox asked.

I gritted my teeth and looked over Lockbox's shoulder. A soldier was coming toward us, far enough away that I couldn't identify him, but I had a strong hunch it was Turuk. I moved away from Emberly. She planted a final kiss on my cheek.

"Thank you," she whispered.

"I'll drop some food on my way out."

By the time Turuk arrived, Lockbox and Emberly were nearly out of sight, making their way to the pump with the light of the small lantern as I stood at the entrance, Lugar in hand.

"Here you go, Sir," Turuk said, trying not to sound winded.

I took the apple and package of warm oatmeal.

"Thank you," I said.

"I thought maybe you'd gone in with them."

"I'm brave, Turuk, not stupid." As I said it, I'd forgotten to lay on the accent.

Turuk looked at me, hardly masking his confusion.

"What do you think?" I said, voice normal. "Do I sound like one of them? Think I could pass?"

"Pass as what, Sir?"

"Just if I wanted to go undercover. Do I sound like a lurper?"

Turuk wasn't amused. "Uncanny, but why would you need to?"

I shrugged, pulling the accent back into my words. "If there's a coup, it would be good to get information. I just wonder if I could convince anyone of anything."

"You're strong, Sir, and I am starting to believe you could convince most anyone of anything. Some people are born leaders. You're one of the few."

I clapped Turuk on the back. "Thank you," I said and then dug into my breakfast.

Turuk and I had sat outside the entrance to the mine for hours, barely speaking as we huddled away from the bitter wind and away from the danger of the darkness of the tunnels.

Though I finished the package of oats, I left the apple untouched. Emberly would like it later. I'd find some way to slip it to her. Or maybe I'd give it to Lockbox and he'd start to remember how I'd shared my books with him and he'd shared his vyco with me.

Wasn't it just typical that the single memory he had of me was the one where I'd left him unconscious? He'd remember more. With time other memories would come back.

Turuk barely nibbled his apple, gaze fixed into the darkness of the mine's opening.

"You've clearly got something on your mind," I said, twisting the palka in my gloved hands.

"Yes, Sir—"

"Drop the formalities when no one's around, okay? My name is Luka."

Turuk nodded. "Luka, this coup has me worried."

"Yeah?"

"The reveal about Commander Markos doesn't sit right."

"I agree. That's why I'm here."

"But Luka, Sir, I mean no disrespect, but did he change?"

I listened to make sure there was no one in the mine, hiding in the shadows to listen.

"What do you mean?" I asked.

"I mean, he was a good man. A great leader. Did that change?"

He may have been baiting me. I eyed Turuk. His blond hair looked darker in the mine.

"What does it matter?" I asked. "Markos lied from the beginning. He was a criminal who dodged the draft and got sent to Zalar for it. Maybe Khizmit shouldn't have tested their serums on the inmates there, but war calls for desperate actions. If he wanted to help Khizmit, he would have then. He changed when they gave him a serum, but not in his heart. That didn't suddenly make him loyal, honest, kind, or good. It made him strong. It made him dangerous."

Turuk looked away from me, down into the mine.

"Why are you here?"

Turuk cracked his neck. "I don't know."

"Turuk."

"For the good of Khizmit," he said with a grin. "Just paying my dues. Putting in my time. Doing what I'm asked to do. Hoping not to die in the process."

I was on my feet in an instant as I heard the rock sailing through the air. Instinctively, I caught it and immediately regretted it. It was larger than my hand and broke multiple bones upon impact.

"Skudge," I said, healing the injuries as quickly as they'd occurred. If Turuk stared at me in disbelief or awe, I didn't notice. My attention was fixated on the figure in the dark and the sound of the second rock that flew through the air. As it whistled toward Turuk's head, I stepped in front of it, catching it in my shoulder.

"Skudge," I yelled, drawing my Lugar. "Drop it or I fire!" I screamed into the tunnel.

I couldn't see who threw the rocks, but I could hear them shuffling. I couldn't hit them. Turuk had his Lugar out as he crouched behind a boulder, scanning the darkness. The third rock sailed towards my face. I shot the boulder, and then the person who'd thrown it.

He began to howl.

In an instant, I had the lurper in my hands. With my grip on his arm, I hoisted him up and carried him to the light of the entrance.

Turuk was silent, pale, and wide-eyed. The inmate was 14 or 15 years old, his striped clothes so stained they appeared to be black.

"How long have you been down there?" I asked.

He screamed in pain, clutching at his calf where the bullet had torn a hole. Based on his appearance alone, I guessed he'd gone missing at least a few days ago and had hidden here, waiting to attack.

"You've got slag for brains," I scolded, and I pulled out my dagger.

"Sir, no, please!" he begged.

"I'm not going to hurt you." I looked at the blood seeping down his leg. "Again."

He wailed, and his attempts to push me away would have worked if I wasn't gifted with serums from both parents. I cut a strip of cloth from my shirt and wrapped it around the wound. With quick hands I cut a second strip from his pants and wrapped it around the first, tying it even tighter.

The boy went still beside me as he saw what I was doing.

"How long were you in there?" I asked, but the boy wasn't looking at me. He looked from the apple to my dagger to Turuk's Lugar.

"Toss that to me," I said, gesturing to the small red fruit.

Turuk did, and I held it out to the boy. He reached out, and as he did, I caught sight of his wrist tattoo in the process.

Lima-04.

He tracked my gaze and pulled his arm back.

"What's your name?" I asked.

"Lima-04," he groaned.

"What do you want me to call you?" I asked, pushing the apple into his hands.

He took the apple and bit into it savagely. I wondered if he'd be able to enjoy it with the horrible pain he must be feeling.

He eyed me with worry as if I was going to take the food away at any moment.

"I still hate you," he said, mouth full.

"Fine," I said, reaching for him.

"Don't touch me!" he wailed.

"I'm taking you to the clinic to get patched up."

"Why not finish me off? Just let me bleed out!"

I scooped him into my arms. "You're no help to Khizmit if you're dead."

"Always for the good of Khizmit, huh?" he spat.

"Just don't die," I said.

"Why?" His heart was racing, faster and faster. I heard it without even trying to.

My words were clipped. "I don't like when kids become corpses."

The boy, taking shallow breaths, tried to eat more of the apple.

"I'll be back soon," I told Turuk. "I'll send a comrade as soon as I find one."

"Yessir!" Turuk said, saluting me. "Thank you, Sir."

"Don't make a big deal of it," I said, and I prayed that he wouldn't.

———

Turuk was pacing at the mine entrance when I returned, his uniform stained with Lima-04's blood.

"That was fast," Turuk said, unable to hold still.

"I couldn't very well leave my comrade out here alone. Armed and dangerous as you are, if any of these lurpers knew…" I trailed off. I'd been speaking in character, as a cruster, but the thought of someone emerging from these tunnels and killing Turuk made my stomach twist.

"Armed, sure. But I don't know about dangerous. I'm not skilled like you."

I could tell from the way he looked at me with awe and a bit of confusion, that he was thinking about the incredible feat I'd performed, stopping the rocks from bashing his head open.

"Lucky," I said. "Let's not discount luck."

Turuk nodded, finally taking a seat on the rocks.

"Never a dull moment here."

"Sir, earlier you said you don't like when kids become corpses."

"I don't."

"That's something I admire about you. You want what's best for Khizmit and what's best for the lurpers, too. You don't want them to suffer."

"I don't want anyone to suffer, Turuk."

"Well, you saying that made me wonder if we might take some of this back to the Oscar and Victor. They've been at it for a while now and…" Turuk's face turned red, whether from embarrassment or anxiety, I didn't know.

A smile came onto my face of its own.

"Yes, Turuk, I think we should," I replied.

He cared about them. About Emberly and Lockbox. He cared about lurpers.

CHAPTER 30
A BLOODY SCAR

I WANTED to go back and hold Emberly, and joke with Lockbox, but I'd have to be content in knowing that they were able to rest back there, maybe even nap while they waited to hear me coming.

I stood, brushing off the back of my pants before lifting the lantern. With a turn of the small knob, a soft click left the fuse glowing.

"You don't have to come, I—"

"Why are you always trying to get rid of me?" Turuk asked. "You picked me as your comrade and yet, you're always trying to get away."

"It's not like that," I said. "I know you'll do whatever I ask, and I never want to put you in a position you didn't volunteer for. Going into the mine with lurpers is dangerous. It's a risk I'm willing to take, but not one I'm willing to demand from you."

"It's much more dangerous without a comrade. I'll come with you." Turuk picked up his apple and a few meal bars. "Besides, I should expect they'll be happy we're bringing lunch."

"Maybe," I said. If any guard had brought me a meal

while I'd been working, I'd have been convinced it was poisoned. That it would kill me.

As Turuk and I entered the mine, memories followed me, threatening to bring crimson into my vision with each curse and each threat that had been my life here. As we drew nearer to the pump, I told Ember and Lockbox to work, I started talking to make sure they heard us coming. To make sure they were working.

"Have you been in here before?" I asked.

"No Sir," Turuk replied.

"Carry your dagger if you'd like," I advised, catching sight of his trembling hands in the swaying light of my lantern.

The next time I looked at his silhouette, I saw the dagger in his hand.

"Victor?" I called. We turned the corner to see Emberly and Lockbox standing at the pump. "Are you working?"

"Yes, Sir," Emberly said.

"And you?" I turned to Lockbox. His anger towards me was different than Flak's or Ice's. His anger was deeper.

Glowering, he didn't even pretend like he was going to give us any respect.

"We brought you some food," I said, extending my hand to Turuk. He dropped two meal bars into it.

I extended one to Emberly who took it and tore it open. In three bites, it was gone. Lockbox hadn't budged. Arms working, he pumped, then stopped.

"Do you want one?" I asked, taking a step in his direction.

"Sure," he said.

I stepped closer and watched, confused, as he threw a small rock at Emberly.

She easily dodged it as I closed the distance between me and Lockbox, situating myself between him and Emberly.

"Do you want the meal bar or not?"

Lockbox reached out for the bar, then dipped his hand lower. I knew he was going for my dagger, but I didn't step back.

He wouldn't, I thought, just as he swiped the blade across my face. It caught my cheek like a hot whip.

Stunned, I lifted my hands to my face.

Lockbox shot forward. As I felt the dagger punch into my side, I dropped the lantern to the floor on top of Ember's, pitching us all into complete darkness. The darkness would hide my hurt. Hide my healing. And in it, I could contain Lockbox without Turuk seeing anything that would damn me.

Emberly hurried to me. "Luka," she gasped, and my name echoed around us. As she said it, she hugged me, and I could feel her apology in the gesture.

With a grunt, I pulled the dagger from my gut and healed it completely. Emberly stepped away as I moved forward, following the distinct steps Lockbox took as he shuffled to the side. I grabbed him by the wrist, twisted until he was uncomfortable, and used the pressure to bring him to his knees. Then to his belly.

My teeth were gritted together as tears beaded in my eyes. "Why?" I asked.

Much faster than I would have expected, a soft click illuminated the area around us. Turuk had his palka extended toward the small space Lockbox had previously occupied. The light in Turuk's hand revealed Lockbox, lying on his side on the floor, arm twisted back as I held his wrist.

Bold red shone from my side.

"Sir, are you hurt?" Turuk asked, bringing the light closer to my side.

"Just my face," I said, turning so he could see the cut across my left cheek.

"But this blood," he said, eyes wide as he assessed my clothes. "There's blood all over you."

"I'm fine," I said. *Skudging idiot!* I should have just healed part of it. But if I'd only healed part of it, Lockbox would be sentenced to death for attempting to kill a guard. Skudge it all! I was covered in blood. Turuk would know. There was no way out of this.

"Sir, we need to get you to the medical clinic. And this Oscar…"

Any inmate who attacked a guard was subject to early termination. If they knew he'd attacked me, he'd be killed. Under normal circumstances, I was supposed to kill him here and now.

"I'm fine," I said. "It's just my face." *Just my face,* I thought.

Ember moved forward a single step, prompting Turuk to point his palka toward her. As the light of the lantern fell across her, she spoke. "Mr. Chief Preemptive Officer," she said, addressing Turuk. "The Oscar wasn't attacking the Lieutenant," she declared. Pointing to her own shirt she said, "He was attacking me."

My blood had soaked her clothes. Soaked bright red into her linens.

"You?"

"Yes," she said.

"Do you need a medic?"

"I don't think so, Sir," she said, voice tentative. She cast a glance at me, then scowled at Lockbox with pure hatred.

"This is a lot of blood. How are you still standing?"

Emberly straightened, somehow managing to look noble and dignified in bloody, striped prison clothes. "I'm a Victor," she declared. "I can heal."

I exhaled so loudly it made Turuk look my way before turning back to Emberly. "What?"

"Lockbox here took the dagger to attack me," she explained. "The lieutenant got in the way, so he slashed his face to make him step back, which he did. Then the Oscar lunged at me, and stabbed me in the side. See this cut in my clothes?" she prodded her fingers through a hole that I had no doubt she'd just made with a sharp rock. "The lieutenant dropped the lantern and then tripped, landing on me. I took out the dagger, accidentally stained his uniform, then healed."

"So, if we test this blood…" Turuk's gaze flitted from me to Emberly. "It will test positive for Victor?"

"Of course," Emberly said. "How else would you explain it?" Her tone managed to also say, "How do you manage to do anything, you slow, stupid crusters?"

"I see," I said, finally getting my bearings. "That explains it."

Lockbox began to rise. "That's not—"

I pushed him back down and placed a knee across his ribs. "Not a word from you, lurper. Take her to the clinic. Check her for injuries. We don't want to lose our final Victor."

"Sir?" Turuk's hands trembled slightly.

"I have this one contained." I put more pressure on Lockbox, forcing him to gasp.

"I'll wait for you, Sir," Turuk said.

"No," I said as I pulled manacles from my back pocket. "I need some time with this one."

I unclipped one of the cuffs and tightened it around Lockbox's wrist.

He tried to speak again. "That's not what—"

"Shut up!" I screamed at Lockbox, slamming his other wrist into place. Because of him, Emberly was going to be tested. She was going to be hurt. They were going to make her prove that she could heal. All so she could protect me. And protect him.

Following my lead, Turuk cuffed Emberly. She complied.

"Don't worry, Sir," Turuk said. "I'll take her alone. What will you do?"

I stood, forcing Lockbox to his feet. "Interrogation. Then whatever I want," I growled.

Turuk gave a quick nod before leaving me and Lockbox beside the pump.

With a final glance to Emberly, I dismissed Turuk, lighting the small lantern again as the beams from Turuk's melted into the darkness.

Emberly had saved Lockbox's life and mine. He wouldn't be punished for attacking her. But she was going to be injured. She was going to have to prove her abilities, abilities she hadn't developed yet. At the clinic, they'd have access to the rapid test.

Maybe they wouldn't test the blood to see it ping positive for Victor and X-ray.

Maybe Lockbox didn't just sentence me to death.

But maybe he had.

———

"Why?" I asked. A few errant tears tracked down my face, some mingling with the blood on my left cheek. I couldn't even heal it now that Turuk had seen the gash.

Lockbox's voice was entirely too casual. "In my memory of you, your face is scarred. Maybe I thought that if I saw you like that, my memory would come back."

I didn't believe him. He couldn't have thought that would work. He just wanted me to hurt. He wanted to embarrass or expose me.

"You healed your stomach like it was nothing," he stated. "Any normal cruster would be dead on the floor. You're a lurper then? For real?"

"You're going to get me killed."

"And that's supposed to upset me?"

"Yes," I said, fingering my dagger. The tip was red with my blood. Blood that would tell the world I was Victor-27, the monster from Predvoi. And Lockbox had gone and spilled it all over my uniform and Emberly's clothes. "You wanted to see what I was?"

"I figured you were a lurper. The way you move. The way you can hear me even from a distance. I can't sort it, though. You're an X-ray or a Victor. Which is it?"

"I'm both," I said. My cheek stung and I could feel blood dripping from the cut. "That's the second time you've used my knife against me. Last time you got my throat."

"You let me."

"I didn't think you'd do it."

"Then you're dumber than you seem."

My voice sounded angry and pained. "You were my cellmate in Predvoi. We played chess, shared books, you gave me boots and let me borrow your koruna for lunch."

Lockbox scoffed. "I don't think so."

A frustrated growl rose in my chest. "What would cause memory loss? You remember a lot of things, but not me. Did something wipe out the last year for you?"

"It's called amnesia, slaghead," Lockbox said.

"Yeah, sure, it's also called memory loss. What causes it?"

"Well, it would seem I have retrograde amnesia. I have lost previously made memories. This type of amnesia affects recently formed memories. Older memories stay longer. Maybe I have a disease affecting my memory." Lockbox stood and took a step forward, manacles clanging together.

"Disease can cause it, but what else? Injury?" I asked.

"Yeah, but they didn't find any brain injury in the clinic. Maybe I have dissociative amnesia caused by trauma. Maybe your attempt to kill me back in Predvoi caused this."

"I didn't cause this," I insisted. "But maybe you had trauma afterward."

"Sure, 'cause having someone choke you unconscious isn't traumatic."

"Listen slaghead, I've had people kick me unconscious

and I didn't get amnesia." I shoved the bloody blade back into the sheath and clipped it in.

"Yeah, well, you can heal, can't you?"

"You said you used to try and get a power migraine. Maybe you didn't feel them, but they were slowly chipping away at your brain."

Lockbox glanced at the pump like he was going to comment about it before saying, "Or maybe you just can't own up to what you did. I bet I got this from you. If you tried to kill me once, you probably tried again."

"Lockbox, I didn't try to kill you. Trust me, if I had, you wouldn't be here!"

He grunted and raised his eyebrows. Gaze lowered, he stared at his cuffed wrists.

"Maybe it's a drug-induced amnesia. They made serums that turned criminals into skrags. Maybe they have drugs to erase memories too."

"Would they have a serum to undo it? Bring back your memory?" *Bring back my best friend,* I thought.

"Why do you care if my memory is gone? You lose some information and hope I have it?"

"No, I lost my friend! Aren't you listening?"

Lockbox kicked at a loose rock, sending it sort of towards me, but it skittered off the ground wildly going to the side and into the darkness beyond.

"What the skudge makes you so sure I'm your bestie? You go from threatening my life to acting like we're brothers."

Brothers. That was it. We were brothers.

"Rich," I said. "You're the one who just stabbed me. What if I couldn't heal? What then?"

"Then I guess we'd both be dead. Listen, it was a calculated risk."

Calculated. He'd gambled with my life.

"You tried to kill me," I hissed.

"I guess we're even."

This approach wasn't working. I had to switch. With a steadying breath, I decided to change.

"I'm undercover, okay? You know that. I've been nothing but honest with you."

"Nothing but honest? I think now you're the one with memory loss. You've been threatening and violent. You've been manipulative and deceptive. Your entire persona here is as a cruster with an accent when you're nothing but a boy from these ratholes."

I stood, yanking off my ushanka as I stood and approached him. "Listen, this isn't easy for me."

"I don't give a skudge what's easy for you!"

Exasperated, I dragged my hands through my hair. "I didn't want to start over with you. I liked what we were. Roommates. Friends. I'd take a bullet for you!"

"Easy for you to say since you'd be able to spit it back out."

I dropped beside the pump, twisting my ushanka in my hands as my gaze fell upon the discarded meal bar. Maybe his memory would come back eventually, but in the meantime, he really didn't have a great impression of me. Much as it killed me, I had to start over with him.

In the distance came the all-too-familiar crank of the elevators and distant hammering and chiseling from faraway tunnels.

"Hi," I said, my voice echoing in the mine. "My name is Luka Drivick."

I waited for him to introduce himself.

"Hi," he said, patronizingly. "Apparently I'm Oscar-16."

I almost told him he was Oscar-17 before, but every time I'd mentioned the past or told him something he didn't remember, he got annoyed. His memory loss had to be gutting him, and when I told him, an Oscar, something I knew that he didn't, it angered him.

"Nice to meet you, Oscar-16." I said, voice monotone. "Would you like a meal bar?"

"No."

"Why?" I said, irritation threatening to spill into my words.

"Because I don't trust you." Lockbox looked like he'd eaten something sour.

"Okay," I said. "What if I open it, take a small bite, and then pass it over?"

"No, it could still be poisoned. You can heal, meaning your body could easily rid your system of toxins before you succumbed to any of the symptoms."

I chuckled. "That's true." I thought. "Hey, you know what, when I was an inmate here, I put some ground-up cement into a guard's cup, and they thought it was poison. Later, the chancellor supreme made me drink it. I told her it wasn't poisoned, and she sort of let on that maybe it was. Do you think she slipped something in herself to see if my body would heal without my knowing how to?"

Lockbox shrugged. "Seems like something she'd do."

"Do you remember her? Dulka?"

"Yes, I remember her."

A moment of silence passed between us.

"I'm sorry about your memory loss," I said. "Not just for me. But for you. Must be pretty slaggy to have so many empty files in your head."

Lockbox's attention snapped to me at the word "files."

"Why'd you say it like that?"

"When we were in Predvoi together, there were times when you were trying to remember something, and your fingers would flip through the air as if you were going through files. I always imagined you were sorting through things like that."

He nodded, nearly solemn. It was admission enough for me.

"I want to help you get your memory back. Maybe if we figure out what caused it, we can reverse it. Will you accept my help?"

"Will you promise not to lie to me?"

"Yes," I said.

"Will you promise not to threaten me?"

"Lockbox, I have to—"

"Will you promise not to hurt me?"

"I don't want to hurt you. I'm offering to help!"

"Fine," Lockbox said, fiddling with his cuffs. "You want me to trust you. Then show that you trust me. Take these off."

I had no reassurance that he wouldn't try to gut me again, but now I was ready. Since we were alone, I could heal without the risk of being found out. If, by some act of insanity and a stroke of insane luck, Lockbox stabbed me again, I'd be ready.

As I turned the key and the cuffs fell away, I made my decision.

"You knew me as Victor-27," I began.

Over the next hour, I told him everything, every detail I could remember from our time together and he sat silently, listening. The only question he asked was, "Have you tampered with this meal bar?"

I assured him I hadn't, and he ate it while I told him about his work as a surgeon in the Lurper Legion.

When I finished, he remained silent.

"Well," I said, expectantly.

"I like your story," he said. "I can't find too many holes in it."

"Too many?"

"You've confided in me. Enough that I'm willing to work with you."

"Great," I said.

"I'll figure a way out of here, Mr. Chief Preemptive Officer, and when I do, I'll tell you."

"Don't call me that. Not when it's just us."

"I will call you that," Lockbox insisted. "That's what you are to me. You have to accept that."

"Fine," I said, holding the cuffs out for him to put on himself. "But it's subject to change, right?"

Lockbox snorted as he fastened the metal around his wrist. "You've got a lot of hope for a lurper. Sure," he consented. "It's subject to change."

CHAPTER 31
A REASONABLE CRUSTER

DOCTOR TRAFT DIDN'T SUTURE my face, he glued it. Said it would heal better that way. I thanked him and asked what happened with the Victor.

"I don't know how she knew she could heal, but she can. We tested it," he said.

I nodded solemnly, not daring to hear what they'd done to make her heal. She'd done it. She'd healed.

It sounded like since she proved she could heal, they didn't bother testing her blood. Though there were many rapid tests in Khizmit, there was still a shortage up here, for now.

After getting my face cleaned up and changing into a freshly laundered uniform top, I wandered the hallways. Should I go back to the cell and talk to Lockbox? Should I check on Ember? My face didn't hurt, but the pain and confusion storming inside me did. Lockbox didn't know me. The crusters here knew that Emberly could heal. I had hundreds of lurpers I needed to liberate and no clue how I was going to go about doing it.

Absentmindedly, I wandered outside through swirling snow to an empty guard tower. I'd been sitting in it, listening to the whistling wind for only a few minutes when the door creaked open and Turuk poked his head in. He smiled apologetically.

"Can I come in?"

I laughed. "Sure."

He immediately stared at my face.

"I saw you put the Oscar back in his cell."

I pursed my lips, remembering to fake an accent. "Seemed a waste to kill him."

Turuk kept staring at my face.

"It's not that bad, is it?" I asked, reaching up to my cheek.

"Luka…" Turuk began and then stopped. "Luka, you're a good soldier. A good man."

"Thank you…" I said, knowing that his words were a preamble of sorts. I waited but then he didn't say anything else.

There was something in the air between us. Some unsaid, unsettling feeling filled the empty tower with more potency as the moments passed.

"What is it, Turuk?" I asked.

"You're him, aren't you?" Turuk's voice held some fear, but not as much as I'd have expected.

"Who?"

He sighed, and his expression shifted. His voice was nervous. "There were some people who didn't believe that Victor-27 was dead."

As he said my old name my back stiffened.

"You're him."

I hadn't given Turuk as much credit as I should have. He was smarter than I'd expected.

I dropped the accent.

"Yes, I was. I'm Lieutenant Luka Drivick now. What gave me away?"

"I've seen you before. With the scar. Even without the evidence that has been piling up now that your face is back to normal, it's obvious."

"Obvious?"

"Sort of. You were stabbed back there, not Emberly. I took a rapid test from the clinic and tested the blood myself. You're the only X-Ray/Victor combination that exists."

I stared him in the face, looking for fear in his eyes or malice in his expression. "Are you afraid?" I asked.

He blinked and swallowed hard, his Adam's apple bobbing obviously. "I've met Commander Markos. I've met you. I've met Emberly Markos. I think...I think maybe Victors aren't exactly what I was always told."

A reasonable cruster. I didn't think such a thing existed.

Turuk considered me a moment and went on. "You're not bloodthirsty or violent. You're not terrifying or menacing... you're just...people. People with some extraordinary abilities."

"Thank you," I said, clapping him slowly on the back so he didn't see the gesture as violent.

The wind howled outside, and I pulled my overcoat on tighter.

"What are you going to do about it?"

"About you?" Turuk asked. "Nothing."

"Nothing?" I asked, guffawing. "I'm a lurper pretending to be a cruster, not some vazzie the chancellors decided could wear this uniform. I'm a boy pretending to be a man. A skrag masquerading as a lieutenant! You're telling me you're not going to do anything about it?!"

I realized my hands were in fists and I'd cornered Turuk.

His gaze flitted to the door and then back to me.

"Who did you tell?" I asked, my voice soft.

"No one," he said, reaching up to remove his ushanka. "I didn't want..."

I watched him scratch the back of his head for a moment.

"What?" I asked.

"I didn't want them to kill you. Like I said, you're a good soldier. A good man."

This whole plan was skudged from the start. Turuk had seen right through me. I was just supposed to come and get Ember and leave. I wasn't supposed to run into Mike and promise to save him too. Lockbox wasn't supposed to show up with his memory skudged. Turuk wasn't supposed to be nice.

My conflicted emotions battled inside as I paced the small space in the tower. The wooden floorboards creaked musically as I strode across them.

"What will I do with you?" I asked, squaring my shoulders in Turuk's direction.

"You won't kill me. You can't send me away. You can't make me forget what I know. I think you have only one option."

"Which is?"

He smiled apprehensively. "I think you have to recruit me."

"Recruit you?"

"You're still working with Markos, right? You're here helping him. Keeping Emberly safe. Planning the coup."

He knew too much. Sirens were practically sounding in my head. He knew everything.

"I want to join your coup. I care about you, Luka. I want to help the Victors." He laughed, "Slag! I can't believe I'm saying it, but I want to liberate the lurpers."

I stared at him in complete disbelief. And yet, I *did* believe him.

"Sir," Turuk said, formality entering his voice again. "High Warden Molnar needs to be briefed on today's events."

Of course he did.

"Okay," I said, then cleared my throat and pulled the accent back into my voice. "Korporal Turuk, I'd like you to relay the series of events to him."

Turuk grinned. "Yes, Sir!"

———

High Warden Molnar struggled to extricate himself from his seat as we entered his office and eventually gave up trying. Turuk and I crossed the room in only a couple of seconds. Since there was only one chair in here besides the one Molnar occupied, and we were here on official business, we stood opposite him at the desk.

Molnar reached his hand out as if we had something to pass over to him.

"Official report?" he asked.

Turuk spoke. "Apologies, Sir. We haven't had a chance to compile it. I'll have it to you by this afternoon."

Molnar dropped his hand and stared at my face, narrowing his fat eyelids. "That'll leave a nasty scar." Then, perhaps feeling bad about his comment he added, "Some women are hopelessly attracted to battle wounds. I know a private who got his right hand blown off and he found a wife within a month of being discharged."

"I'm not worried about it," I said casually. "But thank you, Sir."

Molnar adjusted himself in the seat. "Maybe some men don't mind scars either. I don't mean to assume you're, erm, only interested in women." He glanced over to Turuk and then back to me quickly. "Are you—"

"Sir," I risked interrupting him. "At the moment I'm only interested in keeping these lurpers in line."

"Of course. Terribly unprofessional of me," he apologized. "What happened today in the mine?"

Turuk stood at ease and told the series of events in clipped sentences. "The Oscar jumped at the Victor. She dodged and knocked the lantern from Drivick's hand, Sir. Lieutenant Drivick was quick to have his blade out and pointed at the Victor since she was the bigger threat. The Oscar slammed into Drivick as a clever way to injure the Victor. She was stabbed and as Drivick attempted to maneuver around, he accidently cut his own face."

Molnar nodded, his double chin appearing and disappearing as quickly as Turuk relayed the false series of events.

"The Oscar didn't injure the Lieutenant?"

"No, Sir," I said, knowing that if they knew he had, he'd be dead. "I refused to let go of my weapon, but gashed my own face in the process."

"And you're the one who stabbed the Victor?" Molnar asked.

"When she seemed combative, I was sure to get a weapon between us, according to the Code of Penal Officers."

Molnar nodded again, head bobbing up and down as he considered the tale.

I found myself speaking next. "Seeing as the Oscar took violent action against the Victor, we recommend that he remain in his cell for the next few days as a disciplinary measure."

Molnar agreed. He asked a few clarifying questions, which Turuk was quick to answer. He said nothing about me. Gave no hint of inconsistency in his responses. Here we were in the high warden's office and Turuk didn't out me.

"I'm going to get some rest," Molnar said, finally heaving himself out of his chair. "You two get some as well."

"Yessir!" Turuk and I both said, saluting him as he stood and left the room. The door slammed shut behind him, leaving Turuk and I standing there a bit awkwardly.

Without speaking, we exited the room and began our way through the narrow hallways of the dark prison, the flickering lights as our guide. As we passed cells, I still worried someone would recognize me the way Mike had, but no one said anything. Most of the conversations that I heard in the distance died down as they heard crusters coming.

Turuk and I entered the guard's quarters and found it empty. Captain Caterpillar—I mean Oravec—must have been pulling night duty. I unlaced my boots and moved my overcoat into locker 14.

"Thank you," I said.

"Of course," Turuk said, removing his uniform top and swapping it for a linen one for bed.

"You, uh, didn't answer him," Turuk said.

"Regarding…oh his personal question?" I asked. "I didn't think it warranted a response."

Turuk continued getting ready for bed in silence. Silence that grew and became awkward.

"I don't mind the scar," Turuk finally said quietly. "I know you'll heal it later, but I think you look…really good."

"Turuk," I said, understanding dawning on me slowly. I tentatively placed a hand on his shoulder. His expression grew hopeful. "Just Ember," I said. "I only like Ember."

"Of course," Turuk said a little too fast. "I apologize if—"

"Don't apologize," I said offering him a smile. "You're a good man. You're a good friend to me."

"Of course, Sir. Besides, fraternization and all that," he chuckled.

I laughed out loud at that. Laughed so loud that the sound echoed off the walls probably waking any sleeping officers.

"You're recruited," I said. "I trust you, and I need your help getting these lurpers out."

CHAPTER 32
AN UNWORKED SECTION OF THE MINE

WE HAD to leave Lockbox in his cell as a disciplinary measure, but it worked in our favor since he'd likely be able to get more intel interaction with other lurpers as they came and went. Turuk agreed to go in later and walk him around at a distance so he could socialize and listen. In the meantime, Emberly, Turuk, and I headed back out to the mine.

We entered the same hole as the previous day, still alone as the other lurpers climbed down smaller ratholes, preferring to go where guards wouldn't follow.

The lanterns appeared to grow brighter as we went deeper into the tunnels taking step after step in silence until Turuk stopped and cleared his throat.

"I'll stay here," he announced. The lantern in his hands lit the lower half of his face making his blond eyebrows appear long and black. "Watch the entrance and all that."

"Thank you," I said, dropping my fake accent. "Let us know if someone comes."

The shadows on Ember's face didn't conceal her concern.

"He knows," I whispered. "Who I am. What I am."

"He knows?"

"Yeah, I know, and I can still hear you," Turuk said playfully. "Why don't you two just hurry back and have your long-awaited make-out session while I keep watch, okay?"

A sound of surprise escaped Emberly's lips.

"Yeah, I know. Turn of events." Turuk gave a weak laugh and bent over to set his lantern on the floor. He settled himself onto a large rock and pulled out his palka. "I didn't realize I'd been coming between the star-crossed lovers, or I'd have excused myself weeks ago. I thought—oh, please—you know what I thought. You made me think it!" False anger entered his voice.

"You mean…you're okay with it?" Ember asked.

Turuk threw his hand up and waved it dramatically. "Luka and I are friends, whatever blood he's got doesn't matter to me."

"Thanks, Turuk," I said. "Really—"

"Go teach her to heal or block pain or swap spit or whatever you've been waiting to do, and I'll hurry back if anyone comes down here."

His voice held a bit of fear.

"Are you going to be okay here? Alone?" I asked.

"As long as I know two Victors have my back, I'll be fine. Just don't turn on me, okay?"

I almost made a joke about how easily we could hurt him, but his fear of us was genuine.

"I won't," I said sincerely before reaching out for Ember's hand.

She'd guided me through the streets of her childhood. Shared her traditions with me. Shown me where she grew up, what she ate, how she passed her time. I hadn't planned to share my childhood with her, but I felt like that's exactly what I was doing as I walked down the all-too-familiar tunnels at Rhosivi.

The smell of coal and dust and mold put my senses on edge, but there was an element of predictability in the familiarity of it.

I led her back to more narrow tunnels going deeper than any lurper would go, hoping not to find any bodies along the way. We skirted around a few piles where the support beams had failed and then when I was certain we were truly alone, we did exactly what Turuk had told us to.

This place had been my hell, but as I held Emberly in my arms and ran my hands through her hair, it became something more. Only she could have the power to turn a nightmare into a heaven.

Was it a wise use of our time? Maybe not.

But if we were about to die, there was no better way for me to spend my last moments.

We scarcely spoke as we held each other. Twice she broke into tears, shaking as she tried to keep her sobs silent. I finally asked her why, but I already knew. This place could break even the strongest.

"I'm going to get us out of here," I said.

"He cut my arm," she said and using my finger traced a line from the tip of her shoulder down to her elbow. "And I healed it. With a thought."

"It's amazing," I said, moving my lips to the place she'd been hurt.

"Why didn't Milena heal?"

I shook my head, feeling tears well in my eyes at the memories.

"I don't know."

But I did. She wanted to die human, not live a lurper. She wanted to die with her beliefs intact. She died for her faith in her father like a martyr rather than let her reality be shattered.

There was something noble in it. Something brave and admirable, but I wish she'd have been able to let go and grow.

Not wanting her to sit here and think about her sister, I told her about her father. Kindnesses I'd observed from him. Things I admired.

"Milena told me you were obsessed with me," I whispered.

"When?" she asked, putting her hand on the dark cavern wall, her voice free from sorrow for the moment.

"When we were waiting for the caramels to cool. You were outside with them, and she and I were with your mom, cutting papers. Milena said you were obsessed."

"Of course she did," Ember chuckled.

"Can you make the caramels again sometime? Or does it have to be only on Koliada?"

"I'll make them for you whenever you want. Next time we're back in Khizmit."

I kissed her, long and gently before sitting back up and moving to stand.

"We have to go."

She took my hand, and I pulled her to her feet. Hand in hand we walked back through the tunnels. We were nearly to the section of the mine where I'd been pumping air for ventilation when Mike had come to ask for help and then I'd been confronted by Dent. Guards did occasionally come back here. Though I doubted it would happen, I dropped her hand and moved my hand to my dagger.

Just then a voice cut through from the endless black.

"You two are the least subtle couple I've ever seen," Lockbox said.

I couldn't see him, but I turned to face where I assumed he sat.

"You grew up in Predvoi. How many secret couples could you have possibly observed?"

"More than you'd think." He stepped forward and adjusted his glasses.

"How did you get here?"

"Why do you always ask the wrong questions?"

"This is starting to feel like an interrogation," I said, using the exact words I said to him when we met in the cramped cement cell at Predvoi. My memory wasn't half as good as Lockbox's, but I tried to bait him into a previous conversation to remind him of our past together.

"I ask questions," he began, and I joined him, speaking verbatim as he did.

"It's what I do," we said in unison. "I stay alive in here by knowing stuff so—" Lockbox stopped speaking. I didn't.

"Consider yourself lucky," I finished.

"I think you stole my words." Lockbox's voice carried a happy lilt of incredulity.

"Keep jumping to conclusions and you'll break a limb," I said, repeating something else I'd said when we'd first met.

He smiled. He'd liked it when I said it the first time.

"I'll keep asking the questions if you don't mind."

I grinned. "I don't mind."

"You ready to get out of here?" With some of the confidence I'd seen from him at Predvoi, he leaned against the ventilation pump and jutted his chin out.

I asked. "You lost?"

"You asked for my help." Lockbox narrowed his eyes at me. "Or did you always know a way out and just ask me for the hell of it?"

He made me nervous. I hated to admit it, even to myself, but his swagger and his intelligence did intimidate me. I'd witnessed his methods at Predvoi, but I'd been his teammate then. This side of things was more complicated, and I began to understand how he'd survived. He could have libraries of information in his head that he didn't share.

"I'm sorry Lockbox, but I've got slag for brains. You're going to have to spell it out for me."

"Fine," he said. "Do you know where this pumps air?"

Dent had said it went nowhere. "An unworked section of the mine?"

"No, Victor," he said grinning ear to ear. "This pumps air to the Freedom Tunnel."

CHAPTER 33
BE BOLD

The Freedom Tunnel was a myth made up by inmates with no hope left. It was a story we told to feel better about missing inmates. And yet, Lockbox insisted that it was real.

Lockbox, who wasn't right in the head anymore, believed it was the way out of here for us.

The plan Lockbox presented couldn't have made me more uncomfortable. He volunteered to take Ember's place as the bait but admitted it lacked the same appeal factor.

We had to act fast. We had to hold onto hope. We had to take a horrible risk.

The first step was Ember's least favorite part. Turuk and I stood at the entrance of Ember and Lockbox's cell.

"You don't actually have to do it. You just have to take the fall," Lockbox said, seeming willing to do the nasty job for her. The job required more blood from me. More pain. More masquerading.

"I'll do what I have to do," Ember said, flashing Lockbox a look that made it clear what Roman had meant when he said I was scary when angry. Perhaps it was a Victor trait.

"Three hours and counting," I said. It was time to get the ball rolling. My boots clomped on the floor as I took heavy steps over to Mike's cell.

Mike sat up grinning as I approached.

"Mr. Chief Preemptive Officer," he said happily.

I squatted down close. It was three in the morning, and while most of the guards here were asleep, there were no guarantees someone on duty wasn't going to wander back here.

"We're going to break out today," I whispered to Mike. His eyes lit up with hope. "When we all come into the yard for an execution, I'll give the signal."

"What's the signal?" Mike asked.

"It will be obvious," I promised. "Spread word that everyone should be compliant with cuffs to be in the yard at the time. If there are lurpers still stuck in their cells, we won't be able to get them out. If they aren't in the yard, they'll be left behind." My words sounded callous. There was no way to get everyone out. This was the best we could do. Would the inmates kill each other? Would they kill me?

"You know about the fuses, right?" Mike asked in a small voice.

"Fuses?"

"Before Head Warden Velky left he directed us to set fuses around Rhosivi. Some of us have been going around tearing them up, trying to slowly sabotage what he did, but if Head Warden Molnar wanted to, he could bury the mine."

"Bury the mine?" I asked. Velky had always wanted to bury us here. I should have known that once he was head warden he'd find a way to mass execute all the inmates.

"The fuses are set. I just wanted to make sure you knew about it. If we don't move fast enough, we could get caught in the tunnels, Sir."

"Don't call me Sir," I said, distracted by the image of a thousand tunnels collapsing at once with all the inmates inside.

There were a million ways this could go wrong. A bunch of Charlies might start fighting other lurpers to be compliant.

I didn't even know the designations of most of the inmates here. What about my previous cellmates? Was Foxtrot here? Would he take orders from me? How long would it take Molnar to give an order to collapse the mine?

Behind me, Turuk pulled Lockbox and Ember from their cell and began walking them down the hallway.

Mike reassured me. "I know you've got it figured out. I'll spread the word."

Did I? "Three hours enough time?"

"Yessir," Mike said.

"Don't call me Sir."

"Victor." Mike corrected himself. "Just Victor."

I unlocked his cell and sent him out to scurry around the cells spreading word. I passed my key over to him. "Don't unlock everyone, just the ones who *aren't* scheduled to get released to work today. We need them to have access to the yard when I give the signal and to stay hidden until then."

"Understood," Mike said, throwing up a ridiculous salute.

I knew he'd pass the word along, but I couldn't know what the inmates he freed would do. If they acted alone, they'd die alone and might sabotage the plan. Back in Mike's cell, his cellmate didn't move. If he was faking sleep, he did it well.

My gaze followed Mike as he headed back to the more dangerous inmates' cells before I turned and walked after Ember and Lockbox.

For the next thirty minutes, we gathered supplies. Turuk and I smuggled a few rifles from supply beneath our overcoats. Lockbox told me what we needed, and Turuk and I gathered it up. We picked up enough explosives to blow a tunnel, which is exactly what we had to do, without causing some catastrophic event.

No sign of alarm rose. No warnings. If Mike was hastily liberating lurpers from their cells, they were following orders and sneaking towards exits. Overcoat stuffed, we made our play for the yard. My heart hammered as I walked along the hall. Emberly had been quiet except for her occasional, deliberately slow exhales.

As we stepped out from the prison the bitter wind, ever reliable, greeted us by throwing snow up towards us in the darkness. A single spotlight pivoted across the grounds and found us. The guard controlling it fixed it on us as we walked. Turuk gave a wave, indicating that all was well. That's when Emberly attacked me.

I knew she'd be fast but not this fast. She snapped the palka off my waist and swung it at my arm as I pivoted. I screamed, went down, and reached for my dagger but she got to it first. She swiped at me, caught my arm, and then Turuk cracked his palka over her head, so hard I gritted my teeth. She crumpled and screamed. I stood so my shadow fell over her, making it so the guards couldn't see her, in case someone was taking aim.

We'd been fast enough that none of the armed guards in the towers had time to react and retaliate but the voices from the soldiers above us meant they'd witnessed it. Enough of them had witnessed it.

"The threat is contained!" I shouted, while pulling out the handcuffs I'd brought. I snapped them over Emberly's wrists and dragged her across the snow to the base of the platform near the main exit. Sometimes Velky stood here to address us while we shivered. It was only a few meters across, and no more than twenty centimeters above the ground. It gave little advantage, but enough of one that I'd take it. Besides, the inmates knew to look here. They knew to listen to whoever spoke to them from here. I could use that to my advantage.

There were no trees, nothing that could cast a shadow on her. "Keep that spotlight here!" I shouted to the faceless soldiers in the guard towers. They did.

With Ember bound, I sent Turuk back inside with Lockbox. Lockbox would slip one direction to make sure Mike was able to spread the word of the prison break and Turuk would ask Molnar for a public execution. Molnar would have to come out here. I wouldn't leave Ember's side. Not when she was in this condition. Vulnerable and cold.

Ears trained, I listened for the sound of the rifles. The clicks of any gun's safety getting turned off. The click of a new magazine getting slipped in. Nothing happened. There had to be three aimed in our direction, but no one's heart rate or breathing was so loud to make me think they were going to open fire on her.

The gash she'd made on my arm was deep. I looked at it, realizing I'd forgotten to allow pain in. I dropped all blocks to pain and screamed out. Delayed. So delayed. Maybe no one would notice. Maybe normal men have adrenaline-masked injuries too. My blood stained my whole sleeve red.

Good, I thought. *It'll give the inmates something to see. Something convincing to witness when I need to win them over.*

I called up to the guard tower.

"Is there a medic out here?" I asked. No one answered. "Who can hear me?"

Two soldiers spoke at once. "I hear you, Sir."

"I'm not a medic."

"Go get Doctor Traft!" I screamed, packing my arm with snow.

"I can watch the Victor while you go in!" someone replied from above.

As the only female inmate, everyone knew she was the Victor. With all the eyes on her, no one bothered thinking about me.

"This Victor will not leave my sight until I, myself, have retribution. High Warden Molnar gave me this job. I will see it through."

"Roger that, Sir," came a reply.

The steady *thunk* of the boots of a descending soldier rang in my head until he reached the snow and walked toward us. The soldier, a private, stood before me in blatant terror.

"I'll get the doctor, Sir." He saluted and hurried away.

Step one was complete.

Ember didn't fight. Didn't move. Didn't complain. I knew she'd healed her head and was biding her time.

If she was afraid, she didn't show it.

I kept my eyes fixed on the door to the prison and my ears trained for any sign of a threat to Ember.

The door opened wide, and Captain Oravec accompanied Doctor Traft out into the dim morning light. Oravec had his Lugar in hand. Traft carried a large medical kit.

They stomped over to me, and Doctor Traft got to work on my arm.

"We really should get you inside so I can get this cleaned up," he said, his voice dull and quiet.

"No," I insisted. "I'm not leaving her side until I've had my revenge, and I won't mete it out until I have an audience."

Oravec raised his caterpillar eyebrows at me.

"How'd she do it?" he asked.

"She's fast," I groaned as Doctor Traft injected a numbing agent into my arm around the gash.

"You've lost a lot of blood," Traft said. "You should at least sit down, Sir."

I shook my head, ever wary of the weapon in Oravec's hands.

"I'll watch her for you," Oravec said, glancing toward Emberly. Her short black hair blew around her face in a tangle making her look nearly demonic as she glared at us unblinking. There was something majestic in the role she played. Something beautiful in her power.

"She's not going anywhere," I said. "My concern is not that she'll attack again, but that someone will steal this show from me."

"Show?" Oravec asked.

The door opened again. Four guards exited alongside High Warden Molnar and Turuk. Molnar walked with such fear I wondered if he'd ever set foot in the yard before this. Something told me, from the way he admired the guard towers en route, that he hadn't.

"Status?" He asked, but I wasn't sure if he was asking me, Doctor Traft, or Captain Oravec.

Doctor Traft answered. "Lieutenant Drivick has been attacked quite badly, Sir. I recommended that he come inside where I can stitch him up as necessary, but he refuses."

"Drivick," Molnar said, voice full of compassion. "You ought to listen to the good doctor. We'd hate to lose you."

I shook my head and caught sight of Oravec pointing his gun toward Emberly.

"May I?" I asked, gesturing to his Lugar.

"I'd rather not," Oravec replied. "The Victor disarmed you once. If she takes this, we're all in danger."

"She won't get it from me now. She's chained."

High Warden Molnar dug his hands into his pockets before weighing in. "Go ahead and give it to Drivick. Let him carry out the execution, and we can go back inside."

Oravec passed his weapon to me. I didn't aim it at Emberly—not yet.

"I will do it here. I will do it with this, but Sir, I think we need to do it publicly. With an audience."

Molnar's beady eyes flickered with fear. "Who did you have in mind?"

"All the lurpers here. I think you should bring them all out here to witness the execution. Think of the message it would send. The daughter of the former high warden here."

"It would be bold," Molnar said.

"It's necessary," I insisted. "If we let her get away with this, or put her away privately, the lurpers might come up with some other story. They might allow hope to blossom in their hearts. We can't let that happen. She must die today under their watch."

Molnar looked out at the yard. "You want me to order all the lurpers to the yard? Most are still in their cells."

"Yessir. Bring them out here without any breakfast. Make them stand in the cold. It makes them slow enough without the need to chain them. Disarm any guards on the ground except for their palkas. Get plenty of guards in the towers."

"Disarm the guards?"

"You saw what this one did with my dagger!"

Molnar peered over to see Traft at work putting sutures in my arm. "And where would I be for all this?" He gawked at my injury.

"On the platform, Sir. With these personal guards. I'll be here, and Turuk." I hoped it didn't matter that I used names here around Emberly. He didn't seem to care. She was about to die as far as he was concerned.

"Besides the security risk, it would take a couple of hours, at least!"

"The sun will be up by then, so you don't have to worry about them being shrouded by the morning light, but it'll be cold enough that the lurpers won't cause any problems. They'll be hungry and tired and cold and *compliant*," I said. "Yes, it's a bit of work to get them out here, but it's a few hours of work for months of compliance. It would absolutely devastate their spirits. I think it's quite timely considering all the rumors about Victor-27. Some of these lurpers think he escaped. They might start thinking they can get somewhere, too. I think it would be a bold move, but one that would set you apart as high warden here, Sir."

He considered it as he nuzzled into the thick fur of his overcoat.

"Okay," he agreed. "You can have your retribution publicly and then we will put all the inmates into their cells for the rest of the day. There's chatter coming in from Khizmit that leaves me unsettled." He flashed a look towards Emberly and then turned back to me.

"We'll get the inmates out here to witness the execution and then they're all going back to their cells until all this talk of coups dies down."

I smiled. "Excellent, Sir."

Traft wrapped a bandage around my arm.

"It's been treated for infection and sewn up." He looked over to Emberly. "The sooner we're rid of her, the better. You'll be nothing but scar tissue if she stays."

"When the yard is full, I'll return," Molnar said, stiffly reaching down to place a hand on the hilt of his saber.

"Captain Oravec, will you accompany me?" he asked.

"Yessir," Oravec said, and looked at me. "I'll need that."

Molnar noticed my hesitation in returning it. "Let Drivick keep it. We'll get you another one."

"Thank you, Sir," I said.

"Drivick," Molnar said, shuffling a little closer to me. "When she's dead, will you stay?"

"I don't know," I replied. "I can stay if you'd like me to. Or I can go to hunt the rest of the Markos family."

Molnar chuckled and it came out a mix of surprise and fear. "Stay with him," Molnar told Turuk.

Molnar and his guards retreated inside. I stayed on the platform with Turuk and Ember. The minutes dragged past.

Cell by cell the guards released inmates and drove them outside by the ends of palkas and shouted threats. As the sun rose, the yard filled up, each lurper standing still in their assigned places. They looked like statues as they stood, hopeless, hurting, and angry. Would my words be enough to light a fire in them? A fire warm enough to bring these statues of boys to life? They looked so young.

"Where's Lockbox?" I asked Turuk.

"I sent him on with my key. He should be in his cell. When

they bring the inmates from that cell block out, he'll be with them."

"Ember," I whispered. "Are you—"

"Stop asking if I'm okay," she said playfully. Honestly, how she could sound playful made no sense at all. "I'm fine. It's cold, but I've numbed it so when it becomes painful it disappears and I'm all healed up for whenever you give the signal."

"You're amazing," I said.

The door opened again, and Lockbox led the way, but unlike the other lurpers, he was chained. The rest of the inmates from his cell block weren't with him.

But someone I recognized was.

And someone who must have recognized him.

My hand tightened on the handle of Oravec's Lugar.

High Captain Voboda was supposed to be watching the Oscars in The Grand Palace, so why the skudge was he here at Rhosivi?

CHAPTER 34
NO MORE PRETENSE

By the time the pointed nose and chin of High Captain Voboda turned in my direction, I'd pulled the thick brown ushanka low over my eyebrows and fastened the top buttons on my overcoat to cover the bottom half of my face.

The cruster worked with Oscars which meant he must have gotten the assignment for being clever himself. When he got close enough, he'd recognize me as Private Petrov, the idiot who'd helped Lockbox, that exact Oscar who now walked in front of him in chains, fly away from The Grand Palace on canvas wings.

I gritted my teeth together.

"This is going to go poorly," I warned Turuk. "Change of plans."

"Luka," he muttered. "Don't do anything—"

"Get High Warden Molnar out here immediately!" I hissed. "I'll postpone as long as I can."

The inmates were still slowly being shuffled out into the frigid air. The hum of energy that filled me didn't extend to anyone else, except for Emberly who now sat up, staring towards Lockbox.

Turuk stepped away from the platform and stopped High Captain Voboda en route with a salute.

"Good morning, Sir. Can I help you with anything?" Even from this distance, he sounded scared. Many inmates turned to see Lockbox and High Captain Voboda. While his rank patch would have certainly drawn their attention, I don't think many of them could see it. Most of them looked because it was something, anything to see and hear in this frozen world while they waited for what they surely knew would be a public execution.

"I was informed Head Warden Molnar would be out here," Voboda said. "Where is he?"

"If you wait over there at the platform, he'll be out momentarily."

"I'd rather meet him inside, if possible." Voboda's teeth chattered. The chains rattled in his bare hands. The idiot hadn't brought gloves out.

"We're in the middle of a security situation—"

"I'd say! Look what I found. My missing Oscar, and his numbers have been altered. Who the skudge would ink a lurper?"

"I don't know, Sir," Turuk replied calmly, directing Voboda to the podium.

With a revolver in one hand and Lockbox's chains in the other, he marched towards me. "Lieutenant, please tell me you know something about this."

I maintained a level composure and the accent I'd pulled into my voice since my arrival. "About the Oscar, Sir?"

"I was told an Oscar turned up. There are no records of an Oscar-16 which is why I, myself, came to see what the skudge is going on."

"Yessir," I said calmly.

Voboda stepped closer to me, sending my heartrate hammering. "You heard about the escaped lurper in Khizmit?"

"Yessir. An Oscar from the Grand Palace. You're High Captain Voboda, aren't you Sir?"

"This is the Oscar!"

"Congratulations, Sir," I said keeping my back straight and my sentences short. Another line of lurpers exited the prison and took their places in the yard.

"His wrist doesn't say Oscar-17. It's been changed." Finally, Voboda looked at my arm. "What happened to you?"

"This inmate attacked me." I jerked my head towards Ember. "We're currently assembling all the lurpers for a public execution."

"I don't see why you need an audience."

"You will."

"Excuse me?"

He must not have liked my tone. I didn't care.

"You will see why we need an audience."

The back door opened and Turuk exited, followed by Head Warden Molnar, Captain Oravec, and three other guards.

The yard of inmates stood frozen as the ice around us, but they watched. They waited. They stood patiently even while their nerves were on edge. I could hear it in their breathing and the small shifts in their stances.

"High Captain," Molnar said, rapidly approaching Voboda. "Is this your Oscar then?"

"Yes," Voboda replied, giving the chains a hard pull. Lockbox faceplanted on the ice. He sat up with a cut across his cheekbone from where his glasses had hit. A single drop of blood stained the snow in front of him. "Stay down now, and you'll be able to walk back to Khizmit or I'll break both your legs again and drag you there!"

I stared at the single drop of blood, and it stained my whole vision in red. I looked up to the center of Voboda's face.

Pop!

The snow around me flooded in red. A second passed.

Another second. Then Voboda's body dropped to the ground. The inmates stood in absolute silence and stillness.

"Dr-Drivick?" Molnar asked, his large mouth agape. Oravec raised his new Lugar towards me.

My hand still held the Lugar pointed where Voboda's head had been. Large pieces of his brain melted scattered divots. Whispers from lurpers in the back found their way to my ears.

"I'm sorry," I whispered to Molnar. Slowly I extended the handle of the Lugar to Turuk. "My nerves must have gotten to me. I didn't mean…" I dropped to my knees.

"Raise your weapons," Molnar directed the guards. Most of them hadn't been looking at me anyway. They'd been too distracted by the smatter of gore across the snow. Did he think I'd accidentally shot High Captain Voboda in the face? In a moment reason would return to him. But he didn't have a moment.

I slid forward through the mess and grabbed Voboda's revolver. I shot Oravec in the hand, making him drop his Lugar.

"Drop your weapons!" I bellowed, shouting with my real voice. No more masks. No more pretense. One guard dropped his Lugar. Another guard raised his towards me. I shot his hand. Turuk's Lugar barked and then a guard from the tower fell, crunching into the snow with a disgusting thud.

I jumped at Head Warden Molnar and used him as a body shield against any guards in the towers. I pressed the warm end of the revolver to his throat. "Tell them to drop their weapons."

"What's going on?"

"Tell them to drop their weapons."

"Drop your weapons!" Molnar shouted.

Oravec was screaming, but he'd scooted away to pack his hand and wrap a tourniquet around it.

"Nobody move!" I screamed. Molnar winced.

"The guards in the towers need to throw down their rifles."

"But Drivick, the lurpers could grab them if they—"

"Tell them to throw them down now!" I pressed the gun deeper into his fat throat.

Molnar raised his voice. "Throw down your rifles from the towers."

"No one move until I say to!" I screamed as an older lurper stepped out of his place to reach for a falling rifle.

I fired, planting a bullet in his shoulder. "I said no one move!" The lurper froze.

"Mike!" I screamed. "Mike, are you here?"

A shuffle and then a soft reply.

"Yes," he said. He stepped out of position and raised his hand.

"Bring me three rifles!"

He was fast. He slipped around the standing lurpers, snatched the rifles the guards had dropped, and clambered up towards me, only slowing as he drew near to Molnar. I traded my revolver with him.

"Stay here," I said. "Keep that aimed at Molnar, but don't fire."

I passed a rifle to Lockbox, and one to Emberly, who stood and aimed it at the guards who stood beside us on the podium.

"If anyone moves before I say you can, you will be shot, lurper or cruster I don't give a slag!"

I looked back to Lockbox and Turuk.

"You're clear," Turuk said.

"All clear," Lockbox confirmed, adjusting his glasses.

I stepped out from behind Molnar.

"My name is Luka Drivick, but you all probably know me as Victor-27." Gasps and curse words of shock spread through the crowd. I reached up and removed my overcoat to fully expose my arm. The explosives I'd stashed there fell out and Lockbox snatched them up to carry out with him.

"Look!" I said, directing their attention to the wound as I healed it. "That's your evidence. I'm going to tell you how this will happen. The crusters will stay in place. If you wear stripes and you want out, go to tunnel 33B. If you don't know where that is, head that direction." I pointed straight back to the small opening. "Some of you may have heard that I am here to liberate the lurpers. It's true."

"Drivick," Molnar said. "They can't just leave. You can't just—" Mike reached over and relieved him of his saber. As the long blade left its sheath, Molnar quieted.

"Go now! Follow Lockbox and Ember. I will take up the rear. If you inflict violence on anyone you will be shot." I hoped I wouldn't miss.

I turned to Lockbox. By now he'd managed to unlock his cuffs with Voboda's keys.

"Did I know him?" Lockbox asked, motioning to the body.

"Yes," I said. "Go!" Lockbox and Ember ran off the platform between the rows of lurpers who took a few seconds to realize that I was serious. "Go!" I screamed again, and they did. They pivoted around and followed orders. They didn't stampede or trample, they just ran off for tunnel 33B.

Movement in a tower to the northwest prompted me to send three bullets that way. I don't know what the guard was doing, but he stopped when the lead bit him. Molnar had melted into a puddle of despair at my feet.

"I'm not going to kill you, Sir," I said as the last line of lurpers disappeared into the distance.

"Someone else will," he said ruefully.

I looked up to see Oravec staring at me. Maybe he didn't believe I was Victor-27. Maybe he didn't want to believe that a lurper could put on a uniform and pass as a man.

"Turuk? Are you a lurper too? You can't be..." Molnar trailed off.

"No Sir. I'm just sympathetic to their cause."

"Sympathetic," Molnar said. "Sympathetic is one way to put it."

Turuk and I backed away slowly and then broke into a full sprint, following the trail the lurpers of Rhosivi had left on the grounds. I waited for the crack of a rifle to sound behind me or the steady stomp of boots to follow, but they didn't. Not yet.

I was leaving Rhosivi for good. Last time I vowed to never return. This time there would be nothing to return to. Nothing for anyone to return to.

"We'll bury you!" Molnar screamed when we'd gotten far enough away. "There's no exit that way. We'll blow the tunnels and bury you!"

I knew they'd follow. We had enough time. We had to have enough time!

As I ran I heard Molnar shouting, "Collapse the mines!"

When we got to tunnel 33B, it was packed and ringing with sounds. Crowds of inmates parted as I walked through.

"Work faster!" I screamed looking for a spare pickaxe to join in the work of collapsing our entrance.

A few Hotels began smashing their tools against the walls. In a flash of stripes, the inmates had torn down the support beams around the entrance.

Then it started. Far in the distance came the drumming of boots in the mine. Hundreds of boots perhaps. The pop of rifles rang out. They had to have mobilized every guard in Rhosivi.

"Hurry!" Lockbox commanded. The inmates worked faster, set some fuses, and then we ran.

The explosion was too close. Dust billowed behind us, and the reverberations shook through my legs. I tripped over the inmate in front of me who'd fallen, smothering a few more who'd dropped to the ground in front of him.

We all rested for a couple of seconds as the rocks behind us settled.

"We're safe," someone said.

"We're stuck," another one said.

"They'll dig through," Turuk added, and I looked to see him a few people away. He was easy to spot as the only other uniformed body in the crowd.

"Everyone get up!" I shouted and somehow the inmates obeyed and stood.

"Where are we going?" A few people asked.

"Out the Freedom Tunnel!" Lockbox declared, a few dim lights of lanterns shining off his dusty glasses.

"It's a dream!" someone yelled.

"Then follow your dream and get the skudge out of here before they blow the whole mine!" I yelled back. Lockbox and Ember led the way with their lanterns. Lockbox identified a few other Oscar's and brought them to help lead. I didn't even stop to consider what it would mean if Lockbox had picked the wrong tunnel.

Call it hope. Call it faith. Whatever it was, it numbed pain better than the strongest dose of vyco.

I moved down the side tunnel to the pump and began working it. Up and down. Up and down. Turuk stood at my side as all the rest of the lurpers worked their way down the tunnels. There was no time to pause, not with hundreds of breathing bodies going through the Freedom Tunnel. One pump every thirty seconds wouldn't be enough. I hoped constant pumping would be. Up and down. Up and down.

"I'll take it from here, Sir," Turuk said.

"If they come in, I can heal."

"You won't be able to heal any better than I can when they blow the mine."

I pumped harder as the sounds of the inmates in the tunnel died down.

"This isn't your fight. Go with them."

"No, Luka. It's my fight because I made it my fight. I don't belong with them. One of us will die here and if it's me, it doesn't really matter. No one will really care that much. But if it's you, well, you know what I mean. You're their savior. You're the symbol. You have so much more to offer the world than I do. I'm just a man. You're something much greater than that."

I pumped three more times. "You're wrong," I said, reaching out to embrace Turuk. "I'll care."

"Let me stay. Let me go out as a hero."

"Let you die?"

"Let me save you." He smiled taking hold of the pump.

"You did," I said, picking up the last little lantern left behind.

I didn't know if it was the right thing to do, but I let him. I hurried away down the tunnel after the lurpers of Rhosivi and let Turuk stay alone in the pitch blackness of the mine pumping ventilation for us.

CHAPTER 35
BURNING AND MEMORIES

Every few minutes a soft *pfffft* sounded through pipes above us. I stood there where the tunnel leveled out, listening to the steady puff of air coming through the ventilation. Every pump sounded like Turuk telling me to run. Telling me to go on. Turuk would pump all the air out, leaving none for himself.

When pitching the plan of escape, Lockbox had told me to assign the pumping job to someone else. I'd agreed but I'd always planned on it being me. I thought maybe I could pump until everyone was gone and then I could take a deep breath and run. I should have found an Echo to do it. No, I wouldn't ask anyone to do it. I hadn't asked Turuk, I reminded myself as guilt nipped at my heels.

The Freedom Tunnel could help Turuk escape. He wouldn't pump it forever. He'd follow eventually.

The resounding echo of the detonation behind me shook dirt and large pieces of earth from the walls. The ceiling was low, so the rocks didn't have far to fall.

"Turuk," I whispered, pausing for a moment. He'd buried himself for us. For lurpers.

If Veles or some other God was real, I prayed they'd take Turuk to a paradise peacefully. That his arms would grow tired, and he'd take a moment to rest only to wake in a warm and beautiful city in the skies made for self-sacrificing soldiers. Made for men like him.

Knowing my oxygen was limited, I hurried on, following the distant sounds of the lurpers ahead of me.

"You there?" Lockbox asked.

"That's the second time you've snuck up on me in here," I said as we hurried on together.

"Just making sure you didn't get left behind."

"You…waited for me?"

"Yes, Mr. Chief –"

"Don't," I said.

"I was going to say Mr. Chief Lurper Officer, for your information."

"Sure."

"I was!"

"Will they get lost up there without you leading the way now?"

"Nah, it's just a straight shot to the surface. No other tunnels." Lockbox turned back towards Rhosivi.

"How did the Freedom Tunnel get here?"

The tunnel narrowed and Lockbox had to bend over to squeeze through.

"A group of Mikes, Novembers, and Oscars here worked together to construct the Freedom Tunnel about ten years ago. Rumor was that they enlisted the help of some Golfs, Hotels, and Indias to help dig and lay the ventilation pipes. Most of those who built it used it to escape. Since guards didn't come this way, no one checked to see if the area they'd been told to mine ended up being accurately mapped on the records given to the head warden. The head warden at the time was Markos, and maybe he didn't care either way."

For all I knew, Markos planted the idea of a Freedom Tunnel in their heads.

"Turuk stayed?"

"Yes,"

"Sorry. Sorry you lost another friend."

"It's a recurring theme," I stated. Then worried I'd guilted him, I tried to make it better. "I didn't lose him. We'll hang out again when we're all dead. Might be soon if you keep talking and using up all the air." I gave him a playful push with my elbow.

He didn't stay silent long as the tunnel continued. I listened ahead, some of the clamor of inmates still reached me. They were fast. Good. We had to be.

"What's the plan when we get out, sir?" Lockbox asked.

"Drop the sir and I'll tell you."

"I mean it as a joke, Victor."

Victor. That was progress. I could live with him calling me Victor. "You said we're not far from Vazenia. We'll go there. Rescue some of the inmates." If they weren't all dead, was the unspoken ending. "I was sort of banking on you giving me the rest of the plan."

"That man, Voboda, he broke my legs before?"

"Yes,"

"And I, I'm sorry but, did I…"

"What?"

"I have something like a memory of being in the air. Of flying."

"You flew like an eagle. You glided out of an open window."

"Sounds cool," he said.

We continued. The air felt heavier. My movements slower. *Good thing,* I thought, *that Emberly and the others are far ahead.*

"When you told me everything, it helped," he said.

"Yeah?"

"About our time together. The Outskirts. I'll piece it together."

"I know you will," I said, and just then, a shout of joy streamed through the tunnel back towards us.

The first group made it out. Twenty minutes later, the bright sun broke through a small crevice in the earth that led upwards.

They'd been waiting for me. All the lurpers from Rhosivi had stood or sat with their attention at the hole watching for me to emerge.

"Victor!" They shouted! Some rushed me to embrace me. Others stared on in disbelief. I thought I saw Foxtrot's face, but it was swallowed in the swarm of striped linens.

"Listen!" I shouted, climbing atop a large boulder where Lockbox and Emberly waited for me. As they quieted, I intended to tell them we were going to Vazenia and then to Khizmit to join Markos' coup. But I heard a distant group trampling through snow and ice, hurrying towards us. I narrowed my eyes at the horizon to the southeast and there, through the trees, came an army.

"Someone's coming!" I shouted. "We need to be united. We can't fight each other!"

"Stop thinking we're going to fight each other!" an inmate screamed. "If you're a lurper like us, then stop treating us how the crusters did."

A few voices joined in unison. As I looked upon the group, I didn't see them as a group of dangerous lurpers with a mixture of incredible abilities. I saw boys. Scared, cold, brave boys ready to unite and change the world.

"Get into a formation. Set yourselves up as if this is the prison yard. Take your places facing the incoming force. Use your weapons on my command!" As I spoke, they moved, as if they'd been trained. Some wielded hammers, others chisels or rifles. It only took a few moments for them to get into position. Ember, Lockbox, and Mike stood beside me on the giant bolder overlooking the sparse trees, our army, and the incoming force.

"Who are they?" I asked Lockbox.

"I love that you always think I have the answer," he replied, a bit of teasing in his tone.

We waited for the force to advance. For them to get close enough to see. *Had Rhosivi radioed for help? Could an army from Khizmit have arrived this quickly? Or were these men guards from Predvoi since it was much closer?* Even as I squinted and tried to get my eyes to work at this distance, I couldn't tell what I was looking at.

The uniforms were green and grey.

"We should walk out to meet them," Lockbox said as the air between us grew heavy. "Us three. You're the commander here. We're your cadre."

We'd do what Lockbox said.

"Stay here," I directed Mike.

"Yessir," he replied.

Lockbox, Ember, and I climbed down from the rock and walked down the straight line of soldiers toward the advancing force. My heart pounded as I felt the gaze of a hundred lurpers at my back. It was as Flak had said. These were my brothers.

We left the safety of the formation and crossed the open area towards the incoming force. At a distance, they stopped and a group of six individuals began walking towards us.

A voice called out, "Luka!" and the tension in my shoulders released. Roman could see us. Roman could identify me even though, for me, he stood as nothing but an incoming silhouette.

After several more strides forward the silhouettes all became familiar. Commander Markos stood in the center, with Roman on his right, Alba beside him. On his left were two members of his cadre, Captain Gaborik, his blond curls slicked across his sweaty forehead, and Captain Sakrova whose smile now revealed two missing teeth. Kasia, the smallest of them all, walked at the end.

My heart warmed that Markos' cadre remained loyal after

learning what he was. Emberly sprinted across the distance and leapt into her father's arms. She looked small there, cradled against him. She'd seemed so strong, unstoppable, and capable in Rhosivi but there in her father's arms, she became something fragile. Roman hurried forward, clapping me on the back. Lockbox crept behind us, moving to the left. Was he ashamed to be here? I decided he didn't have a memory of Markos and The Outskirts.

"Lockbox," Markos said, trying to get Lockbox's attention.

"Commander Markos, sir," Lockbox said, visibly uncomfortable.

"We lost contact," he said, reaching out to clap him on the back. "Have you heard from Zuzana? I thought you were—what's wrong?" he asked as Lockbox recoiled.

"He lost his memory." I stated the sad fact. "But it's coming back."

"Show me your arm," Markos said, and Lockbox complied, quickly rolling up the sleeve to show his wrist. "No, not that." Markos pulled the sleeve higher, exposing the inner side of Lockbox's elbow. A series of red ripples extended from a large purple mark there.

"You've been drugged."

"Yessir," Lockbox said.

"How long ago?"

Lockbox said he remembered being in the snow outside Khizmit and a journey in the back of a truck to Rhozivi.

"Some memories are coming back," he said.

"Oscars are remarkable. Hold on," Markos said. "Gaborik," he called.

Gaborik stepped over.

"The medical kit please." He extended his hand and Gaborik handed him a small black bag. From within, Markos extracted a vial with a light blue liquid.

"You'll just feel a slight pinch," Markos said, filling a syringe with the medicine.

"What a surprise seeing you again!" Alba shouted, unexpectedly rushing over to see…me? In her haste she bumped into Markos roughly, making him drop the vial into the snow. All eyes went to the vial, miraculously unbroken. Alba stepped past, making an obvious and deliberate attempt to step directly on it.

Markos grabbed her and moved her away from the vial.

"Be careful," he said.

"I didn't mean…" she said, before lunging at the vial. She failed again to break it.

"Contain her," Markos said, handing her over to Roman.

He took her gently, but firmly into his arms. "Alba, please, explain—"

"Why?" she spat, trying to push away. "I don't have to explain!"

"What's gotten into you?" Roman asked again as she hit him repeatedly. "I'll let you go but hold still until we can figure this out. Please."

She stilled. "I'm afraid, okay? I'm surrounded by all these lurpers. I'm unarmed. I'm scared!"

"I won't let something happen to you."

"Arm me," she said. "Give me your gun. I'll calm down if I just have some sort of weapon in my hand."

Alba and I locked gazes for a fleeting moment. She was horrified of me. And for good reason. It was only a matter of hours before I'd make good on my threat against Khizmit. Not as gratuitously as I'd said. When I'd said those things about making blood run in the streets of Khizmit, I hadn't been myself. I could be, as Kasia had said, morally virtuous. Alba would see that in time.

Roman continued his attempts to calm Alba as Markos drove the needle deep into the purple mark on Lockbox's arm. "Slight pinch, and then, it will burn." By the time he finished saying it, the vial was empty.

Lockbox began to breathe louder and louder. He dropped to the snow; his arm held tightly to his side.

Kasia approached me and I turned to look at her properly. She wore her uniform again, but now that I'd seen her in Emberly's dress, the way she'd moved at DavatNoc, I couldn't look at her quite the same. Quite as neutrally.

"It will bring back his memory," she explained. "But it has to burn up the blocking agents in the drug he's been given."

Lockbox moved his hands to his arms and then his head.

"It burns!" he screamed.

"Will he be okay?" *What if he lost more of his memories? What if this medicine made him remember even less?*

"He will. It will only take a few moments." Kasia smiled. "Congratulations on the promotion, Lieutenant Drivick," she said, looking at my rank patch.

"Kasia," I said, knowing this wasn't the time. "I'm sorry I scared you back in Khizmit. You were right. I wasn't myself. And when…" I looked over to see Emberly standing across from me, far away, fixated on Lockbox as he rolled around in pain. "When you…held me, it helped. I didn't thank you. I've thought a lot about what you said. 'There's no moral virtue in being—'"

"Back up!" Lockbox shouted, looking back to the group of us. *Was he mad at me again?*

We spread out, staring as Lockbox rolled around. I backed up again, notably putting more distance between myself and Ember.

"He'll be okay. He'll be able to answer questions soon," Kasia said returning to my side. "You found Emberly." She looked over in Ember's direction. "That's what matters."

"That's what matters, but it's not all that matters. I just mean to say—"

"Luka," Kasia placed her hand on my shoulder. "We don't need to define anything right now. Focus on the mission. We'll have time to debrief later." She laughed and stepped back, letting some more formality enter her tone. "Someone didn't want Lockbox to remember the past." She looked towards Alba.

Lockbox rolled across the snow, crying out.

"Can't we help him?" I asked. "Give him vyco?"

"It'll only last a minute. Vyco wouldn't work right away. Oscars don't respond to it the same as you do anyway."

Lockbox kept spasming in the snow, screaming. Then, suddenly, he stopped.

He stood.

He sprinted across the snow, rushing towards Alba, malintent in every motion.

Then I saw Alba. She held Roman's Lugar in her hand and leveled it at Roman's head while his attention remained fixed on Lockbox.

"Roman!" I screamed, sprinting forward. *Too slow. Too slow!*

Alba turned the gun to Lockbox just as he mimicked a move I'd done where I'd thrown a closed fist into another lurper's chest. Only Lockbox's closed fist held a blade. Where he got it, I had no idea. It must have been back in Rhosivi. Back when the guards had dropped their weapons.

Eyes wide, mouth partially open, Alba dropped straight back.

Her body hit the ground as lifelessly as a felled tree. The pistol slipped from her fingers. Lockbox was retreating as Roman caught him around the throat.

"What have you done?" Roman screamed, looking past the kid in his grip to the woman he loved. Dead. Dead on the floor. Blood continued to pour from her chest even though her heart had stilled.

Roman's hands were tightening around Lockbox's throat.

I tackled Roman to the side, forcing him to release Lockbox and face me.

Kasia and Ember both approached, and Markos told them to stand down.

"Get out of my way!" Roman bellowed, trying to throw me to the side. I kept hold of the end of his sleeve as he stood and then pulled him back towards me as I blocked his knee with the bottom of my foot. He went tumbling to the side. I landed on top, pulled by the grip I had on his sleeve.

I sat atop Roman as he twisted to the side.

The Lugar. I'd forgotten to get the Lugar before he did. He nearly had it pointed at Lockbox when I flipped around, pinning his bicep with my shin before bending his wrist backward.

"Let go," I said, knowing if he didn't, I'd break his wrist. "Let go. Let him explain himself!"

"Explain—" Roman caught me in the side of the head with his other fist and I tumbled off the side into the snow.

I jumped up and kicked the gun from his hands. I'd expected him to dive after it, but he moved in the other direction, towards Lockbox.

Lockbox was frozen to the spot, staring at the woman he'd killed.

"Killing him won't bring her back!" I shouted, reaching for Roman. He tried to throw me, but I dropped to my back intentionally and with my feet on his hips, threw him over my head.

I looped my arm around his head and his right arm while leaning into his ribs. Pinned. He was pinned between me and the snow. Though he thrashed he got nowhere. I gripped behind my knee with my right arm, holding him in position.

"Let me go!" Roman bellowed, fighting me again. Every time he exhaled, I leaned in harder. With each breath, his lung capacity decreased.

In less than a minute he stilled. His entire body collapsed as if all the muscles released at once.

I released the pressure on his chest and moved away, sure the rage had passed. He let out a long exhale and sat up.

Captain Romulus Kral, the company commander of the Lurper Legion, crawled on his hands and knees through the snow to the body of the woman he loved. His shoulders rocked with sobs as he held her. Crimson tinged my vision as I approached Lockbox.

"What have you done?" I whispered, feeling tears fall down my face.

Lockbox had become a bigger threat than any of us.

CHAPTER 36
SCARS

"ALBA WAS GOING to kill you and me and any other lurpers she could get her hands on," Lockbox explained, voice full of terror. He looked at her corpse held delicately in Roman's arms. Lockbox's voice shook with every word. "I remember it all now. It's rushing back too quickly to explain. She knew I'd remember, and she was going to kill me. To kill him." He pointed his finger to Roman and then, seeing how dramatically it shook, pulled his arm back in. With a shudder, he sat on the ground. Kasia approached him.

"Alba injected you?" Roman asked.

"Yes. And as I was falling asleep, thinking it was a sedation serum, she pulled out another one."

"Why would she sedate you?"

"I remember realizing in that moment that she was here to sabotage it all. She'd come to sabotage the coup. I asked her why, and she said Romulus."

"What?" Roman asked, aghast.

"She said, 'He's why! I didn't have a strong opinion about lurpers before him. But he came into my life, stole my heart, and only after he held it admitted what he was. He manipulated me; conned me into being an accomplice.'" Lockbox could hardly speak fast enough to get all the words out coherently. "You told her Luka was different but she…she saw him that night with Milena. She said Luka was going to flood the streets of Khizmit in the blood of the chancellors." Lockbox turned to me, mortified at the memory and the image. He turned back to Roman.

"Alba said…she said you left her no choice. When she found out you hadn't killed Victor-27 and you'd lied to everyone about it, she couldn't trust you. She couldn't trust lurpers. You'd stashed me at her home. You damned the Markos family, whom she'd come to love. While she'd planned to sabotage the coup for a long time, she wasn't sure she could go through with it once she heard that Ember and Milena were lurpers…but then she met the Victor." Lockbox gestured unnecessarily to me. "She heard firsthand the threat he posed to Khizmit. She tried to console him, if for no other reason than to survive the night."

Roman clenched and unclenched his fist. Lockbox's hand went to his temple again.

"It's not true," Roman declared.

"She said Luka was a demon," Lockbox said, his voice pained. "A monster."

The memory of Milena's death punched back through me. Had I been the one to push Alba past her breaking point? I'd been terrifying that night. She'd been openly mortified at how I'd snapped Erik's neck, and I hadn't shown even a milliliter of remorse. I should have cared how frightened Alba had been. I should have been more in tune with her opinion of me and the things she'd said.

But I wasn't responsible for her betrayal.

Lockbox stared at Alba. "She said she'd kill all the lurpers if she had the chance. She hoped to use me to bring us down. To stop the coup."

"Start at the beginning. They'll understand better if you work chronologically," Kasia said.

Lockbox took another quivering breath and shut his eyes while a few tears leaked out.

"I used the cipher Luka brought back from Commander Alekin. We opened lines of communication and set a new plan. Not to overthrow Khizmit. Not to go through with the coup. We'd lose too much doing that."

"We aren't going to Khizmit?" I asked.

"No, I'll explain. Let me get through this," Lockbox said. "As soon as I could walk and see properly, Markos and I coordinated a new plan. One that required me to go to Khizmit alone. I would tell Zuzana the change of plans. Tell her it was time to leave. First I had to go to Chancellor Eldrat myself to tell him that Markos planned a coup."

"That's true. He's accurate there," Markos said.

"Why him?" I asked.

Lockbox answered. "He'd technically bought me at auction, and I pretended that I'd been loyal to him all along. I told him Markos planned a coup. I brought evidence. Asked him not to send me to the Grand Palace. Offered to be his personal information slave. Eldrat passed the information along. I told him the best way to defend Khizmit would be to pull the Bear and Wolf Legions back to the city walls."

"And he listened to you?" I asked.

"Did you get in touch with Zuzana?" Markos asked.

"No. I couldn't reach her. I didn't deliver the message because of her." Lockbox pointed to the body still held in Roman's arms. "Alba. She came to Chancellor Eldrat and, oh Veles, she killed him, framed me for the murder, and then injected me with a psychoactive drug," Lockbox mumbled. "It's giving me retroactive blackouts. But it's coming back. My memories." He offered me a weak smile. It was the kindest look he'd given me since turning up at Rhosivi.

"I'm sure she meant for me to die, but, well, this lurp doesn't go down easily. She left me alone in that room, with a wiped memory, and Eldrat's blood on my arms. I climbed out through a window and managed to get down part of the wall before I fell. Must have been picked up by some guards outside of Khizmit. They brought me to Rhosivi as an empty shell of what I was."

"Not empty," I said. "Angry. Mean."

"I was afraid," Lockbox said, locking eyes with me. It pained him to look at my face with the scar. "I was afraid of you."

I nodded. Even Roman was terrified of me at times. Lockbox looked back to Roman. "I wasn't trying to kill her," he whispered. "But I was afraid. And she was going to kill you."

I'd seen her with the pistol in hand, aiming at Roman from point-blank.

"Alba wouldn't do any of that," Roman insisted. "She wouldn't drug you."

"We can find out if it's real," Lockbox said. He swallowed obviously. It had to be true. Every word. Lockbox wasn't there with me, Kasia, and Alba that night.

Lockbox continued. "If Zuzana is alive, then call this all a messy mistake from confabulation."

"Confabulation?" I asked.

"Messy mistake?" Roman shouted. "You killed her and you don't even know if your memory is accurate!"

"Confabulation is when someone with amnesia makes up memories to fill in gaps. I'm certain this isn't such an instance," Lockbox said. "My memory is accurate. It's coming back in painful bursts."

"Where is Zuzana?" I asked, seeing the apprehension and fear in Ember's eyes. In Markos' tightly drawn lips.

Lockbox looked to Ember apologetically. "Alba knew Zuzana had been gathering intel on Dulka and told the Parliament House knowing what they'd do. Zuzana knew what her husband was. She knew what that meant for her daughters. Alba was, among other things, horrified at the situation. Roman had implied that Commander Markos had abilities he shouldn't have and that he was going to use his abilities and position of power to overthrow the Chancellors. Roman wanted Alba to get safe. Alba wanted Khizmit to be safe. Safe from Test Criminals and Lurpers and Vaznov, even if that meant she had to betray the Markos family. She's the one who told the soldiers where to find Emberly. Alba believed she had to turn in Zuzana for the good of Khizmit. After all, not only did Zuzana know about the coup, she'd been setting the stage for it here. Once Dulka knew, well ... we all know what Dulka's capable of. I think we all know why Commander Markos hasn't been able to reach his wife. Why he hasn't heard from her."

"No," I said, remembering how confidently Zuzana had left us. *Did she die the same night as her daughter? Was Alba housing the Markos' while plotting their demise?*

"My memory is sound. Zuzana is… I'm sorry."

Markos pulled Ember close before he spoke. "I'm afraid it must be true," he whispered. "I assumed when I lost contact with her. Your mother and Milena are together now. Just as we're together."

A soft, pained sound escaped from Ember, and she buried her face into her father's shoulder as the two stood in the frigid snow. The two of them stepped away.

Roman's tears slowed. The anger melted away to just pain. Just agonizing pain.

Lockbox paused only a moment to allow people to mourn before he continued. "Before I'd been drugged, I considered intel I had been privy to in the Grand Palace. I studied the charts Markos gave me. I thought through it all and then asked for detailed information on individuals. Dulka, Commander Alekin, High Captain Voboda." He swallowed hard when he said his name. "I came to the shocking realization that all of the intel suggested one thing: Commander

Alekin was an original Test Criminal who'd escaped from Zalar."

"Interesting," Kasia said. "I can see that."

"The task force never found many of the original Test Criminals, and I concluded it wasn't because of the lack of rapid tests, but because they weren't in Khizmit anymore. And why would they come back to the city that had imprisoned and experimented on them? Some must have gone to Dovaberg. Maybe they helped them build the ships with iron hulls to break through the ice and settle elsewhere. Many went to Latvani, so why not Alekin? If we had Markos, a Test Criminal, rise through the ranks here, why wouldn't one rise through the ranks there?"

"But why not use their forces to overthrow Khizmit like we planned? Why all the build-up for a coup that isn't going to happen?" I asked.

"Khizmit was never going to accept us. Even if Markos successfully overthrew Dulka, the hatred and fear for lurpers is too strong. Emberly could tell you that from her efforts with the Vasnov Assistance Association."

Ember would have told me if she hadn't just received word of her mother's death. No one cared about lurpers and vazzies.

Markos brushed off Ember's shoulders. "We can't stay here," he warned as Roman removed his overcoat and draped it over Alba's body.

Roman just nodded and stood. The wind blew hard making him shiver.

"Will you bring her with us?" I asked him.

"She's gone," he said. "That's just a body. Buried here or elsewhere it makes little difference." He sniffed hard. "This is going to skudge me up, Luka. I mean it."

"It would for anyone."

"Did you see her? Was she really going to shoot me?"

"Yes," I said, unsure if it was worse to have the woman he

wanted to marry die in front of him in a grisly, violent way, or learn that she'd been plotting his demise. "She really was." And I wouldn't have been there in time to stop it.

"Well, that's something that I'll struggle to make peace with."

"I'm sorry for…all of this."

"You're not the one to blame. I should hope that I've been through enough that I have the moral fortitude to deal with this grief and loss appropriately. I have to pull it together." He sniffed loudly again. "We must all pull together." He embraced me and took a deep breath before he stepped back. "It's good to see you again." A pained smile crossed his face.

I was going to tell him that it was good to see him again too when Markos straightened and stepped away from Emberly to address us.

"Captain Sakrova and Gaborik will take command of the Rhosivi Legion," Markos said. "We will set the pace."

"To Vazenia?" I asked.

Markos nodded his head somberly. "We will check for any survivors and bring whoever we can with us. My hopes aren't high, but you never know. Lurpers are remarkably resilient." He looked at Ember with pride as she wiped a few more tears from her red face.

Would Ice's sister be there? Would she have survived?

"Then we march for Khizmit?" I asked.

"Latvani is distracting Khizmit while we grab who we can and flee."

"Flee? Where?"

"Didn't you listen?" Lockbox asked.

"You threw a lot of information at me at once," I said. "We're not going to Khizmit at all?

Roman looked to Lockbox, not with the anger I'd expected. "Bear Legion is stationed all along the wall and Wolf Legion has flooded the streets," he explained.

Each legion had hundreds if not thousands. I couldn't

remember how many soldiers Markos had said they contained— if he had. The Lurper Legion was small comparatively, I knew that much. "You mean they retreated from The Outskirts? Both legions?"

"Yes," Roman said.

"Because Lockbox told them about the coup." I grew frantic. I'd *never* get back to the Enclave? Never see the trees and lights again? We couldn't take on two legions. Khizmit was safe from us, just like they'd always wanted.

"Of course they knew," Roman said, throwing his head towards Lockbox.

"The coup became a ruse?" I asked. "We're running away?"

Behind us, under the direction of Sakrova and Gaborik, the Rhosivi inmates began to march. Ahead of us stood an army of inmates from Predvoi led by a few members of the Lurper Legion.

"We have a new chance at life. At a future in Latvani. And we're taking it," Roman said, straightening. "They agreed to take us. Harbor us as refugees."

"Why would they take us? Why would they allow hundreds of criminal refugees to enter their land? To live among them?" As I asked it, I knew the answer.

Lockbox is the one who replied. "Research. We agreed to let them study us. We agreed to be a force for them to maintain the border between Latvani and Khizmit and allow them to reverse-engineer the serums. We agreed to supply them with all the files we have and submit to humane testing."

"What makes you so sure it's going to be humane? What makes you trust what Commander Alekin said?"

"Commander Alekin escaped from Zalar," Lockbox said, intentionally not looking over at me. "He's an Oscar."

"An Oscar?" I let the unspoken question linger before vocalizing it.

"Which Oscar?"

"I believe he's…Oscar-17."

Oscar-17. I stopped in my tracks. *Had he seemed remarkably clever to me? Had his intelligence landed him as the commander?*

"You think he's…" *Did he look like Lockbox?*

"Besides," Lockbox picked up. "He's not the only one. Their society openly accepts scrags, lurpers, and vaznov. They've been harboring them for years. We help them advance technologically and they'll let us call Latvani home."

"It's risky," I said.

"Life's risky," he shrugged.

It was. Hope was a risk. Fear was a choice.

"Do you remember me yet?"

"How could I forget my roomie?" he said cautiously, offering another apologetic grin.

We began to walk as Markos shouted orders to the Legion. It would be warmer as we moved south. *Would they celebrate Koliada in Latvani? Would they have caramels and parades?*

Ahead of us, I watched Kasia remove her small overcoat and pass it over to Roman who draped it across his shoulders. She gave his hand a compassionate squeeze and then dropped it but continued in stride alongside him.

Emberly stepped away from her dad. I slowed to have a moment with Markos.

Ember gave us a little bit of space, but as a Victor, I knew she'd be listening anyway.

"Are you going to heal your face?" Markos asked. I wondered when someone would.

"No, Sir. I don't think I will. I don't want to regret the past. I want to be at peace with what happened: the injuries, the pain, the loss, the lessons. Healing it would feel like a mask. This scar, all my scars, they're a part of me. Not something to hide. Does that make sense?"

"You never cease to impress me," Markos said.

I took a few more steps beside him, watching Emberly's short hair swing back and forth with her quick steps. Her hands swung at her side, one gloved, one bare, as if asking for me to join her.

"Well, are you going to take her hand or not?" Markos asked.

"Is that permission?" I replied.

"Yes. Take care of her, please. Be patient and…gentle."

"Yes, Mr. Chief Preemptive Officer," I replied.

"Luka," he jibed back.

"Yessir," I said, and hurried forward, slipping my hand into Ember's. Her fingers were cold and the calluses in her palms dug into mine. We moved away from the group for at least some semblance of privacy.

"It's a miracle. You… out of there … with clean hands," I said, bringing her hand to my mouth so I could drop a kiss on the back of it.

She waited a moment before saying. "I didn't."

"What?"

"Didn't you notice he was missing?"

"Who?"

"You said…" her voice sounded sticky. "You said that if someone came into my cell I should listen to the directions. And I did. And he's gone."

Someone came into her cell. And she'd killed him?

Who?

I thought. Someone had been absent.

The realization hit me. *Razin.* I hadn't seen him. Hadn't heard him.

"He came in…" she said.

"You don't have to tell me."

"We Victors are killers, aren't we? No way around it. We are what Khizmit said."

"We are so much more," I said, reaching for her hand again. She kept her hand in a fist but I wrapped my fingers around it anyway.

"My mother…my sister…gone."

That wasn't all. Alba. Turuk. Raph. Countless others dead. Other losses piled up. My entire childhood. Khizmit. Her home. Our futures there.

"Is this what it means to be a Victor?" she asked, finally opening her hand to wrap her fingers with mine. "To have such pain? To feel dangerous and not trust yourself? To be smothered in loss and grief?"

"No," I replied. "That's what it means to be human."

We continued, snow crunching beneath us. I paused, pulled off my ushanka, and settled it over her red ears. Gently I placed my hand on her cheek and looked her in the eyes.

"We've all lost a lot. Enough that we would each be justified in letting grief envelop us. Letting sorrow and darkness consume us. But I've spent enough time cursing my losses. Trying to find someone to blame. Trying to seek retribution." I tucked a stray strand of hair over her ear and swore to myself that I'd spend the first koruna I made on some new earrings for her. "There will be evil and sorrow ahead, but every now and then happiness will lift us up. We'll feel joy again. Roman said we must pull together. It's not complete compensation for our losses but it's something. We are strong enough to cope."

"I want to be happy again," she said, shutting her eyes and resting her head on my chest for a moment.

"There is happiness ahead. Keep walking. Keep going. We've lost a lot. Big losses. Painful losses. And we will carry our scars," I said, my voice cracking. "But there is more to us than what we've lost."

Hand in hand we walked away from Rhosivi. Away from Khizmit. Away from the perfect vision of a utopia to a future that was unknown but decidedly happy; a future that would have sorrow and evil, joy and laughter. I knew leading the lurpers of Rhosivi, walking with my friends alongside Emberly, that despite the bad, the future would be more than good enough.

Things are about to get personal and long-winded so if that's not your cup of tea, skip to the end. :)

I had my first miscarriage in 2016 and my most recent one last week. In 2019-2020 I did IVF in a foreign country where I barely spoke the language. As difficult and uncomfortable as it was physically—between the self-administered shots, surgeries, plentiful blood draws, and weekly vaginal ultrasounds to check things like the thickness of my endometrium for months—the most painful part was emotional.

Though I'd read about infertility in the Bible, I'd assumed it was as far-fetched in our world as leprosy. My mother easily had 6 kids. Her mother had 6 kids. I had what seemed to me an endless stream of cousins. My best friends growing up almost all had more than 5 siblings. No one in my life had ever been infertile; or at least, they'd never discussed it.

After pursuing all other fertility options over the seven-year period of not getting pregnant the old-fashioned way, my husband and I decided to do IVF while living in Brazil, where the cost was more manageable for our financial situation. I let hope be my guide, my strength, and the image of having another baby was the only thing that kept me taking an Uber to my appointments while my husband took work trips to Guatemala and Colombia. I went to the surgery center, fumbling over a foreign language, where they put two embryos back in. I hoped for twins or triplets (I guess I never wanted to sleep again and for my house to smell like pee). I even convinced myself I had infertility because God wanted to give me triplets and this was a way He could make science do His will.

But IVF failed. And it failed again.

Hope, that shiny damn glimmer of hope, had led me to the most painful emotional place I'd ever been. It had led me down a mysterious path to a new place where I felt it beat me nearly to death with the failure.

No implantation.

No pregnancy.

No baby.

And here I'd gone and picked out names for twins along with a cute nursery theme. (Under the sea with a big octopus. Eight limbs for the eight limbs that having twins in the womb would have been.)

Hope had raised me to cloud nine and then dropped me without a parachute to plummet to my half-dead state. Infertility wasn't what had killed me; it was hope. I felt that infertility was a prison, a punishment I'd done nothing to deserve. I'm a great mom. Why wouldn't God give me more kids?

Cue inmate Victor-27; Luka.

Luka is a prisoner and not because of his own choices. He's punished for crimes he never committed, and could never see himself committing. As a result, fear and hope become tangled in his mind. He even goes so far as to say, "Hope. Lies. What's the difference?". And later, "Hope. The word I hated. Hope and fear were useless to me, or so I'd proclaimed. I'd sworn off hope. It had no use for me. All it did was set me up, lift me up, and then dash me to pieces". When talking with Emberly, Luka finally vocalizes these feelings in dialogue when he tells her, "Hope is the hand that leads you into the darkness of the unknown so it can torture and kill you there without any witnesses."

Though I didn't identify with Luka at first, I later realized that I'd given him all my fears and sardonicism. His voice, my writing style for this work, emerged from my frustration. He was punished for something he'd never done, much like how I was punished with infertility and I'd done nothing to deserve this consequence. Both of us innocent but victims nonetheless.

But, wonderfully, miraculously you might say, I've also let Luka grow with me as I've processed my grief and moved on from that sorrow. Through me, Luka has come to see that hope does have a role and a purpose, and through Luka I've gained invaluable perspective on how hope can be what guides you though hardships that you'd have to go through regardless. Hope is what keeps your head above the water. It keeps you from giving up.

I felt alone and isolated in my infertility, as the infertility community didn't want to accept me since I had two kids. How dare I say I was one of them? And so, Luka had no friends. Even among the prisoners, those who should have understood his sorrow and trials, he was shunned.

The more I opened up about my challenges and the sorrow and the pain and the confusion surrounding my own trial of infertility, I found that I wasn't alone, and that even those who don't have infertility can sympathize with my hardships. And so, Luka got a cellmate who cared for him and helped him.

These themes of dealing with situations outside of our control, deciding how to deal with the emotions of feeling isolated, and misunderstood, are themes relatable to young adults and adults alike. I wanted to be sure I used themes with identity and coming-of-age as Luka escapes from his prison and chases his dreams.

How many of us feel like we're trapped in one way or another? What do we have to do to escape? I want readers to ponder those questions and gain the courage to run away from whatever is keeping them from happiness or success the way that Luka stops hoping for The Judgement Board to decide his fate. Our fate is in our own hands. As a teenager, I didn't really believe that. But that's exactly the stage of life when you begin to realize the power you wield over your future—when you step away from your parents' protection and their rules and routines. It's when freedom hits you full in the face with either blessings or consequences. (Generally, a bit of both.)

I love to write for young adults because I want to entertain and educate them simultaneously. I never would have picked up a self-help book as a teen, nor would I have voluntarily seen a therapist, even though my own father is one. I love therapists, I just didn't want one for myself. But books can get right inside the heads of teens and teach them in a way that's digestible and more subtle. They can convey causes and effects that produce experiential learning.

This idea of seeing hope as the enemy and then switching it around, to see how hope can assist you, is something I know young adults in particular can appreciate.

Hope corresponds with light and color in my story. Luka's life in Rhosivi Mine is full of shadows and darkness. It's dark and gritty with little color beyond the black coal, the dust, and the white flakes of snow. Grey uniforms and black ushankas worn by the guards fit nicely into the bleakness of the story at that point.

It is any wonder with IVF failure fresh in my mind, that Luka grows up in an infertile, frigid desert where there is no life? Is it any surprise that he spends his days digging deeper and deeper not sure if he'll find the source of life (coal) or die in the process? Add in his questions of why they don't trust him with more important tasks in the mine and consider my authentic questions to God of why he doesn't trust me with more children and I begin to feel exposed by how personal this story really is.

When Luka goes to Predvoi Prison, color begins to come into the scene with the introduction of rabbits and more food in the mess hall. The readers feel hopeless with Luka. When he leaves Predvoi and makes his way to Khizmit, it corresponds with a beautiful sunrise which marks the first day of his freedom. That explosion of color corresponds with the success of his escape and the burst of hope he feels as he makes his way. "Dazzling pastels in shades of purple, blue, and yellow streaked through the thin clouds and I stared, unsure if this was the first time the sun and sky had orchestrated such a stunning display or if I'd never been privy to the brilliance before". From then on, the story has more emphasis on colors as we've left a lot of the grit behind us. He still has grit and endures a lot of hardship, like burning his wrist, but here his paradigm surrounding hope shifts, and we leave much of the darkness and misery behind us.

Another breakthrough point with color and life comes when Luka finally enters Khizmit Enclave. For the first time in the novel, the descriptions burst with life, from the ornamental trees to the sweet aromas to the bright lights and colored roofs.

As I take a step back from *Fate's Inmate* to consider why I made the decisions I have regarding plot, theme, language, setting, and character development, I have been surprised and indeed, amazed. Infertility made me consider the relationship between hope and fear. It led me to a setting where I felt like a prisoner in a bleak, cold desert. Luka waits for his freedom to be granted to him, and it isn't, just as I still haven't conceived. But something implanted in my mind and that was this idea of escape. Escape from the prison of tracking cycles going to doctor appointments just as Luka finally accepts that his only shot at a future is through escape, not waiting on the Judgement Board. As it turns out, none of the events or messages are random, and all of it is heavily influenced by aspects in my real life, from my relationship with God to my fertility status.

Luka spent the first half of the book hating the scar on his face and the better part of the middle hiding it, but in the end he wears it. Maybe not proudly, but with some sense of resignation and closure.

Maybe there's something I can learn from that.

Thank you for reading my story and Luka's. I hope you'll share it with other readers.

———

Allow me a brief section of **acknowledgments** as I thank the following people:

-Matt, my husband, for his unwavering love, support, patience, and brilliance. Thank you for taking me to Kosice so I could finish my book.

- My Slovak friend Peter Krajnak for inspiring the location, showing me around his country and city, and letting me borrow his last name for Luka's father.

- My Slovak daughter, Tereza Kendrova, for patiently helping me as I tried to integrate Slovak culture and words into the story and forgiving me for my linguistic mistakes and faux pas.

- My editor and friend Cheyenne Cooley who has believed in my story, and Stag Beetle Books, more consistently than I have.

- Caleb Hafen who truly brought this world to life in the narration. I knew immediately that he had stardust on him. Listening to him perform the audiobooks of Fate's Inmate has been a highlight of my adult life. Let it be forever recorded that if my dream of having this story brought the to silver screen comes to fruition, I implore the casting director to find a place for him, front and center.

Truly excited to see where your life takes you, Caleb. I'm skudging honored to have you as a "comrade."

Warmly,

L. Blaise Hues

FROM THE PUBLISHER

Thank you so much for reading The Final Victor!

We hope you enjoyed the journey and characters as much as we loved bringing them to you. **Please leave a review on Amazon** and Goodreads while the story is fresh in your mind. Reviews are writing fuel for authors and help their books get into the hands of other hungry readers. If you're a big fan of speculative young adult and middle-grade fiction, we invite you to join our street team. Get copies of our books in advance, early access to covers, and other freebies!

Stag Beetle Books

www.stagbeetlebooks.com

ALSO BY L. BLAISE HUES

Legacy of Debris: A Gritty Young Adult Dystopian

Republic of Ruin

Shattered State

Crimson Nation

*

The Eden Compound

*

Kids of Cybercity: A Middle-Grade Trilogy

<u>The Search for Silence</u>

<u>A Voice in the Noise</u>

<u>The Thundering Echo</u>